RESCUING ROSE

RESCUED HEARTS OF THE CIVIL WAR ~ BOOK 1

SUSAN POPE SLOAN

WILD HEART
BOOKS

ISBN-13: 978-1-942265-62-7

PRAISE FOR RESCUING ROSE

"In Rescuing Rose, Susan Pope Sloan has penned a stirring tale of hope and love amid a backdrop of war. The debut novel brings a fresh voice to Christian fiction and unique insights readers are certain to connect with."

— CYNTHIA ROEMER, AWARD WINNING AUTHOR
OF *UNDER MOONLIT SKIES* AND *BEYOND THESE WAR-TORN LANDS*

"Author Susan Pope Sloan has penned a heartwarming tale set during the turbulence of the American Civil War. In the wake of the destruction of Rose Carrigan's Southern home, she and her sister are protected by Noah Griffin, a Union Officer. The chasm between North and South thins along the line of attraction and mutual respect, but the war rages on and certain realities can't be overlooked. The first in a series, I look forward to reading the rest."

— PEGG THOMAS, AWARD-WINNING AUTHOR OF
EMERALD FIELDS

"In *Rescuing Rose*, Sloan has crafted a plot that draws readers into the plight suffered by Southerners during the Civil War. Danger and upheaval tug at the reader's emotions from the beginning. Historical events are woven into the fabric of the story. I recommend this novel to reader of inspirational historical romance."

— SANDRA MERVILLE HART, AWARD-WINNING
AUTHOR OF THE SPIES OF THE CIVIL WAR SERIES

"Sloan debuts with a suspenseful Civil War romance brimming with danger and forbidden longing. Fans of historical romance will light in this earnest tale."

— PUBLISHERS WEEKLY

To my family,
who endured my years of various writing endeavors
and loved me anyway.
I love you all.

"Rejoice not against me, O mine enemy: when I fall, I shall arise; when I sit in darkness, the LORD shall be a light unto me."

Micah 7:8 (KJV)

CHAPTER 1

*S*omething foul was afoot, and this time it was more than a few mice chewing on the machine belts.

Her loom slowed without warning, and Rose Carrigan clutched at the cotton threads tangled in her fingers. The customary high-pitched whine in the room plummeted to a deep growl as all the machines shuddered to a stop. Shuttles paused mid-sweep, setting the bobbins that fed them to dancing on their spindles. Puffs of cotton drifted like falling snowflakes in the still air.

The wide-eyed faces of her co-workers mirrored Rose's bewilderment. A glance at the narrow window to her left revealed the hazy blue of a summer sky. Hours until quitting time.

Whispered questions buzzed but dropped like swatted mosquitoes at a sudden commotion.

A column of blue-clad soldiers burst through the door.

1

The bearded leader glowered at the workers. "Out! Everyone outside, now!"

The order bounced from wall to wall. Pointing their rifled muskets, the Union soldiers swept down the aisles and prodded the workers away from their stations.

Dear God, the war had arrived at Roswell's door. Men with fierce expressions crowded closer. The odor of sweat and filth on their wool uniforms robbed her breath. Memories threatened, but she forced them back.

Rose followed the other weavers into the blinding, blistering sunshine. A sea of blue uniforms circled the factory. Rose threaded her way between her coworkers and groups of haughty soldiers. Snatches of conversations fluttered and fell away. Rumors and speculation of what would happen now. The clamor rose as the crowd swelled.

Rose veered to the left, searching for Celeste. The horde surged around her, and she stumbled. Why didn't she see her? The afternoon heat settled like a cloak over her shoulders and stifled her breath. Fighting the rising panic, she whirled in a circle, seeking the face so like her own.

"Celeste." She raised her voice. "Celeste!"

Out of the chaos, a familiar voice called her name, and Rose turned toward it.

Celeste twisted her way through the press of people.

"Thank heavens you're safe." Rose clasped her sister's hands as the crowd pushed them along to the top of the hill that faced the mill. Although Celeste had turned twenty last month, Rose couldn't shake the feeling of responsibility for her, heavier since the death of their father.

Shouted orders echoed above the rumble of disgruntled murmuring, drawing Rose's attention back to the now-deserted mill. A torch sailed through the air and disappeared into the building's top floor. In moments, fire engulfed the four-story structure. Rose gasped and clutched her sister's arm.

Panic clawed at her throat, urging her to run, but where to? Soldiers and horses formed a living barrier to keep the workers trapped between the fire and a larger phalanx in town.

Black smoke puffed through every crevice, marring the summer sky, its acrid odor drifting across the hillside. With fascinated horror, she watched the structure bow to the flame and crumble into a pile of blackened bricks and charred beams.

Heat from the fire intensified the stifling temperature. Perspiration slid from brows and sprouted in armpits, darkening homespun shirts and blue wool uniforms alike.

It was July, after all. And this was Georgia.

Rose and Celeste, along with the other mill hands, watched in silent terror, transfixed by the sight of such wanton, deliberate destruction. Machinery and ashes of cotton bales lay in scorched heaps on the ground. With the mill gone and the war on their doorstep, what would become of them?

The screen of smoke spread insidiously, stretching its tendrils as far as the eye could see. The crowd shifted, growing restless. Rose cupped her hands over her mouth to block the smoke from her lungs, but her eyes stung and watered.

Celeste raised the tail of her apron to cover most of her face.

A commotion rippled along the edge of the crowd as a uniformed rider guided his horse around the throng. His gaze skimmed over the workers, seemed to assess the scene in mere seconds. Rose lifted her face and dared to meet his scowl. Could he read her scorn, or did he only see the confusion and disappointment that men would stoop to such barbarity?

His jaw clenched, and he looked away. A few words to his men set them scurrying. They pressed against the people and herded them like cattle away from the scene of destruction.

"Go home now." The soldier closest to them moved through the crowd. "You'll get orders for your removal tomorrow."

Celeste dropped her apron and gaped. "Our removal? What does that mean?"

Someone nearby spat a bitter answer. "Well, it's for sure and certain we can't stay here no more. No mill. No work. No food. Ain't nothin' left here."

~

*P*uffs of red dust billowed around Captain Noah Griffin as he spurred his horse away from town on the road toward Marietta. He was glad to leave that wretched inferno behind. Glad he didn't have to witness the horror and despair on the faces of displaced workers as they watched the destruction.

Coward.

He absorbed the truth of the accusation. Oh, he found the courage to act in time of battle. Nobody could say he ran from danger. Like the mythological creature that shared his family name, he flew into the fight, sometimes without proper caution, much to the dismay of his old arms instructor.

The aftermath of battle, however, sickened him. More and more he shunned the celebration after a victory, preferring solitude. He needed the solace of nature to cleanse his soul of the carnage. Destruction that he'd participated in—again.

Another vision eclipsed that of the carnage. The woman who dared to challenge his scrutiny as he searched the throng for his junior officer. Her eyes shot daggers, but tears coursed her cheeks. She couldn't know how he hated when his orders destroyed women's lives, and he did what he could to mitigate the damage. When he joined the military, his goal was to secure the country through law and order. Would that even be possible now?

His current assignment allowed his escape. Whenever General Garrard needed a temporary messenger, he called on Noah. Knowing Noah to be an accomplished rider with a hound dog's nose for direction, the commander relied on his speed and skill.

Right now, though, Noah needed to work off his frustration at the havoc they'd caused in Roswell, inhabited mostly by women. The primary objective of this campaign was to secure the Chattahoochee River. He failed to see how robbing women of the means to feed their children advanced the Union cause.

Movement in the thick stand of pines ahead warned him to stay alert. Without changing his pace, he swept the area for danger. He was at a disadvantage traveling an unfamiliar road, and he braced for trouble.

A dozen yards in front of him, a young buck sprang from the foliage. Noah pulled on the reins as Hercules sidestepped to avoid the deer. The stag halted and stared, as though taking the measure of the intruders. When it darted away, Noah blew out the breath he'd sucked in.

"Thank You, Lord. Guess I needed reminding You oversee everything. Even with the mess we've created, there's still beauty here."

Giving his faithful steed an appreciative pat, Noah adjusted his seat. "Let's get this letter delivered, boy." Both man and beast would be ready for a proper meal and a few hours of rest. They settled into an easy canter, alert to danger on the path.

$\sim$

*R*ose still gripped her sister's hand as they joined their neighbors trudging toward the workers' quarters. Even in this blistering heat, Celeste's cold fingers signaled her deep distress. Rose whispered words from a Psalm she had memorized as a child. "He will give His angels charge over thee." It was a promise of protection, but she grappled with this new reality. The Union Army spread over the area like the foul stench from Marietta's paper mill when the wind blew from that direction.

For months distant guns had thundered near Roswell, but its residents trusted the Confederate forces to stand between them and the howling enemy. After all, the Johnny Rebs stood firm last year at Chickamauga, despite their heavy losses. Surely, they could repel the encroaching enemy again.

The determined bluecoats, however, didn't give up. They'd returned and pushed steadily southward: Dalton, Resaca, Adairsville, Kennesaw Mountain. Residents of Roswell wondered if they would be next. With no railroad, the small town existed only because of the mill.

Rose continued the soft recitation. "They will bear thee in their hands..."

Celeste turned to her. "What's going to happen to us now, Rose?"

"I don't know." She paused at the end of the street to catch her breath. Mothers and children hurried past them, taking different paths to their cottages. "I heard they took down Monsieur Roche's French flag at the woolen mill and held him at gunpoint too."

"Silly man. He should've known that ruse wouldn't work. Why would the Yankees care whether the flag flying over the mill was Confederate or French?"

"I guess he thought a foreign flag might provide some kind of immunity." Setting up mill supervisor Roche as a partner had been a crafty move by the owner, but it still didn't save the building. According to the rumors, they'd shipped finished fabrics and raw materials to other towns as the Union army advanced. It angered Rose that their employers cared more about the goods at the mill than the people.

Rose ran a hand over her face and shook her head. "Ah, no sense trying to figure out why people act the way they do. At least we're alive and well."

"And we still have each other." Celeste placed her other hand on top of their linked fingers and squeezed.

Eyes burning with unshed tears, Rose regarded her sister, now her only family. People often thought they were twins, with their similar size and coloring, though better than two years separated them. She poked Celeste in the side. "Your hair is falling down."

Celeste sniffed and tossed her a look of chagrin. "When isn't it falling down?" She reached up to tuck the wayward chestnut strands back into the chignon. The stringent style didn't flatter, but it kept the hair safe from grasping mill machinery, and it proved cooler in the summer heat. "Days like this, I miss having hoops in our skirts. These petticoats are hot without them."

Rose agreed. Hoops would be cumbersome, not to mention dangerous around the machinery. Finding work in the mills had seemed the best choice last year, with the Federals hovering around Chattanooga, so close to their home in Dalton. With Da sick and most of his congregation leaving, she had convinced him to move so she and Celeste could find jobs.

Resetting a few of her own hairpins, Rose pondered the prospect of yet another move. They had no choice, but this time, it would only be the two of them.

Rose announced her decision as they reached their little cottage. "We are going to gather our belongings so we'll be ready to move out as soon as the army leaves." Her voice conveyed more confidence than she felt. Once again, men who cared nothing for them forced her and Celeste from their home, saw them merely as hindrances. This time, she'd push back.

Celeste started. "But where will we go?"

"Farther south, I suppose. Let's ask Janie where we might find employment." Janie Wilson had stepped in as a mother figure when the sisters came to Roswell. "I imagine others will be thinking the same, so we need to be sitting on ready, as Da would say. The Lord will guide our steps to the right place."

Celeste pushed open the front door. "Did the army destroy the company store and the warehouses? I didn't think to look that way or to ask anyone."

Rose followed Celeste inside and sank onto a cane-straw straight-back chair. "Not as far as I know. But there couldn't have been much left there after Mr. Barrington King divided the provisions." That was one thing the owner had done right by his workers before he left town. At least they'd all have something to eat for a few days.

"I wonder where they'll get enough food to feed that army." Celeste fingered the yellow curtains at the window where she stood.

Weariness pressed Rose. Why couldn't they put down roots for good? All she wanted was a place to call home.

She cast about for a word of hope, something to lighten the darkness hovering around them. Forcing a cheerful tone, she slapped the tabletop. "Well, there is one good thing about this sudden turn of events."

Celeste turned troubled eyes her way and voiced her doubts. "And what would that be?"

Rose's lips twitched, striving for a smile. "We can sleep late tomorrow. No mill to report to at dawn. And packing up ought to be easy since we won't be carting any furniture this time."

CHAPTER 2

$\mathcal{W}$as anything more exhausting than packing a house?

Surveying the disarray of the tiny cottage the next morning, Rose groaned. She pushed the furniture aside to create walking space. Between the heat and working muscles she'd not moved since spring cleaning, her normal energy flagged.

With Celeste hanging clothes outside, Rose gave up the fight. She collapsed across her bed, now stripped of linens. Floating in and out of sleep, she vaguely registered the sounds of her sister moving around the other room, then the closing of a door.

A peal of thunder woke her, and she sat up, groggy and disoriented. She splashed water from the ewer on her hands and face and wandered into the sitting room. It was empty. She peered into the kitchen. "Celeste?"

No answer. Opening the back door, she noted the swiftly moving clouds to the west. Not much hope for a good soaking rain then. Just a quick summer afternoon sprinkle and moisture to add to the heat. Clothes danced on the line to the tune of a balmy breeze. She gathered the personal items but left the still-damp sheets.

Rose closed the door and retraced her steps to the sitting room. A scrap of butcher paper held in place by a pencil caught her attention. "Gone to see Janie and fam."

"No, Celeste." Groaning, Rose crossed the empty room. "You can't be running off to visit folks now." The army commander had passed the word last night for everyone to assemble in the town square this afternoon. Time marched steadily toward that hour.

Rose pinned up her tumbled hair and crammed her old straw hat over it. Spying her father's walking stick in the corner, she grabbed it and headed out the door. The cane would be a poor weapon if she needed one, but it was the best she could find.

Taking the path she and Celeste had traveled many times, Rose avoided the streets and weaved her way between buildings toward what remained of the Ivy Woolen mill. Aware of the increased population about town, she kept her head high and her steps steady.

Janie Wilson had befriended Rose and Celeste when they first arrived in Roswell last year. In her early forties, Janie kept her large family going by the force of her faith and strong personality. Rose and Celeste visited the Wilsons on most Sundays, especially since Da's passing. Ordinarily, Janie would have sent her son to escort Celeste home, but Pete had joined the Roswell Battalion last month. The battalion had left town early yesterday to join General Johnston's troops and guard the bridge across the Chattahoochee River. That move had rendered Roswell defenseless.

Just before Rose reached the block where Janie lived, she spotted Celeste hurrying toward her, head bowed as she climbed the hill.

"Celeste!" Rose rushed to intercept her.

As they met near the crest of the hill, Celeste gripped Rose's free hand. Distress and anger intensified her voice. "Those Yankees burned down the paper mill at Sope Creek, too, along with all the storage buildings."

"Oh, my. Do they burn everything? At least they didn't destroy any of the houses here." Everyone had heard of the burned houses in other towns.

"No, but they emptied out Barrington Hall and Bulloch Hall. They're using those beautiful homes to house their officers. All the paintings, silver, floor coverings, even the piano…everything was divided among the soldiers or tossed like trash onto the lawn."

Celeste paused for a breath and leaned against Rose to adjust her shoelaces. The stench of burned cotton grew stronger as they neared the mill.

Celeste continued her tirade. "Janie said they destroyed the pipe organ and hymnals in the Presbyterian church, which they've turned into a hospital. They damaged Mount Carmel Methodist and Lebanon Baptist too. I guess nothing is sacred in this war. Nothing of value is left untouched." Celeste dashed a tear from her face and pressed her lips together.

Rose was stunned into silence. Occupied with packing, she hadn't ventured beyond their cottage and had no idea the destruction had spread past the mills.

Celeste took a deep breath. "That's not all. The soldiers seized Janie's wagon and told her we're all considered traitors and will go to prison."

"Traitors?" Rose scoffed. "For spinning and carding wool and cotton? For working to keep food on our tables? That can't be right."

Celeste sighed, deflating her anger, and fell into step with Rose. "I guess it's nearly time for the meeting."

Rose bit her lip to keep from scolding. "Why did you take the chance to go to Janie's?"

11

Intent on their conversation and hurrying back home, Rose hadn't seen the gang of men heading toward them until it was too late to veer away. Five soldiers, grinning like a pack of dogs that had cornered a couple of rabbits, spanned the expanse between two apartment buildings. It made Rose think of games they had played as children, one team calling to the other to break through their ranks. But this was not a game she wanted to play.

The skinny man in the center swaggered forward. "Look here, fellas. Two of them Southern belles coming to meet us. We ought to ask them to dance."

Laughter followed. "I don't see much beauty in the women in this town," another called, "but then I ain't real picky. A female's a female." Slowly and deliberately, the two at either end of the line drifted closer. Their movement decidedly menacing, they cut off any avenue of escape. They appeared primed to pounce.

Rose gripped Celeste's elbow and took a cautious step backward. She darted a glance around. The apartment buildings where the mill supervisors lived—commonly called The Bricks —loomed to the right and to the left. No tenants remained there, since the Army held those leaders elsewhere. No help would come from those quarters.

Lifting her chin, Rose forced bravado. "Please, let us pass." She fought the quiver in her voice. "We have to be in the town square, as ordered by *your* general."

"Aw, you got time for a dance or two," the leader wheedled. He spat on the ground with disdain. "Garrard won't miss two amongst so many women. Old Kenny's got a passel of females here to choose from."

The others laughed at his casual slander of their commander.

The soldier crept gradually closer as he talked, his grin stretching a scar on his cheek. His eyes bounced from Celeste to

Rose. He lunged forward, grabbed Celeste's arm, and jerked her to him.

Celeste squeaked in protest and pulled against his grip. "Let me go!"

Anger boosted Rose's courage. She raised Da's walking stick and pointed at the brash ruffian. "Let her go."

It was pure bluster, of course. Her puny weapon and woman's strength would be no match for one, much less five war-hardened soldiers. The display would have been for naught, except another voice echoed the command from the other end of the alley.

"Let her go, Pierce."

Rose tore her eyes from the soldiers on foot to an officer astride a bulky chestnut charger. He was moving toward them. Dust clung to both man and beast. The animal pranced a bit, probably eager to take his dinner and rest, but the officer held him in check.

Rose breathed a silent prayer of thanksgiving but still held the stick waist-high, maintaining her guarded stance.

The leader released Celeste and took a step backwards, raising his hands in a show of innocence. "Now, Griffin, we was just talking with these young ladies."

"Looked to be more than talking to me, and it's Captain Griffin, Sergeant Pierce." He emphasized the two terms of rank. "Now you men head on over to the town square. You may be needed there to maintain order." Authority rang in his voice, brooking no argument.

With sidelong glances at each other, the men did as told. The mounted officer watched until they turned the corner at the end of the building.

A sigh of relief escaped as Rose lowered the cane. The close encounter left her drained and wary.

Beside her, Celeste rubbed the offended arm.

Captain Griffin swung off the horse and ambled toward

them, lifting his hands to indicate he meant no harm. He touched one gloved finger to the bill of his kepi. "Noah Griffin, captain in the Seventh Pennsylvania, United States Cavalry. I trust you are unhurt?"

Rose glanced at Celeste, who nodded. "We're all right."

He stood in the shade of the building. Beyond his considerable height and military bearing, Rose could discern a well-trimmed beard framing thin lips and a nose with a slight hook.

"You ladies best be moving along. Meeting will start soon, and I can't stand here watching out for your wellbeing." His next words scolded. "You should have stayed home and not been traipsing around town, asking for trouble."

He sounded like a teacher reprimanding an unruly student.

Rose bristled at the unfair condescension. Wasn't that just like a man to put the blame on the woman? She gave her sarcasm full reign as she replied, "Well, thank you for your concern, Captain Griffin, but it happens that's where we were headed when those men accosted us."

"Ma'am, I'm happy they didn't get beyond *accosting* you. Every army has its share of miscreants, and you happened to run afoul of one of the worst I know."

Resentment at their sudden vulnerability turned her voice rough. "If you know that, why do you allow them free rein of the town? We were safe here until y'all arrived."

"Rose," her sister pleaded. "He did save us, and we should be going." She tugged on Rose's arm but addressed the captain. "Thank you, sir."

Though she couldn't see his eyes beneath his kepi, Rose felt his gaze bearing into hers for a long moment. He glanced away, dropping the argument and breaking the connection between them. He heaved a breath to indicate longsuffering and turned to Celeste. "You're welcome, miss. Now you really should move on."

The remnants of Rose's anger slipped away as Captain

Griffin bowed in their direction. Her pride still smarted from his disdain, but he had rescued them.

"Yes, thank you," Rose muttered through stiff lips.

The officer nodded and led his mount to the road.

Rose followed Celeste in the other direction but glanced back to see him pause at the building's edge. As if she'd called to him, he looked back once more. His hand lifted in salute before Rose could jerk her gaze away.

CHAPTER 3

*R*ose quickened her steps to keep up with Celeste's pace. Confusion clouded her attention and lingered over Captain Griffin's parting gesture. His demeanor marked him a gentleman, never mind his current occupation. She should have controlled her temper and her response. Her only excuse was her fear.

She prayed she'd never see him again.

As they neared the town square, she focused on their surroundings. Heaven forbid she should lose Celeste in this crowd. Rows of soldiers marked a perimeter and created a barrier against the people jostling for position closer to the front. A few young women dragged along reluctant children. Others assisted elderly parents.

The fragmented families wrenched Rose's heart. Beyond the pull of grief and yearning for her deceased parents, stronger than the twinge of envy directed at those holding their young ones, she ached for those women who carried the burden of providing for a family while war raged around them. How would they survive without the factory? As demanding as the work had been, with its long hours and disagreeable environment, at least it provided food and shelter.

Now they had nothing, not even an idea of what their future held.

She gestured to some boys who climbed into the trees for better viewing. Cedar needles broke loose, and dry mimosa blossoms fluttered to the ground in the humid air. Nobody admonished the boys to spare the leaves and few remaining blossoms. Why should they care about the lawns of people who'd fled town ahead of the invasion?

Honesty forced Rose to adjust her criticism. Barrington King *had* ordered the company store to distribute the remaining provisions to the workers. And the Roswell populace considered the late Captain Tom King a local hero. Reverend Pratt remained in town with his family, even though he had the means to leave.

How easy it was to cast aside those exceptions and paint all the leaders with the brush of cowardice. She'd do well to remember that her family had abandoned Dalton. One always could excuse her own actions with a list of reasons that might seem flimsy to others.

The press of bodies intensified the day's heat and fouled the air. Moisture gathered under her bonnet and on her upper lip. With careful movements, Rose angled her position to allow a bit of air to slip past her bodice.

More people pressed into the crowd. Low conversations hummed around them, some rising with anger and complaint, some falling with anxious speculation. The sound dropped to a low hum as a squad of soldiers escorted several men through the gathering. Whispers identified the mill supervisors, including the overseers Monsieur Theophile Roche of the woolen mill and Olney Eldredge from the cotton mill.

Rose stretched her five-foot-three-inch stature as far as

possible by standing on tiptoe. "Ah, I can't see. When are they going to tell us why we've gathered here?"

"Maybe folks are still coming in. It's difficult to tell." Celeste tried to fan herself with the loose ribbons from her tattered straw hat. "Goodness, it's hot today. What I wouldn't give for a breeze."

Rose swallowed a nervous snicker and lightly punched her sister's arm. "It couldn't get through all these bodies, even if it came straight down from heaven. You could take off your bonnet."

"But then the sun would scorch my head. I wish I'd grabbed my fan." Celeste motioned ahead. "Look, someone's bringing a wagon."

The vehicle stopped among the assembled citizens somewhere beyond her vision. An officer clambered into the wagon bed, where he stood and waved his hands for everyone's attention. The people quieted, and he began to speak, but the long distance compounded by the noise of people shifting around them prevented Rose from making out more than a few words.

The officer stopped now and then as someone raised a complaint over his statements. Rose heaved a sigh of frustration. "If only everyone would be quiet, perhaps we could hear."

Suddenly a female voice rose to a high keening such as she'd heard often accompany the passing of a loved one.

Rose and Celeste exchanged questioning glances, as did others around them. The mournful sound died away, and the officer uttered a few more words, the meaning lost to Rose. Whether he tried to calm the woman or issued orders, she couldn't tell. He bent and disappeared from their sight, his speech obviously ended, but nobody moved. Some activity captured the attention of those closer. A hush fell as the others waited.

The spectators slowly separated, allowing a wagon to pass. Behind the uniformed driver and armed guard, several people huddled between trunks and boxes, their heads bent low and shoulders slumped in defeat.

These humbled people were their leaders, at least those leaders who'd stayed in town. A sense of bereavement surprised Rose. What would become of them now?

Rose bowed her head, feeling the disgrace and humiliation as her own. Why were they singled out for public display? Continuing their jobs should not be counted a crime.

Other wagons slowly followed the first, each pulled by decrepit horses or mules that had to be coaxed into moving. Murmurs vied with the squeaking and creaking of the vehicles as they passed.

"Arrested like common criminals."

"Imprisoned as traitors."

The words rippled over the waiting spectators. Rose shivered at the implications and slowed her breath to fight the threatening panic.

When the procession of wagons ended, those left standing wandered aimlessly, a people without purpose. With no orders issued from the soldiers, they were left on their own. Rose searched the faces surrounding her for any indication of what to do. Uncertainty made her shoulders tense.

Finally, a few weary mothers sat on whatever grassy area they could find and pulled their children close. Some extracted cloth-wrapped bread or cheese. Others shifted by small degrees toward their homes, likely hoping to pass the night under shelter. Men in blue uniforms sauntered among them, turning some toward a group of officers, letting others pass after a brief conversation.

Rose pulled Celeste toward their cottage on Factory Hill. "Let's go home."

They ambled along a crooked path between groups of women. She hoped to avoid any encounter with soldiers. It was not to be. When they were a few blocks from their cottage, two soldiers stepped into their path.

Rose raised a hand to block the sun. Captain Griffin's raised eyebrows challenged her. Of all the people to run into. Heat rushed to her face as she braced for another scolding.

"May we assist you ladies somehow?" The other officer asked the question. His green eyes twinkled playfully, and twin dimples peeked from around a well-groomed auburn mustache.

Rose tamped down her anxiety and raised her chin in a show of confidence. She addressed the captain, whom she thought might be the superior officer. His serious countenance, in contrast with the congenial expression of his companion, supported the notion.

"As a matter of fact, we would appreciate your assistance again, Captain Griffin, if you could provide an explanation for us. We were so far away that we couldn't make out exactly what your commander was saying. Can you explain what this meeting was about? What does your army plan to do now?"

Surprise glinted in the captain's eyes, gray like a winter sky. He'd attempted to remove the travel dust from his uniform, and damp hair curled over his collar. He didn't smile but clasped his hands behind him.

He glanced at them with some reluctance and cleared his throat. He spoke as if reciting a memorized speech in front of a room full of classmates.

"Everyone connected with the mills is to be transported from here to Marietta, Georgia, where General Sherman has arranged further transportation. We understand they...you... will then be put on rail cars and conveyed to points north. The exact location hasn't been disclosed, but we're assured you should be able to find employment there."

"Oh. North. Somewhere." She worked to absorb that information. Confusion mingled with fear. Suppressed memories threatened to surface against her will.

Celeste grabbed her hand and squeezed it for support.

"All your family members go with you, of course." The other officer seemed to be trying to ease her alarm and offer reassurance. "Do you have parents here? Or children? I'm guessing any adult male relatives are"—he cleared his throat—"not currently present."

Celeste answered. "There's no one else. No family. Our father passed last winter, and Mother died before the war. It's just the two of us."

The men exchanged glances. Captain Griffin shifted his stance, leaning slightly toward them. "The wagons that left today will return and be ready to transport others to Marietta tomorrow. You'd be wise to be among those who leave then. While we await further orders, the inactivity may lead some men to mischief, as you witnessed earlier, Miss ..." He paused. "I don't believe I got your names?"

"Oh, pardon my lack of manners, sir." Rose extended her hand out of habit but yanked it back. What was she thinking? One never offered a bare palm, especially when the hand was covered with calluses.

"I'm Rose Carrigan, and this is my sister, Celeste. Our father was pastor of a church up in Dalton until last year."

Her voice failed, memories obscuring her view. From Tennessee, they'd found refuge in Dalton and then Roswell. Now, she and Celeste would continue to some distant town to start over again.

In closed rail cars. She clutched the collar of her dress as her breath grew shallow.

Enclosed in a hulking mass of metal without a means of escape. For hours, days?

How far away would they travel? Her mind reeled at the prospect. Her vision faded and darkness threatened.

"Rose!" Celeste's cry sounded far away.

Strong hands gripped her shoulders. "Miss Carrigan." A gust

of warm breath carried her name, causing a shiver as it swept over her neck. A harsh voice laced with concern. "I believe we should find a place for you to sit."

Captain Griffin guided her to a low stone wall set as a boundary marker. Warmth from the wall seeped into her body. Funny that she had turned cold on such a sunny day. The panic receded as the captain blocked the sun with his body, looming over her.

Celeste knelt beside her, chafing her hands, while the other soldier hovered nearby, looking ready to spring into action.

Rose forced a deep breath. "So sorry. I don't know what came over me." She patted Celeste's hand and attempted a shaky smile.

"The heat of the day, perhaps together with these unusual circumstances." The captain's brow furrowed, and his voice softened.

"I'm sure I'll be fine after I rest a while. I thank you, gentlemen, for your aid. I know you must have duties to attend." She made a feeble shooing motion. How mortifying to have them witness such weakness. She hoped they'd go away and forget this incident.

"Our duty is to watch over the locals. As you are part of that number, our duty is here." Captain Griffin gestured to his companion. "I believe I failed to introduce Lieutenant Cooper Bradley of the Seventeenth Indiana."

The lieutenant executed a proper bow. "Miss Carrigan, I don't mean to be indelicate, but how long since you've eaten?"

Rose tried to recall. "I really don't know. Didn't we eat a bite this morning, Cissy?"

Celeste peered beyond Rose to the looming officer. "Please, Captain, our house is just up the hill there. If you would kindly escort us, we'll be out of your way."

Her words hinted at their earlier experience, when the captain had intervened. When Rose would have protested,

Celeste continued. "I'm sure my sister will be all right once she's rested."

A curt nod of agreement was her answer. "Cooper and I are at your service." He gestured to Rose. "Miss Carrigan, if you will take my arm, I believe we can make our way unhindered."

Rose glanced from one face to the other and saw determination on each. Gathering the tattered remnants of her dignity, she gave in. "Thank you, Captain. I believe a nice cup of tea and a good night's rest will set me right as rain."

She lowered her eyes to conceal her doubts. How could anything ever be right again?

CHAPTER 4

$\mathcal{F}$atigue dragged at Noah as he unrolled his blanket under a spreading oak. Vickery Creek flowed nearby, still swollen from recent rains. He hoped to hear the water flowing somehow beneath the muted nighttime sounds as men and beasts settled after a long day. The scent of burnt wood lingered, but he'd grown accustomed to it. It seemed the army burned something everywhere they went.

Maybe the air would be cooler near the creek.

Maybe a breeze would waft over the water.

Maybe the mosquitoes would feast elsewhere.

Yeah, and maybe he would wake up and find this whole war was a strange nightmare. With a sigh, he stripped off his frock coat and tossed it atop his knapsack, perching his kepi on a nearby rock. He could have joined other officers in a tent or in one of the vacated houses, but he preferred to be outdoors this time of year. Being in the open also worked better with his present assignment.

He settled on his back with his hands linked behind his head. A few stars peeked through the lacy limbs overhead, obscured now and then by a passing cloud. Up the hill, he could just discern the cluster of buildings where the mill operatives, including the Misses Carrigan, lived. He'd arranged with Lieutenant Bradley to place a reliable watch near their front entrance for his own peace of mind. Having played their rescuer twice now, the responsibility for their safety pressed upon him.

They looked much alike, those two, with their chestnut hair and delicate features. Rose Carrigan wore the mantle of the elder, easily assuming responsibility and leadership. Her frame was slightly leaner, coupled with a sharper chin and piercing blue eyes. He pegged Celeste as younger, more because of her manner than her appearance. Her demeanor presented as milder, and she reminded him of a doe with her soft brown eyes. He'd guess no more than two or three years separated them.

Rose reminded him of Katie, his independent, cheeky little sister. *Please, God, watch over Katie while I'm not there to see to it.* Perhaps that was why he'd stepped into the fray between the Carrigan women and Pierce. Edwin Pierce was a troublemaker, much like Noah's cousin Luke. Since childhood, Luke had strutted a cocky swagger that attracted others. A natural-born leader, he used his charm to his own advantage, never mind the cost to others. Edwin and Luke had teamed up for a while back home. They'd terrorized neighbors until Luke's mother moved her family to be near in-laws in Kentucky.

After Noah's encounter with Pierce's band of rowdies, he'd settled Hercules with a good brushing and feed, then hurried to watch the town meeting. Munching a meat pie from the cook tent, he'd happened upon Cooper Bradley on a hill at the gathering's perimeter. Cooper hailed from the same county in rural Indiana. Their friendship had solidified when Noah took Cooper's part against a bully at school.

Something scurried in the leaves above, sending a spray of leaves over his bed. Noah swiped them away from his face as he replayed the reunion. While they shared the latest reports of family, something in the distance captured Cooper's attention. "Well, snap my suspenders. There's a couple of gals who don't look like they dined on pickles and tobacco." He stood straighter and prepared to advance on the females.

Noah grabbed his arm when he recognized the objects of Cooper's interest. Surprised to see the women he'd encountered earlier, he relayed the story to his friend.

"That Pierce." Cooper spat the name as if it tasted bitter on his tongue. "He's like a snake in the grass, sneaky and dangerous."

Cooper shifted his attention to the women. "Perhaps we should make certain they reach their destination safely." He waggled his eyebrows in typical Cooper fashion, always eager to meet the ladies.

Noah chuckled at the memory, but his thoughts returned to his self-appointed wards. Cooper's assessment of the Carrigan sisters resonated his own thoughts. They seemed out of place in this mill town. *Why were they here,* he wondered, *working in that noisy, dusty mill?* Their mannerisms marked them as educated and more refined than most of the other women. Their father had been a minister, he remembered. His death must have left them destitute.

Though pale and poorly dressed, much like the others, in that first encounter, they'd displayed a certain air. Not arrogance exactly, but a quality of dignity even in the face of an uncertain future.

Well, maybe a touch of arrogance, in Rose's case.

Noah smiled. She wasn't afraid to stand up to him, although she managed to do it in a respectful manner. He chuckled as he recalled Rose brandishing her stick to warn the rascals away from her sister. His smile slipped when he recalled her sudden attack of anxiety at their last encounter. That'd been strange. He suspected something had triggered a memory. After four years at war, he understood the sudden panic that could surface from nowhere.

He rolled to his side and growled in frustration. "Forget it, Griffin. You can't afford to be thinking about young women now, not even Katie, beyond a prayer for safety. Sleep is the priority."

He'd head out to meet General Sherman's supply wagons in a few hours. Those wagons should contain much-needed provisions, shipped by train to Marietta. He hoped the contents would be mostly food rather than arms. Food was scarce here, with barely enough to provide for the town's residents, much less the thousands of soldiers who'd descended upon it.

Even if the wagons were full of food, though, it would little benefit the locals. Once relieved of that burden, those same wagons would return with a vastly different cargo: a few bundles of salvaged fabric and scores of unhappy workers, headed for Marietta and the North beyond. For those who'd spent their entire lives in this small Southern town, it would be a strange, scary world. Getting the women away from the heart of the conflict was best for everyone.

CHAPTER 5

SATURDAY, JULY 9, 1864

*R*unning, running, but getting nowhere. Rose kept running and searching for Celeste. Fear drove her. She tried to call out, but her voice wouldn't work. Only small, mewling sounds came out.

She was suddenly waist-deep, surrounded by water. No wonder she made no progress! Running in the ocean, her feet fought for purchase in the wet sand. She struggled for the shore but instead seemed to go farther out. Seaweed wrapped around her legs.

The water was over her shoulders now, and the waves tossed her, sweeping her off her feet. She reached for something. She couldn't see it well but sensed it offered a rescue. Where was it now? She struggled to rise, but someone pushed her down.

"Rose, wake up. Rose."

Celeste's voice burst through the nightmare.

Rose awoke, shivering. How could she be cold in this heat? Sweat drenched her body, her nightgown twisted around her legs.

Untangling her gown, Rose sat up and shook away the remnants of the dream. "Oh, Celeste. I'm sorry I disturbed your sleep."

"Don't be. I wasn't sleeping well myself. This room is stuffy, even with the window open. I wonder if a storm is brewing." She padded barefoot to peer outside. "It's almost dawn anyway. We might as well get on with the day." She turned to Rose. "Are you all right? Do you want to talk about the dream?"

Rose shrugged. "It's the same as before. Running in the ocean, trying to find you, getting caught in the undertow." She paused, remembering. "Except this time, nobody was chasing me, not that I could see. I guess I panicked because I couldn't find you. And something floated above the waves, something I tried to grab, maybe a rope or a piece of wood."

She stood to strip off her damp gown. "Then you woke me up with your yelling. You probably woke up the neighbors and the soldiers on patrol too."

"Oh, I did not yell that loud." Celeste reached to pull Rose's braid.

Rose sidestepped to avoid the tug and darted behind the changing screen. "We'll just ask the guard on duty when we go out. Maybe it'll be that young officer we met yesterday. What was his name?"

"Cooper," she said, then stopped when Rose peeked out from the screen. Celeste executed a delicate wave of indifference and raised her eyebrows. "Wasn't that it? Cooper Bragg or Bradford —something like that. I really didn't pay much attention."

Rose lifted the pitcher and poured enough water to wet her cloth. After swiping it over her body, she tossed the rag aside and donned her clothes. She continued to tease Celeste. "Oh, I think you did. He certainly seemed to be taken with you. What was his rank?"

"I don't believe he said. It was thoughtful of him to put a guard in our area."

"So it was." Relieved Rose had diverted her sister's attention away from the nightmare, she stepped back into the bedroom and gestured for Celeste to take her turn behind the screen.

"Do you think we'll get a place on the wagons today?" Celeste swept up her day clothes and headed behind the screen.

"Hmm. I don't know. I wonder if those people spreading their blankets yesterday were meaning to spend the night there. If so, I imagine they'll be first to get a seat."

Rose took a place at the window. The horizon turned pink and orange as the sun made its ascent. A golden ray spread across the scene. Buildings and trees obscured much of the view, but she kept her gaze on the gap between them. Watching the beauty of God's creation lifted her soul. In the last year, only Sundays came with such an opportunity. All the other days found her at her duty station in the weaving room before the sun cleared the horizon.

Celeste joined her at the window. "All our things are packed and ready. We should eat something now and pack a lunch, or perhaps more than lunch."

"I suppose we should pack all the food we can carry," Rose said, her voice heavy with reluctance. "Then we can mosey down to the town square and see if there's room for us on one of those wagons."

"I don't mind waiting another day. Leaving is going to be difficult."

"I know. I feel the same. Let's have a time of prayer before we head that way. Perhaps we'll get a sense of direction from the Scriptures." Rose picked up the small book of Psalms— Da's larger Bible was safely packed away—and led the way to the kitchen.

"We should visit Da's grave before we leave town," Celeste said. "I wonder if we'll be able to attend church tomorrow. Of course, Da would say we carry the church with us wherever we go, but I always feel such a peace in the chapel here."

Rose sighed in agreement. "I think we're going to need a double portion of that peace in the days ahead. This upheaval wears on body and soul."

~

*N*oah frowned at the soldier who slumped against the building, chin to his chest. Pity for the weary youngster threatened to rise, but Noah squelched it. Tough lessons, not pampering, built character.

Dredging up memories from his youth provided the impetus to issue a message in duty and fortitude. He kicked the youth above his trousers' waistband. Lack of padding around the boy's middle doubled the impact.

"On your feet, Private. I wonder if you know the penalty for sleeping on watch. Are you ignorant or just plain lazy?"

"Sir. No sir. I mean, yes, sir." He scrambled to his feet, staring at Noah with wide eyes. "Was I asleep? I only closed my eyes for a second, I swear, sir."

"I stood here for a full minute watching you." Noah leaned forward, narrowing his eyes. "You do know the penalty for dereliction of duty, do you not? I thought you were a soldier, not a mama's boy."

The boy's shoulders sagged, then he pulled them back, shoring up his defenses to quell a trembling chin. "I am a soldier, sir." He met Noah's gaze.

Good for you, boy. "Then prove it to me. March the perimeter of this block six times before you head to get grub. And do not let me catch you asleep on duty again. I promise you next time, if there is a next time, you will not get off so easy."

"Yes, sir. Thank you, sir."

Noah watched him march away, shaking his head in dismay. *What have we come to that we allow children to pick up guns and fight? This war waxed worse and worse.*

In his periphery, he noticed Cooper approaching. He swung about to face him. "Your last guard had a little trouble staying awake. Where did you find him?"

Cooper lifted his kepi and resettled it, a sign of agitation Noah was familiar with. "He latched onto me as we left Chattanooga, said his family was all gone. The major said to let him stay so long as we could keep him busy. I figured this assignment fit his capabilities. He's got to find his place in this catastrophe somehow."

"I sent him on a wake-up march then to fill his gullet. The boy's much too skinny."

Cooper frowned. "He's probably eating better with the Army than he ever did at home. I wonder what he'll do after the war." He left unsaid the thought Noah could almost hear. *If he survives the war.*

"Why, good morning, Captain Griffin, Lieutenant…Bradford, was it?"

While Noah had talked with Cooper, the Carrigan sisters had launched a stealth attack from the rear. The question came from Miss Rose, a hint of laughter in her dulcet voice. Both women regarded them with cautious geniality.

Noah understood. After all, he and Cooper wore the uniform of the Army that had destroyed their means of livelihood. Yet they'd also displayed a degree of kindness to the women on the day before. Like many fellow officers, they found their duty warred with common upbringing. Courtesy and care, that was how to treat women, not throwing them out of their homes and carting them off like cattle to a more convenient location. He couldn't see such an action advancing the Union cause. It gave these people one more reason to hate every soldier in blue.

"Bradley." Cooper smiled broadly. "How are you ladies on this fine summer morning?"

Celeste blushed and twisted her hands.

Rose chuckled, a gentle tribute to the irony in the lieutenant's voice. "Warm already! It is July, you know." She waved her hand as if to stir up a breeze. The sight of a gloveless hand producing such a dainty action struck him.

"Yes, ma'am, it surely is." Cooper swiped at the perspiration sprouting along his hairline. "Days like this convince a man to make plans for a future in heaven and shun the other place."

Noah watched the women exchange glances, using a silent communication that put a man on his guard. He sensed Cooper tensing beside him.

"Are you a man of faith, then, Lieutenant?" Rose lifted her finely shaped brows.

"I am, Miss Carrigan, although I admit our present circumstances sometimes make me question it." He swept his gaze across the view down the hill. Blue uniforms moved among the dull browns and grays of a weary populace. "I don't believe Providence is much pleased with any of us at the moment."

"Sadly, I must agree with you. We pray daily for an end to this struggle."

Silence reigned for a few moments. Not the awkward silence of unease, but unspoken communion among strangers who could have been neighbors but had met as foes. Or were they foes who had bridged the gap with simple human decency and a common faith?

Noah glanced at Cooper, who usually had a quick rejoinder on any subject. Even his friend's lighthearted approach to life had been shaken. He thought it best to move to more mundane topics. "Well, I'm sure you ladies need to be securing a place in the wagons heading out today. Will you need any assistance getting your baggage down the hill this morning?"

Rose met his question with elegant hostility. "No, thank you, Captain Griffin. Not knowing what we may face on our exile, we've limited ourselves to only as much as we can carry."

Though her words were mild, her tone was cold. Like a chameleon, her attitude shifted with the change in subject.

"I beg your pardon, ma'am." He'd not be baited into displaying unbecoming conduct. "My intent was not to badger you but merely to offer our assistance, should you need it. Since you clearly do not, I bid you good day."

He turned away.

"Captain." Her words halted his progress, and he turned. "I beg your pardon. The stress of this experience has affected my behavior. I am not usually so brusque and rag-mannered." A blush tinged her cheeks. "Please. Allow me to thank you gentlemen again for your assistance yesterday. And for posting a guard nearby last night. I pray God will keep you both safe."

Celeste added, "We're on our way to the cemetery right now, but we'll head to the departure site immediately after. We won't keep you from your duties any longer. Good day, gentlemen." She tugged on Rose's arm.

Noah sketched a brief bow while Cooper lightened the atmosphere with a dramatic sweep of his cap and some clever comment Noah missed. The women swept their skirts in the direction opposite town.

Though their leave-taking was genial enough, somehow Noah felt he and Cooper had been chastised and dismissed. He puzzled over Miss Rose Carrigan's reaction to his suggestions. Every time they met, she bristled and then apologized. Didn't the woman realize he was trying to keep her and her sister safe? Why did she resist leaving when it was in her best interest?

～

*T*he visit to the cemetery didn't dispel Rose's humiliation or anxiety over their circumstances. When would she learn to keep her anger in check? She prayed she hadn't upset Celeste with her forward tongue. Those officers had been polite and helpful, but she couldn't trust them to remain so.

She followed Celeste back to Factory Hill. Neither spoke until a young boy ran up behind them and nearly collided with Celeste.

He skidded to a halt and jerked his cap from his head. "Beggin' pardon, ma'am. Be you Miss Carrigan?"

"Yes," both said. Rose clarified. "We both are Miss Carrigan," she said. "Sisters."

"Oh." He glanced from one to the other. "You'uns do look alike. I'm Johnny. My granny over there sent me." He pointed back to a woman waving from a cottage beyond their own.

"Widow Thompson? She's your grandma?"

"Yes'm. She asked if you would please kindly step over to speak to her a moment."

They followed him to where the grandmother waited, grasping the railing that lined the shallow porch. She smiled, revealing slightly crooked teeth stained from long years of dipping snuff. Many mill workers indulged in the habit, believing it warded off illnesses often contracted in the harsh mill environment.

Rose couldn't get past the smell to try it.

The women spent a few minutes discussing the weather and the widow's health. They commiserated over the circumstances forcing them to leave town and wondered how much longer the war would last.

After several minutes of small talk, Rose turned her attention to Johnny. "This is a fine young grandson you have, Mrs. Thompson." She laid a hand on his shoulder with a smile. "He said you asked to speak to us. What can we do for you?"

"Nothin' for me, dearie. But I promised to beg a favor for another. Emily, Mrs. Anderson, it is. She come to me yestiddy, askin' if I knowed anybody what could write a letter to her man in the Army. So's he can know what happent here after we's all gone."

The older woman shifted her weight to rest against the railing. "I sez to her that you gals could write good, and I figured you to be kind enough to do that for her."

"I see." What a pity most of the mill workers had never learned to read and write.

Widow Thompson awkwardly patted her hands together. "O' course, if'n it's too much trouble."

"It's no trouble at all. Of course, we'll be glad to help with that. I appreciate your kindness and thoughtfulness. You just tell us how we can find Mrs. Anderson, and we'll take care of it right away, if she's still in town. Then my sister and I must see if there's room for us on the wagons leaving for Marietta."

CHAPTER 6

*T*hey missed the wagons leaving that morning. After listening to Widow Thompson for a good half-hour, Rose and Celeste followed her directions and found the Anderson house. Unfortunately, nobody answered their knock.

Rose pointed to the sheets drying on the line. "They must still be in town. Should we delay leaving and try to catch them at home later?"

"We should at least see whether the wagons are here and have room for us," Celeste said. "We promised Captain Griffin."

They finally made their way to the town square, trading the lingering odor of burned wood for the stench of too many humans and animals occupying a small space. Three wagons lumbered away as they crossed the grassy square, now marred by the muddied imprints of many feet and heavy burdens. Wagon wheels carved deep tracks in lawns once maintained with diligence and pride. Like their lives, Rose mused, broken and humbled by circumstances beyond their control.

The town square held only a fraction of the numbers who'd gathered yesterday. A few children ran about, some involved in a game of hide-and-seek. Mothers stood in small groups, visiting and keeping a watchful eye. Despite the rising heat, all took advantage of the rare opportunity to be outside with no demands on their time. This day provided an odd kind of holiday while they waited for the next upheaval in their previously restricted lives.

Blue uniformed soldiers crisscrossed the town with a sense of purpose, ever watching those in plain clothes. Whether they were viewed as repressive guardians or lax jailers, their presence was tolerated with thinly veiled antipathy. In return, the citizens earned suspicion.

Rose and Celeste approached the sergeant who turned away from the departing caravan. He dusted his hands and fished a handkerchief out of his back pocket. Swiping the kerchief across his damp brow, he eyed their approach with disgruntled impatience.

Rose barely uttered a word before he interrupted.

"Last wagons just left. You women will have to wait for some o' those to return. Could be late this evening, so I wouldn't count on getting on one until morning. Best be here around sunup, and don't think to bring no more than you can carry yourself. It ain't our job to tote your trunks and furniture."He turned and stalked toward the nearest building.

Celeste murmured, "I guess someone slept poorly last night."

"Or perhaps not at all. I've heard that too much drink can give one the headache." Rose wasn't as charitable as her sister. Her experience with men besides her father did not inspire confidence in their concern for anyone but themselves. She glared at the man's retreating form.

Celeste fidgeted with her worn reticule, glancing surreptitiously around the area. "Since we have the rest of today before us now, what shall we do? I don't like to stand here in full view of anyone who passes, but neither do I want to sit in our stuffy rooms for hours."

Rose sighed. "I suppose we could check at the Anderson home again and see about getting that letter written."

They made their way back toward Factory Hill, careful to gaze straight ahead, ignoring the ever-present soldiers.

"Where are we going to find paper to write a letter?" Celeste asked. "I don't recall seeing any among our things while we were packing."

"Let's see if Mrs. Anderson has any, although I don't hold out much hope, seeing as how none of them can write. The cost of paper was high even before the Army burned the mills. We may have to beg some wherever we can find it."

"Perhaps one of these soldiers would..." Celeste stopped, realizing the absurdity of what she was about to suggest.

Rose grinned at the notion. "Oh, yes, I can just imagine any of these Yankees would be obliging enough to give us paper so we can write a letter to someone in the Confederate Army. Considering we're all counted traitors, they'd probably accuse us of wielding a weapon." With a burst of mischief, she raised her arm to flourish an invisible sword. "The pen is mightier than the sword, you know."

"Ah, 'behold the arch-enchanter's wand!'"

The girls gasped and whirled in horror at the voice behind them.

Captain Griffin merely offered them a sardonic grin. "I believe that's the next line, is it not?" When they only stared at him, he imitated Rose's gesture. "But perhaps you've forgotten since that part is played by a man. Do you often attend the theater, ladies? Or given your present location, perhaps you merely do dramatic readings? Do you include Shakespeare in your educational pursuits as well?"

Rose wondered if he mocked them or was merely surprised to find such a conversation among mill workers. Da had said she was wont to take offense when none was intended, and she'd already exposed Captain Griffin to her sharp tongue earlier in the morning. She decided to expose her confusion rather than anger. "I'm afraid I don't understand your question, Captain."

"I overheard you quoting an English playwright. 'The pen is mightier than the sword.' I wondered how you came to know the play. I'd been told everything here revolved around the mills with little time for recreation."

Rose lifted her chin. "Our father was fond of saying that. I suppose he read it somewhere. I had no idea where it came from."

Celeste added, "Da loved to read all sorts of things. He always said you could learn something from even the most unlikely people and places." The sweet innocence of her statement contained a prick of truth. Rose glanced away to hide her smile.

Some of the gleam drained from the captain's eyes. "I quite agree, Miss Carrigan. Unfortunately, not everyone holds such a philosophy." He glanced around and lowered his voice. "The end of that speech recommends diplomacy instead of war."

How different life would be if the war had been averted. She and Celeste never would've left Dalton. They wouldn't be here now, conversing with a Union soldier so casually.

Rose recalled the stories she'd heard of the ruthless Union Army. The awful devastation visible here was only a small portion of the calamity across the South. How could she trust this man who kept showing up?

She believed everything happened for a reason, a purpose ordained by God. It was depressing to think He allowed so much death and destruction, but He worked on a grander scale. His plans covered years and decades, even centuries. She could hear her father's voice quoting Jeremiah. "I know the thoughts that I think toward you, saith the LORD, thoughts of peace, and not of evil, to give you an expected end."

The three of them continued up the hill in silence, as if by common assent, toward the sisters' cottage. Her thoughts were mired in somber emotions and questions.

~

*N*oah pondered the disturbing circumstances. After viewing his company with Lieutenant Boyd, he'd caught sight of the Carrigan sisters as they left the town center. If he'd been in charge of removing the people, he would have sent the young single women first.

Every hour spent in this town, now teeming with barely restrained soldiers, put them in danger. After all, some of the soldiers fell far below saintly in the best of circumstances. They were only men. Men who ached with loneliness, who dreamed about their wives and girls back home, longing for the soft touch of a female hand. Men who eyed each woman they encountered as a prize to be obtained, legally or otherwise, and other men who viewed them as a quarry to be conquered and discarded.

And he? Was he any better? In these women he saw his sister Katie, to be sure, a treasure to guard and protect—but still he was a man. The more contact he had with the women here, the more he viewed them as individuals. His compassion stirred for the mothers who balanced toddlers on one hip while grasping the hand of an older child. He pitied the older women with hands and bodies misshapen from long hours at a loom, their faces wreathed in wrinkles, their frames gaunt from lack of proper nutrition.

And yes, he admitted, he found his interest stirred by the few who had emerged unscathed by this harsh environment, whose looks and spirits still survived.

"I find myself amazed at your ability to steal up on people undetected, Captain, and at close enough range to hear a private conversation." Rose kept her voice even but challenged him with her eyes. "Just how long were you following us?"

There she went, sparring with him again. His anger swelled. "I observed you speaking with Sergeant Crane as I left a meeting with my company. You can imagine my chagrin at finding the two of you still in town when I expressly encouraged you to leave as soon as possible. As you saw yesterday, it's not wise to be wandering around unescorted."

"And you followed to chastise us, is that it? Then you heard us discussing our dilemma?"

"Your dilemma? What has happened?" He hoped they didn't detect the edge of concern in his voice.

Celeste patted Rose on the arm. "'Tis nothing alarming, Captain. We have need of some writing paper, as a favor to a friend. Unfortunately, our supply has long been depleted."

Paper. They needed writing paper. Hence the reference to the pen? " I suppose... Well." He thought for a moment, wondering about their need for paper. His duties included relaying messages between Garrard and Sherman, but he had no claim to those writing resources. In fact, he was overdue on his own correspondence. The present quartermaster had become tight-fisted of late, demanding reasons for requests outside normal distribution. He was someone best avoided as much as possible.

The meeting he'd left had been attended by a war correspondent from a Northern newspaper. Newspapermen always had paper available. Perhaps he could beg the correspondent for some paper as a goodwill gesture.

When they arrived at the sisters' home, he broached the idea. "I believe I might be able to secure some paper for you. But in return, I insist on your promise to be at the departure site early tomorrow morning."

"Truly, that was our intention today," Rose said.

Celeste bobbed her head. "Everything is already packed. We'll be on time."

Their gratitude for his offer of assistance was satisfying.

"Right, then. I'll see if I can get the paper and bring it to you here. I think it would be best for you to remain inside until I return. You really shouldn't be wandering about town if you can avoid it."

"Our front window provides a good view of the way we just came. We'll watch for your return."

"Good. It may take a while, as I have another meeting to attend, but I'll return as soon as I can." He started back the way they'd come, his thoughts focused on this new errand. He hoped that newspaperman hadn't left town.

~

"*I* don't like staying in this town when we should be on our way to Marietta." Major Cason stalked around the room crowded with Union officers. He stopped near Noah at the windows overlooking the front lawns of their temporary headquarters.

Noah turned his attention from the setting sun to the major and the room beyond. Maps littered the elegant dining table where his fellow officers occupied the matching chairs. Several lanterns sat in strategic places around the room, along with the crystal chandelier suspended over the table, all ready for lighting when the sun set. No other furniture remained. Like the rest of the house, the room had been stripped of paintings and other portable items, courtesy of the Union Army.

The war correspondent sat apart from the military men, his gaze sharp and his pencil worn dull as he scribbled furiously across his notepad. Noah wondered what he found of interest in the current debate.

"Duly noted, Major," General Gerrard said. "As soon as we

43

get all these females on their way, we can resume normal operations." He passed a weary hand over his beard. "I will be dashed glad to be rid of them. Most should be gone tomorrow, so I'm going to allow the boys a bit of celebration, as promised."

Several voices spoke at once.

"Celebration, sir?"

"I suppose that means raising a toast?"

"What are we celebrating?"

Garrard waved the message he'd been handed earlier. "We have successfully forded the Chattahoochee River, gentlemen. The enemy thought they had routed us by burning the nearest bridge, but they didn't count on Yankee ingenuity and our Spencer carbines. I think that's reason to celebrate. Tomorrow, we will break out the whiskey barrels."

Grins and nods accompanied a buzz of approval.

"But tomorrow is Sunday." Noah's protest left his mouth without thinking. His breath backed up in his chest. He dared to criticize the decision of his commander?

The other men turned incredulous expressions his way.

General Garrard's brows lowered. His fingers tapped the table, the sound echoing in the hushed room. "Hmm. So it is, Captain. We will encourage attendance for everyone at divine services in the morning." He pushed out of his chair and regarded the wary faces around the room. "Then we'll open the barrels. Dismissed."

A collective sigh preceded the rustling of papers and scraping of chairs. A couple of officers hurried to the general's side for private consultation.

Major Cason slapped Noah on the shoulder with a chuckle. "Good try, Griffin. Unfortunately, whiskey is a flashier drawing card than the chaplain's sermons."

Noah attempted a smile, though it felt tight. As the major walked away, he muttered, "And a sight more dangerous." Mixing soldiers and whiskey created a volatile situation, especially with innocent women nearby. He stalked toward the door and caught sight of the newspaperman stashing his satchel.

He skirted the table and thrust his hand toward the man. "Johnson, isn't it?"

He shook Noah's hand but crooked an eyebrow in question. "And you are?" He glanced at Noah's shoulders. "Captain?"

"Griffin, Noah Griffin. I wonder if you could let me have a blank sheet out of your notebook." How ridiculous. An officer begging paper from a newspaperman? But who else could he ask?

"My company is outside town, the quartermaster is likely at supper now, and I only need a sheet or two for a...an unexpected...need. I just thought, since you're here, I'd ask . . ."

Eying Noah with suspicion, the man reached into his satchel, flipped through several pages and ripped one from the binding. Noah lifted a silent thanks as it tore off clean.

"Going to write out your Sunday lessons before bed?" Ah, so *now* he realized who was asking.

Noah met the man's mocking gaze as his embarrassment faded to righteous conviction. "That would be putting it to good use for sure. Thank you, Mr. Johnson. I'll see you at services in the morning. Don't be late. I'm sure you'll want to take notes."

CHAPTER 7

*R*ose kept vigil at the open door of the cottage. Celeste had complained of a headache building and went to bed with a warm cup of weak tea.

The sun was dipping toward the horizon when she finally spied Captain Griffin striding up the hill.

"I'm sorry to be so late," he said as he reached her. "The meeting dragged. I had to beg this from a newspaperman." He held out a single sheet of paper. "I guess even newspapermen have to account for how much they use."

He shifted from one foot to the other. Was he nervous? Worried that he shouldn't be fraternizing with the enemy?

She offered a tentative smile. "It's fine, Captain. We'll make do. I do appreciate your help."

He shrugged off her thanks. "It was little enough. Do you think you could call me Noah? I hear 'Captain Griffin' much too often."

Her brows shot up, but she inclined her head. "All right. If you think it won't be perceived as forward. And I suppose it would be easier for you to call me Rose."

"Is it simply Rose or a shortened form of Rosemary or Roseanne?"

"Actually, it's Rosette. My mother was French. With an Irish surname like Carrigan, she made sure to give us both names to honor her heritage."

"Rosette," he said, musing. "It fits you."

He tore his gaze away and heaved a deep breath, as if expelling the tender sentiments. When he turned back, he'd resumed his serious demeanor. "I will remind you of our bargain, however. I'm counting on you and your sister being on the wagons tomorrow. I have reason to believe some of the men may be rowdier than usual by tomorrow evening."

"Yes, of course." Rose took a step back and lifted her chin. "We plan to be there early. We were prepared to go today, but a neighbor detained us. I'm afraid our conversation and the task took much longer than anticipated."

She hesitated, then forged ahead, determined to make up for her earlier bad manners.

"I suppose we won't meet again in this life, the world being as it is. I want to thank you for all the assistance you've given us. Despite the current circumstances, I'm glad to have made your acquaintance, Noah Griffin."

His large hand engulfed the one she offered. The warmth of his touch surprised her. Palm to palm, she noted the ridges in his, created perhaps by frequent use of heavy tools, and forgot the rough condition of her own. He bowed over their joined hands. "The pleasure is mine, ma'am. I wish you well, you and your sister." He opened his mouth as if to say more, then abruptly turned and strode back down the hill.

~

*W*hat was he thinking? Noah had not behaved at all like himself.

Resisting the urge to look back up the hill, he passed a hand over his face. There was a war going on. This was no time to become romantically entangled, especially not with a Southerner. How had his natural inclination to protect the innocent and helpless become complicated by attraction? He warded off the internal voices answering such questions, voices that sounded much like those of his sisters and Cooper. Although Cooper's voice carried no words. He simply laughed.

Should Noah risk talking to Cooper about this? Once his friend stopped laughing, he might have some advice. Though younger than Noah, Cooper had more experience with women. Women of all ages naturally flocked to him. He was a charmer but in a wholesome way, unlike Pierce and his ilk.

Noah's chest burned. He could blame that on what he'd eaten, but the problem didn't lie there. He arrived at his campsite and found Cooper perched on a nearby stump with a cup of coffee in his hand. Noah couldn't stop the bark of laughter.

"Why don't you appear on the battlefield when I need someone at my back?"

Cooper speared him with a questioning look. "How's that?"

"I was just about to search for you, and here you are. Now if you can materialize at the mere thought, I'm going to call you up for the next battle."

Cooper grinned. "Oh, I see. Kind o' like an angel. Wish I could help you out, Griff, but you'll have to keep appealing to the Almighty for His protection."

Noah rubbed his chest absently as he paced around the campsite. Now that he had opportunity to ask for his friend's help, he wasn't sure how to begin.

Cooper said, "I heard about you reminding the general that tomorrow's Sunday."

Noah raised his head and grinned self-consciously. "Yeah, that was brilliant, wasn't it? Thankfully, he took it in stride. I wouldn't have fared as well with Uncle Billy."

"Garrard is all right in my book. He backed himself into a corner by promising a reward for crossing the river, so he had to come through." He stood and slapped Noah on the shoulder to stop his pacing. "At least he agreed to hold off until the chaplain has a chance to say why the men shouldn't indulge." He peered into Noah's face. "But that isn't what's bothering you, is it? Come now, time to share your burden with ole Coop. Just pretend I'm my father."

Noah reared back in horror. "Your father? Of all people to share my innermost feelings with, it wouldn't be your father."

Cooper chuckled. "Ah, so it's feelings, ey? A woman that's got you all stirred up. Should've known. Which one of the Carrigan ladies is it? Although I think I can guess."

Running his hand through his hair, Noah exhaled loudly. "Rose. She drives me crazy. She takes offense at everything I say, doesn't do what I've suggested, looks down her pretty little nose at me like I don't have the sense God gave a billy goat, acts like I'm her enemy…"

Cooper's raised eyebrows stopped the rant.

"Well, yes, that aside, I don't think she likes me very much. But when I stopped by her house tonight—"

"You went to her house? Uninvited?"

"I was invited. She needed some writing paper, and I told her I'd find some for her."

Cooper's grin made Noah grit his teeth in frustration. "I went to her house to give her the paper as promised."

"All right." Cooper deliberately wiped the smile from his face and attempted a serious countenance. "And then what happened?"

"She said she was glad to have met me and wished me well. It was a definite goodbye. She gave me her hand, and I was nearly overcome with the need to pull her into my arms. But I couldn't, could I?"

"No, I suppose you couldn't. Not now. But things don't have to be over yet. I heard your company is scheduled to accompany the next caravan to Marietta."

"Yeah, but Garrard could pull me aside. My men will carry out their duties whether I'm there or not. "

Tomorrow could present another opportunity to see Miss Rose Carrigan, or at least to make sure she arrived safely in Marietta.

When Cooper left to join his own company, Noah spread his bedroll but gazed toward Factory Hill in the growing darkness.

∼

*D*aylight waned as Rose hurried to the Anderson home. Finding them home, she sat with Emily and her in-laws at the kitchen table, writing while they debated and dictated the letter to Martin. Only when they'd finished the task did she think of needing an envelope to cover and secure the letter from prying eyes.

The elder Mrs. Anderson—Ada, she'd insisted on being called—took care of the matter. She removed a family Bible from a chest and ripped the back page from it. Rose gasped but quickly recovered. The offering was one of those extra blank pages. She never would've considered such an act, but these were unusual times.

Confusion made her stammer. "You have a Bible...but none of you can read or write?" Her gaze traveled from one person to the next.

"It's my mama's Bible, passed down from her folks who came here from the old country long ago." Ada passed the book to Rose for inspection. The woman's dark hair and brown eyes reminded

Rose of her mother. "It ain't in English, I was told, so none of us could read it anyways, even if we had any schooling. I keep it for the family names in the middle part with the colored pages. Took it to the preacher to add the names of the children when each was born."

Reverently Rose turned the pages, briefly examining the family registry before flipping to the front and finding the book of Genesis. "It's in French. My mother was French and taught my sister and me when we were younger, although we rarely use it anymore." She returned the book to Ada with a smile. "I think we'll stick with English for now."

Returning to her task, Rose carefully folded the letter so as not to smudge the words and fitted the torn page around it. "Now we need to write your husband's direction on the outside here," she explained to Emily.

"All I know is he's in the Thirty-fifth Georgia, company G, somewhere in Virginy. 'Twas what the mill foreman said when he told us the news last week. Will that do for the letter?" Rose tried not to show her dismay. What were the chances of Martin Anderson ever receiving such correspondence? "Do you know of anyone else who has family in the Thirty-fifth? Maybe we can get a more specific address from them." She searched the faces of everyone at the table.

The old man's face wrinkled in concentration. Though several decades older than Rose, he'd insisted on being called J.D. "Seems like the place had a man's name, the name of one of them disciples in the Bible." He pointed to the book on the table, clearly pleased to contribute to the cause. "I 'member Preacher Pratt saying so when I took him the bread box I made for his missus."

Mentally comparing disciples' names with towns, Rose suggested, "Jamestown, maybe?"

He shook his head. "That don't sound right."

She continued slowly, trying to recall any Virginia towns

she'd heard of. "Petersburg? Now I recall hearing someone at the mill mention it."

At the family's agreement, Rose wrote the information across the envelope: "Martin D. Anderson, Company G, Thirty-fifth Georgia CSA, Petersburg, Virginia," adding "Please forward as needed."

"We still have to find out whether any mail is getting through. With no way to post it from here, maybe we can find someone who'll know how to get it out." Discretion ruled the day, with every move monitored by the Federal soldiers. Though she couldn't fathom why they'd care about family correspondence.

Rose's finger tapped the letter. "I've written everything here and asked for it to be sent on if he's no longer there. We might ask around as we travel, or when we get to Marietta, see if anyone knows where the Thirty-fifth might be now. You can put this in one of your bags until we find out."

She extended the letter to Emily but didn't release it. "I think we should pray over it first. Ask God to direct it so Martin will receive the news from you."

She regarded the expressions turned her way. Surprise. Embarrassment. Doubt. She read them all but held her ground and smiled. "My father was a preacher. He taught us to pray over everything. It's ingrained in me."

Emily shrugged. "If'n you think it'll help." Cautious hope lightened her features.

"Well, it shore can't hurt." Ada covered their hands with her own, and J.D. followed suit. Rose added her other hand.

"Dear Lord, You are not limited by time and space as we are. We pray You'll provide the means to get this letter to Martin Anderson, wherever he may be, so he'll know what's happening here in Georgia. We don't know what the future holds for any of us, Father God, but You do. We trust You to guide us all according to Your will. Amen."

Rose tucked her pencil into her reticule and made her way to the door. "I'm pleased to have met you all and glad I could help with the letter. I suppose I'll see you again if you're leaving on the wagons in the morning."

"Yes'm, we'll be there," J.D. said, unfolding his angular body from his chair. He opened the door and peered past Rose into the growing darkness. "Should I walk you over, miss? Wouldn't want you to suffer any harm from one of them soldiers wanderin' around."

"Thank you, Mr. Anderson, but I'll be fine. It's only up the hill a bit."

Rose trudged up the hill and, as the ground leveled out, lifted her eyes to marvel at God's handiwork in the sky. War and confusion littered their world, but stars dotted the night sky, reminding her the Creator saw the flight of every sparrow. "He knows the way I take."

Sensing movement to her left, she pivoted right into the path of a soldier. He grasped her arms and barked out a sinister laugh. "Well, that's more like it now, you coming right into my arms. Guess I get my dance after all."

Rose recognized the voice. Sergeant Pierce. A whiff of his fetid breath turned her stomach. She should've accepted Mr. Anderson's offer but figured the old man's presence offered little protection.

Jerking her arms proved useless.

Words were her only weapon. She poured her outrage into them. "Let me go or I'll march right over to your commander's headquarters and report your conduct."

He laughed and pulled her closer.

A scream ripped from her throat as she twisted her face away from his.

A shadow materialized and struck her captor's head.

The sergeant's arms dropped away, and he slumped to the ground.

Rose stumbled to stay upright. Was she safe now? Or merely passed from one predator to another?

"Miss Carrigan? Are you all right?"

The voice wasn't Captain Griffin's, but she'd heard it before. Starlight made his face barely discernible. Captain Griffin's friend peered at her anxiously.

Rose wrapped her arms around her middle and wrestled with the panic. She gulped long drafts of air. "Yes, I thank you. Would you...would you mind walking me to my house?"

His smile bloomed. "Exactly where I was heading, Miss. I'll be taking the first watch tonight." He stepped around the prone form and offered his arm.

Rose hesitated, casting an anxious look at her attacker. "He isn't...dead, is he?"

"No, though some would say he deserves it. He'll come around soon enough, so let's get you home now."

She took the lieutenant's arm and whispered a prayer of thanksgiving. The good Lord had protected her, even using Union men to work against their own.

"I'd prefer not to tell anyone about this incident please, but you can be sure my sister and I will be on the wagons leaving in the morning."

Lieutenant Bradley nodded. "I think that would be wise."

These officers would probably breathe a sigh of relief to watch the Carrigan sisters depart Roswell for Marietta and points northward.

CHAPTER 8

"*I* thought you were heading out with the last wagon train." Cooper picked his way over a fallen tree trunk and caught a low-hanging branch with one hand.

Noah paused in his packing to address the implied question.

"General Garrard held me up while he wrote an update to take to General Sherman." He gestured to his half-packed gear. "As you can see, I'm breaking camp so I can get on the way. Did you get to attend divine services?"

"I did. I thought Chaplain de LaMatyr did a creditable job of keeping everyone awake."

Noah snorted. "Yeah, although Garrard's promise of whiskey seemed to depress attendance by others. Grab that bedroll, would you?"

Cooper handed off the bedroll and crossed his arms. They had played this game before. Cooper would wait for the question burning in Noah's brain. He turned back to his task, determined not to give in. He started counting. Five, six, seven seconds.

"You saw them off, did you?" Noah threw the question casually, but clenched his jaw, betraying the tension he held in check. There was no doubt who was on his mind.

Cooper couldn't hold back the grin. He'd always ribbed Noah about being straitlaced and by-the-book. Noah was the one with the cool head who admonished the other boys to behave. Only once before had he admitted to Cooper his interest in a certain female, and that was in his youth, years before.

Cooper offered his friend a cheeky salute. "As ordered, Captain. Miss Rose and Miss Celeste loaded their baggage onto the eighth wagon, right in the middle of the train, but they chose to begin the journey on foot. I daresay they did so to allow the older people and small children to have a place to ride."

Noah's brow creased. "They chose to walk to Marietta? But it's twelve miles if it's an inch."

"I don't think they'll be racing the entire way," Cooper said, his penchant for irony in full force. "They set off at a speed my grandmother could manage without complaint."

Noah guffawed. "Mawmaw Bradley would be snapping a whip over the lot of them, telling them to git. But the walking itself isn't what concerns me. It's the proximity of the soldiers in the convoy. Could you tell if any other company went with them?"

"If you're asking whether Pierce was there, then no, I didn't see him. I believe his unit is due to head west."

Noah stuffed the last of his gear into his saddlebags and slapped the carrier over one shoulder. The straps of a leather pouch crossed his chest and back, forming an X with his ammunition sling crossing from the opposite shoulder.

"I imagine they'll stop to rest once or twice," he said. "Traveling with women and children will slow down the wagons considerably."

"Without doubt." Cooper followed Noah to the corral where Hercules had already been saddled.

Noah conveyed his thanks to the young soldier on duty and tossed his bags across the gelding's flank.

Cooper slung an arm across Noah's shoulders. "You should be able to catch up to them easily enough."

Noah opened his mouth to argue, then gave it up with a grin. No sense denying the obvious. "I suppose I shall. And what of you? Is your company ready to move out?"

"In a couple of hours. I suppose the major wants to let the wagon train get far enough ahead that we don't overrun them."

Noah adjusted the gelding's load, pulled on his gauntlets, and grabbed his kepi.

Cooper offered his hand with a warning of caution. "Tread carefully, my friend. The war still rages, and the future is unpredictable these days."

"Duly noted. I expect our paths may cross again shortly, probably under less pleasant conditions. God be with you."

"And you, in all circumstances."

Noah mounted the horse and turned him in the right direction. Deeper south and the next battle awaiting them. There seemed to be no end in sight.

~

*R*ose slowed her steps as the wagon beside her came to a sudden halt. She looked up to see J.D. Anderson grip a boy under his arm and swing him over the side. The child wobbled a bit but soon found his feet and lurched into the nearby bushes.

A mounted officer drew alongside the wagon. "Hey, why are you stopping? Where's that child running off to?"

"To empty his stomach in the woods," J.D. answered. "Seems wagon riding don't agree with him."

Before the officer could respond, the boy returned, pale but walking steadily. He eyed the wagon askance. "Maybe I oughta walk." He glanced toward Rose and the other women who'd volunteered to walk at the outset of the journey.

Poor child. Rose stepped closer to the wagon. "I'd enjoy having someone to walk with me, if that's all right, officer?" She waited for the soldier to voice his agreement then held out her hand to the child. "I'm Rose Carrigan. What's your name?"

"John Mark Anderson." He took her outstretched hand but hesitated, waiting for his folks' permission to join her.

Emily Anderson inclined her head. "Much obliged, Miss Carrigan. You mind your manners, John Mark."

They made their way over to the others on foot as the driver called, "Walk on," and the wagon jerked its way into motion again.

"So, you're part of the Anderson family I met yesterday. I guess you'd already gone to bed when I got there. I know your pa's in the army but not much about the rest of your family."

The boy reached into his pocket and withdrew a few pebbles. He tossed them from one hand to the other. "That's my ma, my sister, grandpa and grandma in the wagon. Last we heard, Pa was in Virginy. Ma and me, we work in the mill, or we did 'fore it burnt down."

Rose flashed him a smile. "I worked in the mill, too, along with my sister. See that girl in the green bonnet over there?" She indicated her with a sweep of her hand. "Her name is Celeste."

"Why don't she walk with you? Did y'all argue? Ma says me and Sarah Grace argue all the time. It's because she thinks she's the boss of me, but she's only five, and I'm almost nine, so I ought to be the boss of her."

Rose laughed. She loved his childish honesty. Too bad many

people lost that somewhere along the way to adulthood. How different the world would be if more folks retained it.

She hurried to answer while he paused to take a breath. "We didn't argue. We get along fine most of the time."

Lowering her voice to a conspiratorial whisper, Rose said, "She's involved in a secret mission." Putting a finger to her lips, she motioned for him to speak quietly, indicating the soldiers riding up and down the road as the caravan crept southward.

"What secret mission?" Eyes round with wonder, the boy halted.

Rose gently nudged him forward, then leaned down to whisper. "She's counting how many steps she takes so we'll know how far we walk."

"Why would she do that?" His brow wrinkled then cleared as he understood her meaning. "Oh, so we can know how far it is back home, right?"

"Bright boy. You figured it out right away. When we know how many steps it takes to make a mile and how far we can walk in an hour, then she'll stop counting steps and figure the distance from how long it takes us to get there. Do you understand?"

He frowned in serious thought, nodding. Perhaps appealing to the boy's sense of adventure would speed the trip for both of them.

"We also need to know which direction we're going," she said. "Otherwise, we might get lost walking back. See how the sun is climbing up in the sky over there? That's east, so the direction we're headed now is mostly south."

"How do you know all those things?" John Mark asked, childish skepticism coloring his voice. "I never heard my pa or grandpa talk about any o' that. Are you just making it up, like I make up stories about fighting the Yanks?" He quickly lowered his voice again with a furtive glance toward the nearest soldier. "Ma says I make up too many stories."

"No, I'm not making it up. I promise." Rose signaled a cross over her heart. "You see, my pa was a preacher and a teacher when I was growing up. Like your pa, I'm sure, he was very smart, and he taught Celeste and me about all kinds of things, like history and science."

He took a moment to digest that thought, walking quietly. "Your sister must be up to a thousand steps by now. Grandpa said a thousand is a lot, and we ought to know how to count that high so's not to get cheated in trade."

Rose feigned surprise. "Can you count that high already? I'm amazed."

But none of the family could read. Maybe she could make a difference there.

∿

Nibbling thoughtfully on a piece of bread with some cheese rolled inside, Rose waited for Celeste to sit in the shade beside her. According to her, the convoy had traveled nearly five miles in the two hours on the road. The red-haired soldier said it was about thirteen miles to Marietta, meaning they had three or four more hours to go if they maintained the same speed, and if all went well.

Celeste carried a cup of water in each hand and passed one to Rose. As she sat down, Rose said, "I wonder if we could teach some of these people to read and write once we get to Marietta. From what I can discover, nobody here has even a basic knowledge of letters. They left it to the mill owners and preachers to pass on anything they needed to know."

"Oh." Celeste took a sip of her water. "But didn't someone say there used to be a school in Roswell?"

"Yes, years ago, but evidently teachers were hard to keep in town. The school was closed more than it was open. Only the children of the leading families received any consistent education. They attended Reverend Pratt's school in the Presbyterian Church."

"Wouldn't the workers need to know at least the basics to do their jobs? I never gave it much thought, working in the spinning room."

"Most of the supervisors came from other places, mills up north usually. I guess they found ways to train a few of the men who worked with them. Women have managed homes for years without education, especially in the South, so they probably never figured to need it."

Celeste frowned. "But the world is changing. I heard the North is full of different kinds of industry, more than the South. All of us may need to learn something new, especially with all the losses from this war. How will they get along if they can't read?"

Rose leaned over to pat Celeste's hand. "Just so, dear sister. I know we've never tried to teach, but I think we could at least teach these children to read."

Celeste swallowed the rest of her water. "Just the children, no adults?"

"I think the idea would be received better if we only address the children. Some of the adults might be embarrassed to admit they can't read. Others would insist they're too old to learn."

"I'm sure Janie would be glad to include her children. Peter had the chance to attend school before they moved to Roswell, but none of the others."

Rose nodded. "I remember her saying Peter didn't have the patience to teach the younger ones. What about Phoebe? Do you think she would want to be included?"

"She's distanced herself from me lately, even made some rude remarks, which didn't bother me but upset Janie something fierce. I guess she's getting to that age where she thinks she knows everything. Plus, at fifteen she's suddenly developed a keen interest in men. With all these soldiers around, I doubt we could get her to focus on schoolwork."

"Janie will also need her help with the younger ones."

Rose paused, tapping her chin with a forefinger. "I think parents always want better opportunities for their children than they had for themselves. That's the biggest reason to focus on the youngsters. Also, whatever town we end up in may require the children to go to school. That was becoming more and more common before the war. These children will be at a disadvantage if they don't have at least a basic knowledge of how words are formed."

Celeste regarded Rose thoughtfully. "All right. I agree with you. We were blessed to have parents who provided a good education, and we should share that with others less fortunate." She dredged up a tired smile. "Maybe God had a plan, sending us to Roswell last year."

"He always has a plan, but we might not have figured it out so soon if the Yanks hadn't ordered us to leave. We certainly didn't have the time or energy to take on such a task while working in the mill."

Celeste expressed exactly what Rose was thinking. "All things work together for good. I suppose even losing our home and income."

"Da always said God is our Source. He'll provide a way for us." She stood and replaced the cups in their knapsack. "Well, I guess we should test our idea, and I know right where to start."

They stashed their knapsack and picked their way to the wagon, where the Andersons waited on the call to move out again. John Mark spotted them first and ran to intercept their path.

"Miss Carrigan, are you going to walk again or ride?" Without waiting for Rose to answer, he turned to Celeste. "Did you finish your secret mission?"

"Secret mission?" She glanced from the child to Rose, who

said, "I told him about your secret mission to figure out how far we traveled today."

"Ah, I see." Turning to John Mark, she bent down and whispered. "I figure so far we've traveled about five miles. The soldier told me the trip was thirteen miles. Maybe you can help me figure out how many more we have to go."

He screwed up his face in concentration, repeating the numbers. "We already been five?"

"That's right. And the whole trip is thirteen. Now start counting up from five until you reach thirteen."

Rose shared a smile with Celeste as the boy started counting on his fingers, whispering under his breath until he reached the final number. His crow of achievement rang out as Rose approached his mother.

Emily stood apart from the others, her shoulders slumped, her brow furrowed. Perhaps their plan would be a welcome diversion from her troubling thoughts.

"Mrs. Anderson."

The woman jerked out of her contemplation. "Oh, Miss Carrigan. I thank you for taking up with John Mark. I hope he isn't wearing you out with his chattering."

"Not at all. We're having a grand time. He's a fine boy."

Emily blinked away a sheen of moisture. "Thank you for all you've done. I'd be pleased if you'd call me Emily. It's what I'm used to hearing."

"I'd be happy for you to call me Rose. I have a proposition I'd like you to consider, a plan for your children."

Seeing Emily's surprised expression, she rushed on. "As John Mark and I were talking, I thought it might be good if I could teach your children, and maybe some others, how to read and write. We're all on this journey together, and it may serve us all. None of us knows the future or what awaits us. We're not teachers, but if you agree, my sister and I'll be glad to pass on what we've been taught."

Rose clamped her lips together. Prattling on and on did no good. Her face grew warm as Emily simply stared.

Ada Anderson overheard and spoke her opinion. "Well, I think it's a fine idea."

"Oh, yes. Yes, I agree." Emily gazed at Rose with childlike wonder. "I just never imagined... It's kind of you to offer."

Rose flushed with pleasure. Surely, she and Celeste had discovered purpose in this trial of faith. Making her way to Janie Wilson to offer the same suggestion, she prayed she and her sister would be up to the task. A search among their possessions should turn up a few books they could use. It was a shame they didn't have a good supply of paper and pencils or slates and chalk for writing practice, but they'd find a way to make it work.

She smiled at the thought of Captain Griffin bringing them a single sheet of paper for Emily's letter to her husband. God had supplied that need. She was sure He had a plan of provision for whatever came their way. Even if he had to use the Federal army to supply it.

A verse from James came to mind. "You have not because you ask not." Rose swallowed her fear. She'd find the courage to ask. As soon as she figured out who might be the best person to approach.

CHAPTER 9

*N*oah slowed Hercules to a walk as he spotted the caravan ahead. Now that he was here, he wasn't sure what he would say or do. Rose had bid him farewell as if they'd never meet again. Perhaps that suited her all right, but it didn't sit well with him.

Growing up in the country hadn't prepared him for romantic pursuits. Besides his sisters, the only young females in his world wore nappies, and the older ones had married before he outgrew his short pants. Setting his mind on a military career, he'd immersed himself in study. The longer he dodged contact with females, the more daunting he found them. But his reaction to Rose would not be denied, even if it terrified him.

Was it foolish to pursue her to the next town? Their paths would go separate ways soon. General Sherman's plans included deporting the workers north while he readied the army to capture Atlanta. With his division on the move, Noah could only give Rose a means of contacting him when the war ended. Once the women left Marietta, the decision of any future communication would be up to her unless he could make suggestions for which guards were assigned to accompany the women to their destination.

That wasn't likely to happen, but the thought gave him hope.

He refused to dwell on the differences in their lives, the things that served to drive them apart. North and South, Yankee and Rebel, the conqueror and the vanquished, however that turned out. Instead, he concentrated on their similarities, which boiled down to faith and education. To his way of thinking, those were the most important aspects of life anyway.

But how can I be sure it's enough? She's a Southerner. She worked in a factory that provided goods to the enemy.

A simple matter of location, he reasoned. She worked to stay alive. A woman without a father or husband had few choices. Even if she had relatives elsewhere, how could she and her sister undertake a journey with the war raging around them? From their conversation yesterday, he concluded that the Carrigan sisters had no personal interest in the war, and their reduced circumstances ruled out holding slaves.

Ah, but what were Rose's views on the reasons for the war—States' Rights and the institution of slavery? Would her ideas of social justice conflict with his? And he couldn't claim to be without some form of prejudice himself.

"Enough!" The word escaped his lips unbidden.

The soldier at the rear of the cavalcade whirled on his horse and stared at him. "Sir?" He snapped a quick salute.

Noah returned the salute and waved away the soldier's concern. "I appear to have fallen into Warren's habit of talking to myself. It's quite disturbing."

The man flashed an understanding smile. "I have caught myself doing the same at times. I wondered why you weren't among us at the outset, Captain. Thought perhaps you might be coming with the Seventeenth Indiana."

Noah patted his breast pocket. "Special messages to deliver

on arrival. The writer took a while figuring out what he wanted to say."

A snort of understanding accompanied the lieutenant's nod. "I, too, would choose my words carefully when writing to the general. No need to stir up things more than they are."

"Just so." He saluted and rode up the line farther, slowing as he reached a cluster of women walking beside the wagons. Would he recognize Rose Carrigan without seeing her face? Except for differences in height and girth, women appeared much the same from the rear. They'd been on the road for a few hours now. Had they already stopped for a rest period?

Eighth wagon from the front, Cooper had said. Noah counted as he passed the caravan from the rear wagons. Ten, nine. There! While most of the women plodded like cows out to pasture, he spotted two trim forms with a livelier step, chatting with a young boy who walked between them. He'd stake his next meal on those being the ladies he sought.

Hercules whinnied in protest of the increased pressure on the reins, and Noah corrected his grip. "Sorry, old boy."

As he drew even with the group, the boy darted to the middle of the road. Noah jerked the reins to spin the rearing animal away from the child. Voices rang out in alarm.

"Whoa!"

"John Mark!"

Noah's gaze settled on the youngster, who glanced from the horse to Noah with wide eyes.

He stammered out an apology. "Sorry, sir. Didn't mean to spook your horse." He stuffed an object into his pocket and turned away.

"You could have been seriously injured, young man. What was that you picked up? What could have been worth the danger?"

The women gathered around the boy like broody hens

rescuing a chick. Three of them led him a safe distance away. The fourth turned her anger on Noah.

"Shame on you," Rose hissed. "He's just a child. It's your duty to watch out for the weaker ones. How was he to know you were there?"

"And good afternoon to you, too, Miss Carrigan." Spoken aloud, her surname begged for a childish rhyme with *harridan*. His lips quirked, but he dared not smile. He swept off his kepi and held it over his heart. "My apologies to all you ladies." He gestured to include everyone, "And to the young man. Fear for his safety caused me to speak so sharply."

"So you say." Rather than continue chastising him, Rose merely sniffed and turned to join the others. The wagon had not slowed its pace but plodded along unfazed by their little drama.

Though this wasn't the way he'd wanted to announce himself, he wasn't going to lose the opportunity to renew his acquaintance with Rose and company. He swung from Hercules's back and fell in behind the women, horse in tow. Their pace was decidedly firmer than moments before, militant even. A few soldiers could learn something from them.

He decided to address the younger Carrigan this time. "Good afternoon, Miss Carrigan I trust this journey has not been too hard on you?"

Celeste's gaze bounced from Noah to Rose to John Mark and back again. She offered him a faint smile. "I am faring well enough. 'Tis not the journey as much as the heat that wears on me."

He could feel Rose's glare, though she stared straight ahead and ignored him altogether. Let her fume awhile. He signaled from Celeste to the other women for introductions. She didn't smile but obeyed.

"Janie and Emily, this is Captain Griffin. He was kind enough to come to our aid back in town. Captain Griffin, Mrs.

Janie Wilson and Mrs. Emily Anderson. Mrs. Anderson is John Mark's mother."

Another young woman pushed her way into the group.

"And this is Phoebe Wilson," Celeste said.

Noah acknowledged the women, but his courtesy was mostly met with grudging civility. Only young Phoebe seemed happy to meet him. The slender blonde pulled her braid over her shoulder, gave him a saucy smile, and batted her eyelashes. "How do, Cap'n?"

Encouraging the girl's flirtation would bring more trouble than he could afford. He turned his attention to the boy. "So, John Mark, is it? I daresay these ladies are not well pleased with either of us at the moment. I'm relieved we have both escaped unharmed from our, uh, dramatic meeting."

"Yes sir." He glanced at his mother. She nodded, and he smiled back at Noah. "I thought I saw a gold piece on the road, but it was just an old bullet casing."

"Ah, that's what you picked up then?"

"No sir. When I got closer, I saw this arrowhead." He drew the arrowhead from his pocket and offered it to Noah for inspection. "Thought it might be from one of them Cherokee what used to live here."

Turning it over in his hand several times, Noah released a low whistle. "I think you may be right, John Mark. It looks mighty old and could be valuable. Some people collect these, you know. In fact, I might be interested in buying it from you."

An idea formed, one that would give Noah an excuse to visit the boy again, and perhaps his female entourage as well. "When we get to Marietta, I'll find my friend Cooper, and he can tell me what it might be worth. His pa has a collection, so he would know."

"Really? You'd give me money for it?"

"If it's truly from an Indian arrow, sure. You hang onto it for now, okay?" He handed the object to John Mark. "Keep it in your pocket and don't lose it."

"Yes sir!"

Noah lifted his head, his gaze colliding with Rose's. Her eyes conveyed bewilderment and suspicion, and maybe a dozen or two questions, but he chose to ignore those for now. He sent her a smile. "Has the company stopped for the noon meal yet?"

CHAPTER 10

Marietta, Georgia
Sunday, July 10, 1864

*N*oah ate with his young friend to avoid the women's suspicious glares. Deciding he'd spent enough time there, he galloped into Marietta ahead of the wagon train and delivered General Garrard's carefully worded message to Sherman's aide-de-camp. That general, he was told, could not be interrupted while planning strategies with his fellow commanders. Their raised voices in the house they occupied droned. Noah didn't care to linger and learn the outcome of their voluble discussion. He turned to leave but pivoted back to ask a question.

"Where are we putting the female mill workers coming from Roswell? I passed the latest party on the road, and I know this is at least the third group to arrive."

"They're being housed in the military academy, which the Confederate cadets evacuated before our arrival. You've seen it, I suppose, on your earlier visits."

Noah scratched his chin. "I thought Major General Thomas was using it as headquarters for his Cumberland boys."

"He's using a portion and putting the workers in other buildings." The man wagged his head in pity. "I wouldn't want to be in his or Colonel Gleeson's shoes, having to put up with so many prisoners, even if they are women. He may soon have to find other places to put them if their numbers keep growing."

The aide returned to his duties, and Noah set out for the military school's campus. The size of the complex made it the perfect place to house large companies, but he doubted it was suitable for families or even single women. Like other military structures, it likely consisted of large dormitories with a dozen beds in each room. Little privacy.

The scene, when he arrived, looked vastly different from the last time he'd passed the facility. The buildings that housed the workers appeared to be converted classrooms. Evidently, General Thomas's troops occupied the barracks. No chivalry there.

Several women endured the afternoon sun, attempting to launder garments using whatever equipment they had or could appropriate. Others huddled in doorways or shady areas while they watched children involved in a game of hopscotch.

Guards stood nearby, observing everything.

Noah approached a guard near the children's game. A sling dangled from the man's neck, his arm tucked inside. He watched the activity with studied nonchalance.

"At ease, Private," Noah said. "I'm here merely as an observer."

The young man lifted his weapon and executed an acceptable salute. "Yes sir. Thank you, sir."

Noah asked a few questions about his assignment and how many people were lodged in the buildings. After learning where he might find the officer in charge, Noah led Hercules in that direction, but a shout drew his attention to the end of the street.

Several wagons stopped to unload passengers. Scores of women and children swarmed the area. This couldn't be the group from Roswell. By his calculations, they still had another hour before they reached Marietta.

Watching the women stumble from wagons, he wanted to curse. Where were they going to put all these people? His upbringing prevented the words slipping past his lips, but his mind reeled with them.

He hailed a soldier who dismounted from one of the wagons. "Where have these folks come from, Sergeant?"

The man saluted and lifted his arm to catch the drops of perspiration tracking along his brow. "A place called New Manchester, where the Sweetwater Cotton Mill was destroyed. We was ordered to burn it and bring the workers here so they can be sent north on the train."

"That was Major Tompkins's assignment, wasn't it? How many?"

"I heard there was two hundred what worked in the mill. Don't know how many brung their families, but we loaded maybe a dozen wagons. A good many of the folks walked the whole way. Sixteen miles it was, but we split it into two days."

Noah pinched his lips together to keep from blurting out his irritation. The destruction of the mills had created more work for the Army and heaped on heartache for these people. "Thanks for the information, Sergeant. I'll see if I can find out what they plan to do with the other families coming from Roswell."

The man swiped his kerchief across the back of his neck. "I'll say this, Captain, them women are tough. They'll find a way to make it work."

"I pray you are right. Marietta's population is already over-flowing." Spurred by the growing number of wagons, Noah pivoted, mounted Hercules, and set off to find Colonel Gleeson.

The colonel would be hard pressed to find places for this many refugees.

~

*M*arietta. The name that had been issued as a prison sentence a few days before now promised blessed rest for the weary travelers from Roswell. Once pronounced a curse, the name had become a benediction.

The caravan slowed as it encountered other wagons, mounted riders, and pedestrians along the rutted streets. Despite her fatigue, Rose observed the town with interest. Storefront signs indicated an industrious population. They passed a milliner's shop, an apothecary, and a tobacconist, as well as an imposing bank. Several windows, however, displayed signs announcing changes to the shops' business, such as Quartermaster's Office and Army Post Office. Beyond the rooftops, men worked on new construction. In every direction people swarmed like locusts of biblical proportions.

Blue uniforms everywhere.

A cavalry officer made his way down the line toward them. He stopped at each wagon to give directions, waiting for the people walking alongside to clamber aboard the packed beds. As he drew closer, recognition dawned. Rose groaned. Did he plan to follow them forever?

Celeste leaned around Janie's generous figure to peer at the traffic. "Why are we stopping? Oh, my, it's Captain Griffin again." She glanced at Rose. "He pops up at the most unexpected moments."

"I've noticed. It's most disconcerting." Rose plied her fan, then quickly slid it shut, unwilling to display the sorry item in town. She kept it because it was her one remaining fan. Tattered and stained, it was a remnant from a former life. Life before the war.

She pulled back her shoulders and gathered her wits, preparing for the coming encounter. Somehow, despite his bouts of kindness, Captain Griffin represented the entire Federal Army. Enemy was perhaps too strong a term. Nemesis. That was the word. His presence put her on guard. What ulterior motives could he harbor against her?

He approached the wagon nearest them and spoke to the driver, gesturing the directions. Both men saluted, and Captain Griffin rode past them to the next wagon, ignoring Rose and Celeste entirely, though he stopped to speak to John Mark behind them.

Rose's defenses fell away. After insinuating himself into her affairs, why would he ignore her now? Perhaps he'd tired of the game.

Celeste peeked over her shoulder at the group behind them. "Well! That was unexpected. I guess he must be quite busy now that we've reached town."

"Undoubtedly. Thank heavens for small favors." She lifted her chin and faced forward.

Celeste turned away, but not fast enough to hide her smile.

The wagon driver bellowed above the noise of the traffic. "Hop aboard, ladies! We don't want to lose you this close to the end of the trail."

He halted the team, and Mr. Anderson stood to assist the women. Rose and Celeste clambered after Emily Anderson, gaining their precarious seats before the wagon lunged forward again.

Rose glanced around. Janie had joined the rest of her family on the wagon in front of them. Ada Anderson held Sarah Grace in her lap, but there was no sign of the woman's grandson.

"What about John Mark?" Rose asked.

Emily gripped the edge of the wagon as it rocked and pointed back the way they'd come. "He's riding with Captain

Griffin on that big ole horse. I never seen the boy so happy. I guess they's a few good men in the Federal army after all."

The wagon pushed through the town and turned down a tree-shaded lane. Elegant houses lined either side of the road, their yards dotted with great oaks and tall, spindly pines. The lawns and flower beds showed signs of neglect. Goldenrod and milkweed littered the uncut grass. The blossoms of pink and blue hydrangeas drooped in the afternoon heat.

Rose's spirit sank at the sight of the negligence, assuming the houses had been abandoned by their owners—Southerners who'd deserted town and left it to the mercy of the enemy army and occasional squatters. A sad legacy.

Feeling the wagon slowing to a stop, she noticed the one ahead had pulled into the yard of the house just ahead. A moment later, their driver alighted and motioned to the passengers to leave the wagon bed. Mr. Anderson positioned himself at the tailgate, where he could hand the ladies to the soldier waiting to lift them off. Much to Rose's surprise, the soldier was Captain Griffin himself. When had he caught up to them?

He set Celeste on the ground and reached for Rose. She gasped as he placed his hands at her waist, heat rising from the twin points of contact. Corresponding heat flushed her face. Fighting for equilibrium, she blurted out the first question she could articulate as her feet hit the ground.

"Why are we stopping here?"

"This is where you'll stay until there's room on the train." He released her and marched up the short walk to the house.

Rose followed him to the porch, where several more women watched their approach, their brows furrowed with curiosity. Her gaze swept over them, finding no familiar faces, hearing no words of welcome.

Flashing a tenuous smile, Captain Griffin offered a general introduction. "Ladies of the Roswell mills, please meet these ladies from the Sweetwater Mill in New Manchester. I regret you'll have to share these living quarters for a day or two, but I think you'll find them more agreeable than the military academy where many of your fellow workers are staying."

He turned to address the soldiers who hefted large bags of foodstuff from another wagon. "I believe the summer kitchen is accessible through the rear door."

All the women stared as the men passed by, carrying more staples than Rose had seen in months. At least they would eat decently while they stayed here.

Rose struggled to understand. "Captain Griffin, do you mean for all of us to occupy the same house until...until advised otherwise?" Her troubled gaze flitted over the assembled company.

He nodded curtly and moved from the porch to a lower step.

"Temporarily. Well, I'll leave it to you folks to complete the introductions and decide on sleeping arrangements." He gestured to the soldiers still unloading the wagon. "Private Jones and Private Allen here will assist you as needed. I'll try to check with you again tomorrow. Good day."

~

*R*ose's gaze followed Captain Griffin as he strode away. Leaving the field of battle, she thought, but the irony didn't escape her. She couldn't fathom his behavior. Perhaps the stress of war had affected his mind.

After the caravan had halted for a rest on the trail, he disappeared as suddenly as he'd shown up. Only John Mark had known of his departure. The boy proudly announced that Captain Griffin had to move ahead of the wagons to make sure everything was ready for them.

Thinking of John Mark, Rose saw he was approaching a young boy with the Sweetwater crowd on the porch. The others were already introducing themselves. Celeste and Emily stood behind Rose, observing the interactions. Rose shook off her woolgathering and extended her hand to the nearest person.

"I'm Rose Carrigan. The journey must have rattled my manners."

The auburn-haired woman took her hand with an understanding smile. "Olivia Spencer. No apology needed. We've only just arrived ourselves, and everyone is weary beyond measure. I daresay this must be your kinswoman, a sister perhaps?"

Olivia moved to take Celeste's hand and introduced them to Lydia Gibson, a buxom woman with straw-colored hair. Around them, others were exchanging names and handshakes. John Mark and the younger boy dashed off to explore the upstairs while warnings to behave followed in their wake.

Thunder rolled in the distance. A slight breeze carried the clean scent of rain, and sprinkles warned of an impending summer shower.

"I suppose we should move inside as well," Olivia said, "and figure out the sleeping arrangements. I counted seven beds upstairs, complete with pillows. I declare it's a miracle, but everything seems to be untouched by the army. Lydia and I were about to tour the downstairs area when you arrived."

Seven beds and thirteen people, if Rose had counted accurately. They could make do.

Olivia introduced them to her aunt, an older woman with silver strands lightening her auburn hair. "Edith Wynn," she said. "And this is Shiloh." She pulled the young woman with dark, curly hair to her side.

"That's my husband, Isaac, over there." Edith pointed out the shorter man with white hair. In spite of their contrasting appearances—Isaac had a slight build where J.D. was tall and gaunt—they talked amiably. She turned back to Olivia. "Now if you ladies will take care of the sleeping quarters, Shiloh will help me get things started in the kitchen. I can't wait to dig into those sacks and see what we can do with such bounty."

Working together, the women found linens for the beds and worked out the sleeping details. Rose found comfort in the familiar tasks of making beds and helping serve the meal. The routine reminded her of how people of the church banded together whenever a family was in need. Women divided the work between them according to their natural inclinations, while the men shouldered the heavier chores. Or did as their wives bid them, she mused with a smile, watching both Ada Anderson and Olivia's Aunt Edith give specific assignments to their spouses.

After a simple supper of bean soup and cornbread, the group gathered in the parlor while the rain cooled the air outside. Quiet conversations led to discoveries of similar backgrounds and skills. Fatigue soon overtook them, but nobody suggested moving upstairs yet, reluctant to disrupt the tenuous sense of unity. As the room fell silent, Olivia's Uncle Isaac brought out his Bible. He cleared his throat before addressing the weary gathering in a hesitant voice.

"With all the upheaval we've been through, I'm sorry to say we've completely missed honoring our Creator today. If it's all right with everyone, I'll read a short passage of Scripture before we turn in for the night."

Nods and murmurs of agreement encouraged him to go on. Rose sat forward to listen and discreetly observe the others. The Anderson family clustered together near the fireplace, John Mark leaning against his grandfather's side while Sarah Grace sat between Emily and Ada. She wondered about their knowledge of Scripture since none could read. She wondered if they listened out of courtesy or real interest. No matter, at least God's Word was proclaimed.

The two younger women from Sweetwater had chosen low stools, leaving the claw-footed chairs for Celeste and Lydia Gibson, who insisted on being called by her given name. All four gave their full attention to the reading, and Rose sensed they treasured the familiar custom. Edith sat with her husband on the settee, absently patting his shoulder in encouragement. Olivia's young stepson, Wade, curled up next to her on the hearth rug. She smoothed his brow as he sank deeper into sleep.

"Matthew six, verse twenty-four says, 'No man can serve two masters...'"

Her mind wandered, reviewing events of the last few days. She chastised herself for irreverence. Fatigue did strange things to one's mind. She tuned in to the words again.

"Take no thought for your life, what ye shall eat, or what ye shall drink, nor yet for your body, what ye shall put on."

Rose found the familiar words weighty with meaning. Hadn't she caught herself lately thinking overmuch about those exact things? How were they to eat? Would the clothes they'd brought be sufficient? Her silent confession and repentance blocked out the voice again. By the time she finished, the man had reached the end of the chapter.

"Take therefore no thought for the morrow, for the morrow shall take thought for the things of itself. Sufficient unto the day is the evil thereof."

"How true," Rose said. The last few days had brought unexpected concerns, many of them evil, but also some new opportunities and potential friendships. She could only wait and see what the coming days would bring.

CHAPTER 11

he next day arrived early for Rose, and the Scriptural warning of potential for evil loomed over the wayfarers at the house in Marietta.

Awakened by a noise outside, she lay listening, waiting for the sound to come again so she could identify it. When nothing followed, she arose and knelt beside the window, careful not to disturb Celeste on the other side of the bed. Across the room, Emily Anderson curled around her daughter. The four younger women from Sweetwater occupied the next room, and the older couples took two of the smaller bedrooms, with the boys in another.

Rose moved the lacy curtain aside an inch, barely enough to peer into the pre-dawn stillness. A crescent moon rode above the roof of the next house, its pale light dimly outlining the trees and buildings visible from her vantage point. A slight breeze danced among the leaves of the oak and sent a few pine needles sailing against the windowpane. Nothing moved in the yard below. The faint wail of a distant train whistle emphasized their remote location.

As she released the fabric and turned away, the noise came again. Ah, 'twas the scraping sound of a tree limb against the house. She sighed. The wind must have shifted.

Accustomed to early hours, Rose wouldn't attempt to lie down again. She slipped on the dress she'd worn the day before, pinned up her braid with a few hairpins, then picked up her shoes and crept to the door. Careful not to wake the others, she made her way downstairs, where she sat on the bottom step and fastened her shoes.

A shadow moved in the dining room. Rose gasped, then swallowed a chuckle as she realized someone else had risen early as well.

Lydia offered a weary smile from her place at the table. "Good morning. I see you also get up with the chickens."

Rose chuckled. "A lifetime habit that's hard to break. Da used to say he had to wake up the sun and the roosters. Even if he'd been up late with a family at a wake or sitting with a sick parishioner, he was still the first one in the kitchen, putting on water for coffee or tea." Sweet memories cascaded in quick succession, bringing a smile.

"Sounds like he was a wonderful father. As was mine, for as long as I had him. Oh, there's still a bit of cornbread under that dish, if you're hungry."

Rose helped herself to a square of bread and dipped a cup of water from the bucket sitting on the sideboard. She pulled out a chair at the table and sat across from Lydia. "You lost your father at a young age, then?"

Lydia pressed her finger to the scattered crumbs and nodded. "When I was nine, but he was near sixty. Mother was his second wife, and I was the youngest of six. What I remember most is his gentle nature and his distinctive laugh."

Edith and Shiloh entered the dining area and helped themselves to the leftovers.

"What a blessing to have such a pleasant place to spend the night," Edith said. "The soldiers in our area stripped the crops from the field and even came into the houses to seize whatever they wanted. Finding this place in such good order is a miracle."

Rose blinked. "They didn't burn down your mill, then? We didn't know they were coming our way until the soldiers burst into the mill and ordered us out."

"Not right away," Lydia said. "They must've been there a week or more before Major Tompkins announced he was going to burn it down."

The women finished the last of the bread. Edith brushed a few crumbs from the table into her hand. Her quiet voice carried the weight of authority. "Since we don't know how much longer we'll be here, I think we'd best cook up double portions of food we can carry with us. Biscuits and such."

Lydia looked at Rose. "I don't know how much time you folks had to pack your things, but the soldiers rushed us out with hardly any notice. Even though they'd camped in the area for several days, the order to move out was a hurried affair. If Millie and I hadn't started packing the day before, we wouldn't have half as much as we have now."

"Why did you do so?" Rose asked.

Lydia blushed and glanced at Edith, who answered for her. "The Good Lord told her to, just like he did my Isaac." Edith chuckled and wagged her index finger. "Only difference is Isaac resisted and wrestled with the Lord for a few days. Lydia had the good sense to hop right on it."

How good of God to warn these folks in advance and put her right in their midst. Even if it was by the hand of the Federal army.

Edith pushed away from the table. "Well, those biscuits

won't make their selves, so we'd best get on it. You ready, Shiloh?"

The shy woman bobbed her dark head and started for the door.

"Do you want some help?" Rose asked.

She and Lydia stood, volunteering to join them, but Edith waved them away. "No, the summer kitchen is a good size, but there're so many bags and barrels in there right now, we'd be bumping into each other. Why don't you check the root cellar and pantry to see what's there we can use?"

Rose hesitated. "Should we do that? I mean, surely the people who lived here will return sometime."

Bowing her head and planting her hands on her hips, Edith said, "I figure it this way. Those folks who lived here took all they wanted or could carry with them. Nobody knows how long they'll be gone or even if they'll make it back. We left most of our possessions at home. I won't begrudge anyone who goes into my house and makes free use of what I left there. These are desperate times."

As Shiloh followed Edith out to the kitchen, Lydia turned to Rose. "I believe she has the right of it. If anyone in need happens to end up at my house, I'll be glad for them to take whatever they find, especially any food that might not keep. Truth to tell, there's a few things I wish they would carry off, like my ugly kitchen rug." She grinned and gestured toward the door. "Let's get to that root cellar."

Olivia came down the stairs as they passed. "I heard Aunt Edith order you to scout the cellar. I'll help with that." She snatched a lantern near the back door. "I think we might need this. Who knows what kind of creatures might be hiding down there?"

Rose shuddered at the implication but followed the others outside and into the underground space. The stale air and dark memories stole her breath. She stayed close to the exit while the other women roamed deeper, examining the shelves. Her foot touched something that rolled away. A basket. She bent to pick it up, realizing they should have brought containers to carry out whatever they found.

Lydia's voice called back, "Rose, are you wearing an apron?"

"I'm not, but I found a basket here on the floor. Do you need it?"

"Yes, there are several jars of honey or preserves here. We could—"

Olivia's voice interrupted her. "Oh, my goodness! Lydia, Rose, come here."

The urgency in Olivia's voice propelled Rose farther into the cellar, her focus on the light cast by the lantern. When she reached the other women, she followed their line of vision to a shape on the floor. Someone lay there, unmoving. Rose prayed the person was only asleep.

～

*N*oah changed position on the hard bench at the back of the room, struggling to stay awake for the officers' reports. Morning duties began early, and the days stretched long in summer. Shorter nights compounded the constant fatigue, and the incessant heat drained his energy. Although the fields of Indiana were plenty warm in July, at least the nights brought some relief. Here in Georgia, the heat went on and on.

Just like the officers giving their reports, making it hard to pay attention to their words.

A poke in the ribs made him start and turn to the culprit with a sharp word at the ready. He managed to keep his voice low. "Coop, what're you doing here?"

Cooper nudged him to make room on the bench, and Noah slid over. "Captain sent me in his place. He's indisposed."

Noah's eyebrows rose but he refrained from asking. Whether the man had overindulged or suffered from one of the diseases that stalked the army, he wouldn't demean a fellow officer with speculation.

Movement at the front of the room caught his attention. Colonel Gleeson stood to report on the state of the mill operatives. He smoothed his moustache with two fingers and referred to a report as he spoke, his Irish brogue commanding attention.

"Forty-five men from the mills in Roswell and forty-three men from the Sweetwater Mill in Campbell County were arrested and brought to Marietta, along with a large number of women and children—"

"How many?" a brusque voice interrupted.

Colonel Gleeson addressed the speaker. "Our estimate is roughly seven hundred persons, all told. The women are uneducated and not capable of signing their names on a register. We thought it unnecessary and not good use of our resources to have our men record every one. Besides, the prisoners will be here only a few days. I will instruct General Webster to take a census when they reach Nashville."

Noah started to rise in objection, but Cooper held him down. "Blast it, they are not all ignorant!" He whispered his frustration to Cooper. "I know of at least two who are educated and would be glad to record those names if they were asked. As it happens, they're planning to teach the youngsters with them to read and write."

Cooper's green eyes sparkled with curiosity. "Are they now? And how did you discover that nugget of information?"

Noah fidgeted in his seat as Colonel Gleeson answered questions from other officers about the female prisoners.

"I made friends with a boy, and he told me about their plans. Which reminds me, I want you to examine an arrowhead he found to see if it's worth anything."

Colonel Gleeson raised his voice over the hum of various

conversations. "Most of the families are housed at the Georgia Military Institute. Some are in abandoned houses. General Dodge is arranging for some of the women to serve as nurses in the field hospital."

The presiding officer banged the table to cut off the discussion. "However," Gleeson said, "from Nashville, most of the operatives will be sent by train to Louisville and then across the Ohio River to Indiana. They should be able to find employment there, and they'll be off our hands." He flicked his wrist as if shooing away an annoying insect. "General Garrard, what progress have you made at the river?"

The casual disregard for those displaced families irked Noah, but he pressed his lips together to prevent a retort. His mentors had stressed the importance of keeping good records, and preserving families carried even more weight. Such a cavalier attitude demonstrated the officers' lack of concern for those in their care. With their men away, the women and children had no way to contact them.

He hoped the Carrigan sisters carried through with their plans to educate the youngsters. Perhaps they'd extend the offer to the women as well. Then they could contact family members and share their new location, wherever they landed.

Could he assist them with those lessons?

The familiar vibration and chug-chug of a train nearing the station spurred him to action. The refugees' days here were uncertain.

CHAPTER 12

$\mathcal{R}$ose cowered as Olivia swung the lantern closer to the prone form. When the light reached the man's face, he leaped to his feet and brandished a long knife. "Stay back!"

The women retreated several steps and huddled together. Rose took in a shaky breath. "We mean you no harm. We're only collecting some f-food."

Lowering the arm with the weapon, the man ran the other hand over his face. "Sorry. I wouldn't hurt any woman, but you'uns gave me a scare, you did." His gaze swung from one face to another in the dim light. "Who are you and what are you doing at my house?"

"Your house?" Rose exchanged glances with her companions. "We were under the impression the family had abandoned it."

Olivia said, "The Federal army brought us here. We were taken prisoner at the mills they captured and burned."

The man cursed under his breath and dropped to his knees. "The town is truly in Yankee hands, then? I'd heard they was coming this way. I had to come back and see for myself." He paused to catch his breath. "Begging your pardon. I'm Sergeant

Seth Morgan, Eighteenth Georgia infantry. I've been walking for days, hardly sleeping at all, got here about daybreak, hid in here until I knew how things stood. Thought maybe I'd catch my folks before they left town."

Lydia sank to the floor to face him, her skirt billowing around her. "I'm Mrs. Gibson. These're Mrs. Spencer and Miss Carrigan. We don't want to disturb you, but you'd best stay out of sight if you're wearing the gray or butternut. There's Federal guards all around here, and they'll jump on you like ticks on a hound dog."

Rose stepped forward with her basket. "We'll just gather a few things and then leave you to rest, Sergeant. That is, if you don't mind us taking some of your stores."

He waved them away and lay down again. "Take whatever you need. If the family's gone, they won't mind it going to help fellow Southerners. If someone could come later and wake me up?"

"Yes, and we'll bring you something to eat." Olivia helped Lydia to her feet. "Sleep a while now." Her suggestion was unnecessary, as his breathing grew shallow with slumber.

With silent steps, they gathered several jars and left the storage room. They passed Shiloh and Celeste carrying platters of hot biscuits and a crock of syrup to the house. Celeste smiled at them. "If someone can bring the pot of grits when it's done, we can all have a hot breakfast this morning."

"We'll get it," Rose said, following the others to the kitchen. Of more importance than breakfast, though, they needed to warn Edith about their surprise visitor. They crowded into the kitchen and told Olivia's aunt about their discovery in the root cellar.

Edith kept her voice low. "The fewer people who know about this, the better. We'll carry on as usual for now. I suggest one of you check on him in a few hours and see if you can find out what his plans are. Likely he won't be wanting to stay here long with matters as they lie. We dare not cause trouble with the guards. Once he's gone, we can be at ease."

"Celeste and I thought we'd take the children outside this afternoon," Rose said, "and hold our classes near the small garden. We should be in full view of the cellar door and able to watch it while we teach. If anyone approaches it, we can distract them."

The others offered to take turns checking on the outdoor classroom. Since the guards kept their duty on the street outside, even taking their meals on the front porch, the women decided it should be no problem to keep their cellar occupant a secret.

~

"*N*ow, children, let's see what you remember." Rose used a stout stick to write the letter K in the dirt where she and three children huddled on a blanket. "What is this letter?"

She studied their faces as they pondered the answer. John Mark frowned in concentration while Sarah Grace scrunched her lips to one side. Wade Spencer propped an elbow on his upraised knee, tapping a finger to his chin.

Janie Wilson's children had joined them for class, coming over the yard from the neighboring house escorted by fifteen-year-old Phoebe and one of the provost guards. Phoebe showed no interest in learning. She claimed her task was to watch over three-year-old Tommy, who currently napped on a blanket in the shade. Phoebe's attention centered on the young man in uniform. The two conversed in low tones in a friendly manner. Perhaps too friendly. Should Rose speak to Janie about it?

Celeste sat a few yards away with Janie's two younger daughters.

The children had been attentive when they started lessons

earlier in the day, but the rising temperature sapped their enthusiasm.

Shiloh rescued them when she stepped onto the back porch and called, "Supper!"

Boys and girls scrambled to their feet and scampered away while Rose and Celeste picked up blankets, slate, and chalk. Even with limited equipment, their project to teach the children proceeded as planned. Parents and children alike greeted the idea with enthusiasm, especially with so many people sharing each house. The lessons kept the children occupied and out of the adults' way while they divided chores. Everyone's spirits lifted when they stayed busy and contributed to the group's welfare.

Rose helped Phoebe round up her siblings. The soldier lifted sleeping Tommy and handed him to Phoebe. As they crossed the lawns to the next house, they looked like a family. Even the weapon resting on the young man's shoulder could be interpreted as a means of protecting his clan instead of a threat to keep them in line.

How deceptive appearances could be.

Celeste waited on the covered back porch, where they deposited their few teaching instruments. Knowing Edith would see the men and children served first, they took some time to discuss each child's grasp of letters and numbers.

Celeste touched Rose's hand. "Why did you keep glancing toward the house all afternoon? It's not like you to be so jumpy. Are you expecting someone?" Tilting her head, Celeste batted her eyes and smiled.

"What? No, of course not." Rose waved away the suggestion. "Even if I were, people do not go around the house to the back yard. All proper visitors know to knock at the front door."

Celeste observed her with narrowed eyes. She was much too perceptive. "Are you keeping something from me?"

Blowing out a heavy sigh, Rose drew her sister back into the yard and gave a whispered account of the early morning trip to the root cellar.

"Oh, my. No wonder you've been on edge all day. Has anyone checked on him since then?"

"Lydia took him a meal about midday. She said he barely finished before sleeping again. Poor man was exhausted." Rose pressed her lips together. "I suppose it'll be a day or two before he'll be up to leaving, so we'll have to stay vigilant."

Nodding, Celeste glanced at the house. "I suppose we should go in before someone comes hunting for us."

They washed up and headed into the house, passing John Mark and Wade as they rushed outside to play. Rose shook her head in wonder. "My, they certainly have a load of energy now that class is over."

Before she and Celeste could join the other women at the table, however, male voices raised in greetings drew their attention to the parlor. All the women paused in place, looking as if they played a game of statues. Rose could barely breathe. Only the women's eyes moved, darting from one to another, anxious questions clearly expressed there.

Being closest to the hall doorway, Rose forced herself to investigate. Her progress was halted by a familiar face as she entered the hallway. "Captain Griffin." Her hand fluttered to the skin over her heart.

"Miss Carrigan." He removed his kepi with one hand. The other supported a box tucked under his arm. For a moment, neither of them said anything. Then his gaze moved beyond the door to the dining area where the other women remained immobile.

"Ladies. Good day to you. Please, don't let me interrupt your meal. Something smells good." His gaze wandered to the table. "Looks good, too."

Nobody moved or returned his greeting.

"I, uh, just wanted to drop off this box of paper. I thought you could use it, uh, teaching the children." He thrust the box toward Rose.

She didn't take his offering. "How did you know we were teaching the children?"

"John Mark told me about your plans yesterday. I think it's a fine idea. I remembered you're short on paper and requisitioned a box from the quartermaster."

He pushed the box toward her again, and this time she accepted it, acknowledging his efforts to help. Again. As if he'd adopted their little band. Or perhaps he helped others, too, as he could. He continually surprised her, going out of his way to assist them.

Just as he had done yesterday, bringing us to this house. How astounding.

The women revived and returned to the task they'd abandoned at the interruption. Most were still wary and kept their distance from the Yankee captain.

Edith Wynn took a step forward to welcome him. Rose had already dubbed Edith as "the peacemaker" for her steadying influence on everyone.

"Captain, your gift is much appreciated," Edith said. "Would you care to join us at the table? The men and children have already taken their meal, but most of the ladies have not."

Rose covered her gasp with a strangled cough. Did Edith forget that a Confederate soldier—this man's enemy—hid in the cellar? She noticed discreet nods from Lydia and Olivia as Celeste put another plate on the table. Emily and Ada kept their distance. Shiloh and Millie must have eaten with the earlier crew, as Rose could see them through the window toting dishes toward the kitchen.

The captain began to demur, but Olivia pushed to Edith's side. "Please do join us, Captain. That is, unless you think it will cause you problems. After all, this food came from your officers." She gestured to the table. "We'd like to hear any news you might be able to share."

Rose set the box of paper on the sideboard and turned to find everyone seated except Captain Griffin. He waited to assist her, just as if this were an ordinary dinner. He'd wormed his way into their good graces—well, most of them. A few seemed torn between reluctance and hunger for news of the battlefield.

Was she the only one who found his attention disturbing? In spite of his kindness, she was reluctant to trust him, and not just because he wore a blue uniform. The memory of another patronizing gentleman made her wary. She'd been young and too naïve to suspect his ulterior motive for courting her. Such solicitous concern for her welfare had transformed into a weapon of control and destroyed her reputation. Would Captain Griffin's involvement only bring more of the same?

ould dining with these women harm Noah's reputation if word got back to his commanders? He'd been too stunned by the invitation to refuse. Did these women claim no loyalty to the Confederate cause, or did they simply have no means of knowing how the war fared? Surely, they were as eager as he was for it to end.

With dishes passed around and plates filled, understanding dawned as he regarded the faces at the table. The war had taken nearly everything from them. Their concern now was survival and keeping their families intact, including their menfolk who were away at war. With no means of communication readily available, the family fabric tore apart and frayed.

He swallowed the cornbread that lodged in his throat and chased it with a sip of water. His gaze circled the table. "Any news I can share must be sadly outdated. I haven't seen a newspaper in a week or more. You must know our army has secured the Chattahoochee River, the primary reason we came to Georgia, along with the railroads between Marietta and Chattanooga."

"Do you know anything about casualties in Virginia?" The

auburn-haired woman dashed sudden tears from her eyes. She was a member of the Sweetwater bunch. "My husband is a doctor, a surgeon with the Thirty-fifth Georgia, in Petersburg."

A gasp from the women farther down the table delayed his answer. All eyes turned to the woman he recognized as John Mark's mother. "Petersburg! That's where my Martin is, with the Thirty-fifth also."

Surprised comments flew around the room.

"You don't say."

"How come you didn't mention it before?"

The older woman who'd invited him to dine now beamed. "Isn't that just like the Lord? Putting together folks who have men in the same place."

In the discussion that followed, he learned those two were the only families at this house with men currently attached to the Rebel army. The one named Lydia had lost her husband last year at Chickamauga. The older women, along with their husbands, were relatives of the younger women who had worked at the mills.

With the meal over, Noah prepared to take his leave and turned to Rose, who had spoken little during the meal. "Please tell John Mark I haven't forgotten about his arrowhead. Cooper hopes to get by here tomorrow to take a look at it. If it's worth anything at all, one of us will purchase it for Judge Bradley's collection."

Rose began collecting dishes. "I'm surprised he hasn't come in to see you. The boys must be involved in their game."

A commotion drew everyone's attention to the backyard. Noah pushed his way to the door. Women quickly spilled out of the house behind him. John Mark and the other boy froze in their places outside a circle drawn in the sand, pebbles strewn on the ground around them.

Although the shouting had stopped, the source of the trouble lay sprawled a short distance from the kitchen. Beneath Private

Allen's knee squirmed a youth in baggy clothing, his face in the dirt, his body heaving. Noah wasn't sure if he was crying or simply exhausted from the tussle. Noah stopped mere inches from the two on the ground.

"Let him up, Allen."

The soldier shifted and pulled up the miscreant, still holding the stranger's hands behind his back, though his struggles had stopped, and his head hung forward in defeat. "He was stealing food from the kitchen, Captain. I caught him when I was returning mine and Jonesy's dinner dishes."

When the youth made no attempt to deny the charge, Noah reached out to touch his shoulder. The reflexive flinch combined with the mop of dark curls raised Noah's suspicions. That kind of response indicated someone familiar with abuse. He gripped the shoulder anyway, his hand closing over the thinness under the dark coat.

"Look at me."

The head lifted mere inches, bringing the thief's eyes approximately even with Noah's collar.

"Look at my face."

With obvious reluctance, the thief obeyed, raising the face for a full inspection. Noah's instincts warred between pity and anger, observing the delicate face with tears tracking over the tawny cheeks. The dark eyes darted away, hesitant to meet his gaze.

Noah heaved a sigh. What he had here, he suspected, was a runaway slave.

A mulatto, female runaway.

His hand dropped from her shoulder. Confronted with this new problem, Noah scrubbed at his short beard and turned around to find Rose close behind him. Her eyes met his and communicated her grasp of the situation.

"Captain Griffin, I think we should feed this young person at once. If you want to question our, uh, visitor, it can surely wait a few moments."

"You're quite right, Miss Carrigan. I'll let you ladies take over that task. Private, you may return to your duties." Noah turned to the boys. "John Mark, I'd like to take another look at that arrowhead you found, if you'd fetch it."

As the soldier left and the young boys scurried inside to find the treasure in question, two of the women joined Rose to escort the new arrival to the kitchen. Noah caught Rose's arm for a moment and whispered, "Thank you."

Surprise lit her face. And apparently rendered her speechless. Color flushed from her neck to her dark hairline as she nodded and hurried away.

~

*E*mbarrassment made Rose's cheeks bloom with heat. He'd thanked her, but her primary thought had been to break up the gathering. They were all much too close to the root cellar and making enough noise to draw the attention of anyone who happened by. She felt they walked a perilous path between two camps.

She took no part in either side of the war. Caught in the middle between the two armies, she cared naught for their arguments to justify slavery, to condemn or defend states' rights, or to explain the differences in economic concerns. She hated how it affected people. She hated knowing one person hid in the root cellar of his own house at this moment and another nearly starved while fleeing a system that devalued her worth to the rank of property.

She hated that Captain Griffin would be forced to treat one as an enemy and had no idea what to do with the other. She hated that she must keep the secret of Sergeant Morgan's presence from someone who'd come to her aid more than once.

Shaking off those depressing thoughts, she followed the other women to the summer kitchen. Keeping the cooking fires in a separate building made for more comfortable living in the warmer months. Inside, Edith and Shiloh tended to the girl, who gave her name as Dorcas. Across the room, Lydia and Olivia talked quietly. To Rose's relief, Celeste had asked the other women to help her search for more clothes for the girl, leading them all back into the house.

Lydia picked up a covered platter and slipped to the door. She tilted her head toward the house, indicating the plate was meant for the stowaway in the cellar. "I'll stay in the cellar until one of you lets me know it's safe to come out. We don't need any more excitement this evening."

Rose tried to appear busy as Lydia ambled toward the house until she veered off to the cellar. With a quick glance around, she lifted the door and disappeared.

Olivia joined Rose outside the kitchen. "It might be good for you to speak with the captain since you seem to know him best. Let him know we'll keep the girl here tonight while he decides what's to be done with her. Find a way to suggest that she stay with us and continue her journey north in safety."

Rose frowned. He was a leader of men, used to giving orders. Though his kindness had surprised her, she was wary of his motives. "I'm not sure he'll listen to my suggestion."

"He probably won't if you come right out with it. Make him think it's his idea. Men like to make the decisions, you know." She gave Rose a meaningful wink.

Rose scoffed at the proposal. "Subtlety isn't one of my gifts."

Olivia simply smiled. "I've seen the way he looks at you, dear. Just be your normal charming self, and he'll follow you anywhere."

Rose shook her head. That was the last thing she wanted to do. "I'm afraid I fly off the handle more quickly with him than anyone I've ever met. Our acquaintance has been rocky.

Somehow he sets me off..." She clamped her lips tight as she caught sight of him coming out the back door.

Olivia pushed her gently forward. "Believe me, that's a good sign. Now go to it."

~

*N*oah met Rose in the yard as she left the kitchen. She seemed almost hesitant to approach him. Was he so fearsome? He thought they'd begun to build a friendship. Determined to be pleasant, he smiled as she drew closer.

"Well, Miss Carrigan. It's been quite an evening, hasn't it? How fares the runaway?"

"Dorcas is being fed and cared for. It's fortunate she chose this house. The other women are kind, and we'll make a place for her with us. Celeste is leading the charge to find more clothes, and I'm heading upstairs to make up a bed for her."

Noah's shoulders relaxed as the tension drained away. "You set my mind at ease. I know she'll be safe here with you folks. I was surprised by the way everyone rallied around her."

Rose tilted her head in thought before responding. "As an educated man, Captain, surely you're familiar with the poem 'No Man is an Island?'"

"Of course. John Donne was a favorite of Professor May, one of my mentors."

"Then you should understand what binds us together. We are women, most of us here, some with children and elders to care for. We are Southerners, Captain. Not Rebels, mind you, Southerners. We are caught up in this...this awful . . ."

When tears sprang in her eyes, he found himself wanting to draw her into his arms. He settled for grasping her shoulders. "I understand. Truly, I abhor this war as much as you. But here we are, and we make the best of it."

She lifted her chin. "We take care of our own. Perhaps you

could wait a day or two until Dorcas has recovered before sending her away. Where do you plan to send her?"

He rubbed the back of his neck. "I don't know. I've never encountered this before. Some units have contracted former slaves as guides, but only men. Truthfully, I'm not sure those guides are any better off than they were before. But a female is another matter entirely. I'd rather not take her where she'll be mistreated. Do you have a suggestion?"

Rose stepped back. "Me? You're asking me what to do?"

Noah chuckled. "I have two sisters. You women always have a suggestion. You just never come out straight with it."

He delighted in the coy smile she sent his way. "I believe you have found us out, Captain. Actually, we thought Dorcas might stay here and go with us when we leave. Surely one more woman among so many will not be remarked upon."

"I'm sure you're right. In fact, the army has no official count of the mill operatives. Her skin color might bring notice. I don't recall seeing any others with dark skin. Of course, I haven't seen everyone." He held back a yawn.

"The right clothing will help. I see you're tired, as we all are. Perhaps a good night's sleep will clear the way."

He grinned. "You are correct. I'll take my leave. Good night, Miss Carrigan." He handed her onto the porch, bowed, and turned to make his way around the side yard to his horse. When he looked back, Rose was watching.

Her regard warmed him to his toes.

~

*R*ose held her breath, going cold when he turned to catch her watching. He stopped right by the cellar door, then waved and continued to the front yard.

Sagging with relief, Rose slipped inside and met Celeste as

she descended the stairs, her arms full of clothing. "You found something for the girl?"

"Millie is about the same size and donated generously. Unfortunately, with Millie's condition progressing, she'll be the one needing more clothes soon. I guess we'll see what we can cobble together for her while we're here, however long that may be."

Celeste started for the door, but Rose held her back. "I noticed the armoire in our bedroom is full of clothes, and the door won't close completely. Sergeant Morgan said for us to take any food we need. I wonder if he'd mind our appropriating some of those garments to outfit Millie."

A nod and a smile preceded Celeste's answer. "We could ask him."

"Why don't you drop off those things for Dorcas, then go to the cellar and tell Lydia she can come out. While you're there, you can ask the good sergeant about the clothes."

After punctuating her orders with a hug, she shooed Celeste on her way. "I'm off to create Dorcas a place to sleep. I expect she'll be ready for it right away." She ran up the stairs before Celeste could find a way to reverse their roles. Rose simply couldn't bring herself to visit the cellar again tonight, and Lydia needed to be rescued from her temporary prison.

Prison. The word halted her steps. They all were held captive in this house, their prison. A lovely one, to be sure, but confining just the same. With their movements restricted and observed by the provost guards, not knowing when they might be moved or where, Rose could understand the despair of others held in confinement.

She opened a few cabinets in the upstairs hallway before she found extra bedding. After pulling it to the space she planned for Dorcas, she snapped open a folded blanket and paused as it floated and settled.

They'd just traded one prison for another. The mill held

them captive almost as much as this house. They'd worked fourteen hours a day, every day but Sunday. Paid in currency only good at the company store. Dependent on the owners and unable to leave for lack of resources, they were undervalued as surely as Dorcas or any other slave. No wonder she'd taken the risk to run away.

Rose and Celeste should have been so brave.

As the other women came into the house, Rose stood at the top of the stairs and waited for them to reach her. Celeste led the way and beamed as she caught Rose's eye. "He said we're welcome to anything we need. Perhaps we can search through the clothes tomorrow."

Lydia touched Rose's arm before she could follow. "From what I gathered, the clothes in that room belonged to his late wife. We might be doing him a favor by taking them away."

"How recently did she pass?"

"A couple years ago, I think," Lydia said. "He joined the Army soon after her death."

A roll of thunder closely followed the streak of lightning visible through the windows. The stamping of several pairs of feet climbing the stairs indicated a close to any private conversation.

"Looks like there's a good downpour on the way," Olivia said as she gained the landing. "Maybe it'll make for a cooler night."

Rose's thoughts drifted to Noah. Had he reached his destination before the storm rolled in? After the strange events of this evening, though, what was a little rain?

CHAPTER 14

*R*ose regarded the rain-splashed windows with unease. The gloom depressed her spirits, and based on the other women's faces, she wasn't alone in that. The rain made them prisoners twice over, and it didn't seem ready to let up anytime soon.

In the dining room, Rose found Olivia with papers spread across the table, her hand moving confidently over one page. Rose halted in the doorway, her ready greeting dying on her lips. The woman from New Manchester could write.

Lifting her head, Olivia blushed. "I hope you don't mind that I purloined a piece of paper from the box. I know it's for your classes, but I'm afraid it might be a while before I get another chance to write my husband."

Rose sat at the table across from her. "No, of course not. I'm just surprised. Most of the women from the Roswell mills can't read or write, which is why Celeste and I offered to teach the children. I should've figured a doctor's wife would have some education, and it's obvious Wade is ahead of the others already. Forgive my presumption."

Olivia patted her hand. "Nothing to forgive. The people of New Manchester were blessed to have a regular school since I was a young girl. My aunt and uncle always encouraged us to attend whenever we could." A look of pain marred her face for a moment.

"You didn't get to attend much? But you write beautifully." Rose indicated the flowing script on the paper.

"My sister, Camilla, was often sick. She was crippled and missed so many days that it was hard for her to keep up. Then Shiloh came to join us, and it was easier for Aunt Edith to teach us all at home, where we could take care of each other."

Rose recognized the pain of losing someone close. "Your sister was younger or older?"

Taking a deep breath, Olivia summoned a sad smile. "Younger by nearly six years. She died last year. Her body just couldn't handle sickness in her weakened condition. We were blessed to have her fourteen years."

Sympathy swelled, bringing with it Rose's darkest memories. Most days she kept them at bay. "I'm so sorry. Losing anyone is hard, but it's especially hard to lose a young person." Tears welled up with the familiar burden.

Olivia's gaze softened. "You sound like someone who knows that pain." She laid aside her pencil and gave Rose her full attention. "What happened, dear?"

Rose swiped her damp cheeks. Perhaps speaking of the accident would ease her guilt. She bowed her head, pleating her fingers in the skirt of her dress. "We lived on a small farm, but Da also served as the local church's pastor. During harvest, he'd assist our neighbors, and Mama would watch the smaller children so their mothers could help with the work."

"Our community did the same, pitching in to help everyone," Olivia said.

Rose continued. "When I was eleven, one day near the end of harvest, we had four or five children in the house. They were restless, not being allowed outside because it was muddy from recent rains. Mama had struggled with some sickness the day before and suddenly turned worse. I didn't realize she was in the family way."

"Oh no. Did she lose the baby?"

"Yes." Rose took a deep breath, struggling to keep her composure while she finished the story. "I panicked. I told Celeste to go for help, which meant I was solely responsible for the little ones."

She paused to take a sip of water. "While I was busy changing a couple of nappies, a four-year-old boy slipped out of the house. I searched for him, went to the door and called his name, but I couldn't go outside to search for him, not with all the other children there and Mama so ill. It seemed like hours before Celeste returned with Da. He'd already sent for a doctor for Mama, but now he had to hunt for the lost child."

Olivia squeezed her hand. "I take it the child was hurt."

Rose cleared her throat. "The boy loved horses and was trying to get to them, I suppose. But he stepped too close to an irate cow that sent him flying across the yard. I wasn't allowed to see him, but he suffered a serious head wound. He lingered a couple of days before he passed away." She covered her face, remembering the awful wails of the child's mother. "It was my fault. I should have kept him in the house."

"You were a mere child yourself, Rose. In a moment's time, adult responsibilities dropped on your shoulders. I don't see how you could have acted any differently. Surely nobody blamed you for such an accident. You must forgive yourself."

Rose didn't dispute Olivia's supposition, but she remembered the accusing stares, the drop in church attendance, the heavy cloak of grief shrouding their little community before her father was asked to resign as pastor. She'd learned the importance of taking responsibility for her actions.

"I know you're right, but doing it is another matter altogether."

Olivia sighed. "How well I know. When Camilla died, I kept wondering what I could have done to keep her here longer. But God's grace covers us. We have to trust that everything happens for a purpose."

They fell silent while Olivia read over her letter to her husband. Finally, after adding a few more words and her signature, she folded the paper over twice and slipped it into her pocket.

The action nudged Rose's memory of another letter. "If you don't mind my asking, how do you plan to send that?"

Leaning across the table, she gave Rose a conspiratorial smile. "Sergeant Morgan. The way I see it, God brought him here as a means of contacting our men in Virginia. Do you suppose Emily will want to send a letter to her husband also?"

"I know she will because I wrote it for her before we left Roswell." She shook her head in wonder. "We had no idea how we'd get the letter to him. She's been holding on to it until we find a way. I never expected to discover someone this quickly."

Others began to wander into the room, so Rose and Olivia stood to help with the preparations for breakfast.

Olivia touched Rose on the arm. "Would it be all right to take one more sheet of paper? I always try to include a picture from Wade in my letters to Evan."

"Of course. And that gives me an idea of how to keep the children busy today."

"Good. Let me know if I can help. This rain may affect their behavior."

Rose grinned and pointed her finger at Olivia. "I'll hold you to that."

~

"*W*hat's holding up Colonel Gleeson? This rain is getting harder by the minute."

Noah smirked at the complaining officer, who huddled in his rubber raincoat while water gurgled from the building's eaves. The fellow, a former classmate, had expected to be pampered in the Army as he'd been by his parents. Before Noah could form a reply, another answered. "Oh, some private rushed in before you got here. Seems he had a matter of misconduct to report. Gleeson said for us to wait. Specious tale-bearing greenhorn."

As soon as the words left the man's mouth, the door opened, and the group pressed forward to drier quarters. Noah hung back, letting the others go in first. He'd suffered worse conditions than rain.

Pushing against the flow, the private who left kept his head down, forgetting—or refusing— to salute his superiors. Something about him triggered Noah's memory.

"Private Allen?"

The younger man raised his eyes to meet Noah's then dropped away. "Cap'n," he murmured with a nod, keeping his hands in his pockets. Hunching his shoulders against the rain, he turned and hurried on his way.

Noah stood in astonishment, frowning over the abrupt meeting. A hand clapped his arm and shoved him inside. "Didn't your mama teach you not to stand in the rain, Griff?"

Cooper Bradley released Noah's arm and attempted to wipe the dampness from his own jacket.

Noah shook his head at his friend in consternation.

"No?" the lieutenant asked. "Now I don't believe that for a minute. I think the issue is it didn't penetrate that thick skull of yours."

With a wry laugh, Noah cocked his head and gave Cooper

his full attention. "You are right about that, I suppose. Some things continue to amaze me. Are you still acting for your captain?"

They searched for seats in the crowded room but found none. Leaning against a wall near the door, Cooper displayed a wide grin. "Nope. The major has fallen ill as well. You can be sure I'm keeping far away from them, getting my orders through the window from the doctor or nurse."

"Gentlemen!" Gleeson's call to attention prevented further conversation.

Numerous reports and assignment changes later, the meeting wound down. Noah's orders would take him east to the line of the Chattahoochee while Cooper's company went south toward Atlanta. They turned to leave, but Gleeson's call stopped them. "Captain Griffin, stay a moment."

"I'll wait outside," Cooper said.

Noah approached the colonel. "Yes sir?"

Gleeson peered over his reading glasses. "You may have noticed the private who was here before the meeting?"

"Yes sir. Private Allen is one of the guards over the operatives from the mills." He tempered his words and kept his opinion close to his chest. It wouldn't be wise to remark upon the casual treatment of those "prisoners."

The colonel heaved a weary sigh. "He reported what he deemed an infraction and conduct unbecoming an officer. You've been visiting the mill operatives at one of the houses left vacant, I take it?"

Noah frowned. "I took the initiative to assist in settling the mill operatives in houses when the Institute became overcrowded. I learned a few of the women who can read and write are serving their fellow citizens by teaching the children. To assist, I obtained a box of writing paper for the children to practice their letters and took it over to them."

"The private said you had a prolonged visit." Gleeson raised his eyebrows to make it a query rather than a statement.

"When I arrived at the house, they were just sitting down to dinner and graciously invited me to join them. I accepted as a gesture of good will. A short while later, Private Allen discovered a thief in the summer kitchen. He apprehended the person, which turned out to be a female runaway slave."

"Go on," the colonel said.

Noah blew out a breath. "The women there all gathered around her and offered to let her stay with them. Not knowing our protocol for dealing with female runaways, I agreed it might be best for her to remain there for now."

Gleeson tugged at the dark mustache that bracketed his mouth. "That seems sensible enough. I don't know that I would have acted otherwise."

"Colonel, if I may offer a suggestion? It seems the easiest way to deal with this would be to let the girl continue with that group as they travel north. Since she's a runaway, I'm certain her destination aligns with theirs."

Colonel Gleeson frowned. "I'll think on it and let you know."

"Thank you, sir. I appreciate your consideration and depend on your wisdom." Noah slapped his kepi against his leg and faced the door.

The colonel's voice halted him. "Captain, unlike the private, I think your actions are to be commended. You might be interested to know I have recommended you for a promotion."

Surprise rendered Noah speechless for a moment. "I'm honored. Merely having your approval is a great privilege."

With a thin smile and a pat on Noah's shoulder, the officer pointed him to the door. "Let's keep it that way, shall we?"

Still in a daze from Allen's accusations and Gleeson's vote of confidence, Noah saluted and stepped outside. Raindrops pelted his face and slipped past his coat's collar. The rain had brought blessed relief from the Georgia heat. He kept to grassy areas to avoid the water-filled grooves in the road.

Regardless of the colonel's good will, Noah had better guard his steps in the future. *Let not your good be evil spoken of.* It was a lesson he thought he'd learned long ago, but obviously not well enough.

CHAPTER 15

*D*espite the rain, the children's lessons continued, thanks to the paper contributed by Captain Griffin. He'd also included a few sturdy pencils, some chalk, and charcoal sticks. Someone at the neighboring house discovered a couple of tarpaulins, so Janie's children gathered under those and sloshed their way from one porch to the other. Whether Janie thought the lessons more important than the weather or the children had grown too rambunctious for the adults next door, Rose deemed it a good sign for their progress.

The weather did make the children somewhat fractious, and Rose ended up devising a game at Olivia's suggestion. Recruiting more adults from the Sweetwater party, they paired each child with an older person to find items of different colors and shapes, which they recorded on their papers.

Finally, the children settled at the table to draw pictures for their parents. Edith and Ada surprised them with a batch of cookies, a rare treat in such hard times and much appreciated. When a break came in the weather, the Wilson crew gathered their pictures to leave.

Rose stood on the porch as they tramped down the steps.

Tommy marched to the nearest puddle, but Phoebe pulled him back.

Celeste called Rose and motioned her upstairs to the room where they slept. "Sergeant Morgan said we could take whatever clothes we need. I didn't say anything to him about Dorcas, not knowing whether his family had slaves or his thoughts on the matter."

Rose hugged her. "My wise sister. I knew you could handle it. Let's see what we can find for Millie."

"Did I hear my name?" Millie poked her head around the doorframe.

Celeste whirled toward the blonde. "You're just in time. Because you gave so much for Dorcas, we got permission to see what will fit you from this armoire." She led Millie to the armoire and started pulling out all the sturdy garments.

Stepping back, Millie regarded Celeste with wariness. "What do you mean you got permission?"

Rose asked, "Didn't Lydia tell you about the soldier in the cellar?"

The girl's eyes widened. "No! What's he doing in the cellar?"

Celeste gripped Millie's arm in warning. "Shh...he's not a Federal man. This house belongs to his family. He hid in there when he discovered the town filled with Yankees. He'll be returning to his unit soon as it's dark."

Rose raised her eyebrows at the news, but she'd be glad to wish Sergeant Morgan a hearty Godspeed. "He's going back tonight?"

Celeste nodded. "It's too dangerous for him to stay any longer. Too many people around."

"That's the gospel truth," Rose murmured. She turned Millie toward the tall cedar chest. "Come on, little mama. Let's see what we can find here for you."

They delved into the contents, rejecting all the lovely silks and satins, though each found something among those to greatly admire. Soon they piled up several items for Millie to try on. Skirts, bodices, full dresses. Even petticoats and shifts littered the surfaces of beds and chairs in the room.

Lydia came to the bedroom door, Olivia and Dorcas following closely. "What's going on here?"

"We're finding clothes for Millie." Rose regarded Dorcas thoughtfully. "Hmmm. We should also consider looking for things to help Dorcas get past the guards." She started pulling open bureau drawers.

Olivia and Celeste joined in the hunt.

Lydia was perplexed. "Just what are we tryin' to find?"

"Oh, an old bonnet, gloves, bits of lace to bring that neckline up higher." Rose muttered as she searched a box of fabric remnants.

Millie joined in, giggling. "This is the craziest shopping I've ever done."

"Aha!" Olivia's cry had all heads turning her way. She held a small jar aloft, beckoning Dorcas to her side. "Rice powder."

She found a small brush, dipped it in the jar, and lightly spread it over the girl's face. "I hope it won't make you sneeze. When I was a girl, a lady I know would sneeze for a full minute after she applied powder to her nose." She pulled the brush away and regarded her handiwork, then turned Dorcas to face the others. "What do you think?"

Rose scrutinized the dusted face Dorcas presented. For a moment, she saw another, younger face of the same golden color—a girl she'd called her friend until Rose's family moved. She blinked, and the image changed. "I think it'll work, especially when we add the other items."

The others added their endorsement until a tear slipped from Dorcas's dark eyes and tracked a line down the dusted cheeks. Olivia pulled the girl into her arms. "Hey, it's only for a while, until we get far enough north that you're not in danger."

Dorcas waved away her concern. "It ain't that, missus. I just ain't never had anybody be so good to me as you all. Givin' me dresses and the like. Countin' me as one o' you so I can get away." She hid her face in her hands, effectively ruining Olivia's artistry with more tears.

The four women gathered around her, murmuring assurances. At last Lydia cleared her throat for their attention. "So long as Dorcas stays in the house, she won't need to wear the powder. When word comes for us to leave, we'll help her prepare. Now, let's clean up this mess. It's almost dinner time. The others will wonder what's become of us."

～

When he headed out to visit Rose and the other women, Noah glanced at the sky and realized it must be about dinner time. The rain had slowed to a drizzle in the last hour, but gray clouds spread as far as he could see above the trees and rooftops.

He sighed. The women would think he expected to be invited to dine with them again. He hadn't intentionally planned his visit for this hour, but the rain had conspired with his superiors to keep him at headquarters until now.

At least John Mark would be happy to see him. Cooper thought the boy's arrowhead was worth a dollar, which he was prepared to offer if John Mark wanted it.

He pulled Hercules to a stop at the gate as a flash of lightning preceded a rumble of thunder in the distance. The two men he'd spoken with yesterday lifted their hands in greeting but headed indoors. Though most of these refugees were women, the few elderly men left in town had accompanied their wives and daughters. What else were they to do? There was no work for them, even if they'd been able-bodied. Some of them might not survive the journey.

Private Jones left the porch to greet him and take charge of the horse.

"Just hold him here, Private. I shouldn't be long."

Realizing he'd made the same statement on his last visit, he amended his statement. "If I'm not back in ten minutes, please remind me I have a meeting in an hour. I'm sure the dinner inside will be more inviting than what awaited me back at quarters, and the view far better, but I must not stay." Finding the front door open, he issued a perfunctory knock and sauntered inside.

It was a madhouse. Where he had encountered mild domesticity yesterday, today's atmosphere closely resembled the circus his friends had persuaded him to sneak into as an adolescent. He halted in wonder behind the older men.

Like him, they stared in consternation at the flurry of activity now on display. John Mark and Wade chased some small creature, while a little girl pressed into her mother's skirt in terror. Beyond them, several women clustered around two younger women, who turned in circles to show off their outfits.

The scene transported him back in time. His mother always insisted the men of the house admire his sisters' new dresses for special occasions, and his younger brothers could always find some mischief. The last occasion had been Eliza's wedding, which he'd barely made, traveling on furlough from his company in Tennessee to Indiana. He hadn't seen his family since.

A feminine gasp brought him out of his reverie. In the sudden silence, everyone turned his way. He caught sight of the runaway and focused on her.

"Well, now, don't you look different." He searched the group for Rose and Celeste as an anchor. While the other women's faces flushed with embarrassment or excitement, Rose paled. He flashed her a smile. "I see you ladies were able to find more suitable clothing for our young friend."

The one with darker skin smiled. He racked his memory for her name. Something from the Bible, but it eluded him.

The other girl fairly glowed with excitement. He remembered the young blonde as being aloof and sullen—and obviously pregnant—but now she chattered giddily.

"We found that some of my things were perfect for Dorcas, and I was glad to let her have them, knowing I won't be able to use them for a while, if ever again. Then like a blessing from heaven, I learned Sergeant Morgan said we could take whatever we needed, and I found these wonderful things…"

She stopped suddenly and glanced around at the others, whose expressions had changed while she prattled. Noah reran the girl's sentence in his mind and came up with the reason.

"Sergeant Morgan? I don't recall him. He told you to take whatever you wanted from where? When did this happen?"

The auburn-haired lady from Sweetwater stepped forward and put her arm about the blonde's waist. "I believe the name wasn't Morgan but Munsen. He's one of the guards who escorted us from New Manchester the other day." She frowned. "No, maybe it was Monroe or Morris. Is Morgan what I told you, Celeste?"

Celeste bit her bottom lip. "I thought that was the name you said. Could be I misheard it."

Rose stepped up beside Celeste, taking charge. "Well, whatever his name was, the point is we were concerned about making use of anything we found along our journey, and Mrs. Edith said she thought we could take what we needed but no more. After all, we'd be glad for anyone who entered our houses to do the same."

Several nodded, and the elderly gentleman from New Manchester added his bit. "None of us can take any of this earthly stuff with us to the next life anyway. We might as well share with one another while we're here."

Noah's head was beginning to ache as he tried to follow the

conversation. Something strange was going on, but he couldn't discern what. Giving up, he addressed the group at large. "Well, I'm glad you found what you needed for Dorcas. My superior officer seemed to think leaving her with you is a good choice for the moment. If that changes, I'll let you know. I know I can trust you all to take care of her."

He glanced around the room. "Now, where did John Mark go? I have good news for him about his arrowhead. I want to tell him before I leave since I may be gone a few days."

~

"I have to get back to camp, to my unit." High color flushed Seth Morgan's cheeks, and his eyes blazed with a glassy stare in the distance.

"No, you don't." Rose panted. "Not today." It took all four of them—Rose, Celeste, Lydia, and Olivia—to restrain him.

Lydia slapped the wet cloth against his neck, trying to douse the fever.

Rose had hurried to the cellar with his dinner after finishing her own. When she found him thrashing and mumbling in his sleep, she'd been alarmed. Slipping out of the cellar, she glimpsed Dorcas headed to the kitchen. The situation had called for quick action. "Dorcas, will you please ask Olivia to meet me in the root cellar? I need her opinion on something down there."

Though curiosity sparked in her eyes, the girl complied immediately. Somehow Olivia had alerted Lydia and Celeste. All three rushed into the cellar. As though they'd known and helped each other for years, the women set to work subduing their strong patient. Finally, he dropped into a fretful sleep.

"What do you think it is?" Rose and Lydia looked to the doctor's wife for answers.

Olivia shook her head. "I'm not sure. Could be influenza or

pneumonia. With the heat and the recent rains, plus his exhausted state when he arrived, either is possible."

Lydia crossed her arms and leaned against the one wall without shelves. "Well, one thing is sure. He's not able to leave now. It could be days before he's able to stay upright."

"So, what do we do? How can we help him?" Celeste glanced at the others.

Rose pursed her lips and sighed. "We'll have to take shifts, staying with him or at least checking on him more often." Christian duty sometimes meant self-sacrifice, but dread filled her at the prospect. She could deal with soldiers out in the open, as the last week had demonstrated. Her courage quailed, though, to think of being in a close place with a man again, even one as incapacitated as Sergeant Morgan.

She'd managed to keep the full truth from Da and Celeste, and diligent prayer had sustained her over the past four years. Still, just thinking about being shut up in a dark place quickened her heart rate. Feeling her breath grow shallow, she fought to keep the terror at bay.

She focused on Olivia's voice. "Let's search the house for medicine. Although, not knowing for sure what ails him, we'll have to exercise caution in giving it. Aunt Edith may have some advice. Beyond that, my husband would recommend broth and tea."

Celeste, always the compassionate one, volunteered to stay with him awhile. As the others reached the door, Celeste hummed an old hymn, as she would for a sick child.

Taking Lydia and Rose by the arm, Olivia slowed their steps. "It may be time to let the others know about him." She tilted her head back the way they had come. "If what he has is catching, they should know to watch for signs of sickness. Especially among the children."

"You're right," Lydia agreed. "But let's tell them individually, not all at once. I'll tell Millie."

Rose offered to tell the Anderson adults. "Let's keep it to this house for now. With the Wilson children coming over for schooling, we can watch them for any signs of illness."

Olivia sucked her bottom lip in thought. "I'll let Aunt Edith and Uncle Isaac and Shiloh know, of course. What about the guards? Do you think they'll notice anything different?"

"I don't think so. Captain Griffin's away for a few days, and the guards don't usually bother us as long as we're inside," Rose said.

Lydia snickered. "And as long as they're fed."

Rose and Olivia shared her humor. "We'll do our best to carry on as usual. And cover everything in prayer."

"Amen to that."

CHAPTER 16

*S*omebody's prayers had worked. Rose lifted a silent thanks as she and Celeste watched Sergeant Seth Morgan walk the perimeter of the root cellar. Three days ago, he could barely lift his head to sip the soup and water the women poured into him. Now he chafed at the delay of waiting until sunset to leave.

Celeste passed him his haversack, reciting a list of the food she'd packed. "But you should eat again here before you set out." She pointed to the plate he'd set aside.

The man grinned at her. "No wonder those Yankee guards don't bother you gals. You fill them with food and flash your pretty smiles, and they lose what little wits they have."

Celeste giggled.

Rose's senses went on alert. She narrowed her eyes and studied the man as if she could discern his motives simply by staring.

Neither he nor Celeste seemed to notice her behavior. They seemed oblivious to her presence.

Rose cleared her throat to gain their attention. "Your uniform is packed at the bottom of the sack, clean and mended. You should leave it there and wear your civilian clothes until you reach North Carolina."

"Yes ma'am. I agree."

Celeste released the coat and hat she held. "I found the hat and jacket you wanted in your room. You might want to smudge them with dirt, though, to make it harder to see them in the dark."

Rose didn't give him time to answer. "Someone will let you know when it's safe for you to leave. C'mon, Celeste. We need to help with supper."

Taking the lead, Rose mounted the steps and held the door aside for Celeste to follow. But a figure emerged from the trees.

Panic made her gasp and release the door .

Beside her, Celeste rubbed her arm where the door had grazed it. "Ouch, why'd you...oh, hello, Phoebe."

Rose recovered her poise. "Phoebe, did you need something?"

The girl peered at them, curiosity on her face as she glanced at the cellar door. Tossing her braid behind her, she pulled a stuffed toy from her skirt pocket. "Tommy left his bunny here. Mama sent me over to search for it. What're y'all doing in the cellar?"

With a casual motion behind her, Rose said, "Oh, just looking to see what's down there. We've been able to use a few of the stored items, but mostly what's left is old and funny look-ing, like somebody didn't know how to keep it from spoiling." She held crossed fingers in the folds of her skirt and chose her words to keep from telling a complete untruth.

Phoebe frowned. "I best be getting back before Mama sends

the guard after me. I sure don't want to have to talk to *him*." She sniffed and flounced off toward the other house.

Celeste pierced Rose with a questioning gaze. "Old and funny looking? I assume you meant Sergeant Morgan?"

"Well, he is, or at least he would be in Phoebe's eyes." Rose grabbed Celeste's hand. "C'mon now. Time's a-wasting."

Later, after supper was consumed and dishes cleared away, the four women who'd attended the sergeant returned to the cellar for a final farewell.

Seth rose from his pallet to meet them. "Is it time?" He reached out and brushed the arm of the woman closest to him, which happened to be Celeste.

Rose scowled at the familiar gesture.

"Not yet," Celeste said, blushing and sidestepping out of his reach. "The sun won't set for another hour, but the wind is blowing in some clouds, so we thought we'd best come on down. Here's the watch we found upstairs. You can use it to see the time." She held it out, and he took it.

Olivia retrieved a packet from her apron pocket. "I found a small piece of oiled cloth to wrap the letters in. We're depending on you to get them through. And please tell anyone you meet from our area what's happened."

"I won't forget," Seth said, his gaze sweeping across them. "Women from Roswell and New Manchester are being sent north on trains, likely to Nashville."

Lydia pressed a knotted piece of cloth into his hand. "A few coins we collected in case you need to purchase something."

Rose thought he might have choked up a bit at that. He cleared his throat and tried to joke away the somber atmosphere. "Too bad there's no horses I could buy to make the trip go faster."

He raised serious eyes to each one. Eyes that had seen far too much for a man not much older than Rose. What did war do to a man?

"I'm not anxious to return to the fighting," he said. "But I'm ready to accomplish my mission and have this war brought to an end."

Every voice echoed that sentiment, and the women slipped away. Rose looked heavenward and wondered which mission would finally prevail in the end.

~

*N*oah, along with a dozen of his men, rode into Marietta late in the afternoon, glad to be done with this latest mission. The three days at the river line had dragged like wet wool and strained his spirit like the mud that sucked on his boots. Despite the heat, he welcomed the sun's kiss on his back as they rode into town.

Two stops, and then he could find a place to bathe and don clean clothes. Poor Sergeant Fowler could barely hold his head up since he'd sickened an hour ago.

Finally, they reached the house-turned-hospital, and Noah and two others helped the sick sergeant inside, where he promptly collapsed at the doctor's feet. Once Fowler was settled, Noah dismissed the retinue and made his way to General Garrard's temporary office.

He caught the general on his way to dinner, so he delivered a hasty oral review as well as the paper with his written report.

Garrard stashed the paper in his breast pocket and turned to leave. "Oh, by the way, Griffin, we shipped out a bunch of the Roswell people while you were gone. You and your men should be able to find a decent place to sleep now. I'd advise you to rest while you can. General Sherman is moving men out for the capture of Atlanta."

Noah's heart raced. He could only murmur a word of thanks as Garrard pivoted and strode away. His mind whirled with the news. He'd known the mill operatives were bound for points north, but he hadn't realized they'd be leaving so soon.

Thoughts of Rose lingered. Like a stubborn melody, she haunted him both asleep and awake. How would he find her again if one of those trains had carried her away?

Calling himself all kinds of a fool, Noah hurried through the streets. Leaving Hercules to his deserved dinner and rest at the stable, he requested another horse to be ready in an hour. He picked up a plate of food for himself and bolted it down before rushing to clean up and change into a fresh uniform. Dashing off a few lines on paper intended for letters home, he folded and stuffed it in his trouser pocket. An hour later, he made his way to the house where he hoped to find Rose and company still in residence.

The gathering clouds played hide-and-seek with the sinking sun. He prayed the rain would hold off until after his visit.

Some of his anxiety slipped away as he neared the house. Two guards lounged casually against the porch columns until they caught sight of his approach and jerked to vigilance. He recognized Private Jones but not the other. Both hurried to the gate.

He tossed the reins to Jones. "Just let him graze. I won't be long. Where's Private Allen?"

"He, uh, got transferred to another duty location. This here's Private Langley."

Noah greeted the other man then pointed at Jones's uniform. "I see congratulations are in order, Corporal. Well deserved."

"Thank you, sir."

Willing himself to patience, Noah tilted his head toward the house. "How have things been around here? It seems quiet."

"No problems here, sir," Jones said. "The women stay busy with cooking and sewing and teaching them young'uns their letters. The men and boys come out to jaw with us sometimes. They're not a rowdy bunch like some I've seen. And they keep us fed, so I ain't got no complaints, even with sleeping here on the porch."

Noah clapped him on the shoulder. "I would've gladly swapped sleeping quarters with you these last few days. Camping on the riverbank might sound like an adventure to youngsters, but these old bones are feeling their age."

Private Langley grinned. "Did the Rebs let you sleep? I heard they like to kick up a fuss in the evenings."

"You heard right, Private. Mostly I took naps when I could get them. I'm glad to get back here." He lowered his voice. "Although I hear we shouldn't get too settled. Uncle Billy is planning for the next campaign. You gentlemen may get reassigned as soon as these folks are shipped out."

The two younger men exchanged glances but merely answered with the obligatory, "Yes, sir."

With a quick salute, Noah covered the distance to the porch and knocked on the front door. He briefly wondered why the door was shut on this warm day but abandoned the thought when John Mark's grandfather pulled it open and invited him inside.

As he took in the domestic tableau, the bubble of apprehension in Noah's chest slowly deflated. Two women sat on a sofa, occupied with some needlework. He recognized the pregnant blonde and the shy one with curly dark hair. Chagrined that he didn't remember their names, he merely nodded. They returned the gesture with quiet murmurs of greeting.

The other man, the one from the Sweetwater group, leaned over the three children who huddled around a low table near the window. The children concentrated on their paperwork so intently, they didn't realize he was there until he commented on their writing.

John Mark jumped to his feet, sending his pencil rolling to the floor. "Oh, Captain Griffin! Did you find any arrowheads while you were away?"

Noah laughed and tousled the boy's hair. "No, I'm afraid I didn't, not this time. But I'll keep an eye out. Looks like you're doing some good work there."

Wade Spencer faced him with a wide grin. "I'm drawing a picture for my pa. Ma always puts one in with her letter when she writes him."

"Me, too," a soft voice added. It was the first time the little girl had spoken to him, and Noah was charmed.

"How thoughtful of you. I'm sure both your fathers will be pleased with your pictures." *If they ever get them.* Mail service for the Union had slowed, but it was practically non-existent for the Confederates. He supposed the task kept the children occupied and hopeful.

Voices from the dining room grew closer, and Noah looked up in time to see John Mark's mother and grandmother stop at the threshold. Three of the Sweetwater women came up behind them, surprise evident on their faces.

"Why, Captain Griffin!" The senior woman swept around the others with her hand extended. "What a surprise. I'm sorry you're not in time for supper, but there's a bit of cornbread left, if you'd like a bite."

He accepted her greeting with a wry smile. "No, thank you. I ate before I came over. When I got back in town, I heard some of the mill workers and their families had been sent north, and I wondered whether you folks had gone with them or were still here." He nodded to the others who followed like ducklings behind their mama. "Evening, ladies."

In his peripheral vision, he saw the auburn-haired woman slip away. Would she insist he eat? That would be stretching the famous Southern hospitality to the limit, wouldn't it? Then he realized Rose and Celeste hadn't accompanied the others. The astute woman had probably picked up on his interest there.

His supposition proved right when the Carrigan sisters entered the room, followed by a young girl he didn't recognize.

Their expressions seemed more wary than surprised. Celeste offered a subdued greeting as she passed him and pushed between the two on the settee. The other girl moved to the corner where the children continued to draw. Seeing her there nudged his memory. She stayed at the other house with the rest of Rose's neighbors from Roswell.

Rose approached him and offered a warm hello, although her smile seemed strained. Some pain or worry dulled her eyes. He caught only a glimpse before she lowered her head, but he sensed the tension.

"Olivia tells me we could be leaving soon," Rose said. "Do you know when that might be?"

Ah, the news of their imminent departure was what caused her concern. He remembered how upset she'd been when he gave her the message back in Roswell. At least now she and Celeste had companions, perhaps friends, in these people who shared the house with them.

As Noah opened his mouth to reply, a shout rang out from the front porch.

"Hold, thief! Come back with that horse!" The thud of boots running along the porch and down the steps emphasized the trouble. Pounding from galloping hooves indicated a chase.

Everyone inside sprang from their places and rushed to the door. Noah sprinted down the steps to meet Private Langley in the road, his head down and his arms hanging at his side in defeat. Corporal Jones stood several yards farther away, staring down the road, his rifle lifted to shoot. But no shot followed.

Noah turned to the private. "What happened here?"

Raising his head and bracing for a reprimand, the younger man blustered, "He got your horse, sir."

Disbelief propelled Noah forward, anger scorching his vision. "Do I understand that someone stole my horse? No, not *my* horse, mind you, the *army's horse*, while two Union guards sat on their..." Aware of the women crowding behind him,

Noah forced himself to watch his words. "While you sat on this porch?"

"Yes, sir."

Onlookers spilled onto the porches of the nearby houses.

Corporal Jones reached them, panting and angry. "I couldn't get off a clean shot, sir, not with him riding through the yards and into the trees. As the senior guard, I take full responsibility. I should have kept the horse in sight 'stead of letting him graze beside the house."

Noah ran a hand down his face. He was the officer present. The horse was his responsibility, and he would bear the indignity of reporting the theft to his superiors.

He turned and noticed the people watching, their faces grim. Frustration pushed him forward. "Do any of you know who would dare to steal an army mount?"

The girl from next door stepped forward. "It must've been that Rebel what was hiding in the cellar here."

CHAPTER 17

*R*ose fought the urge to run and hide from Noah's piercing, angry eyes. She held herself erect, firm in her belief that she'd done nothing wrong. Her Christian duty involved helping those in need, not taking sides in a political battle. The victim in this unfortunate struggle would be her growing friendship with Captain Griffin.

He'd waved off the guards from the other houses and herded their entire party back into the house. Giving stern orders to the guards to return to their posts, he shut the door and faced the sixteen Southerners. For a moment he merely stared at them, anger and disappointment evident on his face. Inhaling sharply, his countenance eased somewhat.

"John Mark, Wade, and the little Miss Anderson, please step forward."

"Sarah Grace," Emily whispered, gently urging the children to stand in front of her.

Noah regarded them solemnly. "I have a question for you, which I expect you to answer honestly." He glanced toward the adults and added, "No one will punish you for telling the truth. Do you understand?"

Although uncertainty stamped their features, the children nodded and answered in unison. "Yes sir."

"Do you know anything about a man, a soldier from the other army, hiding around here anywhere?"

Three heads swiveled in a negative response.

"You never saw or heard anything about anyone hiding hereabouts?"

Another negative response.

"All right, I believe you. Please go outside with the soldiers on the porch. Don't wander off now because it'll soon be dark and time for bed." He opened the door and waited for the children to exit before closing the door again.

He pointed to Phoebe and Dorcas. "You and you. Please tell me your names again."

His voice vibrated with tension, though his words issued no threat. Each girl gave her name, Dorcas trembling, Phoebe with defiance.

"What do you know about anyone, soldier or not, hiding around here?"

Rose was surprised when Dorcas stepped forward and answered first. "I never seen nor heard anything about nobody hiding here, Mass...uh, Cap'n Griffin. I swear on my Mam's grave, or on the Bible, if'n you need." She cast a look at Isaac, who clutched the Book to his chest.

"No need for that, Dorcas. You may join the children outside."

He waited for her exit before turning his expectant gaze on Phoebe. "What do you know, Miss Phoebe Wilson?"

Rose held her breath as the girl licked her lips, the one sign of awareness that she may have caused herself as much trouble as she intended for the others. Dread created droplets of moisture along Rose's hairline and upper lip. Realizing her heartbeat had increased, she started silently reciting Scripture about peace and safety.

With a sudden burst of animosity, Phoebe pointed to Rose and Celeste. "I saw them two comin' out of the cellar just before supper today. They looked guilty, like they's hidin' something, so I snuck back after they went in the house. I went down in the cellar to see what was down there and saw him, sleepin' on a pallet."

Noah kept his eyes on the girl. "And he had on a Confederate uniform?"

Phoebe hesitated. "Well, no. But why else would he be hiding out down there?"

Noah shrugged with apparent unconcern. "He could be a deserter from either army, or just a no-account thief searching for a place to rest. He could have gone in there after the Carrigan sisters left, like you did."

Phoebe's nostrils flared, and her eyes shot angrily toward Rose and Celeste. "No! I tell you, they was hiding him. There was a blanket and pillow and…and a stack of dirty plates near the door."

Rose had to hold her tongue. *Now she's gone to embellishing, to convince him we're up to no good.* When did the fifteen-year-old start seeing her and Celeste as rivals?

Rose cast a desperate glance toward Noah to find him studying her with a frown. He blew out an exasperated breath and waved Phoebe away. She quickly retreated to the door but paused to fling a triumphant look at those remaining. Confused by the girl's obvious bid to cause trouble, Rose couldn't take time to ponder the reason.

Noah motioned to Millie and Shiloh. Before the young women could obey, Lydia pushed her way forward. "Millie had nothing to do with this."

Olivia joined her. "I'm the one who found him and took care of him."

"He was too weak to move," Rose said, "sick and exhausted from walking for days."

Noah raised his hand for silence, and Rose stopped.

"All of you were in on this?" His gaze moved beyond them to the Andersons and the Wynns, who maintained a stoic silence. Isaac and J.D. faced him with solemn expressions, refusing to abandon the women. Ada put an arm around Celeste, who wept at her side.

Edith Wynn's calm voice broke the silence. "Really, Captain, how could we turn a man out of his own house?"

Noah's brow wrinkled. "His house? This house was his? Then he was a Rebel soldier, as Miss Wilson said."

Rose took a step closer, reached her hand toward him, then dropped it. "Sergeant Morgan heard the Yankee army had taken Marietta, so he traveled from Virginia to check on his family, not realizing they'd fled."

She motioned toward Lydia and Olivia. "The three of us found him when we went to the cellar hunting through the stored items. He was asleep but wakened long enough to tell us who he was. We thought to let him sleep to gain his strength before setting out again."

Noah trained a hard look on her. "That's called aiding and abetting the enemy."

So much for reasoning with a man. "What does it matter? We've all been labeled as traitors and taken as prisoners anyway. Deprived of our livelihood, moved from our homes. We're just biding our time here until your army can ship us out."

Her mouth trembled, but she firmed it up. *I will not cry. I will not cry.* "We did not ask for this war. We have no cause to refuse help to anyone in need, no matter what color they wear."

Something flared in Noah's eyes. Anger perhaps, or guilt, or pain? Maybe all of those. He seemed to collect himself before he turned and headed toward the door. He looked back, much as Phoebe had done, to take one parting shot. "I thought I'd earned your trust. Now I see I was mistaken."

He swung the door open.

Rose staggered at the finality in his voice. "You weren't here."

But the door banged shut, and Noah gave no indication he heard her words.

~

*H*er words followed Noah to the porch and up the street. His fury drove him on the march back to the buildings now housing General Garrard's corps. The invading army. However righteous he considered the Union cause, he had to allow that not everything had been done in righteousness.

Deprived of our livelihood, moved from our homes.

He viewed the spreading sea of blue as the residents must see it—a growing cancer taking over the once-flourishing landscape.

We're just biding our time here.

Noah knew that was true, and it sparked his anger again, this time directed at himself. How stupid could he be to allow himself to get entangled with the locals, to consider some of them friends and even more? Cooper had warned him. His own sense of duty chastised him again and again. Any relationships forged in this godforsaken war were doomed to failure.

Until your Army ships us out.

Like a swimmer treading water, he couldn't maintain this impossible situation. The inevitable wave would surely overtake him. What was the saying? Time and tide wait for no man? Only two weeks before, Roswell had been simply a place on a map, a target to be obtained. There was no indication its capture would turn his world upside down. Any day now, Rose would board a train bound for the distant North, and he would move to another Southern town with orders to capture it.

She would be lost to him.

He shoved his hands in his pockets in defeat. His fingers came upon the scrap of paper intended for Rose. The paper where he'd scribbled names and addresses of his family members, in case she ended up near them. In the disaster of today's visit, all thought of passing it along to her had deserted him. Likely he'd never see or hear from her again. The same war that threw them together now pulled them apart.

He kicked a discarded can to the roadside and realized he stood at the corner where the quartermaster presided over army supplies. Never again would he be able to beg the man's favor, not after Noah told him about the stolen horse. Though it would wrench his heart, he'd offer Hercules as restitution.

Two loves lost in one day. How much could a man bear?

~

*L*ost.

The word echoed in her mind as Rose turned into the comforting arms of Edith Wynn and let the tears flow. Life kept dealing one loss after another, but not only her. Everyone in this room had lost so much. She wept for their losses as well as her own.

The other women rallied around her, murmuring their support and consolation as she battled the suffocating sorrow. Isaac Wynn patted her shoulder in a fatherly manner, which only served to remind her of the loss of her father. Fresh tears bloomed with the pain.

Willing them to stop, she joined Olivia and Lydia on the settee. J.D. Anderson called the children inside, along with the younger women who ushered them upstairs to settle down for the night.

Celeste sat on the floor beside Rose, leaning against her sister's knee, and the remaining adults sat or stood nearby. By unspoken consent, they knew the time had come for a family meeting.

Isaac assumed leadership as the spiritual elder. "While I don't think any of us acted for any reason other than Christian charity, perhaps we should have let Captain Griffin know that Sergeant Morgan was on the premises."

Lydia patted Rose's hand. "But the captain's visits were always brief, before today. It seems every time he comes by, things go wrong."

Ada Anderson heaved a sigh. "I guess we could've told them guards about it, but who knows what they would've done?"

J.D. shook his head. "Corporal Jones said Private Allen got moved 'cause he tattled on the captain for eatin' supper with the women and not turnin' in the runaway."

"I should have told him," Rose said. "If I'd explained it to him right away, maybe he'd have understood."

Lydia snorted. "Most likely not. Men!" She glanced at Isaac and J.D. and amended her statement. "*Some men* act first and think second."

Isaac cleared his throat to curtail the comments. "Idle speculation is useless at this point. Now we need to figure out how to move forward."

Olivia roused from her contemplation. "I think that's what we probably should do. Move forward. As much as I hate to leave Georgia, maybe it's time to go."

"What do you mean?" Emily's voice trembled as she looked around the group.

"Hmph." Edith seemed in agreement with Olivia. "Take the bull by the horns, so to speak. Pack up our things and head to the trains. It seems to me the Lord keeps urging us to make the first move."

Isaac draped an arm around his wife's shoulders. "We can see if the guards can get a wagon to haul us and our goods to the station."

Rose clenched her hands as her heart lurched, but she had to agree. Staying here wouldn't improve matters. Maybe they'd been lingering out of fear, clinging to the familiar as long as they could hold on.

It was time to leave town. Time to take a leap of faith into the unknown.

CHAPTER 18

*T*he Lord's Day, and here they were, getting ready to leave town again. Rose held her sorrow at bay and surveyed the front room one last time.

Everyone in the house had risen before dawn to prepare for the journey north. After packing up their personal possessions, the women assembled bundles of food for the group. The men completed some minor maintenance, their way of repaying the owners for use of the property and other items.

With the chores completed and baggage ready to load, Rose and Lydia stepped onto the porch to talk with the guards. Steeling her nerves, Rose took a deep breath. "Corporal, we have a request to make."

Corporal Jones leapt to his feet. Private Langley followed more slowly, eyeing them with suspicion.

Rose launched into her speech. "All the occupants of this house have discussed our situation and decided we should be among the workers leaving on the next train. If you'd please have someone fetch a wagon to transport us and our belongings, we're prepared to leave right away."

The soldiers stared at her as if she'd taken leave of her senses.

Lydia took up her part. "Your general brought us here with plans to send us north. We see no reason to linger when you must be needed elsewhere. If there's more fighting coming this way, it'd be best for us and your army to move us out of the way."

Corporal Jones slapped his kepi against his leg. "That may be true, ma'am, but we ain't got the authority to move you without direct orders. I heard the trains been taking some of the prisoners 'most every day, but we don't know the plans to move you. And we can't leave our post to go ask."

Rose fought her frustration but didn't back down. "I don't suppose you'd let one of us go ask about it."

He shook his head and gave her a penetrating look. "No ma'am, and it'd be downright dangerous for you to do so. Even for one of them men in there. Even if you knew where to go and who to ask, which I don't."

Lydia touched Rose's hand and jerked her head toward the front door. "Let's go back inside and tell the others."

They stepped into the house and shut the door. It was getting stuffy with the windows and doors closed, but it helped keep the house free of dust and debris. And afforded them some privacy. Expectant faces turned their way.

Rose shook her head. "They won't send for a wagon. We'll have to wait and see if anyone comes by. Surely somebody will bring news soon."

Isaac motioned them to a seat. He'd been reading a passage of Scripture while Rose and Lydia approached the guards. "Let's have a time of prayer, shall we?"

His voice rang out clear and strong as he prayed for guidance and protection. Rose added her silent prayer for help to trust God through this difficult season.

Isaac continued. "A man's heart deviseth his way; but Jehovah directeth his steps." *Please, may it be so.*

$\sim$

*N*oah lengthened his steps through the streets of Marietta with a new sense of resolve. He'd have to hurry to make the meeting now, having wandered farther than planned. After a restless night, an early morning walk seemed the best way to settle his mind. Even before dawn, with fog slithering from the lowering clouds, the heat was oppressive. It echoed the gloom in his mind. Neither the heat nor the heartache promised any relief.

Noah slipped inside the crowded room as the adjutant banged on the scarred table to start the meeting. The atmosphere shifted from restrained respect to tense energy.

General Thomas began. "Our contacts have confirmed that the Rebel leaders have replaced Joseph Johnston with John Hood. The cat-and-mouse game is over, gentlemen."

Amid excited murmurs, someone shouted, "Hurrah."

Thomas raised his hands and continued. "Our own General McPherson was acquainted with Hood from their days at West Point. He tells us Hood will push for a direct confrontation." He proceeded to give each company orders for immediate deployment to communities east and south of Atlanta.

As the meeting broke up, General Garrard caught Noah's arm. "Griffin, you're with me. Tell your men to assemble at the Military Institute in an hour. We're headed south to take out the railroad east of Atlanta."

"Yes sir." Noah answered automatically, but the mention of the railroad triggered a jump in his heartbeat. Would trains be leaving Marietta to carry more mill workers north? The question rang in his head as he passed the word to his company. Noah quickly completed the familiar tasks to ride out. A persistent feeling urged him to detour by the depot. He should take the note he'd forgotten yesterday.

As much as Marietta teemed with chaos, he discovered it multiplied at the depot. Wagons clogged the roads, forcing pedestrians and mounted soldiers to weave their way through the spaces between. Both military and railway employees labored with off-loading crates while clerks recorded the tallies and matched the accompanying manifests. Guards observed the activity with varying degrees of interest.

Noah waded into the disorder with caution.

A shout from behind made him spin around and barely miss getting clobbered by a crate toppling from a wagon. With the level of noise here, he marveled he'd heard that shout. He supposed he owed his good fortune to the experience of battle, as well as divine protection.

The smell of a street vendor's roasting onions and sausages reminded him of the passing time. He should abandon this foolhardy errand and return to his unit. Just as he started to retreat, a wagon several yards ahead moved closer to the tracks. It was loaded with baggage, and several women stood to disembark. Recognition slammed him.

Before he could move, another wagon blocked his view. This one also carried women, children, and trunks. He struggled to move around it, pushing his way through the mass of people. Women glared at him. Children's eyes widened in apprehension. One burly guard refused to move until he noticed the rank on Noah's shoulder.

"Sorry, Captain, sir."

Another voice addressed him, this time from behind. "Captain Griffin!" It was the old man from New Manchester. A swift glance confirmed other males from that band. In the other direction, the women had already entered the freight car. He had no time to linger. The men could be his last chance for connection.

He approached the guard. "Sergeant, where are you taking these men?"

The young man snapped a salute. "Sir, these prisoners are being transported to Nashville to General Webster. They'll be joining those who left the other day."

"Where are the women?"

The guard pointed toward the wagons still unloading baggage into the freight car. "Women and small children go in one car, men in another. They'll meet up again in a day or two."

Young John Mark pushed between two of the men. "Cap'n! You found any more arrowheads?"

Noah attempted a smile and shook his head, assuring the boy he'd continue searching. Seeing the other boy clinging to his elderly relative, Noah sank to his haunches. Wariness warred with the tears standing in the boy's eyes. The poor lad must wonder what was happening.

"You take care of your Uncle Isaac here until you get back to your Ma, okay?"

Wade firmed his lips and bobbed his head in response. He imagined the boy was torn between wanting to go with the women and proving he was big enough to be with the men.

Noah cut his eyes to John Mark and whispered, "You're keeping your coin safe?"

The boy patted his pocket. "Yes sir."

"Good. You may need it later." He stood and spoke to the entire group. "God be with you all." Similar words echoed the bittersweet sentiment.

Noah stuffed his hands in his pocket and found the wad of paper he'd never removed from the day before. The guard's attention settled on another old man who appeared to be growing faint. Grasping the paper, Noah spun around and caught Isaac's arm. "Give this to Rose, in case you get that far."

A light of understanding shone in Isaac's eyes as he crammed the paper into his own pocket. "Will do, Captain."

The trains heading north would provide these people some safety at least, unlike the places where he was bound.

⁓

*B*linking rapidly, Rose peered into the dark cavern of the rail car. Pushed deeper inside by the press of bodies behind her, she kept her eyes trained on Celeste's white bonnet, her guiding beacon as she entered the sunless chamber.

Precious little light seeped inside. Placed high in the walls, the few windows looked as if they'd not met a cleaning rag in months. At least when they rode in the wagons, they could watch the scenery and breathe clean air. Shut in this iron prison, they were deprived of both.

Rose dropped her bags and clutched Celeste's hand as she sank to the floor. They huddled between trunks and bundles of sheet-wrapped clothing. Closing her eyes, she concentrated on breathing slowly. If she could block out the image of the hulking black locomotive and pretend they still rode in the wagons, perhaps the panic would subside.

"This makes me appreciate Jonah's days in the great fish," Celeste whispered with a shudder. "It's so big and dark. And full of…"

"Shh! I'm trying not to think about it."

The sigh from Celeste floated softly across her cheek. "Rose, maybe you should talk about what—"

A blast of the train's whistle drowned out the rest of her words. The hiss of steam preceded a violent jerk that sent a few loose items sliding across the floor. The clacking of metal wheels along the track accelerated until the car settled into a rocking motion. The noise prohibited normal conversations.

With the passage of time, Rose's anxiety abated, and she leaned against the car wall.

Beside her, Celeste removed a biscuit from her worn reticule and broke it, giving Rose half. She ate, remembering a verse from the story of Elijah: "Eat, for the journey is too great for you." *Aye, it is too great, Father. Give us strength and peace amid this turmoil.*

Despite the train's constant clamor and cramped conditions, Rose reclined against a pile of stuffed pillowcases. The stress of the past week left her drained. With her eyes closed to restrain the panic, the rocking motion lulled her to sleep.

She awoke later to discover the train wasn't moving, and she could hear conversations going on around her. In the darkness she could make out only odd shapes.

Celeste stirred beside her and stretched away from the trunk she'd been leaning against. "Have we arrived then?"

"I don't know. I suppose someone will let us know if we have."

The car's side door slid open to reveal a blue-velvet sky studded with stars. Two soldiers hooked one end of a metal ramp at the opening while another held a lantern and leaned into the car. "If anyone needs to answer the call of nature, you can get off here while we take on more water. Just don't wander off in the dark."

Rose stood and helped Celeste to her feet. "I will go if only to stretch my legs. Let's see if Millie needs any help. Oh, there's Olivia and Edith."

The women assisted one another, finding the others from their little group as they gained solid ground. When they reached the guards, Edith asked, "What is this place?"

"Chatt'nooga, Tennessee, ma'am. It's about a hunnert miles due north of Marietta. If it was full daylight, you could see the mountains over thataway." The guard pointed to their left. By his accent and obvious pride in the area, Rose figured he was a native Tennessean. He pointed out their location at Market Street, illuminated by occasional lamps in buildings along the road, and the First Presbyterian Church a few blocks away, now serving as a hospital.

Rose digested the information. Chattanooga was forty miles north of Dalton, where her family had lived before moving to Roswell. Would the train continue east to Knoxville or west to Nashville? As far as she could recall, the Federal forces controlled both cities. Both routes would be through mountainous terrain.

One thing was certain: The farther they traveled, the less likely it became that any of them would see Georgia again anytime soon.

The genial soldier added, "We had to use this building here for a hospital last year, so it's a mite cluttered, but it ought to serve your needs."

The guards allowed them into the brick building a few at a time. As Celeste made her way to the women's private area, Rose joined Millie and Lydia. Janie Wilson stepped into her path and launched into speech.

"Rose, I heard about what Phoebe did to y'all, and I'm powerful sorry. I don't know what's got into that gal lately 'cept she's wild about soldiers. I expect she sees you and Celeste as competition for their attention." She swept her gaze over the landscape dotted with only a few men and several dozen women. "As if either one of you would have a Yankee!"

Rose chose her words carefully. "I'm sure it's not easy being fifteen and having few choices of available men. With the war on, any serious relationship would have to be postponed. Being sent North, we don't know what'll become of any of us.'"

She thought of Noah Griffin, and grief washed over her again at the pain in his eyes. His words beat a steady rhythm of sorrow in her heart. *"I thought I'd earned your trust. Now I see I was mistaken."*

She pushed aside the tortuous image and focused on the present.

"She started playing up to one of the guards in Marietta," Janie said. "Said that captain kept showing up at your door, and I guess she decided to aim for a higher rank."

Rose didn't know how to answer. She spotted Celeste visiting Lydia a few yards away. "Look, there's Celeste waiting for me. Come and say hello."

Celeste greeted Janie with a hug and introduced Lydia. "How have you been? Where are the girls and Tommy?"

"Oh, they done gone back to the car where we got our stuff. Sadie weren't feeling well and wanted to lie down. All the others are as well as can be expected, what with all this upheaval." Janie turned toward the train with a huff of resignation. "I guess I'd best get back there before they start bickering again over who sits where."

After they said their goodbyes, Celeste turned to Rose. "Lydia's worried about Millie."

"Is she having problems?"

Lydia twisted her hands. "She's uncomfortable, of course, but she's hardly eating and turned weepy, worrying about the birthing and the baby's daddy."

Rose squeezed Lydia's hands. "Perhaps Olivia and Edith can help. I'm not good with those things, but I'll certainly pray and do whatever I can to assist you."

"We ought to move closer together, if we can," Celeste suggested, "so all of us can be there if we're needed."

"I'd appreciate that," Lydia said. "I can't tell you what a comfort is to have y'all for friends. I don't think I could handle this alone."

A porter swung his lantern and told them to board the train.

Rose gulped and pushed down the threatening fear. "All right. It appears we're getting ready to load up now anyway. Let's see what we can do."

CHAPTER 19

"*Y*our men all set to go? The general is ready to move on." Garrard's aide alerted Noah as he made his way down the line to urge the company on its way.

Since they were near their first destination, breakfast had been quick and cold. Their task lay ahead: miles of track running from Atlanta to Augusta to be demolished in the blistering Georgia sun. Destroying the rail system would cripple the Rebels and, they hoped, hasten the war's end.

Noah guided Hercules to fall in line. The finicky animal allowed nobody else to ride him, a fact that both gratified and disturbed Noah. He'd have to find another way to reimburse the army for the lost gelding. Meanwhile he endured the glowering countenance of Captain Rankin, the assistant quartermaster.

His thoughts turned to Marietta. He replayed the scene from two days past and felt again the crushing disappointment of betrayal. Berating his boneheaded stupidity, he couldn't imagine why he'd risked that trip to the depot.

Hercules needed little direction from Noah. He followed the other riders as he had the last three years. Noah, however, struggled to keep his mind on his present circumstances. He chastised himself for such dereliction of duty. Attacks could come from anywhere, at any moment.

When their route took them through the shadows of spreading live oak trees, he blessed the shade. The relief could cost them though, if enemy forces hid within. The pine trees clustered close together but grew straight up, casting their needles and cones to create an endless cushion on the ground.

Trees grew everywhere in Georgia. He missed the open fields of Indiana, where only an occasional stand of trees interrupted the view of sprouting corn for acres on end. What would Rose think of his family's farm? Would she miss the green rolling hills of the South?

Catching himself, he squeezed on Hercules' reins, which caused him to sidestep and toss his head. "Sorry, old boy. I'm not good company today, am I?"

Amused laughter rumbled from the rider behind him. "Sleeping in the saddle, Captain? Or just daydreaming about some gal back home?"

Chagrinned, Noah slowed his mount and faced his sergeant, an older man he admired for his easy-going nature and down-to-earth wisdom. "Daydreaming about home, for sure. But there's no girl waiting for me there, Fowler."

"Oh? Then I guess Rose must be your favorite flower."

Noah frowned. "When did I speak of Rose?"

"In your sleep last night." The man gave him a pitying look and confided, "You fairly shouted it out, like you was angry or trying to warn her of something. Woke three or four of us nearby. But don't you worry about it, Cap." The man urged his mount closer and winked. "Your secret is safe with us. Keep dreaming."

∾

Nashville, Tennessee
Monday, July 18, 1864

*R*ose emerged from the depths of her curious dream. The sensation of running and searching for Celeste had ceased as a wave appeared to wash over her head. Strangely, she had lain back against the wave, finding a sense of peace, letting the water carry her and calm her anxiety.

The screeching of metal against metal penetrated the fog of sleep. Peering around in the gray light, she remembered her current circumstances and marveled at the lack of panic. The feeling of serenity lingered from the dream, and she recalled a verse from Isaiah. "Thou wilt keep him in perfect peace whose mind is stayed on Thee."

Yes, Father, I will keep my mind on You. Thank You for the assurance that You are with us, no matter where we go. And thank You for new friends to share this difficult journey.

Her gaze roamed over those friends. Olivia and Shiloh bracketed Edith, each slumbering on quilts they had created in better years. Next to them, Dorcas and Sarah Grace curled on their sides an arm's length from Emily and Ada. Lydia leaned over Millie, who struggled to sit up. Their traveling situation clearly made her condition more difficult as time progressed.

Throughout the car, women were beginning to stir, anticipating the opportunity to leave the rail car, if only for a brief respite.

Beside her, Celeste stretched her limbs discreetly and murmured a drowsy greeting. In all they'd experienced since the war began, Celeste had maintained her gentleness and optimism. Though Rose assumed the role of leader and protector, and worried that she failed regularly, Celeste never complained.

In a surge of gratitude, Rose caught her sister in a hug. "Good morning, Cissy, and thank you."

"For what?"

"Just for being you."

Celeste returned the affection with a saucy smile. "I tried to be someone else, but it didn't work out well."

Rose giggled as she stood. "You are very good at being you."

The scrape of metal announced the sliding of the rail car's door. Morning sunlight flooded inside, and soldiers placed portable steps at the door.

Rose shielded her eyes from the brightness but welcomed the rush of fresh air.

A grim-faced porter leaned into the opening. "All right, folks, welcome to Nashville. Gather all your belongings and clear the car as quick as you can. We have goods to load for the troops back in Georgia. General Webster's orders say you're to wait in the depot for further word as to where you're going."

In a flurry of activity, women and children alike hefted their baggage, eager to leave their current confinement. Guards stood on either side of the exit. Rose wondered whether they were there to assist anyone having trouble navigating the descent or to discourage deviation from the pathway. She slipped her arm through the handles of her valise so she could lift her skirts to descend. Her other hand gripped another case while her arm wrapped around a bulky bundle. Others had devised similar methods of negotiating their way down the steps and across the tracks between them and the depot.

Rose and Celeste deliberately walked ahead of Millie and Lydia, with Dorcas and Shiloh immediately behind them. The other women flanked Sarah Grace and brought up the rear. Once inside the building, they worked out a system of minding their possessions so each person could visit the necessary.

Olivia scoured the scene for her son and uncle. "I wonder if they'll let the men join us now. I hate not having Wade with me."

Rose shared her concern. In a matter of days, John Mark and Wade had found a place in her heart, as had the shy Sarah Grace. Their mothers must be distressed at the separation, even though their male relatives had promised to watch them closely. She'd also learned Isaac and J.D. had slight physical limitations, which must worry their wives. Naturally, neither man would admit to any weakness.

After several anxious minutes, Celeste spotted the men coming their way. "There they are." Wade dashed ahead, and Olivia bent to wrap him in her arms. John Mark pretended to be more reserved, but his smile included them all.

"How did you ladies fare on the journey?" Isaac's question reached out to them as the men followed more slowly.

Isaac greeted his family with eager hugs for each one. Sarah Grace climbed right into J.D.'s arms to claim his attention.

Edith settled into Isaac's embrace with a tired smile. "We've had better days, but the Lord watched over us and kept us safe."

"Well, we might as well settle down to wait a while," Isaac advised. "We heard one of the guards saying he wasn't sure where that general would put us."

J.D. put Sarah Grace down and folded himself into position on the floor, setting the child in his lap. "Seems Nashville is already overrun with people leaving their homes and coming here to find work."

Concerned murmurs acknowledged the news.

Rose pressed her lips tightly as her calm seeped away under the pressure of worry.

Others followed J.D.'s example and found places to sit. In silence, the women dug through their baggage to find cheese and bread for everyone to share.

Pausing before taking his own seat, Isaac fished something out of his pocket and handed it to Rose. "I was instructed to give this to you, Miss Rose."

Rose looked at the paper, which had names and locations

written in bold handwriting. They meant nothing to her. "I don't understand. Who asked you to give this to me?"

"Captain Griffin. We saw him at the depot in Marietta just as we were all getting on the train. He said to give it to you in case we get that far. I didn't get a chance to read it myself, so I don't know what he meant about getting that far."

Rose studied the paper again and understood. "I believe these are his family members. He spoke of a sister named Eliza. Oh, and this must be Lieutenant Bradley's family. It seems Captain Griffin thinks we might go as far north as Indiana."

"Does the rail go that far?" Celeste asked. "I thought Nashville was our destination."

"I don't know. I noticed one sign said Louisville, Kentucky, is on this line. Indiana would be north of Louisville if I remember correctly. That would put us three states away from Georgia."

Olivia peeked around Celeste. "Someone said we're bound for the Ohio River. That's the border between Kentucky and states northward. I guess they want us plenty far away from the South."

~

RAILROAD LINE SOUTH OF STONE MOUNTAIN, GEORGIA
WEDNESDAY, JULY 20, 1864

"*W*e'll start ripping the line here and go as far as that line of trees to the east." Major Hendricks pointed to the train tracks. "Then we'll pile up the ties and rails for a bonfire. Kent's men will bend and twist the hot rails so the Rebs can't repair them."

The instructions passed down the column, and the men set to work. Not bothering to set up camp, except for one food tent, which the men would visit in small groups, they merely stashed their gear near the horses. A small creek meandered through the trees, flowing toward the Yellow River and providing water for man and beast alike.

After the skirmishes of the last two days, Noah welcomed this location's relative quiet. The task before them would be physically challenging, but at least this destruction focused on metal and wood, not flesh and blood.

Rank mattered little in times like this. Noah assisted with breaking up tracks, cutting up fallen trees, and hacking off large branches to fuel the fire. Although he'd removed his wool jacket, he couldn't stem the perspiration pouring from the rim of his kepi and dripping off his beard. Discarding his shirt was out of the question. He wouldn't add sunburn to the weapons of this merciless heat.

Taking his break about mid-morning, Noah collected a plate of beans and cornbread and filled his tip cup with water. He joined Sergeant Fowler and Corporal Newsome in the shade of a tree atop a little rise several yards from the tracks.

Sergeant Fowler grunted as he lowered himself to the ground. "Wouldn't want one of those ties to fly off from a careless strike and interrupt our fine dining."

The men attacked their meal, enjoying the respite from the sun. Newsome pointed to a structure in the distance. "Reckon that's attached to the railroad up there?"

Noah considered the area, visually measuring the line of rail and the distance to the building. "Nah, it's too far away. See how the tracks start veering to the right? By the time they reach that point, the building would be at least a quarter mile away. It's probably a farm. I don't see any crops, though it looks to have been cleared for something."

"Could be tobacco or groundnuts there," the sergeant said. "Both grow close to the ground, not tall like wheat or corn."

Coming from a farming family, Noah's interest stirred. "Is that so? I don't believe I've ever seen those plants. I know of tobacco, of course, but I don't know about groundnuts."

153

Fowler drew a shape in the dirt using a short twig. "Some folks call 'em peanuts. They come in pods like green peas, but the pod itself is rough, almost like tree bark. Mostly used to feed the livestock, although some folks boil 'em and eat 'em, I hear."

"Interesting. I'll have to tell my father about that when I write. He's always reading about different crops and farming techniques. Maybe he'll want to check into it."

The sergeant frowned and stroked his beard. "Don't know if they'll grow up North, Cap. It could be risky. Some things only grow in certain areas. Not everything can be uprooted and transplanted elsewhere." He seemed to give extra meaning to his mild words.

Noah's gaze snapped to the older man, but he'd picked up his dishes and started down the hill. Did Fowler have more than plants in mind with those remarks? He'd ask about it later. For now, he had work to do.

He collected his items and followed the men down the hill.

While he worked, he thought of transplants, both people and seedlings. General Sherman's order to send the Georgia women North had seemed reasonable on the surface. It put the women beyond the region of conflict, providing greater safety for them and one less worry for the army. But it threw them into a world vastly different from the one they knew. Would they find employment and housing? How would they cope with the North's harsher winters?

For his own peace of mind, he needed to believe the women could survive the move, though the prospects were limited for those with no education. His thoughts drifted again and again to the events of the last two weeks. From the time he rode into Roswell, life had thrown him into a spin. Why had he let himself trust the locals? Isaac and J.D., who'd made him think of his father. John Mark and Wade and Sarah Grace, who'd tugged at memories of his siblings and his own childhood. And the women.

Especially the women.

Though he forced his mind back to the present, like a naughty child it kept returning to Marietta. The work demanded more of his body but left his thoughts free to wander...and wonder what he could have done differently.

Someone shouted a warning. He looked up, squinting and throwing up an arm to shield his eyes from the glare.

Too late. The object glanced off his right elbow, flipped and smacked the left side of his head. A moment of stunning pain, then darkness descended.

CHAPTER 20

*R*ose stepped from the rail car at their final destination. Dark clouds obscured the sun, threatening rain and making the late afternoon feel like evening.

Or perhaps it was the smoke from all the nearby chimneys.

Several buildings boasting three or four stories emitted the black exhaust associated with the factories she'd heard about. The biting odor recalled the fire that destroyed the mills less than a month before. Her eyes watered, either from the stench or the memory it evoked.

She couldn't give way to melancholy. She had to be strong. Gripping the bags with her few possessions, Rose allowed the crowd to push her along the tracks. The press of people grew even denser as the women made their way through the depot, following the guards who'd met the train.

Beside her, Celeste gasped as they exited the building and nearly collided with a boy chasing a pig. The crowd shifted to allow both runners to move beyond them. The stench of people and animals in close quarters vied with the industrial odors, a confusing assault on her senses. A warm breeze chased the clouds and sprinkled them with drops of rain as their group waited for the street to clear of traffic.

"What in the world is that place?" The question came from Millie, who moved to Rose's other side. Both Rose and Celeste turned to look where Millie indicated.

Directly across the street, a group of brick buildings sat behind a wooden fence that enclosed the entire block. As they studied the complex, a gate opened, and two men emerged from the barricaded structure. Between them they carried a cloth-covered litter, which they loaded onto a waiting wagon.

"Hospital, maybe," Rose said. "But not for the town's residents, I'd guess, with that tall fence around it. Could be a sanitarium, I suppose."

When the way was clear, they crossed to the other side and passed a large iron gate bearing the sign "Union Army Prison."

"Oh, my," Millie whispered. She gripped Rose's arm with her free hand. "Do you suppose...?"

Rose leaned close to the girl. "Don't fret. We're not going there. See, the guards are crossing the street again." The signposts read Tenth Street and Broadway. She read them aloud, committing the information to memory for any future need.

Their destination, however, appeared to be within sight of the prison. A newly constructed building sat square in the block facing the prison gate. No banner or marker graced the entrance. The guards led them into a lobby and down the drab, gray hallway on the right, passing several open doors. Inside those rooms, Rose glimpsed other women sitting on cots or around tables. Oil lamps lit the dark areas.

Windows in the stairway at the end of the hall offered little illumination as they climbed to the second floor. The guards stopped at the top of the stairs to give instructions.

"You can choose which room you want. Each of them has a

dozen beds, a couple of tables and several chairs, and some chests o' drawers. The men and boys will be put in rooms on the first floor since there's not as many of them."

The guard explained about the kitchen and other facilities available at the refugee house "Two water closets on each floor," he said, "but the water hasn't yet been run to this building. You'll have to get water from the well."

Rose and Celeste exchanged looks at that. What good was a water closet without water?

"There's no water pump?"

"Not yet." He dismissed their concern with a shrug. "We hope to have the gas lines in working order before the weather turns cold."

Olivia peppered the guard with questions. Their group took a room near the far end of the hall.

"The guard said Wade and John Mark might be able to visit us if we take this room, so you can continue your lessons." Olivia said. "They'll be sleeping in a room directly below us. It's not ideal, but at least they'll be close enough we can care for them if they get sick. Are you single ladies all right with that?"

It was fine with Rose. She was just glad to have a bed. Along with the other women, she dropped her baggage beside a cot and lay on the narrow mattress.

She'd chosen the bed between Celeste and Dorcas. "Ah, this is heaven after that rail car."

After a few moments, most of the others were asleep. Tired as she felt, Rose could only sleep in the daytime if she was ill. She sat up, removed her shoes, and padded in her stocking feet around the room, inspecting the furnishings.

How would they manage meals? Was there a staff in the kitchen or was it merely available for the residents?

A timid knock at the open door drew her attention. Janie and Phoebe Wilson stood there. Janie twisted her handkerchief, and Phoebe directed her gaze around the room as Rose hurried to greet them.

"How are you doing? I lost track of you when we left Nashville. Have you found a space to settle in this building for a while?"

Janie glanced at the sleeping women and kept her voice low. "Yes, we put up with the others from the house in Marietta. Except Phoebe here. That's to say, there's not enough beds for us all, and I need to stay with the younger ones. Might there be room for Phoebe to stay with y'all? I'd feel better for her to be with folks I know. If y'all don't care, that is, and if you have room." Her voice trailed off as she cast a worried gaze around the room.

Rose sent up a quick prayer for grace. "Of course she can join us. That is, if she wants to. What do you say, Phoebe?"

The girl turned to her with lifted brows. Obviously, she hadn't expected to be consulted on the matter. Resuming her expression of unconcern, she shrugged. "I reckon I have to sleep somewhere."

Janie expelled a breath of relief, and Rose pointed to an unmade cot. "There's one bed vacant on the left side there. You can use it."

"We'll go get her stuff from the other room then. Me and the young'uns are in the third room from the other end of the hall." She pulled Rose into an embrace. "Thank you, dear. I know you'll watch after her."

Rose wandered back into the room and plopped down on her cot. Did life never get easier? How was she to forget what happened in Marietta if she had to see Phoebe every day?

Do not forget. The voice wasn't audible, but it rang clearly in her mind.

But the memories still brought pain and guilt. Perhaps this was her penance for betraying Noah's trust, to remember. *Lord,*

I'm sorry. Please forgive me. She whispered that prayer often. Why did she not feel the assurance of forgiveness?

But she knew the answer. The one to ask for forgiveness was far away, and she might never get the chance to ask it in this life.

Outside the rain turned into a downpour, but noise from the street continued to drift past the window. Their room faced the Union Army Prison, set in the middle of business and industry. How would she be able to sleep in this strange place?

~

A FARM NEAR BLAKE'S MILL, GEORGIA
THURSDAY, JULY 21, 1864

A woman was singing. Noah registered the sound as he drifted to consciousness. A pleasant voice, but the melody wobbled as if she wasn't sure of it. What was that song? He ought to know it, but his head hurt too badly to dwell on the question.

Why did his head hurt? Why was he in a real bed where he could hear a woman singing in the next room?

He opened his eyes but saw nothing. At least he thought his eyes were open. Easing one hand up to his face, he touched bandages. His fingers found the edge of a bandage hanging over his eyes and pushed it up. Bright sunlight made him wince, but he forced himself to blink rapidly, as he'd learned to do while exploring caves back home. His vision adjusted enough to make out a few items in the room.

A pine dresser with drawers that didn't sit properly. A mirror on the wall above a shaving stand that held a bowl and ewer. Pegs on the wall but no clothing, apart from his own jacket, trousers, and kepi. His hand crept to his chest. He'd been stripped down to his small clothes and covered with a light quilt.

The pain increased when he turned toward the window, but he couldn't see beyond the length of blue-striped curtains. A man's room then, he supposed, judging by the shaving items and plain furnishings. A man who wasn't in residence, probably away in the war.

The war. Where in the world was he? Still in the South or sent home to mend? But no, this room wasn't familiar to him. He deliberately slowed his breathing and listened for the woman's voice again. It ebbed and flowed, as if she were walking back and forth. Why didn't she sing the words louder so he could tell where he was? A Southern accent would prevail even in song.

The melody paused as another voice rumbled. Coming from the same direction as the singer, it sounded masculine. The woman answered in a soft Southern drawl then stopped. Detecting steps coming his way, Noah released the bandage and pretended to sleep. He needed to gather more information before letting anyone know he was awake.

He heard her creep nearer, sensed her leaning over the bed. Then she moved away, closing the door behind her. "He's still out of it," she said, "but you'd best stay out of the house until his men come back for him."

Ah. So he was still in the South. His men had brought him here and planned to return for him. But what had happened?

Sounds from the other room indicated his temporary guardians were gathering items. He made out some mutterings about water as something metal clattered against another object. Maybe it was wash day. Noah waited to be sure they'd moved outside before he resumed his limited investigation.

He touched the bandage again, moving his fingers gingerly over the area until he noted a large bump near his left temple. Alarmed by the size, he poked around it until he discovered a damp piece of cloth plastered beneath the wrapping. Maybe the knot wasn't so big after all.

Relief left him weak. The sunlight shifted and warmed the full length of his body. In moments he slept again.

The aroma of something cooking woke him. He moved the bandage aside and blinked. The waning sunlight was demonstrated by bright patches against the far wall. He must have slept for hours. One shadow moved. Not an apparition but a person, placing something at the foot of the bed.

She glanced up to find him watching her. "Oh! You're awake at last. I was feared you might sleep on another day or two."

"Wha…" Noah cleared his throat to try again.

"I 'spect you need a drop to wet your whistle before you can ask questions." She rushed to the ewer and poured water into a chipped earthen cup. Moving to his side, she helped him sit up enough to take a few sips, then piled the pillows behind his head before letting him down again. He adjusted the covers to preserve the woman's modesty.

"Where am I exactly?" His voice sounded rusty.

The woman moved around the room, touching the curtain, replacing the cup next to the pitcher, and moving to the foot of the bed again. "Well, I can't say 'zactly, but it's 'bout half a dozen miles to Blake's Mill to the north side and half a day's ride to Decatur on the south side. O' course, that's riding Comet the mule who don't care how long it takes to get anywhere if there's grass to be found on the way."

A chuckle followed the last comment, but Noah detected a hint of anxiety in the sound. She moved back into the shadows.

Noah's eyes refused to focus properly, so he couldn't tell if she was young or old. Her hair hung loose, like a young girl's would, but he'd noticed some of the poorer, older women in the South didn't keep to the conventional chignons. Noah concentrated on her words, filing the distance in each direction but responding to her last remark.

"Your mule is named Comet? I guess that's a bit of irony, a jest?"

"For certain it is, but we say he's named for one of them reindeer in the story of St. Nicholas." She started toward the door, but Noah needed to find out more about his circumstances.

"Speaking of names," he said, "I suppose I should tell you mine and thank you for taking me in, ma'am."

She spun around. "The men what brung you here told me who you are, Captain Griffin. And I'm Nancy Herring. I need to go check on the soup. I'll be back directly to bring you some supper."

A short time later Nancy returned with a cup of steaming liquid and a small biscuit on a tray. "There's small bits of vegetables but it's mostly broth." She set the tray across his quilt-covered legs.

Noah took a few sips and followed Nancy's movements around the room, pondering which question to ask first. She'd pulled her hair back, and as his eyes focused better, he thought she might be close to his own age. She certainly didn't exhibit any signs of diffidence, neither blushing nor gaping at his state of undress, though clearly attempts to maintain common decency had been made.

He took another sip of broth. "Can you tell me what happened to me?"

She looked over her shoulder with surprise. "You don't remember?"

When he shook his head, she paced back to the bed. "The men said a rail tie broke loose and slammed you in the head. It seems y'all been tearing up the railroad all around here so's to keep our Southern boys away."

Faint memories of such work danced across his brain. "And your house was close by, so they brought me here, I guess." He touched the bandage around his head. "Who attended my wounds?"

"Well, somebody wrapped it in an undershirt doused in

water before they brung you here. Once we got you settled, I replaced that with cold rags and kept them in place with that strip from an old blanket. We ain't got no doctor around here anymore, so we do the best we can."

Noah lowered the cup. "I've eaten as much as I can, ma'am. It was mighty good soup, and I thank you for your kindness."

She took the tray. "Well, your men did give me some coin for takin' you in. Not that I would turn away a body in your condition, even in that uniform. And to be honest, I ain't foolish enough to spurn payment from the devil, not with things bein' the way they are."

She shifted the tray to one hand and shut the door behind her with a snap.

Noah leaned against his pillows and sighed. "I guess the devil now wears blue."

CHAPTER 21

"*W*hat are those blue-coated devils up to now?"

The whispered words jerked Rose's attention from the buckets of water at her feet. She'd set the buckets down to wrap her wide apron strings around her hands for a better grip, and to protect her palms from raising blisters. Five other women paused at their chores as well.

Rose gazed toward the Army prison where several guards flanked a small group of prisoners as they marched down the street. "They're carrying out Governor Burbridge's orders, I'd say. Four prisoners to die for every Union citizen killed in the state." Her heart sank and her stomach roiled, threatening to rid itself of the little it held.

She shook away the brimming tears and tightened the cloth across her hands. Picking up her buckets, she rasped, "Best be about your tasks, ladies, if you want to eat and bathe."

The others snapped back to their business before harsher reprimands could come from other quarters.

Rose could feel the questions following her, however. How did she know what was going on? Was she currying favor with the guards? Who put her in charge? After all, she'd only been there two days, unlike some of them who'd arrived on earlier trains from Marietta.

With their precious horde of paper, she and Celeste planned to continue working with the children. Yesterday she'd asked one guard to pass along available newspapers, no matter how old. She combed them to find any articles she could share with the children, to challenge their reading abilities and even pose problems for arithmetic lessons.

In the process, she couldn't ignore the political news and opinions. Her early exploration discovered various reports and editorials disparaging her fellow Southerners. But she could harness the anger those roused. She would channel it to bolster her determination to survive this time of testing.

The war has to end sometime—may God make it soon—and I plan to emerge a conqueror, no matter which army claims victory.

She carried her buckets into the building and set them down at the foot of the stairs, taking a rest before covering the final stretch to the room down the hall. She dipped one corner of her apron into the water and pressed the cool fabric to her brow and cheeks.

A masculine chuckle arrested her movement. The rustle of clothing and whispers drifted from the alcove in the stairwell.

Rose deciphered the sounds easily enough. A guard engaged one of the women in a secret tryst, taking advantage of the afternoon hours designated for quiet to accommodate the young children and the elderly. Though she considered it a dangerous action on the woman's part, Rose had no desire to embarrass them all with her arrival.

She affected a hacking cough before lifting the buckets and slogging noisily up the first few steps. The guard offered a curt greeting as he passed her on the stairs, keeping his eyes averted.

At least he had the sense to flee the scene discreetly. Rose plodded down the hall and glimpsed someone in a blue skirt dart into the third room.

Curiosity prompted her to look that way as she passed, and she nearly dropped her pails. One person stood in the aisle between the cots. Everyone else was either sleeping or occupied with needle work. The girl peeked over her shoulder, perhaps to see if she'd been discovered.

When Phoebe saw Rose pause at the door in surprise, she lifted her chin and smiled. Rose did not return the gesture.

~

A FARM NEAR BLAKE'S MILL, GEORGIA
FRIDAY, JULY 22, 1864

Noah opened the bedroom door and leaned into its jamb. He'd never known getting dressed to be so tiring. At least his dizziness had subsided. He moved slowly to keep that problem at bay.

When Nancy Herring had announced she'd be gone for an hour or more to visit a neighbor over the hill, he decided to test his mobility. After wrestling with his trousers and camp shirt, he chose not to attempt the boots. He peered in the mirror to view the damage to his head. The knot stood out in all its purplish glory, and his left eye looked like he'd gotten the worst end of a fight. A few years before, those would've been prizes to boast of. Today he only wondered how long they'd keep him from wearing his hat.

Visions of fellow soldiers who'd lost limbs or lives humbled him. "I'm no more worthy than they were, Lord. Thank You for Your protection." Even so, he figured he'd suffer some ribbing from his men about his "war injury."

He moved from the bedroom and crossed the kitchen to the

back door. He had a hunch he might find an outhouse, which would be a better choice than the chamber pot under the bed. He hurried in case his hostess returned sooner than expected. Outside he was surprised to see a couple of sheds and a small barn with the outhouse beyond it. As he passed the barn, a familiar whinny called to him, and he detoured to that building.

He had to blink in the dimness, but he knew better than to leave the barn door standing open. That lesson had been learned through several punishments in his youth. Hercules called to him again from the first of two stalls.

"Hey, boy. Am I glad to see you. Guess you set up a fuss and convinced them to leave you here, huh?"

The two visited for several minutes before Noah searched around the barn. No other animals shared the space, though there seemed to be sufficient feed for Hercules's current needs. All his equipment was missing. Even Hercules' army-issued saddle. Either his men had kept it with their tackle, or Nancy Herring had carted it off to sell. He'd have to confront the woman and hope his company soon finished their assignment and came back to get him.

Still perturbed over his missing gear, he bid Hercules farewell and pushed at the barn door.

"Stop right there!" Though not spoken loudly, the man's words came with confident authority.

Still inside the barn, Noah paused with his hand gripping the wooden closure.

"Close the door unless you want to get snake-bit," the voice ordered again.

Before Noah could reverse his motion completely, he detected a rattle, then a loud whack. After a mighty sigh, the voice came again. "You can come out now, Ma."

Noah pushed the door open to find a young man holding a three-foot snake by the tail, its severed head lying a few feet from the barn.

"Oo-whee! Guess we can add some meat to the soup pot now." Admiring his catch, the youth didn't look up until Noah spoke.

"I guess your ma would know how to do that?"

The hero jerked and lost his grin at the sight of his house guest. "What're you doing out here? You're supposed to be convalescin' in the bed. And where's Ma?"

Noah chose to ignore the first part of his speech and focus on the last question. "If your ma is Nancy Herring, she said she was going to visit a neighbor over the hill."

"That'd be Grandma Pemberton. She's laid up from a spill she took yesterday."

The confused expression still lingered, so Noah stepped forward, offering his hand by way of introduction. "I'm Noah Griffin—"

"I know who you are, *Captain Griffin of the Federal Army.*" The words were laced with venom.

The snake killer stood as tall as Noah, but his frame was slight, giving the impression he'd barely gained his majority. He regarded Noah warily, with perhaps the same regard he'd given the snake. Wiping his free hand against his trousers, he relented and accepted Noah's outstretched one. As if compelled beyond his better judgment, the younger man finally muttered his own name. "Sammy Herring." He pressed his lips together.

Noah thrust aside his own unease. For the moment, they were under an unexpected truce. "Pleased to meet you, Sammy. And I thank you for taking care of that critter. I guess that means you and your ma essentially saved my life twice now."

Sammy withdrew his hand from Noah's grip and nodded self-consciously. "Sure enough, though you'd best get back to bed afore Ma catches you roamin' around outside. And I'll commence to cleanin' this critter."

Figuring he'd been dismissed, Noah pointed to the other building. "Is that the outhouse?"

Sammy grinned. "Yeah, but you might keep an eye out for any more of these slippery sidewinders."

~

Louisville, Kentucky
Friday, July 22, 1864

*C*eleste huffed in exasperation as Rose finished relating her suspicions of Phoebe. "I guess we're going to have to keep a close eye on that girl. Do you plan to tell Janie?"

Rose echoed her sister's sigh. "Not yet. I don't want to get her into trouble without clear evidence. Phoebe already considers us her rivals. Bearing tales on her would just make her resent us more. Besides, it might hurt Janie and drive a wedge in our friendship."

Nodding, Celeste added a few more stitches to the skirt she was mending. "What about the guard? Should you let his superiors know about it?"

Rose's snort probably answered that question. "I can predict how that would turn out. The blame would come squarely back on Phoebe, or us, or her mother. It seems the woman always gets the blame in such cases."

She examined a shirtwaist she'd washed earlier. Scrubbing had faded the spot enough to render it acceptable. Not that it mattered. With only one spare, she'd have to wear it, stained or not. She glanced up in time to catch Celeste with a pensive expression on her face. "What is it, Cissy? You look like you want to say something but don't know if you should."

"You've caught me out. You always do." She hesitated a heartbeat then plunged ahead. "Do you remember the first time we met Captain Griffin? When those men cornered us near The Bricks in Roswell?"

This was not a direction Rose expected the conversation to take. Too many times she'd found herself thinking about the events of the last two weeks and the flight from Roswell to Marietta. "Of course, I do. Why do you ask?"

Celeste bit her lip. "I saw one of those men here. The one who grabbed me that day."

Rose stiffened. "Honey, are you sure?"

"He had a distinctive scar on his left cheek." Celeste drew a finger down her cheek to indicate the place of the scar.

I remember.

Rose shivered. "And you saw him here? When? At the depot or on our way past the prison?"

Celeste bit the thread trailing from her needle and dropped her sewing. She laid her hand over Rose's and directed her gaze straight into Rose's eyes. "No. Here. In this building. I think he's a new guard." She swallowed hard. "He recognized me too. He stared and had this evil smile...like he knew something."

Rose tried to reason away her fear. "All the soldiers stare at you. At all the women, to be truthful, but especially you, sweet sister." Rose patted Celeste's arm. "You don't realize how lovely you are."

Celeste captured Rose's hand. "Not like that, Rose. His eyes almost glowed with evil. It frightened me, but what he told the man beside him was worse."

Rose swallowed, pushing down the fear. "What did he say?"

"He said I had a sister, and he was looking forward to teaching us both a lesson we'd never forget."

Attempting a smile, Rose stood to her feet. "Then we are forewarned to be on our guard. Perhaps we should alert all the women to watch out for him. And we'll be careful not to get caught alone while he's around. The enemy won't find us an easy mark."

∽

A FARM NEAR BLAKE'S MILL, GEORGIA
FRIDAY, JULY 22, 1864

*N*oah rambled around the farm, exploring the outbuildings but moving carefully to accommodate his condition, while Sammy worked on his unexpected catch. Noah had the feeling Sammy observed him as carefully as he watched Sammy, although each worked to appear unaware of the other's scrutiny.

For all his youth, Sammy didn't give the impression of innocence. The war had forced many youngsters to grow up before their time, but Sammy exhibited some characteristics of one who'd seen battle. He tried to cloak his experience, but his cover slipped from time to time. The sudden vacant stare at nothing might be slight, except to another who'd suffered the same. Some battlefield scenes never faded.

Oddly enough, it had been the handshake that alerted Noah. When Sammy wiped his palm across the seat of his pants, Noah noticed the fabric and color. He'd seen the same fabric across Tennessee and Georgia. Decorated with bars and buttons, but mostly smeared with mud and blood.

Roswell Gray. The Confederate uniform.

The sight stunned him for a moment. Not only because Sammy's trousers shouted it out, but because of the memories suddenly rushing across his mind.

Roswell. Marietta. Rose. How could he have forgotten those days?

He touched the knot near his temple. Could it have been a dream? In his condition, he couldn't be sure. He should get out of the sun and concentrate on regaining his strength. Perhaps he'd be rescued from this place soon.

Before he could cross the threshold, a boom vibrated across the yard. Whether thunder or guns, Noah couldn't tell for sure.

His gaze found Sammy's but veered to a figure hurrying down the grassy knoll. Nancy Herring had returned, and Noah aimed to get some answers from his reluctant hostess.

CHAPTER 22

*H*urrying to take her turn on the food preparation and serving line, Rose barely missed colliding with a guard who stepped from the staircase. The man gripped her shoulders—to steady her, she supposed—as she mumbled an apology. When he continued to hold her in place, she glanced up and went cold at the mocking humor in his eyes. The scar Celeste had mentioned clearly identified him.

"Let me pass, please." The phrase so closely resembled what she'd said to him a few weeks before. Noah's command echoed in her head. *"Let her go, Pierce."*

"Pierce." She added his name, hoping it would call forth the same memory. Or at least shock him into releasing her.

His eyebrows shot up in surprise then lowered as his lips twisted into a grin. "Ah, Noah Griffin's paramour, I believe. I'm flattered I made such an impression."

"Don't be, and don't make assumptions about my character on the basis of yours." She jerked out of his hold and turned sideways to slip past him. "I'm expected right away in the kitchen."

In a sudden reversal of attitude, Pierce played the part of a gentleman. "Please, allow me to escort you safely there." His grip on her arm belied his friendly tone. "After all, we should become better acquainted since we're living together under the same roof."

Rose kept her gaze straight ahead as they covered the distance to the kitchen. She knew he was baiting her, and her best course of action would be to ignore him.

Pierce dug deeper. "And we have a mutual acquaintance in ole Griffin. Did he tell you he and I grew up together?"

Only by divine power did she manage to keep from responding.

"Oh, yes. Noah and Cooper Bradley as well. I saw you and your sister with them in that mill town. We all went to the same country school in Indiana. Noah's cousin Luke was a special friend of mine until he moved away. Ah, we had some good times tormenting the people of the county."

He leaned toward her with a sinister grin, his fetid breath fouling the air. "Noah was the leader, you know. Always running to trouble and then running away, leaving Luke and me to get caught."

They arrived at the kitchen, but he pulled her close enough to whisper, "I owe Noah for spoiling my fun, and you and your sister are going to help me repay that debt."

With belligerent force, he shoved her into the kitchen. "Here's your other helper, Mrs. Harper," he said to the woman in charge. "I found her trying to shirk her duties, hiding under the staircase. You'd best watch her close."

Rose stumbled and caught herself against the wall, mortified by the lies he told. Protesting would be useless, though. Her word against a guard's. Rose's best defense would be to apply herself to the work and demonstrate her worthiness. Without a word, without looking at the others in the room, she made her way to the kitchen manager, keeping her back straight and her head high. The woman made a curious smacking noise with her lips but otherwise said nothing. She thrust a basket of potatoes into Rose's hands and motioned to the pot of water on the counter.

Keeping her attention on the work, Rose tried to ignore the curious glances and whispers soon buzzing around her. She couldn't tell whether they believed Pierce's accusations, but no one spoke to Rose. The faces she'd glimpsed were new to her.

After she finished preparing the potatoes and dumped them in the pot, she turned to ask for another task. A figure blocked her path again, but it wasn't Pierce this time. Instead, Phoebe faced her with a smirk. "Guess you're not so high and mighty, after all," she hissed before flouncing away.

Rose had not one but two enemies to beware of. She closed her eyes and rubbed the spot on the arm Pierce had gripped. No doubt she would find a bruise there tomorrow. Today the bruises on her heart and her reputation needed attention.

～

DECATUR, GEORGIA
SUNDAY, JULY 24, 1864

*N*oah stretched his legs along the bare floor and leaned back against the wall, closing his eyes. Voices floated around him in this room, his fellow officers in discussion, but the journey from the Herrings' farm had taken a toll on him. His head ached from the injury, and his strength still lagged. His bruises showed no longer purple but ranged from dark blue to greenish yellow. The knot on his head had shrunk from goose egg to quail egg in size.

Though relieved to be with his comrades again, anxiety

troubled his spirit. This house, the home of one Miss Mary Gay and her family, bore silent testimony to the destruction wreaked on innocent citizens by the Union Army. Attempts to restore order to the furnishings failed to cover the damage and blatant contempt heaped on the locals by the overzealous advance units.

Miss Gay had asked about his injury and offered cool cloths for his comfort, but otherwise she and her household kept to another room. His fellow officers treated her with gracious deference, which he found curious until Major Campbell described his first meeting with the woman.

"We arrived sometime after the advance units, who utterly vandalized the property. When I asked Miss Gay about her staunch loyalty to the Confederacy, she boldly confessed the truth of her commitment to the rebellion. She then proceeded to enumerate all the sins of the North and the patience of the South in waiting for concessions promised but never realized. I admire such a woman as that. You probably will also note her care for all who come to her. She seems to turn away no one in need, regardless of color or allegiance."

The description of Mary Gay, Noah decided, could be applied to other women he'd met recently. His mind replayed the scene at the Herring farm two days earlier, when Sammy had killed the rattler.

Nancy had blanched when her gaze moved from Sammy to Noah, with her secret out. The boy, however, merely showed her his trophy, bluntly stating that he'd saved Noah's life by hindering his trip to the outhouse.

Nancy glanced from one to the other with uncertainty. She addressed Sammy. "Why don't you put the meat in the pot on the stove, then go take off the parts we can't eat? I don't want that snake head and rattles left in my yard."

When the boy obeyed without comment, she turned to Noah. "I guess you and me should have a sit-down talk inside."

"Yes ma'am." Noah gestured her to precede him in the house.

As soon as Sammy left the kitchen, Nancy collapsed onto a chair at the table. Her shoulders drooped in defeat. "So, you know about Sammy."

Noah pulled out the other chair and sat. "I heard you talking to someone yesterday while I was still laid up. You said he needed to stay away from the house while I was here. I assume that was Sammy?"

Nancy nodded and pinched her lips together. "Thank the good Lord he wasn't here when your men brought you in. He'd gone huntin' and noticed the horses in the yard from his cover in the woods. He knew better than to come home until they left. He even waited 'til dark."

"His trousers seem to be Confederate issue."

"They are. He ran off last year with a neighbor's boy to join up." She lifted her worried gaze to him. "The thing is, Sammy ain't quite right. At times he acts like any normal eighteen-year-old, but he'll change quick as lightnin' and act like he's six again. Most times he's easy-goin' and happy, but he has moments of strong anger."

Noah figured Sammy's mercurial moods had caused trouble with his fellow soldiers and superiors. "Your army sent him home when they couldn't control him?"

Nancy shook her head. "I don't rightly know. He says he's on furlough, but it's been months now, and nobody's come lookin' for him. I imagine they're not eager to get him back, and I aim to keep him here where I can watch after him."

Noah spent a few minutes in thought before he spoke. "I saw my horse in the barn. Are my saddle and tack here, or did my men take them?"

"In the barn."

"But I didn't see it, and I did a thorough search."

For the first time since he'd met her, Nancy smiled. "Did you look up to the loft? We strung it all up like a hog for safe keepin'. Didn't want anybody runnin' off with it."

Noah returned her smile. "Very clever. What about my weapons and camp gear?"

"Oh, they took them things. It wouldn't do to leave weapons in a Rebel house, you know."

"As I thought." He spread his hands on the table. "You must tell Sammy to make himself scarce when my men come to get me. No matter where he is, he's to get where they can't see him. If you'll help me get the horse's tack down today, I can be ready to ride out and meet them before they get too close. That way they'll be less likely to run into Sammy."

Nancy placed her hand over his. "Thank you, Captain Griffin. I figured there had to be a few good men in that Federal Army somewhere. You're proof."

Now, sitting in Mary Gay's house in Decatur, Noah realized that good men and women lived in all places. They didn't always agree on matters, especially when matters of judgment collided with political dictates. No clear lines truly separated them.

Different life experiences yielded different viewpoints and expectations. Just as different soils supported a variety of plants —tobacco and groundnuts here, corn and wheat there. The question was whether people could survive transplanting better than the crops they raised.

With those thoughts in mind, Noah gave in to his body's need for sleep and dreamed of the homeplace, fields ripe for harvest, his family welcoming him home with hugs and kisses, even the grandparents who had passed years before.

It didn't strike him as strange to see them because dreams made everything possible. Even the end of war.

∾

LOUISVILLE, KENTUCKY
MONDAY, JULY 25, 1864

*R*ose stood at the window as dawn chased the darkness away. Raising her eyes above the line of buildings, she could see the changing colors in the sky. The display reminded her of a kaleidoscope she had seen as a child. The smallest twist of the tube brought new patterns and colors. Her mind shifted just as easily, remembering the stained-glass windows in a church, and then her final days in Roswell. The day after her run-in with Pierce and the rescue by Captain Griffin, she'd stood at the window in the cottage there, much as she did now, watching the sunrise.

Where was Noah now? Did he hold her in contempt? Would he ever understand why they had acted as they had? Surely, he must have come to understand her reasoning, else why would he have given Isaac the paper?

Mulling over the evidence, she discerned three truths about that missive. First, he committed the information to paper, proving he'd considered what the future might hold for their little band. Second, he'd made the trip to the depot, taking time from his duties and obviously expecting to see one of them there. Third, he'd instructed Isaac to give the paper to her. Was it only because he knew she could read the message, or could it mean more?

He cared for their wellbeing, or at least that of someone in the group. He had grown fond of the children and took an interest in their education. Yet he'd shown concern for her and Celeste before he met any of the others. Did she deceive herself in thinking he paid particular interest to her? Had she grown so pathetic as to imagine an attraction where none existed?

Noises behind her told her the others had awakened. She turned away from the window in time to see Dorcas slip out the door, heading to the water closet, she presumed.

Sympathy set Rose to praying for the girl. Dorcas confided she'd used the last of the rice powder yesterday and dreaded how people would treat her when they saw her true skin tone.

"We will stand with you, dear," Edith had assured her. "At least you won't be sent back to any owners. God has seen you this far. He won't let you down now."

Similar comments met Rose's warning about the guard named Pierce. She'd chosen their Sunday church meeting, including the men and boys, to make the revelation, asking the others to pray for her to have wisdom in dealing with the man.

"I thought it best to inform all of you in case he expands his scheme to include you. He won't hesitate to spread his lies about anyone, just as he has about Celeste and me."

As they left the gathering, Rose asked Celeste's opinion about everyone's reaction to her account. "I thought Emily looked nervous and disturbed, didn't you?"

Celeste frowned. "As soon as you mentioned having a concern about one of the guards, Ada scooted closer to Emily and started patting her knee, as if to calm her down."

Leading the way upstairs, Rose hesitated on the landing. "I saw Dorcas and Shiloh exchange worried glances. That's to be expected, I guess, since they're both so young. And I wouldn't be surprised to learn Dorcas has suffered already at the hands of such men."

"I'm glad Mr. Isaac and Mr. J.D. heard about it as well," Celeste said. "Just knowing they'll support us makes me feel better."

Rose sighed heavily. "Too bad Phoebe wasn't there. I worry about that girl."

"I confess I was surprised when Janie said Phoebe had volunteered to sit with Clara to let Janie attend the gathering. Maybe she's finally beginning to think of others."

"I pray that's true. Janie could use her help with the younger ones, especially now."

To Rose's dismay, as days passed Phoebe's behavior showed no signs of improving. The girl often interacted with the guards more than wisdom allowed, and she delighted in flaunting her misbehavior. Rose prayed for her own restraint as well as for Phoebe to see how her rebellion hurt her family and invited danger.

She comforted herself knowing that matters often got worse before they improved. Such seemed to be the case with her friend's daughter.

~

DECATUR, GEORGIA
MONDAY, JULY 25, 1864

General McPherson had been defeated. Reports varied, with both armies claiming victory, though each incurred heavy losses. General McPherson's death dealt a severe blow to the Union.

Noah remembered the old saying about the darkest part of the night being just before dawn. He prayed it was true because any Confederate victory meant the war would continue to rage. There was no way President Lincoln and the United States government would give up and allow the Southern states to establish a new country.

Generals Garrard and Stoneman adjusted their plans to continue the raids to the south of Decatur. Even with the commotion of loading the wagons and saddling horses, Noah found himself in line to express his gratitude to his hostess. He swept his kepi off and bowed when his turn came.

"Miss Gay, I'm learning that you women are the world's peacemakers. I pray the time is not far off when this country learns to listen to your wisdom."

She clasped his hand, smiling slightly. "I shall join you in that prayer, Captain. May God protect you."

"Thank you, ma'am, and you as well."

He quickened his step to take Hercules's reins from Sergeant Fowler. The animals sensed the men's energy and pranced, ready to be off after a few days' rest. He and Fowler fell into line with the mounted men. The familiar rhythm of Hercules's gait and the rumble of the moving cavalry provided an odd atmosphere for contemplation.

At last Noah put words to his thoughts. "What do you think the world would be like, Sergeant, if women had the same rights as men?"

Shock registered on the older man's face. "How's that, Cap? You think women ought to be the same as men?"

"I mean, what if they could vote and hold property, as the suffragists advocate? Surely, you've heard of them. They've been spreading those ideas for several years."

The sergeant rubbed his nose and scratched his beard. "Well, I'll deny it if you tell anyone, but here's what I think. They couldn't do much worse in this world than what we men have. And they'd be much easier on the eyes." He winked as he spurred his mount ahead.

Noah laughed out loud, feeling better than he had in days.

CHAPTER 23

"*H*ow are you feeling today, Clara?"

Rose approached the little girl's bed in the room set up as an infirmary within the refugee house. They weren't sure what had brought on the illness that seemed to target the younger ones. After finding Janie worn down from caring for her ailing youngsters, she and Celeste had volunteered to relieve her as much as they could. Celeste went to visit Tommy on the side designated for boys. Each sister brought paper and pencils in hopes of entertaining the children.

Clara's thin frame testified to the lack of proper nutrition, but her eyes lit up as she noticed the items in Rose's hand. "I'm better today, thank you, Miss Rose. Are you going to read to me?"

"I'm going to do better than that. You and I are going to write a story. Then we'll practice letting you read it so you can share it with the other children after you move back to your room."

"Really?" Clara pushed herself up against the pillows. "That will be so fun."

"Now we do have one rule." Rose smoothed the girl's hair away from her face, discreetly checking for fever. "If you start feeling tired and need to rest, we'll stop, even if the story isn't finished. We can always finish it later, all right?"

The girl nodded her eager agreement, and they started discussing who would be the people in their story. Rose let Clara dictate the action, recording the story in words she was sure the girl could recognize with little prompting. Clara's mighty yawn told Rose she should encourage an end to the story.

After folding the paper twice, she slipped it under the girl's pillow. "Now you can dream about your story, and we can add more later if you want to."

Clara blinked sleepily. Before Rose could move, the girl caught her hand. "Thank you, Miss Rose. You're the bestest teacher in the world."

Seeing Celeste peek around the curtained area, Rose put her finger to her lips and shushed Clara playfully. "Shh. Don't let Miss Celeste hear you say that."

Clara giggled and waved at Celeste. "You're both the bestest. I can't wait to get back to your class."

Celeste patted the covered legs at the end of the bed. "And we're ready for you to get well. You get lots of sleep now. We'll see you again after supper."

Rose waited until they'd entered the hallway before voicing her question. "Are we having supper? I thought they said we had the last of the food at breakfast."

"One of the churches learned about our predicament and brought a pounding. There's flour, butter, eggs, and a large crock of milk."

"Thank the Lord, but I hope they feed the sick and elderly first, at least the ones who are able to eat." Rose tapped her fingers on her chin. "We need medicine for the sick. I wonder if we could be permitted to hunt around town for work. Then we could purchase some. Without a doctor coming around, we'll have to care for our own."

Celeste frowned. "And refugees are still coming in, from other towns as well as the last of the mill workers. With our numbers increasing, I think the officers would be glad for us to find work, especially if it enables us to move out of here."

Arriving at their room, Rose agreed. "We can ask. I wonder if others in our group will want to join us."

Emily stepped away from the bed where Sarah Grace napped as Ada and Edith arrived from checking on their boys and men. The five women circled to give their reports.

Edith gripped her waist and stretched her back. "The boys seem to be fine so far, and the men are holding their own, though not quite as energetic as usual. I don't think they're sleeping well."

"Probably from hearing others being sick," Ada said. "I thought most adults might've had measles as children. It seemed to strike every few years when mine were little."

"But not all of them have spots," Celeste said, "and influenza can be just as deadly."

Olivia joined them. "Especially since there's no medicine available and they can't keep anything down."

Rose glanced toward the bed where Sarah Grace slept. "How's she doing?"

Emily couldn't keep the concern from her voice. "Just a slight fever and stomachache so far. She and John Mark both had the measles 'bout three years ago, so that's one worry gone."

Rose chewed her bottom lip before broaching her idea. "Celeste and I plan to ask for permission to look for work in town. We need some way to get medicine for the sick. We still have the winter to think about, unless this war winds down quickly. And if the town authorities keep dragging their feet about getting the gas and water lines working here, things could get worse in a hurry."

At their alarmed expressions, she tempered her words. "I don't mean to borrow trouble, but it behooves us to be prepared for whatever happens."

Edith gave a decisive nod. "You're right, Rose. I'm sure my family will want to cooperate with that. We'll figure out who's to stay with the children and who's to find work."

"We can do the same," Ada said.

"With Celeste and me, that should make at least four of us, and we also have Dorcas and Shiloh to help out, so maybe half a dozen to hire out. Let's pray our efforts meet with quick success."

Emily's expression mirrored her concerns about finding employment. "I don't know how many here would be willing to hire Southerners. I heard some of the folks from hereabouts saying they wish we'd go back to where we come from."

"That might be a problem," Rose said. "But we have to try."

~

Louisville, Kentucky
Saturday, July 30, 1864

*T*he smell of burning food assaulted Rose's nose and teased her empty stomach as she and Celeste climbed the steps leading to the stately brick house. She was exhausted—more mentally than physically—from two days of searching for work.

Edith and Olivia had secured positions at the hospital, thanks to their experience and association with Dr. Spencer back in Georgia. A local undertaker hired Isaac and J.D. to help build coffins and transport bodies of the deceased.

Shiloh and Dorcas had volunteered to stay with the children, and Shiloh helped them with their schoolwork. Ada, Emily, and Millie worked together doing laundry and mending for a few customers, mostly soldiers stationed nearby, which allowed them to stay at the home and take over the kitchen duties for those working in town. That morning Lydia had found work as a baker's assistant. That was only two days a week, but at least it was something.

How ironic that everyone had secured employment except her and Celeste, who'd proposed the idea. Rose had counted heavily on at least one of them finding a position as a teacher or a clerk, but she came face-to-face with stubborn discrimination. Being female set them up for disappointment as soon as they walked through the door. Adamant refusal met them as soon as they opened their mouths and revealed their Southern roots.

Frustration and fatigue urged them to halt their search for the day, but honor and dogged determination drove them to apply at the houses in town, inquiring among the more prosperous citizens. Pausing to adjust the waistband of a skirt that persisted in sliding, Rose scrutinized her sister's appearance. "Straighten your bonnet. Ready?"

At Celeste's nod, Rose rapped on the door, which promptly swung open as if someone expected visitors. The smell of burning food rushed at them, making her eyes smart. Blinking rapidly, Rose took a step back to gaze up at the giant standing at the threshold. His stone-faced appearance did not give her much hope.

"Yes?" He drew out the word in an astounding bass voice.

Stiffening her spine, she looked him in the eye. "Good afternoon. I am Miss Rose Carrigan, and this is my sister, Miss Celeste Carrigan. We're inquiring as to the possibility of employment."

The man lifted his eyebrows, but it worked wonders on his expression. "Can either of you cook?"

An hour later, she and Celeste had washed the last pot

from their "job interview" and followed their guide to stand before the elderly lady to whom it was served. The meal they'd put together was simple because of the limited time, but they'd marveled at the supplies available to them. Being able to satisfy their own hunger as they worked proved an added benefit.

The lady of the house, Mrs. Coker, laid down her fork and dabbed at thin lips. Papery skin covered the delicate bones of her face and hands. Though age sat heavily on her shoulders, she resisted it with a straight carriage and careful manners. Mrs. Coker must have been lovely in her prime.

The older woman cleared her throat and issued her proclamation. "Acceptable. I require three meals a day, beginning at eight in the morning. Come again tomorrow and we'll discuss the particulars after breakfast."

Rose and Celeste shared a look of relief. But the difficult part lay ahead.

"We're truly thankful for the opportunity, Mrs. Coker," Rose said, "and trust that we can come to an agreeable arrangement. However, I feel we should tell you about our current circumstances."

The lady raised her eyebrows but didn't speak.

Plowing past her reservations, Rose continued. "We're staying in the refugee house down on Tenth Street. We were brought here several days ago from Georgia."

The woman's mouth fell open. "You're prisoners? Murdering Rebels here in my house?" Her voice rose as she gripped the collar at her throat. Rising from her chair, she called for her servant. "Herbert! Herbert, come here at once!"

Alarmed, Rose and Celeste scurried toward the door. Their way was blocked by the giant who'd ushered them inside earlier.

Mrs. Coker demanded to know how he could betray her so.

Herbert pled his innocence.

"These...these creatures are Rebel prisoners! How did they

escape and come to my house? I will be murdered and robbed blind."

"No, ma'am." Celeste took a step forward and answered in her quiet voice. "We weren't arrested for any wrongdoing. We're only mill workers who lost our positions when the Federals burned down our mill. The Union Army brought us here against our will, but we've never harmed anyone."

The woman stopped her ranting, at least, and Rose rushed to add more convincing facts. "Our father was a pastor who moved to Georgia when we were girls. He passed on last year, and we took positions in the mill to provide for ourselves. Then the Union Army brought us here."

Celeste stretched out a hand in supplication, stopping short of touching the woman. "Mrs. Coker, would we have told you about our circumstances if we intended to do you harm?"

Seeing the woman waver, Rose pressed on. "We're hunting for work to help buy medicine for some of the children in the home who've fallen sick."

Mrs. Coker listened to their words. Accepting the glass of water Herbert presented, she sipped while her eyes darted from one to the other as if to detect any subterfuge. At last, she lowered the glass to the table and folded her fingers, directing her comments to the manservant. "Herbert, you will accompany these ladies to the refuge home and confirm their story with the people in charge. If you find what they've said to be true, I will consider hiring *one* until Hattie recovers."

She shifted her attention to Rose and Celeste. "You understand this is a temporary position to fill in for my sick servant. When she's better, I'll decide whether to retain you."

Mumbling words of agreement and thanks, Rose and Celeste gathered their bonnets. Herbert fetched his own hat and escorted them out the door. Not a word was spoken until they reached the house on Tenth Street. Rose prayed Lieutenant

Goodwin would be in the office alone when they arrived. He was the most reasonable of the guards.

Celeste tugged on Rose's hand and whispered that she needed to go straight to their room, so Rose accompanied Herbert to the office.

Unfortunately, it was Sergeant Pierce at the door. He leaned against the doorjamb, listening to Lieutenant Goodwin, who sat inside the small room. Not the person she wanted to see. Pierce moved aside at their approach, eyeing Herbert with unease.

Ignoring him, Rose spoke to Goodwin. "This gentleman would like to speak with you, Lieutenant." She didn't explain Herbert's errand, hoping Pierce would assume she merely escorted the visitor to the office as a courtesy. When Pierce walked away, seemingly disinterested, she released a breath of relief.

Herbert verified the circumstances leading up to the Carrigan sisters' presence in Louisville and explained the offer of employment. Satisfied, Herbert turned to Rose. "I shall be here to collect you and your sister in the morning at six-thirty, Miss Carrigan."

"But Mrs. Coker said she would hire only one of us."

"Just so, but I know a place where the second sister might find a position."

His demeanor never changed, but somehow Herbert seemed to have taken a liking to the Carrigan sisters. She decided he'd be scandalized if she kissed his cheek, so she merely offered her hand. "Thank you, Mr. Herbert. You are a truer gentleman than I've met in a long time."

Rose walked him to the building's front door and started up the stairs. Her bubble of joy burst as she spotted Pierce on the landing. He reached across the space to block her path.

Rose stared at him with a show of calm expectance, refusing to ask him to move out of her way.

"I hear you've been looking for work." His gaze raked her from head to toe.

Though her fingers fisted in her skirt, she wouldn't allow him the satisfaction of witnessing her fear.

He inched closer to her and whispered his coarse suggestion. "I fail to see why you'd hunt out there when you could easily find pleasurable work here, with me."

Tempering her response, she leveled him with a look of disdain. Neither fear nor rebuke would accomplish anything. "You mistake your appeal, Sergeant. I find no pleasure in your presence. Please remove your arm." She could have kicked herself for including "please" in the last sentence. All those good manners her parents had insisted on certainly did not aid a forceful presentation.

From Pierce's reaction, however, the first part of her speech hit the mark. His eyes narrowed. "On second thought, I doubt a cold fish like you would know how to enjoy certain carnal activities. Lucky for me, there are others here who do. Sweet young things who are anxious to please."

Icy fingers spread through Rose. She remembered seeing Pierce and Phoebe together as they left the dining area the night before. Would he abuse the girl to punish Rose?

He moved away but issued a parting threat. "And I will have my revenge yet, Miss Carrigan. You can count on it."

CHAPTER 24

*R*ose marched toward the refugee house. The six blocks between the Louisville Library and the refugee home had become her time for prayer and reflection. The walk also gave her a chance to view the town from different perspectives. Today, however, she detoured several blocks to drop off a book at the courthouse for her supervisor at the library, Miss Pringle. Leaving early also meant she wouldn't be there when Vernon Fordham, one of the library patrons, made his weekly visit. A blessed relief.

Careful to project an impression of knowing her surroundings, she noted the buildings on her route and the businesses housed within them. She enjoyed the sounds of ships on the Ohio River, though she'd never ventured this far before. Miss Pringle's warning not to go farther than Jefferson Street reinforced her natural caution. She knew better than to wander there alone.

Making her way to the refuge house, she reflected on the

difference between working at the library and her former employment in the cotton mill. The day passed much faster when one enjoyed the environment, not to mention the shorter hours left more time for other activities.

The work gave her satisfaction and a sense of accomplishment, almost as much as knowing the coins in her pocket would help to relieve the war-time family around her. Thanks to Mrs. Coker and Herbert, Rose and Celeste spent their days at tasks they truly enjoyed. They'd known, without much discussion, the position with Mrs. Coker better suited Celeste, who enjoyed cooking and other domestic duties more than Rose. It had the added advantage of removing Celeste from Pierce's reach. Even in the face of the elderly lady's persnickety nature, Celeste maintained her serene temperament. The second position Herbert told them of matched Rose's drive and curiosity.

If Herbert had known her from birth, he couldn't have found a better position for her. Though the pay could have been better, being surrounded with all manner of written material came close to her idea of perfection. Whenever she had a break in her duties of shelving and cataloging items, she searched for books to read to the children, reviewed the magazines to see which outlandish fashions captured the attention of those with money, and anxiously devoured the newspapers for word on the war. She scanned the list of the Federal dead and wounded, holding her breath lest a familiar name should appear. Though it was a painful task, she would give much for a Southern paper to find news that might cheer her friends.

She noted dozens of men coming from the train station as she neared the corner of Tenth and Magazine. With her attention distracted, she must have strayed too close to the street.

A Federal soldier grabbed her arm and pulled her back. "Whoa, sweetheart! I think you'd better hold onto me as you cross this street. We wouldn't want to see you laid out on the ground, but I'd be glad to lay you out on my bed."

A few of the men snickered. She glared in their direction and jerked her arm from his hold.

"The only one laid out will be you." She glanced at the two chevrons on his uniform coat and added, "Corporal. When I complain about your treatment to the officers at the house over there."

The comment produced the desired effect. Complete bafflement. Bullies like this one expected desperate pleas or hysterics, so her best defense was to surprise them with a combative reply. Her caustic tone sometimes went too far.

"Ah, Slocomb, she ain't no doxy you can buy with your coin," one of the men jibed.

"Nor your good looks," another said, bringing on a smattering of laughter.

Many of these men were unarmed and poorly dressed. No smiles or taunts came from them. *Confederate prisoners!* The realization rocked her and sent her gaze scanning the faces.

"Miss Carrigan?" The call came from deep in the throng of bodies swarming around her.

Jolted to hear her name, Rose dared to step closer to the crowd.

"Miss Carrigan! It's me, Pete Wilson." The voice grew stronger. Could Janie's son really be here?

She searched the faces, looking for the speaker. Pete's height topped hers by only a few inches, making it hard for her to spot him among the taller prisoners. "Pete?"

A skinny man pressed forward to face her. Overlong hair covered his ears, meeting his reddish beard. As Rose scanned his face, Pete's smile transformed the scraggly person into the boy she remembered. "Yes'm. It's me along with a couple more from the Roswell Brigade—"

The soldier who'd grabbed her earlier interrupted. "Hey, you sorry Rebs, get out of the road. You're holding up traffic." He scowled at Rose.

The prisoners obeyed, surging to the sidewalk and carrying Rose with them. She quickened her steps to keep up. "Pete, your mother and sisters are at the refugee house, right across the street there."

"Oh, thank the good Lord! They're all right? What about Tommy?"

"Yes, yes, Tommy's there too. Look, I'll see if I can get Lieutenant Goodwin to arrange for you to see them."

A burly man crowded between her and Pete as they pressed onward. "What about my wife and girls, Miss? Wife is Charlotte Stewart. Do you know her?"

"Oh, yes, they're here as well. I'll include them in the request for a meeting." She pretended not to see tears spring into the man's eyes and yet felt a corresponding moisture in her own. "Oh, I know they'll all be so glad to see you!"

The men reached the prison gate and moved inside, and Rose stood still, amazed at this unlikely meeting. Surely God had orchestrated this!

She hurried across Broadway. Most prisoners remained at the Louisville Union Army Prison only a short time before they were transferred farther north. Obtaining permission for the families to meet could take a few days. There was no time to waste. Witnessing the happy gathering would boost everyone's spirits.

～

LOUISVILLE, KENTUCKY
SUNDAY, AUGUST 14, 1864

*M*uted sounds of joyful reunion spread from the families to the onlookers in the yard at the refugee house. Sympathy swelled Rose's heart. The fervent hugs and kisses pressed between parents and children resurrected painful memories. And heavy in the air was the knowledge that this meeting was temporary. Would the ache of separation be lessened or made worse by this?

At least they found comfort in knowing their loved ones' situations. Rose observed the genuine pleasure of Olivia and her family as Janie Wilson introduced them to Pete beside the polite restraint of the Andersons as Walter Stewart approached. Yet, something beyond a courteous greeting passed between them.

Emily's hands flew to her face, and she collapsed into Ada's arms.

J.D. fell to his knees, pulling John Mark and Sarah Grace to his side.

Within moments, the others gathered around the distraught family to offer their assistance. Alarmed, Rose joined the crowd but hesitated to press nearer.

When Olivia and Edith urged Emily and Ada toward the house, trailed by J.D. and the children, Rose searched the remaining faces.

Walter Stewart explained. "Martin Anderson was killed. We heard the day we was captured at Jonesboro." He wagged his head in sorrow. "We was so close to home."

So close to home. Did Emily's husband even get the letter they'd written? Had Sergeant Morgan been able to deliver it when he returned to Virginia?

Isaac Wynn grasped Rose's hand and gestured to others to do the same. "Let's pray for the Anderson family. They'll need the comfort of friends to handle this heartbreak. We'll also ask God's protection for Pete and Walter as they continue on their journey."

When the prayer ended, Rose drifted toward the house, her shoulders sagging as she mourned on Emily's behalf. A light tap on her arm brought her head up. Expecting to see Celeste, she found Phoebe instead.

"I just wanted to thank you for gettin' us some time with

Pete." An air of humility transformed Phoebe's tear-streaked features into beauty. "It means a lot to Mama and the young'uns. And I…uh…I'm sorry for the spiteful way I treated you and Miss Celeste."

Rose folded the girl in her arms, tears springing to her eyes. "All is well. I'm glad y'all got to see him. We're thankful for that."

∼

WALNUT CREEK BETWEEN JONESBORO AND MCDONOUGH, GEORGIA
SATURDAY, AUGUST 20, 1864

*N*oah lifted his head, wishing his vision could go beyond the clouds. "Lord, forgive my presumption that I know what's best. You showed us that only Your love can change men's hearts, not force. I submit to Your wisdom and mercy, asking only for an end to this awful conflict and the wisdom to know what I should do when it's over." His mind darted to thoughts of Rose, but he put them away. He couldn't afford the distraction.

A game of chase with the Confederates around Jonesboro and Lovejoy Station brought the Seventh Pennsylvania and Fourth Michigan to a perilous place, hemmed in on all sides, surrounded by the enemy. General Minty announced a daring move—a saber charge through the adversary's camp, setting himself in the lead. The men responded by spurring their mounts, cheering, and brandishing their sabers like madmen. Noah wondered whether their reactions resulted from fear and visions of the horrors of prison or from an attempt to intimidate the Rebels, who often attacked with their famous Rebel Yell.

By some miracle, the Union forces prevailed. Then they'd pressed on to Walnut Creek to get a better vantage point. Now they waited behind the hastily raised breastworks, their horses strung along Jonesboro Road to their rear.

No sooner had Noah whispered his prayer than he spotted the enemy in full array. Artillery burst from both camps. Noah's eyes and throat burned from the smoke. Pine needles rained down and lay strewn across the trenches. Red dust kicked up in his face, blurring his vision. Sometimes, the red haze took on a more sinister aspect as the deadly missiles found their marks in human flesh. He barely registered the accompanying cries amid the wail and staccato barrage of assault.

How long the exchange went on, Noah couldn't say. His focus had narrowed to the area directly in front of him. At last, the enemy fell back, but they could surge again at any moment.

Captain Dixon rode up beside him, and Noah set his weapon aside to take a long draft from his canteen. "You delivered the prisoners to the Third already? Seems like you just left."

The other man plucked a pinecone from his horse's mane and started pulling it apart. "Funny thing about battle, ain't it? Time just disappears. It could be seconds or hours."

Noah stretched his limbs as far as he could and rotated his neck. "And now that it's over, for the time being, I'm feeling the effects of not sleeping for two days." Yet he knew sleep wouldn't be possible until they put more space between themselves and the Rebs. He worked to keep his mind alert. "What was that explosion I heard awhile back? Did you hear it?"

Dixon tossed aside the mutilated pinecone. "One of our cannon canisters burst. Another one had to be moved because a shell got stuck inside it."

The two talked, waiting for word to come either to move out or defend their position. Soon enough they were firing again, repulsing two more assaults before orders signaled a change in location. At the same moment, the heavens opened and rain poured down as if spurring them on their retreat.

After they sloshed their way through the town of McDonough, they hurriedly set up camp near a river. Noah wrapped himself in his sodden blanket and fell across his bedroll. Nothing short of a rifle to his head would keep him awake. Sleep pulled the curtain of darkness across his mind and blocked out the discomforts of his body. He would address those effects later.

∽

SUNDAY, AUGUST 21, 1864
LOUISVILLE, KENTUCKY

*R*ose woke up shivering. Rain pounded the roof, and clouds held back the dawn. Based on the moaning wind, it was quite a storm. She'd heard local citizens talking about the tornado that hit the town in August of 1854, causing the Third Presbyterian Church to collapse during Sunday services. Intrigued, Rose had found an old copy of *The Daily Courier* and read the news account of the event. That was not a smart decision for a person who didn't fare well in storms.

She couldn't lay all the blame for her shivers on the rain, although the sound of it probably had prompted her dreams. Strange it was, how her old nightmare continually transformed itself since the mill's destruction. Water always figured prominently, usually in the form of a river or lake, but lately her concern in the dream had turned from escaping something to searching for something or someone. This time that person had stared her full in the face.

Noah.

She chuckled grimly at the irony. Since his name was Noah, he should be her means of escape, shouldn't he? A place of refuge and safety. Yet he fought the water in her dream, and he searched for something too. She let her mind wander that path a few moments before firmly pulling it back. No future lay that way. She regretted they'd parted as they had, broken trust and hurt feelings on both sides.

She turned her thoughts to prayer, as Da always said when someone weighed on her mind, it was a call to pray for the individual. She asked God to protect Noah. The scripture in Isaiah came to mind. "When thou passeth through the waters...and through the rivers, they shall not overflow thee."

She supposed waters and rivers represented trouble. When she applied such a meaning to her dream, it made sense. Comfort from the words in Isaiah soaked into her being. Whatever trials lay ahead, she would draw strength from those words.

Already she could hear traffic on the street and figured the rain must have moved away. Chores awaited.

Even on Sunday, even for prisoners and refugees of war, responsibilities beckoned.

CHAPTER 25

*R*ose glanced up at the sound of voices at the front desk of the library, then quickly looked away.

Vernon Fordham let the heavy oak door thud behind him, guaranteeing the attention of every person in the building. With a flourish, he slapped his load of newspapers on the desk in front of Miss Pringle. "Good morning, ladies. Good news in the papers today."

He paused for the best theatrical effect. When he didn't elaborate right away, Miss Pringle picked up her cue. "What good news is that, Mr. Fordham?"

Rose paused in her task of pasting cardholders in the back of new books. If she tried to ignore him now, Vernon would seek her out to make sure she heard his news. He took delight in provoking her. She turned his way with a questioning expression.

He patted the stack of papers on the desk. "The city of Atlanta is now in Union hands, what's left of it."

Rose caught her breath but held back her cry. In truth, it should be no surprise. Under siege by Sherman's army for weeks, the city had held out longer than she'd expected. Though she'd heard scores of people had fled to Atlanta as the army displaced them from other towns and farms, she had no connections there.

Wouldn't Vernon be surprised to learn Union soldiers figured among the few people she knew who might be in the area?

She found a few moments after lunch to view the papers Vernon had collected from the train station. *The New York Times* dated September fifth announced that "The Fall of Atlanta" had taken place on September second, secured by the Department of the Cumberland cavalry. She pushed it aside to read the September sixth edition of *The Daily Pittsburgh Gazette* and an article titled "The Capture of Atlanta." Rose scanned it, finding mention of Generals Garrard, Minty, and Whipple as well as Sherman and Slocum. Several smaller towns had been the site of various skirmishes. Railroads changed possession, people deserted their homes, hospitals overflowed, and prisoners included civilians as well as soldiers.

In her mind she saw the mills burning again, the looting of houses and trampling of grounds in Roswell. Was it only two months before?

She shook her head to erase the vision. Two months, four hundred miles, and one strange experience after another. Her life had twisted beyond recognition. The war had upset her world and challenged her beliefs.

"So, I doubt if you'll be going back to Georgia anytime soon, hmm?" Vernon reached across her to pick up a newspaper. The action brought him much too close, trapping Rose between the desk and the wall. She stiffened and let the papers slide from her fingers. She answered without facing him.

"I doubt anyone with intelligence would venture to travel

anywhere near the conflict. Excuse me, please. I must get back to work."

Adopting a great show of chivalry, Vernon moved aside but grasped her elbow in the process. "Of course, Miss Carrigan, I wouldn't wish to jeopardize your position."

She allowed him to escort her to the worktable. To pull away would only bring attention to them, which would delight Vernon and embarrass her. As soon as he released her arm, she moved into the chair without waiting for his assistance.

Undeterred, Vernon leaned over the table, palms placed near the pile of books. "You should consider the advantages of staying in Louisville. I'm certain I can provide you with ample reason, not the least of which is financial security." He straightened and touched her shoulder with his fingertips. "Think on it."

Though Vernon took every opportunity to press his suit, and Rose rebelled against the pressure, he did not repel her as Pierce did with his threats and innuendoes. Perhaps she should consider Vernon an eligible suitor. After all, she'd turn twenty-two in December. She had no prospects of permanence anywhere else, and marriage would provide a measure of protection.

Her thoughts wandered as her hands performed the routine duties. Protection and security had flown out the window with the war, considering how many married women lived in the refuge home, separated from their mates. Even before their husbands had left to join the ranks, those women worked daily jobs also, at least so long as their health allowed them to work. What had happened to the biblical model of marriage, the kind her parents had modeled?

Rose glanced at Vernon. Why hadn't he joined the Union cause? He claimed a bum leg, but his limp was hardly noticeable. How odd that someone who loudly proclaimed to espouse the righteous cause would be content to miss the action.

An odd memory surfaced from years ago. A neighbor's prized rooster screeched at all hours as he strutted the perimeter of his yard and proclaimed his superiority. One day a stray cat stalked right up to the wire fence to investigate the noise. With a flurry of feathers, the rooster sought safety on top of the coop and left his charges to their fate.

She smiled at the comparison, her image of Vernon forever tainted.

Turning her thoughts back to the news of Atlanta, Rose offered prayers for everyone in the heart of the conflict. Here in Louisville, surrounded by several Union camps, the refugees lived on a protected island. Safe from the ravages of war, they battled unseen enemies: illness, hunger, depression, and despair.

Above all loomed the haunting questions. How did their loved ones fare? Would she and her sister ever return to Georgia? When would this war end, and what would they do when it did?

∾

*R*ose entered the refugee home with caution and peered down the hall, anxious to avoid any contact with Pierce. She grimaced when the door snapped shut and echoed in the silence of the entry.

From the nearby office, the squeak of a chair alerted her to movement in that direction. She scampered toward the stairs but paused when Lieutenant Goodwin called her name.

"Miss Carrigan? I thought it might be you. Would you step over here please?"

Tamping down her apprehension, Rose complied and stopped in the office doorway.

Lieutenant Goodwin picked up a letter from his desk and extended it. A thin smile accompanied his raised eyebrows and obvious curiosity. "This was delivered today. Since it's addressed to you, I assume you can read it for yourself? If not, I'll be glad to read it to you."

Rose stretched a trembling hand toward the letter. Who would be writing to her? She flipped the envelope over for identification. She found only her name and the dubious direction "Roswell Mill deportees, care of General Webster, Nashville, Tennessee. Please forward."

She pondered the letter, eager to hurry away to open it.

Lieutenant Goodwin asked, "Do you need me to read it for you?"

"No, thank you. I appreciate your thoughtfulness, but I can read it myself." She rolled the paper until it fit into her pocket.

Rose forced a smile to her face. "I thank you for giving it to me personally." Without waiting for his reply, she bypassed the stairs and headed for the rear door. Whether it signified good or bad, she thought it best to read in private.

She hurried to a bench near the edge of the yard and removed the paper. Stains and folds marred the envelope, a testament to its to having passed through many hands.

Blowing out a breath, she pushed one finger under the seal and broke it open. She turned the sheet over to find the signature first. Her heartbeat quickened, but she forced herself to read each line from the beginning.

August 26, 1864
Roswell, Georgia

Dear Miss Carrigan,

I hope this missive finds you and your sister well, along with the other friends that accompanied you on your journey north.

You may find it odd that I write when I have no firm knowledge as to your current location, but I have been feeling a most urgent prompting to do so for several days. I am trusting our Almighty Father to see that it reaches you somehow, for I know that He watches over you as He does me. It is my earnest desire to seek your forgiveness for the way we parted and hope for a reconciliation at the earliest opportunity.

The occasion that brought me to this moment and gave me the courage to put pen to paper, which I firmly believe was part of a Divine Plan, was finding myself in the same location as when we first met. At this moment I am sitting at the table inside the cottage where you lived only a few weeks ago. When I learned we were headed this way, I determined to come and see how your little house had fared in your absence. It looks as you left it, I imagine, with the addition of a layer of dust. I hope you will not think ill of me when I say I walked through it, imagining I could see you and Miss Celeste seated at this same table or preparing a meal in the tiny kitchen.

Before I leave town, I will walk down to the cemetery and pay my respects to your father, as I know you would like to do.

A stray mark on the page indicated an abrupt movement had interrupted his writing. The message resumed.

August 28, 1864

We have now moved our camp farther South, from which we can send patrols as far as Marietta. My visit to the cemetery was brief, as we left immediately after securing the area.

I hope you will be inclined to read on, for I should like to tell you about some of my experiences since last I saw you.

My division left Marietta the same day as your train, except

*we traveled east to approach the railroad from that direction.
We made camp at the base of that huge protrusion of rock,
aptly named Stone Mountain. It is such a stark landmark,
surrounded on all sides by acres of trees. It made me think of
how I always pictured the giant in the children's story of Jack
and the Beanstalk, that is, a bald pate with a circle of dark hair
surrounding it.*

*From there we turned west again. Our task was to dismantle
the railroads leading from Atlanta to frustrate communication
and supply efforts among the Confederate forces. It seems we
had barely begun working when a freak accident struck—quite
literally. From what I was told, one of the rail ties flew through
the air, probably propelled by another projectile. On its way
back to earth, it struck my right elbow, flipped end over end,
and struck me the second time on the head, knocking me sense-
less for more than a day.*

*In the meantime, General Garrard received communication
from General Sherman to ride post-haste to Covington, which
was some distance to the Southeast from our current position.
Because I was in no condition to ride, my men took me to a
nearby farmhouse to be cared for until they returned. I hope to
have occasion in the future to share with you concerning my
experiences at that farm as it would be difficult to put into
words at this time. Suffice it to say, I was urged to reconsider
my attitude toward you at our last meeting. That is not to say I
had not struggled with my actions between those times, but
suddenly I found myself placed in a similar situation and
making a similar choice as you made last month. Perhaps I will
have opportunity to describe that time in greater detail in the
future.*

Many of the days that followed the accident remain somewhat

*muddled. They passed much the same, as far as routine goes—
riding from one location to another, trading fire with the
opposing armies, setting up camp, breaking down camp. Only
two incidents stand out clearly. One is meeting a grand lady by
the name of Mary Gay, whose house in Decatur was comman-
deered by our officers. She reminded me of you, not in looks but
in spirit. The other, not so pleasant, is crossing the Cotton
River north of McDonough. The bridge over the river was out,
and the river overflowed its banks so that we had to swim our
horses across. Without help from the Almighty, we all would
have perished.*

*My time here grows short, and I see that I have written a great
deal, so I will close. Perhaps I will have opportunity to write
again later. Until then I remain—*

Your friend and humble servant,

Maj. Noah Griffin

A later date. Rose glanced back to the beginning. August 26.
Two weeks before. Noah's visit to Roswell would have taken
him away from Atlanta, at least for a few days.

The feeling of wonder spread from her heart to her fingertips. Her face grew warm and tugged a smile as she read the
words again. He'd been promoted, yet he took time to write.

She whispered a prayer of thanksgiving and folded the letter.
She would share it with the others. Maybe it would somehow
allay the other news she had to share. The fall of Atlanta did not
bode well for those with family near the city.

CHAPTER 26

North Georgia near the Alabama state line
Monday, September 26, 1864

*N*oah squatted at the creek bed and stirred a stick in the red mud. The arrowhead resisted, held in place by the suction of saturated ground. He stood and thrust his boot heel at one end to force the other end out of the mud. With a great *slurp*, the object broke the earth's force enough for him to grasp it. In a few steps, he leaned over the rocks to wash away the mud to reveal his prize.

"Whatcha got there, Major?" A skinny corporal displayed his toothy grin as he sauntered over to Noah's side.

"Oh, just an old arrowhead that was buried in the mud here." Noah turned it over several times, noticing the smooth texture and faint markings. He had no idea of its value, but he slipped it into his pocket for safekeeping.

"I never took you for one to collect that sorta thing," the young man said.

Noah slanted a half-smile. "I have a young friend who does. He'll be well pleased to get it when next I see him."

Drying his hands on his neckerchief, Noah squinted toward the horizon where the sun spread its colors like an exotic bird. Though the heat lingered, the shrinking daylight hours signified summer's decline. "Must be getting close to dinner time. We'd best grab some food before those boys across the way start firing again."

After consuming the questionable mixture served up as beef stew, Noah picked his way through the aisles between tents, aiming to snatch a quick nap. Sergeant Fowler lounged at the entrance to his temporary quarters, a loyal guard dog to Noah's privacy. He stirred as Noah nudged him with the toe of his boot.

"I hate to disturb your beauty sleep, Fowler, but my legs will stretch only so far."

The sergeant guffawed. "There ain't no amount of sleep going to pretty up this old face, Major. That's why God gave us men beards, to hide the ugliness." He scrambled to his feet and plucked an item from his breast pocket. "This came in the day's mail while you was out scouting. I figured you'd want to see it right away."

He slapped the envelope into Noah's palm with a brief salute before ambling away. Puzzled by the man's behavior, Noah flipped the thin packet over to examine the writing. His breath caught at the name in the upper corner. *R. Carrigan.*

He stumbled into his tent and tore into the envelope but paused before withdrawing the paper. This was a good sign, wasn't it? That she sent a reply? Surely, she wouldn't write to rail at him.

He pulled his camp chair near the tent flap to catch the fading light and opened the single sheet.

Sunday, September 11, 1864
Louisville, Kentucky

Dear Major Griffin,

How surprised I was to receive your letter, and how opportune it was, coming on the same day I learned about the fall of Atlanta. I believe it was God's way of assuring me that you yet survived, despite so many falling on both sides of this terrible conflict. I am exceedingly grateful you are well.

You are not the only one who requires forgiveness for how matters were left in Marietta. How often I have replayed those events in my mind and discovered ways I might have acted differently. Unfortunately, the past cannot be undone, and the only way any of us can move forward is to seek and bestow forgiveness. That I do now and pray the same of you.

I appreciate your visit to my father's grave on behalf of Celeste and me. I have often wondered how matters stand in Roswell, whether anyone stayed behind, if anyone coming behind us was able to make use of things we left. I pray it may prosper again in the future.

Naturally, I shared much of your letter with our company here, as we all think highly of you and were glad to hear of your wellbeing. The children found your description of Stone Mountain entertaining and used it as the subject of their artwork. We were distressed to learn of your accident and pray for your continued recovery.

As for our own news, some of us have been blessed to find paying positions in the city. We sought work soon after arriving so we could buy medicines for the children who fell ill. Though we are well protected from the continuing battles, we are susceptible to the same illnesses that plague the armies. Oddly enough, the place where we are housed was designed to become a hospital, but it has yet to be supplied with the proposed gas and water facilities. I know not how we will fare if we must remain here into the fall and winter. Some of the refugees have journeyed into Indiana, and we have considered taking that risk if matters do not improve.

We are very thankful to have good shelter and work to provide our group a little beyond what is available to us here. We extend to you our good wishes and hope to see you again sometime in the future.

I am signing on behalf of all your Southern Friends in Louisville.

Rose Carrigan

Noah wiped the moisture from his eyes and refolded the letter. "Thank You, Father. Even in this dark time, Your light offers hope for a brighter future."

∾

LOUISVILLE, KENTUCKY
FRIDAY, SEPTEMBER 30, 1864

*R*ose stifled a yawn and blinked for clearer vision. The afternoon sun streamed through the library windows, making dust motes dance in the beam cast across the desk and onto the floor. Its warmth conspired with the quiet of the room and her tedious sorting task to tempt Rose to a short nap. A turn around the room should break the spell.

Shoving away the heavy oak chair, she stood and arched her back. Coffee's delightful aroma teased her nose. Before she could investigate, Vernon loomed in front of her, a steaming cup of the brew in his hand.

He smiled at her questioning look then took a sip. So much

for thoughtful gestures. She pointed to the drink. "I believe I shall follow your example and get a cup for myself." She noted his fallen countenance as she turned away and strolled into the tiny kitchen.

"Oh, I say." Vernon's voice floated behind her. "I could have brought you a cup."

She poured the liquid, added a lump of sugar, and speared him with a steady gaze. "But you didn't, did you?"

He stopped in the doorway, blocking her exit. "I didn't know you wanted any." Surprised innocence raised his voice to a whine.

"You didn't think to ask." The thoughtlessness she kept encountering pricked her anger. She stirred her coffee with more vigor than necessary.

The lack of common courtesy wasn't limited to Vernon, she admitted, but he exhibited his arrogance on a regular basis. Rose considered it strange for a man who coveted her attention. Perhaps she'd been spoiled. *Oh, make up your mind, Rose. You're suspicious of a man who treats you with consideration, then get angry when one fails to do so.*

Here, then, was the crux of the matter. Since reading the letter from Noah, Rose couldn't bear to think of Vernon as a suitor. She should find a way to tell him to apply his dubious charms elsewhere.

Reining in her thoughts, she realized Vernon waited for her response. Had he asked her a question? "I'm sorry, I was wool-gathering. What did you say?"

He huffed. "I said the weather is beginning to change and winter will be here before we know it. You should give serious consideration to moving from that disaster on Tenth Street. With my connections, you know I could set you up…er, you and your sister, of course…in something much more comfortable."

Alerted by something in his voice, Rose regarded Vernon with suspicion. "With your connections?"

He spread his lips in a broad smile.

"You could set me up. Just what are you proposing, Mr. Fordham?"

"Well." He cleared his throat. "What a strange choice of words, Rose. I am not *proposing* anything, merely *offering* an alternative to your current situation. I own a number of small cottages that are available for a very reasonable agreement."

Ice stiffened her spine as Rose set down her coffee cup and lifted her chin. "Mr. Fordham, I may be a displaced Southern woman, but I am not ignorant. Nor am I desperate. I find your *offer* repugnant and demeaning. You may exercise your great influence by having me dismissed from this position, but your authority stops there. I will not be bought or taken in by your sweet-sounding words."

Rose pushed past him, marched to her desk, and snatched a blank piece of paper. Vernon would never let up as long as she worked here. Her hands shaking with fury, she wrote out her resignation, gathered her personal items, and marched to the front doors. Sometimes it was best to quit the field of battle.

~

Near Dallas, Georgia
Thursday, October 6, 1864

*E*xhaustion made Noah's hands shake, but he grabbed the lamp and positioned it close to his cot. Tearing off a bite of jerky and chewing slowly, he collapsed onto the camp chair. He let his head loll. Perhaps he dozed. He didn't know for sure, but peace enveloped him as his wordless prayer floated heavenward. Another day preserved. *Thank You, Lord.*

Sometime later, he stretched and worked out the kinks resulting from his awkward position. It was fully dark now, so he lit the lamp and pulled the crumpled paper from his pocket to read what he had written before yesterday's battle.

October 5, 1864
New Hope Church, Georgia

Dear Miss Carrigan (and company),

I will snatch a moment to write a few lines before the day's duties pull me away. I was delighted to receive your letter of September 11 and learn how things go for you and all my friends from Marietta.

Though we have been on the move nearly every day and engaged the other army often, I have no news worth sharing. Weariness plagues everyone until we can scarcely think beyond the next moment. That's a dangerous place for any soldier, even more so for a leader who must watch for those who report to him. Forgive my depressing words. I think I must blame the memory of this place, where our army suffered a grievous defeat earlier this year.

We have followed General Hood westward while General Sherman continues east toward the coast. I feel as if we keep fighting over the same area again and again. We'll take it for a while and then lose it again. How long can this go on?

Noah smoothed the paper against the table's surface. He shouldn't pass on his gloomy disposition, though he could find little to cheer about. Perhaps if he abandoned talk of the war, it would lift the mood. Writing about his family should help.

October 6

I apologize for the dismal tone of the words I wrote yesterday. I imagine you deal with worries I know nothing of—worries placed on you because of the war also. From here out, I will offer whatever I can in the way of cheer and encouragement.

One welcome bit of news came to me yesterday: I have become an uncle! You may add your felicitations to those pounded upon my back when I broke the news to my men. Of course, I had nothing to do with the happy event. In fact, I had tried to persuade Eliza not to marry Ben, but she wouldn't heed me. And though I still insist he isn't good enough for my sister (no man could attain that measure), he has acquitted himself well. I understand they have a substantial house and now the added attraction of a nephew. You can be sure I will take my responsibilities as uncle very seriously and join my parents in spoiling him as soon as I can.

Back at the homestead, I have another sister. Katie is of an independent nature, much like you, I think. She must be nearly nineteen now, but I continue to picture her as a cheeky girl of thirteen. My stepmother (Mary) has one son (Jesse) from her first marriage. Jesse is with Grant's army somewhere in Virginia. Along with Mary, Pops, and Katie at home, I have two younger brothers who are commonly referred to as the Two Terrors because of their antics, although I suppose they are as well-mannered as most boys at eight and ten. They do make life interesting!

You may tell John Mark that I have two arrowheads to add to his collection. I don't think these are valuable, but they are well preserved, thanks to the mud around the Chattahoochee River. I would have completely missed one had I not seen an old dog nosing around the area. He didn't let me near until I tossed him a treat, and now he seems to have adopted me. As you can imagine, the men tease me about gathering up animals for the ark.

Please give my best regards to all the company there. I remember you all in my prayers as I trust you will keep me in yours.

Your Friend and Servant,

Maj. Noah Griffin

At this point he hesitated, tapping his pencil against the table before he plunged onward.

Please do not share the remainder of this letter with the others, as I write it to you alone. Dear Rose—I wonder if I may presume to address you as I think of you? I expected to forget you as time and distance grew between us, and yet I find I cannot. You are with me in every waking moment and in my dreams. Have I surprised you or caused you disgust? If so, simply let me know and I will speak of it no more. However, if you are agreeable, I would like to call on you as soon as we may be within speaking distance and see whether we might pursue a closer relationship for the future. I await your decision.
—Noah

With determination, he addressed the envelope and stuffed the carefully folded letter inside. He would see it posted in the morning. If he dared. Perhaps he would regret the decision to share his heart. If so, he would rip away the last part before releasing it and risking rejection. Morning often changed one's mind about things.

CHAPTER 27

"*A* decision made in the heat of anger often leads to regrets, but I don't see what else you could have done, dear." Edith placed a cup of coffee on the table and slid the sugar bowl toward Rose.

Rose grasped Edith's hand for a moment in gratitude. "Thank you. For the coffee and the commiseration."

Sitting in the empty kitchen while others rushed off to chores struck Rose as the height of laziness. Having Edith with her made it a blessing. The older woman deserved a day of rest after attending a difficult birth during the night.

Rose kept her gaze on the liquid in her cup as it changed from darkest pecan brown to the shade of stewed apples while she stirred in the sweet cream. Sighing, she confided her concerns.

"Vernon Fordham wields some power in town, so he could use his influence to prevent me from getting a position elsewhere—at least anything that would make use of my education.

It's too bad I waited until school was well under way before I saw through his overtures."

Edith laid her hand over Rose's. "Don't you worry about that, dear. We're doing all right here. As much as you want to take on everyone's burden, you must realize it's too much for you. Let it go. The Lord will work out everything in His time."

A noise drew their attention to the doorway. Phoebe peeked into the room and smiled when she saw them. "So, this is where y'all are hiding! I been looking all over." She sauntered to the stove, touched the coffee pot with the back of her fingers, and snagged a cup from the cabinet.

"You just returned from taking the children to school?" Edith relaxed against the back of her chair, taking her coffee with her.

"Yes'm. I think the newness of school is wearing off. They didn't step as lively as they did when they first started. The boys especially wanted to drag their feet."

Rose frowned. "I hope none of them is getting sick again."

Phoebe joined them at the table, adding a liberal helping of sugar to her cup. "I don't think so, they just…oh, Miss Rose, I plumb forgot why I was hunting you down. There's a gentleman in the office wanting to see you."

Alarm sizzled through Rose. Her eyes met Edith's across the table. Surely Vernon wouldn't come to the refugee house. She pressed her lips together to control her response. "What did this gentleman look like?"

Phoebe took a sip from her cup before she answered. "I'd say he's quite handsome and not too old."

Rose refrained from rolling her eyes. Phoebe considered most men over the age of twenty to be handsome.

"He's taller than Pete, maybe as tall as Mr. Anderson, but his hair is dark where Mr. Anderson's is nearly white."

Impatience growing, Rose hastened to the main point. "Did he give his name? And you say he asked for me specifically?"

"Yes'm. He particularly asked for Miss Rose Carrigan, said his name was Turner and Herbert sent him. Or was his name Herbert and Turner sent him?"

Rose sagged. Whoever Mr. Turner was, if Herbert sent him, he should be safe. Herbert had suffered remorse when he learned about Mr. Fordham. He hadn't known the man had connections to the library. Herbert had supported Rose's decision to leave her employ, even though it left his friend, Miss Pringle, in a bind. To compensate, Herbert had probably canvassed everyone he knew to find her another position.

She rose and carried her cup to the sink. "I hope you didn't leave Mr. Turner cooling his heels in the hallway, Phoebe."

"No, ma'am, I took him to Lieutenant Goodwin's office. Goodwin and Pierce got called to the prison to help with new arrivals."

Praise God for that. Please keep them away until I can speak with Mr. Turner and learn what he wants with me. "Thank you, Phoebe. Miss Edith, I thank you for the company and the advice. I shall do my best to do as you say."

At the front office, Rose tapped on the doorframe. "Mr. Turner?"

The man whirled from the window. His dark hair was well trimmed and absent of gray. A tan greatcoat was draped across his left arm, contrasting with the dark blue of his suit. Holding his bowler in one hand, he stretched the other toward her in greeting. Bluish-gray eyes lit as he spoke. "May I presume you are Miss Rose Carrigan?"

She met his touch briefly and nodded. "Yes, I am. I understand Herbert sent you?"

"Right you are. I was delighted and relieved to hear that someone with your education was seeking a position."

"Perhaps we could sit and discuss the particulars." She gestured to the chairs facing the desk.

Mr. Turner waited for her to take her seat and lowered his

frame onto the other. "I need someone to serve as governess to a four-year-old girl while my mother recovers from a fall. I realize four is young for a governess, but my daughter is rather precocious, and I'd like to begin her education early. I warn you, though, Victoria keeps us hopping with her clever antics."

"I see." Rose tempered her spurt of excitement. "Please pardon me if my questions seem intrusive, but I'd like to understand your situation before I agree. Your wife is in residence at this time?"

He winced as if struck. He cleared his throat and struggled to speak. "My wife died last year. My mother has been staying with us for a few months, caring for Victoria while I'm away. You see, my business requires me to travel for days, sometimes weeks at a time, so I'm not often home. I do my part for the cause by arranging shipments of food and supplies."

"I'm sorry for your loss, Mr. Turner. You said your mother is recovering from a fall. Is she able to get about at all? The reason I ask is to know whether she could manage if, heaven forbid, Victoria became ill or injured herself? Do you have other servants who could care for her in such a situation?"

"I have a cook and housekeeper, but both are near my mother's age. I doubt they would be much help in an emergency. Mother isn't yet able to leave her bed without help." He glanced at Rose. "Perhaps I need to employ two women, a governess for Victoria and a day nurse for Mother. I certainly wouldn't want to put such a burden on one person."

"I believe that's wise. I can enlist the aid of another woman here at the refuge house. If you'd like, we can visit your home and work with your mother to see how we might arrange matters."

The man stood from his chair. "That would be marvelous. Would you be able to come tomorrow? If so, I'll send my carriage around to get the two of you in the morning. Shall we say nine o'clock?"

Rose stood also, glad to find him so agreeable to her suggestion. "Certainly. We can discuss all the details then."

Mr. Turner bowed. "Thank you so much, Miss Carrigan. I'm glad Herbert suggested you for this position."

She walked as far as the outer door with him, then headed upstairs to share her news. From habit, she glanced out the window at the landing. Seeing Mr. Turner talking with Lieutenant Goodwin and Sergeant Pierce near the gate, she pressed her lips together. Maybe Mr. Turner would limit the information he shared with them. It wouldn't do for Pierce to know her business. She watched until the men exchanged a few words and Mr. Turner took his leave.

Flying up the stairs, she put away her worrying thoughts and went in search of Emily Anderson. Emily had been ill and distant since learning of Martin's death. She emerged from her shell of gloom a few moments at a time, finding little joy even in her children.

Da's prescription for such melancholy included a busy schedule and focus outside oneself. Rose hoped it would serve in Emily's case.

Near Summerville, Georgia
Tuesday, October 18, 1864

*T*wo letters. A fat one from his mother and a thin one from Rose. Noah drummed his fingers on the table and debated which one to open first. He desperately needed something to lift his cloud of melancholy. His mother's letter would serve the purpose, for she always found some cheerful tidbits to share, regardless of circumstances.

He stared at the other letter and brushed his fingers over the elegant writing. The sight of his gnarled, work-roughened hand against the smooth paper suggested the improbable success of his desire. Rose, like her name, represented beauty and life. His spirit dragged, defeated by the death around him, scarred and hardened by the work of war.

He pulled his fingers away before he left stains on the cover. Once opened, his world would shift, his future set on one course or another. How had she responded to his request, his bid for her favor? Did he want to know?

Coward. Of course, you want to know. Open it. Now.

Obeying the voice in his head, he tore into the envelope and tugged at the single page. The paper seemed to spring open. He scanned it hungrily for a hint at her answer, picking out phrases, skipping over the nonessential pleasantries.

We are well...new position...pressed for time...anxiously waiting to see you again. Ah, here was a crumb of encouragement...most agreeable to your suit.

His heart stuttered then sped up. Closing his eyes, he savored the moment before reading more.

Will you think me forward to sign this as I do now? Sincerely Yours, Rose

He looked at the date she'd written at the top. October 11. Counting backward, he figured she must have written as soon as she'd received his letter. Blowing out his breath, he gave a shout of relief and carefully folded the paper until it fit snugly in his breast pocket. There it would stay until he could see her again face to face.

~

LOUISVILLE, KENTUCKY
TUESDAY, OCTOBER 18, 1864

*R*ose examined the papers Victoria pressed into her hand. "What's this?"

"Pictures for you, Miss Rose." Leaning over the arm of Rose's chair, the little girl pointed to the one on top. "See, it's a rose, just like your name. And there's the bench in the park where we walk sometimes." She pointed to another paper. "This is the doggie we saw walking with his lady and the gen'leman smoking his pipe."

Victoria wrinkled her nose at the memory of the smell from the pipe. "I'm glad Papa don't have a pipe, but sometimes Grandpapa gets one of them brown sticks and smokes it."

Rose managed to keep from smiling at the image. "A cigar?"

Victoria pumped her shoulders to indicate indifference. "I guess. Grandmama tells him to go outside with it." She flipped to the next paper, where several stick people held hands.

"And who are all these people?" Rose asked.

The child pointed to each one. "You, me, Grandmama, Miss Emily, Papa, Grandpapa, Hetty and Bitty."

Hetty and Bitty were Caroline Turner Richardson's young daughters from her second marriage. Victoria had trouble saying "Tabitha," so the girl's name became Bitty.

"Oh, how nice, but you should draw one with just your family. You know Miss Emily and I are only here until your grandmother is better."

A downcast face met this reminder. "I know. Then I have to go back to Grandmama's house again."

"You don't want to go?"

Blond ringlets flew as she shook her head adamantly. "I want to stay here with Papa, even if he does have to go away sometimes."

"Well, Papa is here now." The masculine voice interrupted from the nursery doorway.

Victoria squealed and raced to the door. "Papa! You're home."

Mr. Turner picked up his daughter and pecked her cheek as she patted his face. "Yes, I am, and I'm hoping the new man I hired will keep me from having to go away so much."

Chubby hands barely missed his nose while Victoria clapped with gladness. "Hooray!"

Rose left her chair and slid the papers onto the child-sized table. "Welcome back, Mr. Turner. I trust you had a successful journey."

"I found a young man in Missouri to take over our western shipments, which should cut my travels in half, leaving me more time with this little monkey." He tickled Victoria's ribs, making her squeal in delight.

"Excuse me." Emily stood in the doorway. "Mr. Turner? Mrs. Richardson sent me to see if that was you what arrived. She wants to see you, if it'd be all right." Emily paused to catch her breath, her hand resting against her bosom. "She started to climb these stairs herself, but I thought it best for her to stay put."

Mr. Turner's gaze was arrested by the sight of Emily in the door.

Victoria wriggled from his arms and ran back into the school room.

Rose spoke into the awkward silence. "Would you like me to ask Cook to take tea to Mrs. Richardson's room?"

The man snapped to attention. "That's a fine idea. Thank you." He turned to go, but Victoria returned and shoved her papers at him. The four of them stood at the top of the stairs.

"Papa, I want to show my pictures to you and Grandmama and Miss Emily." Victoria held up the one with all the stick people. "See, here's everybody in our family." Holding up the drawing for her father's inspection, she identified all the people by name as she had for Rose.

Mr. Turner directed his twinkling gaze at Emily and then Rose. "Well, since Victoria has declared us all family, I suggest we dispense with the formalities and drop the titles. If that meets with the approval of you ladies?"

Emily's evident surprise must have mirrored Rose's own expression. Most Southerners used honorific titles, if not the more accurate ones, for anyone older or in a higher position. "Would it be proper, though, given that you're our employer?"

"Well," he hedged, "we can at least limit the formal addresses to public situations. You know I call everyone else in the house by their given names. Except Mama, of course, and Miss Beatrice prefers plain Cook instead of my joking Busy Bee."

Emily kept her eyes down and shifted from one foot to the other. Perhaps a less formal atmosphere would help her relax.

Rose lifted her hands in surrender. "To be honest, Mrs. Richardson—Caroline—mentioned the same idea already. All right, we shall try it your way."

"In that case, my name is Lucas." His eyes drifted to Emily again as he swept his arm toward the stairs.

Such an unusual man. What was going on inside his head?

~

Leesburg, Alabama
Friday, October 21, 1864

*N*oah stumbled into his tent as the sun began its descent. He collapsed at the fold-up table and swept aside the jumble of items lying there. Maps, pencils, and letters heaped together, a testament to his recent inattention to order. He barely remembered the days when he could locate any item in moments. The army expected its men to keep everything in order, but the demands of war eroded that discipline. Ammunition and weapons ranked highest on the list of priorities; everything else was dispensable.

Noah considered the reports trickling down about changes. General Sherman had other fires to burn besides pursuing Hood's army around Alabama. Having secured all but one avenue across the Tennessee River, the commander left General Osterhaus to continue the chase while Sherman himself turned back to Georgia. His aim was to crush Georgia and the Carolinas under his heel. He'd leave the cat and mouse games to Lee and Grant.

Rumors of a Confederate meeting a few miles south of their position in Gadsden put everyone on alert. A more direct battle could be brewing. The recent skirmishes at Little River and Blue Pond served only to frustrate everyone, making no real difference to either side.

Noah had learned to seize the brief moments of lull for tasks postponed on most days. This time he had letters to write. He quickly penned responses to his mother and sisters, mainly to assure them he continued to walk the earth and had not moved to a more peaceful realm. Never had he mentioned his hopes for a future with Rose. Such news should be planned to the best advantage of a good reception.

At last, he snagged another piece of paper and wrestled with words to answer her last letter. He closed his eyes to conjure her picture. Was she truly as he remembered, or had time and distance enhanced the curve of her cheek, the blue of her eyes? He shook away the vision. No matter. His heart insisted she was everything he needed.

He resolved to grasp the future. When this wretched war ended, he planned to do everything in his power to create a better world. One where he could raise a family in peace and safety. Thus determined, he started writing.

My Dearest Rose.

CHAPTER 28

*R*ose peered at the tiny infant, finally asleep after complaining loudly at the mistreatment she had suffered on her journey into this world. Wrapped in the blanket Lydia had labored to knit all summer, she snuggled safely in her grandmother's arms.

Rose grazed her fingers over the downy brow and marveled at the perfection of God's creation. The blanket rose and fell with tiny puffs of breath.

Rose had arrived a few minutes after the delivery, a disappointment and yet a relief when she heard how many hours Millie had endured. Celeste had met Rose and Emily as they hurried up the walkway.

"Shiloh brought me the news at Mrs. Coker's," Celeste told them. "I made enough sweet rolls to get her and Herbert through breakfast tomorrow so I can stay the night if needed. I hope there's still a bed available for me."

Emily spoke before Rose could answer. "If there's not, I'll put Sarah Grace in with me, and you can have hers."

"Thank you," Celeste said. "I'd like to stay and help if I can, although I haven't been around a baby in a long time. Y'all might have to help me remember how to hold one."

Rose added, "Just what I was thinking. I wish I could stay, but I have to get back to Mr. Turner's house before dark."

"At least Mrs. Richardson promised to send the buggy around for you," Emily said. "I wouldn't want you to have to walk these streets alone at night."

Emily took her turn admiring the babe, then slipped away to find her own children. It took some coaxing and encouragement, but Millie managed to nurse the babe enough to calm her down before they both slept from exhaustion. With their charges resting, Ada, Edith, and Olivia slipped away to snatch a few hours of sleep.

Celeste sidled up to Rose while Lydia lifted the baby and sank onto the single chair, softly humming a disjointed melody.

Rose chuckled. "I don't think Lydia's going to share her treasure yet. Not that I blame her. What a lovely miracle."

"The result of much pain and struggle, however." Celeste gazed at the exhausted new mother. "Edith told me Millie's pains started yesterday but subsided and then increased around noon today. It makes you seriously consider the cost of motherhood, does it not?"

Rose looped her arm around her sister's waist and leaned into her side. "All of life comes the way of pain. Birth, death, war. Even the food we eat cost someone a day's toil. I suppose God gives us the greatest treasures to compensate for the suffering."

That quiet conversation came back to her a few days later at the Turner home. Victoria and Caroline Richardson were working on a gift for Lucas's birthday, so Rose and Emily headed downstairs for a cup of tea. Nearing the kitchen, Rose recognized the tantalizing aroma of onions sizzling in butter. As she opened her mouth to remark upon it, Emily blanched and turned away, pinching her nose and dashing for the kitchen door.

"Oh, no, I can't take that smell!"

Rose started after her, heard the pitiful retching in the yard, and turned back. In the kitchen Cook gave her a damp cloth. "She'll be needing this, and I've a cup of sweet tea you can take also."

Perplexed, Rose accepted the offering. "Thank you. How is it you already had this prepared?"

"She's been doin' that ever' day for a week now."

"Has she? But she hasn't shown any other symptoms of sickness as far as I know."

Cook gave the browned vegetables a quick stir as Rose started toward the door. "No, she's healthy enough, 'Tis just the babe inside protestin' the smell of food."

Rose balked. "A babe? But how can that be? We've only been away from Georgia..." Wisdom reared its warning as Cook raised her eyebrows to stop the questions.

"Some women never get sick at all. Some suffer the whole time." The older woman lifted her shoulders to indicate the matter wasn't worth discussing. "With others, it comes and goes willy-nilly." She pressed the cup into Rose's other hand and pushed open the door.

Emily leaned against the porch rail, nestling her head on her bent arms.

Rose pushed the cloth between Emily's fingers and tentatively offered the cup. She wasn't sure whether the tea's rich aroma might trigger another round of nausea. "Cook sent some sweet tea for you."

Dragging in a shuddering breath, Emily lifted her head. "I guess there's no hiding the truth now, is there?" She wiped her face and took the cup in trembling hands.

Rose gestured to the bench a few feet away. "Let's talk, shall we?"

The wooden structure sat in the morning sun, absorbing its warmth until the neighboring trees lifted their bare arms to interfere. Rose sat next to Emily. Unsure how to phrase her questions, she waited to let Emily set the pace of the conversation.

Emily's voice was low as she began. "You remember the day we all left town for Marietta? I woke up early that day, before the sun was up, thinking I needed to go to the woods and forage for some herbs we might need on the journey north. I snuck out of the house with my basket to see what I could find."

Rose listened carefully as Emily spoke to the ground in front of them, wisps of hair straying from the cap she donned each morning. She paused to swipe the cloth over her mouth and sip the tea.

Rose could guess where this was leading. "That was the day the soldiers broke out their whiskey rations, as I recall."

Emily nodded. "The one who snuck up on me smelled like spirits. I'd started wondering if I might run into any snakes or other critters in the underbrush. That's what I thought the rustling noise was when I heard it. Then afore I knew it, he grabbed me from behind and said, 'What you doin' here?' I was so scared, I couldn't speak, but I tried to get away. Then he moved his hands and felt that I was a woman, so he jerked me around and…he…"

Rose reached toward Emily but stopped short of touching her. With the woman's mind gripped in memories from the past, she might be startled. "It's fine. I understand. He took you against your will."

A tortured cry broke from Emily. "But what will that matter when everyone finds out? I'll be labeled the worst kind of woman, like them women in that other house down the street." She turned desperate eyes to Rose. "Will they make me go there, the soldiers I mean? Will I have to leave my children and family?"

"No, Emily. Nobody's going to make you move or leave your children. You're not like those women who sell themselves. You were violated, forced to endure a terrible, criminal act."

"But I worry 'bout what everyone will think of me. I ain't a bad woman, Rose. Maybe I ain't good like you and your sister, but I ain't never intentionally done anyone wrong."

"This child you carry, though conceived in an awful way, is innocent, just as you are." Rose placed her hand over Emily's. "I don't know how much you know of the gospel, whether you're a believer. The Bible says that none of us is truly good, but God loves us anyway. This may seem like a difficult burden to bear, but God can bring something good from it."

"But what'll I tell everybody about...my condition?"

"Listen to me." Rose took Emily's hands and met her eyes. "You're the widow of a fallen soldier. For all anyone else knows, Martin could've been transferred to another company and gone to Georgia or Alabama. He could've slipped away for a few hours before the Yankees came and took us away. You don't owe people any explanations. You are still Emily Anderson, and when your baby comes, he or she will be an Anderson. Mind, I'm not suggesting you tell any lies, but neither do you have to answer to anyone who asks. People may speculate for a while, but they'll soon forget about this in the face of their own troubles."

~

LADIGA, ALABAMA
SATURDAY, OCTOBER 29, 1864

*S*peculation buzzed in the camp. Would they be pulling out again?

Like his fellow officers, Noah had gathered the equipment numbers from his men. Rifles, bayonets, ammunition, mounts, uniforms, knapsacks...everything had been counted and evaluated. He'd passed the information to his superiors, who would tabulate and consider whether the army should remain or withdraw for refitting.

He dared not voice his expectations. If other companies turned in numbers similar to his, running low on everything, the Seventh Cavalry would kiss Alabama goodbye in a matter of days. Thoughts of escaping the endless drudgery of war figured largely in Noah's dreams. Knowing they'd aim for the Seventh's home base in Louisville, where he could see Rose and perhaps take her to meet his parents, only made him more anxious to leave the South.

And yet he hated to leave a task incomplete. News from the other fronts filtered down the line. General Sherman still flexed his strength in Georgia, plotting his strategy, while Grant and Sheridan tried to out-maneuver Lee in Virginia.

The presidential election was ten days away. With Frémont now out of the race and McClellan disagreeing with his fellow Democrats about a peace treaty with the Confederacy, Noah figured the Union would stay the course and reelect Lincoln.

The war would drag on. Who could tell how long? Nobody had expected it to last beyond a few months. Unfortunately, the two armies mirrored each other in strength and stubbornness. Whoever survived faced the monumental task of rebuilding this devastated land.

While I mused, the fire burned.

What a strange bit of scripture to come to mind. He thought it was from the Psalms, but he'd have to look it up to be sure. What did it mean?

The buzzing around him had morphed from whispers to bustling activity. A man raced by, waving and shouting, "Time's a-wasting! Pack up to head north for refitting."

Noah sat back in wonder. So much for the chain of command. News like that was bound to incite a flood in moments. He laughed aloud at the nudge given him by the Holy Spirit. "Okay, Lord, I get it now. Stop pondering the time away. There's work to do. Packing up the entire company."

And a train to take me home.

~

LOUISVILLE, KENTUCKY
SATURDAY, NOVEMBER 5, 1864

The blast of a train whistle drowned out Emily's words. Rose caught the other woman's arm before she crossed the street in front of the wagon bearing down on them. After it passed and the whistle faded away, she asked Emily, "What were you saying?"

Emily sighed. "It's just my imagination, I feel sure, but, well, Mr. Turner worries me. He looks at me like he knows more about me than he's been told. It gives me a strange feeling."

"Hmm. Maybe he heard us discussing your reading lessons and simply wonders why you never learned to read."

"Could be." But she didn't sound convinced. "I know it's fanciful, but it's like he can see right into my head."

Another thought occurred to Rose. "Then again, he might be wondering if you'd be willing to let him court you."

Instead of the astonishment Rose expected to see, a blush spread across Emily's cheeks, accompanied by a vigorous head-shaking. "I don't think a man with his education and means would consider a woman like me. Not even if I didn't come with a passel of young'uns and elders to care for."

235

"But you wouldn't object to it, if he did, would you?" Rose covered her own surprise at the tacit admission. She considered the situation objectively. "He's a nice-looking man, and he's kind. In fact, he reminds me of someone else who showed us kindness…"

Her voice trailed off as an odd thought occurred. From the first meeting, Lucas Turner had put her in mind of Noah. That probably accounted for her feeling at ease with him rather than suspicious, as she tended to be with strangers.

Scoffing at herself for creating ties out of nothing, she caught the last of Emily's answer.

"…like Captain Griffin. I have to admit not all these Yankees are what I 'spected to find here. Not that I don't look at each one with misgiving and wonder what they're thinking."

Rose knew what Emily meant. She reached for a memory that floated at the dark corners of her mind, elusive as the wispy clouds overhead. It had something to do with Pierce.

They halted at the corner of Tenth and Broadway, waiting for a coach-and-four to pass. When the vehicle cleared their vision, Rose caught her breath at the sight across the street. At the entrance to the refugee house, two soldiers stood face to face, their postures stiff as if embroiled in an argument.

One man looked up when she and Emily neared, and Pierce's taunting laugh rang out as he motioned toward the women. "Well, here she is. You can ask her yourself." He spun back to the front door, spewing evil glee until the door closed on him.

Noah turned troubled eyes her way.

Rose stood transfixed, joy and trepidation warring within her.

Emily rushed forward and gripped his hand. "Captain, no, I mean Major Griffin, it's good to see you again."

"Hello. Mrs. Anderson, isn't it? I'm happy to see you are well, as I trust so is your family."

"We're all middling along." She glanced uncertainly from Noah to Rose. "Well, I'd best see to the young'uns. I hope you get a chance to call again. I know John Mark would be glad to see you."

Noah swept the hat from his head and bowed. "I plan to be around a few days, so a visit with the children will be on my schedule."

Emily darted inside the house, and Rose battled down her misgivings to offer a genuine smile. "Welcome to Louisville, Major. You look well. I trust you received my letters?"

Relief lightened his face as Noah returned her smile. "Thank you, Miss Carrigan, I did."

His gaze shifted to the street and around the porch. "Is there a place where we can speak in private?"

~

*S*omeplace to talk in private, he'd said. Noah grimaced as he followed Rose around the brick, multistoried building to the walled-off yard behind it. Talking figured little in his plans. What he wanted to do involved sweeping Rose into his arms and keeping her there. Then again, since his little chat with Pierce, he might grip her shoulders and shake some sense into her.

Questions buzzed in his head like flies in a cow pasture. How did Luke figure into this picture, or was he involved at all? Could Pierce be spouting off lies again? And how in heaven's name had Pierce finagled his way into a position at the refugee home?

Rose stopped at a wooden bench near the far fence line. She sat and Noah paced, wondering where to start. He glanced back toward the house and noted the windows on the upper floors. So much for privacy. At least nobody could hear what they said.

"Will you please sit down?" She touched the bench beside her.

His eyes roamed her face hungrily as he lowered his frame onto the bench, angled so he could see her expression. His knee brushed hers, but they didn't adjust their positions.

She tilted her head. "You look much the same as I remember, and yet different."

Noah clasped her hand and raised it to his lips. "You are more beautiful than I remembered. My dreams were a poor substitute for reality."

A hint of pink brightened her cheeks before she dropped her gaze and her voice. "So, you haven't changed your mind about courting me?"

"I hope you are still amenable?"

"I am."

Noah gently squeezed her fingers. "I do have a few questions, however. As you saw when you arrived, Pierce played his favorite game of prodding my ire with what I suspect are lies and half-truths."

"He has a knack for that with me also, probably with everyone. He likes to bully people and cause trouble."

Noah dropped her hand to stand and commenced pacing again. "Why didn't you tell me in your letters he was here? I thought at least you were safe from his kind." He gestured around the enclosed facility.

"What good would it have done? It would only cause you worry, a distraction that might expose you to danger. Besides, Celeste and I warned all the women about Pierce so we could protect each other."

"That's good thinking. As for what he told me today, I can't credit it at all. He said you had taken up with my cousin."

"Your cousin?" Bafflement rang in her voice. "I have no idea who—"

"Luke Turner. Pierce said you visit his house frequently."

Her jaw dropped. "Lucas Turner is your cousin? Well, no wonder he seemed familiar."

"It's true? You've visited his home?"

Rose stood and stepped in front of him, blue eyes commanding his attention. "Emily Anderson and I have been employed to work at his house. I teach and care for his daughter, and Emily assists with his mother, who's recovering from an injury."

Noah gripped her arms, giving full vent to his worry. "Rose, you can't trust Luke. He's as bad as Pierce. They ran together as kids and caused trouble everywhere. I'm sure he's convinced you he's noble and kind. That's the way he operates. Where Pierce bullies, Luke uses subtlety and charm. I won't have you falling prey to whatever scheme he's running."

CHAPTER 29

*R*ose pulled herself from Noah's grasp and faced him down. "Do you think I'm such an easy mark, such a poor judge of character?"

Ah, but she had been in the past. She was much younger then and too quick to trust. Memories brought on panic. Rose turned away to hide her distress.

Noah slid his palms along her upper arms to halt her withdrawal. "No," he said. "I don't mean to disparage your judgment. But I know Luke, what a charmer he can be. You wouldn't be the first he's deceived."

And it wouldn't be the first time I've been deceived. She shook away the inner voice. "But he's been kind to Emily and me, and he's definitely devoted to his daughter and family."

"What of his wife?"

"She died last year. From what I gather, she was sick for a long time. They came to Louisville to be near a certain physician. Cook said Lucas was beside himself for months after her death. I can't believe such a man would be evil."

"Rose, he's my cousin. I know him. My family tried to help Aunt Caroline after Luke's father died, but he rebelled at every turn. If nothing else, his association with Pierce should tell you something about his character."

"That's just it. There is no association that I can see. Neither he nor Pierce have indicated they know each other." She stopped to consider. "Not that I would ever mention one to the other. But Pierce has a way of finding out everyone's business, as evident by his accusations about me. Emily and I go to his house together and…"

She paused as sudden inspiration flashed. "I know! You should go with us tomorrow and see for yourself."

A dark frown formed as he glowered. "I don't think you want to put Luke and me in the same room."

Rose studied him a long moment. "How long has it been since you saw him?"

Noah rubbed his chin. "Probably close to a dozen years."

"When you were children?" she cried in disbelief. "How can you judge a grown man by his behavior as a child?"

"A youth," he amended. "A tree doesn't change directions in the way it grows."

Exasperated, she threw up her hands. "Of course, it does! If it's deprived of sunlight on one side, you can correct its growth by clearing out the obstruction. Perhaps losing his father affected Lucas deeply." She recalled a recent conversation with Caroline. "He credits his stepfather with turning him around."

When Noah didn't reply, she issued the invitation again. "Caroline is giving a party for Victoria tomorrow, for her birthday. She's invited Emily's children, and I'm going to help. You could go and judge for yourself whether Lucas is the same person you knew."

He didn't refuse, so she pressed on. "Besides, it would give us a chance to be together, and we might be able to slip out to the garden for a stroll. It's much more private than here."

To prove her point, she directed his attention to the trio of children hurrying toward them. John Mark led the procession,

Wade and Sarah Grace behind. Noah's eyes lit in comprehension. He bent to whisper in her ear, "I'll be looking forward to that stroll in the garden, Miss Carrigan. Do not renege on me."

"Why, Major Griffin, I wouldn't dream of it."

No further discussion followed as Noah turned to defend himself against the nursery attack.

~

Louisville, Kentucky
Sunday, November 6, 1864

*T*he children led the way, barely restrained by their older companions, who flanked the line. Everyone had dressed in their best outfits—the clothes with the fewest stains and patches—and flocked to church for morning services. Rose's admiring gaze strayed more often than it should to Noah in his smart uniform. With him in their midst, they earned a few stares and a more genial acceptance than usual as they filled the two back benches.

Of their group, only Lydia and Dorcas stayed behind to help Millie with baby Amy, who was too young for such an excursion. While going to church always met with eager anticipation, the promise of a party raised everyone's spirits even more. The weather cooperated with abundant sunshine and gentle breezes to endorse outside activities.

Ostensibly serving as the group's rear guard, Noah and Rose strolled behind them as they headed to the Turner home. They discussed the minister's sermon and what had filled the time during their separation. Neither mentioned the test awaiting them at their destination.

When they reached the house, Emily took a brave step forward to introduce her family when Caroline answered the door. Victoria danced behind her, trying to see beyond her grandmother's skirts. "It's Gertie's day off, and Cook is icing the cake," Caroline said. "Besides, I could hardly keep Victoria still, as you can see."

"Mrs. Caroline and Victoria, these are my children, John Mark and Sarah Grace. And this is Ada and J.D. Anderson, my mama and daddy-in-law."

Well acquainted with Emily's withdrawing nature, Caroline took over. "It's so nice to meet you. Lucas hasn't returned from the train station yet. He went to pick up my girls and husband, who didn't want to miss out on the celebration."

Caroline turned to Celeste. "I know you must be Rose's sister. You look so much alike."

"Yes, ma'am," Celeste answered. She took over the remaining introductions.

With the entry filling up, Caroline turned to Victoria. "Why don't you take the children to the play area out back?"

The youngsters sped off, and Caroline urged her visitors farther inside. "Let's retreat to the parlor." She started that way then suddenly stopped. "But where is Rose? Didn't she come?"

"Indeed, I did." Rose spoke from her place near the door where Noah, still hesitant to intrude, stood partially hidden by a tall philodendron. "I hope you won't mind that I brought another guest along. I confess I insisted he come when I learned of your connection." She stepped forward, pulling Noah beside her.

Caroline's hands flew to her mouth, her eyes wide. "Oh, my! Can it be?"

Noah slanted an abashed half-smile. "Hello, Aunt Caroline. I'm glad to see you're recovering well from your recent mishap."

The others stepped aside as Caroline reached his side and stretched up to stroke his face. "Noah, you look so much like your father, I almost thought it was James standing there. Give me a hug, you naughty boy."

Noah laughed and embraced his aunt.

Rose breathed a sigh of relief. *One down, one to go.*

Caroline beamed. "Well, this day is going to be one to remember." She tugged Noah's arm as they continued to the parlor. "Come and sit by me for a while before Lucas returns. I know he'll be eager to bend your ear. It's been so long since we saw you. You know my brother is a poor one to write, but Mary sends a letter from time to time."

She took her seat. "Please forgive me, everyone. I'm a poor hostess to neglect my other guests. But tell me, how did Noah come to be with you?"

Explanations started and fell away as the front door opened and two girls rushed into the room. Caroline stood to embrace them. "And here are my daughters, Hetty and Tabitha." The girls curtsied but didn't sit.

"Papa and Lucas are taking care of the carriage horse and Victoria's surprise," the taller one said, glancing around the room. "Where is Victoria?"

"Outside in the yard with her new friends. Go on out and meet them. You can make your bow to our other guests when you come in to eat." The girls scurried off before she finished speaking. Caroline returned to her seat so the men could resume theirs as well. "I suppose the prospect of playing with new friends is a greater draw at that age than a mother who's been away for several weeks."

Rose squeezed next to Celeste and Olivia on the green sofa, with Shiloh claiming the matching ottoman. Edith, Emily, and Ada occupied the couch next to the fireplace. J.D. and Isaac chose the flanking claw-footed chairs while Noah angled his long legs away from Caroline's rustling skirts on the shorter settee. Having everyone together in the formal parlor reminded Rose of their first gathering in the house in Marietta. Did her friends feel the tension emanating from Noah, or did the tasteful display of relative prosperity account for the uneasiness she detected?

Before the conversation could gain momentum, the sound of the front door opening put Rose on alert. She glanced up to see Lucas pause in the doorway to the parlor, smoothing his jacket sleeves.

"Sorry I'm late, everyone. I trust Mama has welcomed you profusely and seen to your comfort. I'm eager to meet..."

He paused as Noah stood to assist Caroline to her feet. Both spoke at once.

"Hello, Luke."

"Lucas, look who's here."

Lucas stared a long moment before grinning broadly and striding into the room. He grabbed Noah's outstretched hand, then pulled him into a brotherly embrace. "Noah! Man, I can't believe you're here! What's it been, ten, twelve years?"

Rose released her breath and lifted a silent prayer of thanks. Maybe this would work out all right.

~

*N*oah choked back an onslaught of emotions. Wonder. Relief. Joy. A stirring of distrust and bitterness threatened to surface, but one glance at Rose made him quell the negative thoughts. For her sake, he would endure the embrace and even circle his free arm around his cousin. He sent a smile her way as her face lit with pleasure.

In a flash of enlightenment, he understood what his stepmother had told him over a decade ago when he said he wouldn't have anything else to do with Luke. She'd paraphrased the famous passage in First Corinthians as her basis. "Love keeps no record of wrongs. That's why God forgives us again and again, why we must forgive each other over and over. Love wants what is best for the other person, and it delights in seeing them happy."

He sent Rose a playful wink. Her eyes went wide, and her cheeks flushed pink before she glanced away.

Noah cleared his throat. "A long time, Luke."

Luke pushed away but gripped Noah's shoulders and raked his gaze over his uniform. "And you've made major." He passed a finger under his nose and blinked away the tell-tale moisture. "It's good to see you, cousin."

Luke faced the rest of the company. "And welcome to all of you. We're so glad you've joined us to celebrate my daughter's birthday. She is overjoyed to have visitors. Mama, when do we eat?"

Chuckles lightened the mood as Caroline took charge again. "I've asked Cook to seat the children at the family table. The rest of us can make our way to the dining room." Following her lead, the ladies rose as the men offered their assistance.

Noah claimed Rose and Celeste while Luke maneuvered to Emily's side, forcing J.D. to escort Ada and Edith.

Noah exchanged a look of surprise with Rose. She only raised her eyebrows and shrugged.

Luke guided Emily to his mother's side and offered Caroline his other arm. She placed her hand atop his. "I do wish that husband of mine would come inside. He's probably sneaking a last smoke on the porch."

As if to refute Caroline's claim, the front door opened.

"Oh, here he is now." Caroline shifted to intercept her husband in the hallway. The couple engaged in a brief embrace and whispered exchange before Caroline turned to introduce him to the group at large. "Everyone, this handsome rascal is my husband, Jonas Richardson." She swatted him playfully. "You, Jonas, will have to learn their names while we dine."

Conversation started at a slow, awkward pace but soon relaxed into a natural rhythm. The major topics revolved around the refugees' journey from Georgia and how Noah had come to know them. Beyond a simple statement of his stepfather setting Luke "on the straight and narrow" when Jonas and Caroline married, Lucas steered away inquiries about earlier years. A silent message passed between him and Noah. She hoped it might promise a future conversation, and she took heart at the prospect of one relationship mended in this day of unexpected reunions.

Cook recruited the children to collect the adults' dinner dishes while she brought in the raisin-spice cake, drizzled with honey and adorned with a fat candle in its center. The youngsters polished off their slices, then raced outside to play and admire Victoria's gift of two gray kittens. The adults lingered over the rare treat of cake and coffee.

Noah leaned near Rose but spoke loud enough for others to hear. "Miss Carrigan, I believe you promised me a turn in the garden."

Her pulse sped up as she turned his way. "Why yes, I did, Major. Far be it from me to renege on a promise. Perhaps we'll avoid being run down by a group of frolicking children on the way." Noah pulled out her chair, and she stood and placed her hand on his arm.

He picked up her banter and the shawl he'd placed nearby. "Never fear, fair maiden. I'll protect you from the roving ruffians."

She tossed him a playful grin. "And who, pray tell, will protect you?"

Lucas scraped back his chair. "As your host, Miss Carrigan, I suppose the duty falls to me to be sure no harm comes to either of you. Would anyone else care to join us? Miss Emily, perhaps you'd care to enjoy this rare November sunshine?"

Rose couldn't be sure how Emily answered because Noah rushed her out the nearest door and down the path, out of sight of the house. A laugh escaped as he pulled her along. "Noah, slow down. You're bypassing the autumn flowers. They're over by the stone benches."

He stopped by a sturdy oak and turned her into his arms. "You mistake my intentions, dear heart. The only flower I have any interest in is this Rose. I find I'm enchanted by its smell."

Words deserted Rose at his roguish behavior, and she shivered when he put his nose near her ear and stroked her cheek. "I love to touch its bloom, and I can only guess how it might taste."

Before he could put action to those words, a child's scream rent the air. They turned to find Lucas and Emily rushing to the cluster of children around a sobbing Hetty. The child gave a tearful account of seeing a strange man by the gate.

Lucas questioned the other children. "Did anyone else see this man?"

"No," John Mark said. "We was huntin' for hidin' places."

"Show me where you saw him, Hetty."

While Rose and Emily calmed the girl, the men investigated. They returned to the group, having found no sign of an intruder.

"It was probably just a curious passerby. Hetty tends to be a little excitable." Lucas shrugged away the possibility of danger. He slanted a knowing look Noah's way. "I daresay she spoiled your trysting moment."

"And yours as well," Noah returned. "Be advised I consider myself a guardian for all these folks and will not take kindly to any disrespectful behavior."

The men regarded each other silently for a moment, weighing the matter of assumed responsibility. At last Lucas raised two fingers to his brow and snapped a smart salute. "So noted, Major. You may count on me to support you in that role as well."

～

*N*oah hadn't expected his cousin's support, and he still doubted Luke's purported transformation in character. Did he expect to improve his social standing by using the more proper form of his name? Lucas or Luke, what did it matter? People didn't easily change their natural tendencies. Despite the air of genial acceptance, his body hummed with the tension of an underlying current of unspoken words between them. For Rose's sake, he'd keep his opinions to himself but remain vigilant.

Rose squeezed Noah's arm and pointed skyward. Clouds gathered against the blue background, diminishing the warmth of the late afternoon. "Looks like rain might be moving in. We'd best make our way back."

Luke offered his carriage, but they refused. After all, they could walk the distance almost as quickly as they could ride. They raced against the coming rain. A few drops caught them as they mounted the steps and crowded into the front hallway of the refugee house. They'd barely closed the door when a sudden downpour rattled the windows and pounded on the roof.

Their noisy arrival drew the guard's attention and propelled him into the corridor. Assuming an air of studied casualness, Pierce observed their good-natured chattering as they dashed the water from wraps and shook off hats and bonnets. "Well, I see you Southerners managed to dodge the storm on your Sunday outing. Too bad it didn't wash you away with all the other rats."

His words quieted the friendly prattle and prompted looks of disgust from the women. Rose turned away, pulling Noah along beside her. "I need to run upstairs for a moment. If you don't mind waiting here, I think the rain will soon play itself out. You can join the men in their room if you like."

He read the worry in her eyes and shook his head. He wouldn't let Pierce goad him. "I'd best be on my way. A little rain won't bother me, and I have to report to the colonel tomorrow morning."

The rest of their party scurried to the stairs, but Pierce was watching them. All Noah could do was press her hand. "I'll be back in a day or two. If the weather is nice, perhaps we can take a carriage ride."

Her relief brought on a smile. "That would be nice. Take care."

Noah's gaze followed her as she ascended the stairs, waiting to be sure she couldn't hear what he was about to say to his fellow soldier. His aversion to Pierce was so strong, he usually went out of his way to avoid the scoundrel. Knowing the man prowled the same halls as Rose and her companions compelled him to issue a warning.

Noah pivoted on his heel and stalked to the office where Pierce leaned against the doorjamb. "It's a low-down snake who enjoys tormenting helpless women and children, Pierce."

"And you would know about that, wouldn't you, Major?" He fairly spat the last word. "You didn't care how you treated my sister Alice, and you pretend to be so perfect. I heard how you visited them at all hours when they were detained in Marietta. How you joined them for dinner and took 'em gifts. Which one was you trying to sweeten up? Or do you plan to have 'em all?"

Noah clenched his fists to keep from taking a swing at the man. Pierce thought all men were cut from the same cloth as he was. Summoning his inner strength, Noah ignored the accusations. "Do you have spies everywhere? Is that how you remained in the army this long? Be warned. One day you'll be caught in your own evil devices."

Pierce straightened from his leaning position and snarled, "You won't be seeing it."

"Maybe not. But I'll find out somehow."

Noah turned to the door to leave, then whirled around to point his finger in Pierce's face. "Meanwhile, I'd better not hear of your mistreating any of those people you just insulted. I know how to deal with snakes."

If he heard Pierce had done anything to Rose or her friends, he would report him to his superiors and have him removed from duty. At the very least, Noah wanted him gone from the post at this house. But seeing Pierce blanch, Noah realized the man imagined the worst possible end.

He didn't bother to correct the mistake.

CHAPTER 30

*N*oah whistled as he mounted the steps to the refugee house and opened the front door. Had Rose received his message in time to prepare for an outing? With the weekend free, he planned to spend as much time in her company as possible.

He peered into the hallway cautiously, hoping Pierce had business elsewhere. He didn't want that bad apple upsetting his time with Rose. Noah had mentioned to his superiors about moving Pierce, citing the man's frequent harassment of women. It might take several hours to complete the process, but at least the wheels were turning.

Noah lounged near the door until he spied a young girl coming down the hall. "Good afternoon, miss. I wonder, do you know Miss Rose Carrigan?"

"Yes, sir." She proudly displayed a gap-toothed smile. "You want I should call her for you?"

"That would be most helpful. Tell her Major Griffin is here. Thank you."

The girl dashed up the stairs, and Noah turned to gaze out the window. The carriage he'd ordered wouldn't be ready for another hour, but he didn't want to delay seeing Rose. They could stroll toward the river, perhaps find a place to sit and talk.

"Major Griffin?"

Noah spun to find Olivia Spencer at the base of the stairs. "Good afternoon, Mrs. Spencer. I suspect Rose is not quite ready?"

"The thing is, she's not here." She gave him a troubled smile. "She had a note from the lady at the library where she used to work. It seems Miss Pringle suddenly took ill and asked if Rose would take her place for a few hours. Was Rose expecting you? I can't imagine she'd go without letting you know."

"I sent a note around a couple of hours ago."

"That was about the time she left. Your note is probably on the desk in the office. I'm sure you can visit her at the library until it closes. It's easy to find." She motioned toward the depot. "Go straight down Broadway until you get to Fourth. It's in the next block, corner of Fourth and York."

"Thank you, ma'am. I appreciate your kindness in letting me know." He grabbed his hat from the coat tree, pulled open the door, and sprinted down the cement steps. The sight of the prison across the street dampened his spirits, a daunting reminder that war still raged beyond this protected town.

Putting those depressing thoughts aside, he covered the few blocks and turned on Fourth. The stately library reminded him of peaceful times and higher pursuits. It fit perfectly with his image of Rose. Too bad she'd felt she had no choice but to give up her place there.

Noah pulled open the heavy oak door and stepped into the hushed atmosphere. The smell of print and leather evoked pleasant memories. Taking a quick look around, he found the sole occupant at the lending desk. It wasn't Rose.

The eyes that twinkled at him from a long, thin face topped by a graying bun bespoke a kind nature. "How may I help you, sir?"

He glanced around the room again, then back at the attendant. A name plate set at an angle on the desk. Its bold letters announced her name. "Are you Miss Pringle?"

"Yes, I am." She emphasized her answer with a precise nod. "And you are?"

"Major Noah Griffin. I'm looking for Miss Carrigan. I was told I could find her here."

"Oh, Miss Carrigan left us some weeks ago, I'm afraid. Quite abruptly too. Did you ask for her at the refugee house?"

"Yes. She's not there. I was told she received word that you were ill and needed her to take your place for a while."

Miss Pringle's hand fluttered to the cameo at her throat. "Ill? Why, I've not been ill in years. Not since the cholera outbreak of Forty-nine. I can't imagine why anyone would send a note that I was ill. Even if I were, we've hired another girl to help in Miss Carrigan's place, so I wouldn't need to enlist her aid at all."

"I see." Something was amiss here. "Well, I thank you for your help, Miss Pringle." On a sudden thought, he turned back to the woman. "Did Rose, er, Miss Carrigan know you'd hired another girl?"

"Not likely. She hasn't been back here since she quit." With a little frown, she added in a sad voice, "Not even to read the newspapers."

Nothing made sense. It was as if Rose played a prank on him. Or someone else used her to upset his plans. A memory of Pierce and Luke laughing at him surfaced. Noah's anger flashed like a lamp turned fully on. He fought to keep his voice even. "Thank you again, Miss Pringle. I believe I know where to look now."

He let the door slam behind him as he sped down the street. Unrestrained, his fury carried him across town until he reached Luke's house.

He burst inside and went straight to the study.

Empty.

He whirled to find the housekeeper staring at him in terror. "Where is he?" he shouted. "Where's Luke?"

Stricken, she pointed to the parlor. Before Noah could follow her direction, Luke hurried into the hallway. "Noah? What's wrong? Why are you—?"

Noah's fist connected with Luke's jaw. His cousin's shocked face mirrored his own feelings. His lack of control embarrassed him, but he had to press on. "Where's Rose?"

"What are you talking about?" Luke worked his jaw.

Jonas and Caroline hurried into the room.

Taking in the scene, Jonas positioned himself between the younger men while Caroline examined Luke.

"Have you lost your mind?" Jonas asked.

Pumping his fists, Noah looked from one to the other. "I believe I have. Or I'm going to if I don't find Rose soon."

Caroline pinned him with a cold stare. "Rose isn't here. And what has that to do with Lucas?"

Luke shot him a knowing chortle "The man's besotted with her and seems to think I might have moved in on his territory."

The housekeeper appeared with a cold cloth for Luke. He gingerly placed it against his jaw.

Luke spoke over the compress. "I'm guessing you didn't find her at the refuge house? What makes you think we might know where she is?"

Noah sank onto the bench in the entry, letting his hands dangle between his knees, his rage spent in the face of Luke's reasonable questions.

"Olivia Spencer said Rose received a note saying she was needed at the library where she used to work. I went to the library, but she wasn't there. She hasn't been there in weeks. I'm afraid Pierce might've abducted her to get back at me."

"Pierce." Luke slid the cloth from his face, and Noah recognized the anger descending. "Wait a minute. You didn't think I'd help Pierce make off with her, did you?"

"I confess it crossed my mind. I struggled with it all the way here, wondering why you'd get in cahoots with him again, with all you've got to lose." He swiped a hand across his face. "I'm sorry. I don't know what came over me. You can hit me back if you want to, but wait until we find Rose."

"I think I'll pass the pain on to Pierce myself, if he's to blame."

Jonas laid a hand on Noah's shoulder. "I think you should give it some thought before you tear off across the country in haste. Is there anyone else who would wish to harm Miss Carrigan?" He turned to his wife. "Caroline, you might know better than we would."

Caroline shook her head, but Luke spoke up. "What about that man at the library? The one who insulted her with his offer?"

Noah drew in a sharp breath. "She turned him down and quit the job. I suppose that might make a man want to strike back at her."

Jonas's brow furrowed. "Or take her by force."

CHAPTER 31

*P*ain radiated from the back of her head as Rose emerged from sleep. She tried to swallow against the tightness in her throat, but her mouth felt dry and rough as a corn cob. She blinked to force her eyes to focus.

Why was it so dark? Usually, the sun streamed through the slender opening where the curtains didn't meet. Had she been sick? Trying to recall her latest movements increased the pain in her temples. She moved to swing her legs over the edge of the bed, pausing as the room swam in her vision. Her fingers encountered the cool smoothness of some fine fabric, silk or satin, she guessed. Certainly not the quilt she was used to.

Where was she?

Pushing the hair from her face, she discovered the remnants of a chignon, now in desperate disarray. Alarm raced through her. No matter how sick or tired she was, she never went to bed without releasing her hair from the uncomfortable confines of pins and ribbon.

Movement in a dark corner increased her anxiety. "So, Sleeping Beauty awakens."

Rose gasped and turned toward the shadowy form. There

was something familiar about the slurred voice, but she couldn't place it. Perhaps drink affected the normal cadence. The clink of glass and sharp odor of alcohol confirmed her theory.

A wave of cold fear threatened her usual composure. Gripping the coverlet, she struggled for a measure of peace. A verse in Isaiah came to mind. "Thou wilt keep him in perfect peace whose mind is stayed on Thee." Her breathing slowed to near normal as reason returned to override the fear.

The man made his way toward her. The bill of a cap shadowed his face.

The man extended a tin cup toward her. "Imagine you must be thirsty. Chloroform does that to a person."

Rose shrank away from the offering, which elicited the man's laughter.

"It's only water. The good stuff is for me. 'Sides, you need to be aware enough to eat when the food gets here."

Thirst tore at her throat. She grasped the cup. After confirming it was indeed water, she gulped, studying the man as he slumped back to his seat. A blue uniform, to be sure, but she couldn't make out the insignia. She must've grown lax in her vigilance, but she should've been safe at the refugee home.

Her head pounded as she tried to place the voice. "Why did I get chloroform?"

He laughed as he picked up the whiskey bottle. Recognition slammed into her. Pierce. Covering her gasp with a cough, she kept her thoughts to herself.

"The stuff knocked you out good. I thought it might be too much, but Vernon wanted to be sure you slept the whole way here."

"Vernon?" Rose nearly dropped the cup. "Vernon Fordham?"

Pierce laughed again. "Knew that'd surprise you. I met Vernon years ago, before the war, then I hunted him up when I got to Louisville back in August. Found we had a lot in common, especially after you got on down at the li-berry."

Taking a moment to digest this information, Rose sipped the water again. She glanced around the dark room, now able to make out a few pieces of furniture. Two narrow beds, the table with two chairs, and the padded chairs flanking the fireplace. A dresser and armoire hugged the far wall.

The sounds of traffic on the street and muted voices from the room below told her they must be at an inn or a boarding house. The furnishings boasted modest affluence, except what inn or rented room came with satin sheets? She regarded the fabric gathered in her hand. Gold satin sheets at that.

She needed to figure out how to get away.

"Why have you brought me here?"

Pierce slammed down his glass and hooted. "You ain't figured it out yet? No wonder Vernon was so determined to take you, you bein' such an innocent. When you refused his generous offer last month, he started working out a plan."

Keep him talking. Maybe appeal to his own agenda. "But…why are *you* here? I don't understand why you'd want to help Vernon if his plan is to get me away from the refugee house. You won't be able to harass me."

He swirled the liquid in the glass. "There's plenty others left to use my charms on. And it gives me great pleasure to interfere with anything or anybody related to Noah Griffin. Since Luke got religion and turned against me, I figured I'd throw in with Vernon's plans for you."

A knock at the door brought Pierce to his feet. "That'll be our food. Don't get any silly ideas about running away. It's cold this close to the river, and you ain't got shoes nor cloak."

Rose hoped the person with the food was a servant. Maybe she could somehow communicate her predicament. Heaven help her if it was Vernon. She trained her eyes on the door as Pierce pulled it open.

∾

*N*oah opened the door and donned his hat. "We'll meet you back at the refugee house within the hour."

Luke followed, Jonas and Caroline behind him.

"Do you doubt my ability to charm Miss Pringle?" Luke asked. "I'll have all Vernon Fordham's information in a matter of minutes."

Jonas joined Noah on the street. "If Lucas can't get the woman at the library to talk, I'm sure Caroline can. Let's hope Miss Carrigan's sister knows something."

Though Noah itched to tear out after anyone who'd harm Rose, Jonas's plan made sense. Miss Pringle might be more forthcoming with a man asking for Fordham to discuss a business proposition. Her reluctance to give information about Rose could be an attempt to protect someone. He prayed the woman wouldn't notice the slight resemblance between him and Luke.

Jonas and Noah took the open-air curricle while Caroline joined Luke in the closed carriage. Trying to view this expedition as a reconnaissance mission, Noah used the short ride to gather his wits. He blessed Caroline for the prayer she'd insisted on saying before the four of them left Luke's house. Shiloh's offer to watch the girls gave Caroline the chance to assist and be on hand for the sake of propriety.

Though it was only mid-afternoon, there was no time to waste with dusk arriving earlier each day. Noah chafed at the traffic on their road. A delivery wagon in front of the city hotel cost them precious minutes. When at last they pulled up to Mrs. Coker's house, Jonas took the lead and used his identity as part owner of the mercantile to grant them entrance.

The man who led them inside offered a seat in the parlor.

"No, thank you," Jonas said. "We're wondering if Miss Carrigan's sister might be here by chance. Major Griffin had planned an outing with her, but she isn't at the refugee home. We thought perhaps she missed his note and came here."

Frustrated by the continuing delays, Noah said, "Or she may have been abducted."

Herbert blanched. "Miss Rose? No, she hasn't been here in several days. I'll call Miss Celeste so you may speak to her. She may have some information."

He hurried down the hall and soon returned with a white-faced Celeste. "What's this about Rose being abducted?"

"We don't know for sure." He told her what had happened.

Celeste clutched Noah's arm. "That man at the library. Mr. Fordham. He was angry when Rose turned him down."

Herbert's sneer overrode his customary decorum. "My guess is Vernon Fordham didn't like being rejected. I regret I ever told Miss Rose about the position there. I had no idea Mr. Fordham had any business with the library, though he does like to poke his nose into everything. If I'd known..."

"Mr. Fordham is one suspect," Jonas said. "Lucas and Caroline are at the library now, hoping to get information about his holdings so we know where to search next."

Celeste said, "Do you think Sergeant Pierce could have a hand in this? He's threatened us more than once. But where would he take her?"

"I don't know," Noah said. "We wanted to check with you first in case Rose was here. We're going to meet Luke and Aunt Caroline at the refugee house to see what they've found out. Is there anywhere else she might have gone?"

"Not as far as I know."

"We're going back to the refugee house."

Celeste began untying her apron. "I'll come with you."

"No." Noah stopped her with a touch. "Please. She still might show up here, and I wouldn't want to put you in harm's way."

"But Herbert will be here."

Herbert nodded when Celeste looked his way.

"He'll take care of Rose and get her back to the refugee house. I promise I won't get in your way. You might need me."

"But we're in the curricle."

She lifted her chin and narrowed her eyes. "I'll squeeze between you."

~

$\mathcal{R}$ose scooped up the mixture of stewed vegetables, forcing the food past the lump in her throat and praying it wouldn't come back up. She'd need her strength to act when she got the opportunity. The clashing odors of cabbage, onions, and whiskey only made it harder to swallow the meal.

Pierce apparently found the food to his liking. He shoveled in bite after bite, pausing now and then to wash it down with water since his supply of spirits had dwindled to fumes.

He nodded to her still full bowl. "It beats what passes for dinner in the refugee house for certain. This is what a supply of coin can do, buy the best meal in the inn, even if it is on the river." He stopped suddenly and tilted his head, listening.

Rose heard scuffling in the hall, but the noise receded and faded into stillness.

She had no idea whether the boy who'd delivered their meal had understood her silent message. As soon as he glanced her way, she'd mouthed "help" and pressed her hands in an attitude of prayer. Pierce had pulled a coin from his pocket and flipped it to the boy while taking the tray.

The boy gave no sign he understood.

Dear God in heaven, why was she facing this again?

Pierce glanced at his pocket watch and scowled. "Vernon better get on back here. He knows I got guard duty tonight, and Goodwin won't be happy if I'm late."

Though she dreaded to ask, Rose cleared her throat. "Where did he go?"

"Go?" Pierce scoffed. "He ain't been here yet. Far be it from Vernon Fordham to dirty his hands with real work. No, he pays for what he wants done, then shows up to collect the reward. I don't know where he gets the blunt, but he always has plenty and makes sure everybody knows it."

"I noticed that about him also. He likes the attention."

"That's for certain." Pierce pinned her with a frown. "He don't like to be refused. That's where you made your mistake. You should've taken what he offered. Not that I care. You played right into my plan."

"How so? I don't understand." Although she could guess. The more Pierce talked, the more she'd learn about her location. Maybe something would trigger an idea for how to get away.

He stacked the dishes on the tray. "We'd been waiting for days to find the right time to grab you. Vernon found a note stuck in a book at the li-berry. Seems the old lady started writing to see how you're getting along but never finished it, probably forgot where she put it. Anyway, I wrote the rest, copying her hand and asking you to go take her place."

No wonder the writing had looked different halfway through the note. She'd assumed it was due to Miss Pringle's illness.

Pierce chuckled at her expression. "Fooled you good, didn't it?"

"You knew I'd rush right over to help her."

He slapped his knee. "They don't call you Miss Goody-Goody for nothing." He cackled, then suddenly frowned. "Trouble is, while you went to get your cloak, another note came from Griffin. Naturally, I took it and threw it in the trash. Knowing he was on his way to take you riding, we had to move fast. I didn't know how quick the chloroform would knock you out, so I figured a hit on the head from my pistol would help it along."

"Why do you hate me so much, Sergeant Pierce? What did I do to cause that, besides trying to protect my sister? How could I know whether you would harm one of us?"

"Oh, it ain't you I hate. You're just a means to an end. I figure hurting you will get back at Griffin for his interference in my life. Mine and my family's."

Rose couldn't deny the relationship between herself and Noah. Perhaps she could convince Pierce that Noah was innocent of the charges he held against him, or at least not worth the effort of hatred. "What did Noah do to interfere with your family? Whatever it was, it must've happened before the war. And you've carried that grudge all these years. Don't you know hate does more harm to the hater than his victim?"

"Don't matter now. Revenge is gonna be sweet, and the day has finally come."

He prowled the room, glowering. He knocked over one of the spindle chairs and sent it skittering across the room.

Rose scurried to the far corner to avoid his agitated wandering.

"As for what he did," Pierce said, "he turned my best friend against me. He made sure I was put in jail for a little prank while he and Luke got off scot-free. But worst of all, he left my sister with child. She pined after him nearly to death."

The news hit her like a physical blow. Her stomach roiled with nausea, but surely this couldn't be true. Pierce had lied about her, so he could be lying now. She wondered if he had some sickness in his mind that made him believe the lies he told. He had a warped view of the world and how justice was served. Had the war done that to him?

Rose had no answers. She huddled in one of the chairs near the fireplace. She closed her eyes and prayed silently. *Father God, please help me. Show me a way out of this predicament.*

Pierce strode to the window and jerked aside the curtain. He peered into the gathering dusk. "If Vernon don't get here soon, I'll have to figure out what to do with you. This close to the river, it'd be easy for someone to drown."

Rose shivered. She believed he could do it.

CHAPTER 32

oah unfolded the paper John Mark pressed into his hand. The boy leaned against the refugee home's doorjamb, spent from his race of several blocks, while Noah read the terse note.

VF at LL. Come unseen.

"Who gave this to you?" Noah asked.

He trusted the boy, but someone could be using him to throw off their search. He waited for John Mark to catch his breath.

"Mr. Turner," he said, wheezing.

"And how did you happen to see Mr. Turner? Where were you?"

Jonas tugged at Noah's arm. "Give him a minute, Major. It appears he's run a ways."

The boy panted. "From the schoolhouse." He continued, punctuating his statement with deep draws of breath. "I stayed after the others left...so the teacher could show me how to do them tables." He heaved again. "I was leaving when Mr. Turner come up...and told me to run here fast. Said he had to get back to the library...so's he could follow somebody."

Noah passed the note to Jonas to confirm his interpretation. "Fordham is at the library now."

"Luke must believe Fordham is up to something shady if he wants us to remain out of sight." Jonas stroked his chin. "We can park the curricle up the street and pretend to be inspecting the wheels."

"Good plan. Let's go." He started toward the door.

Jonas pulled him back. "Exchange your jacket and hat for something less noticeable. Perhaps Isaac will let you borrow his coat and wool cap. The two of you are near the same size."

Noah begrudged any delay but agreed with Jonas's wisdom. When he returned from Isaac's room, he hurried past Jonas. "Let's go."

John Mark still lingered near the door. "Major Griffin, you're going to find her, ain't you? Miss Rose, I mean?" The worry in his eyes fueled Noah's resolve.

Noah gripped the boy's shoulder. "We are, John Mark. No matter how long it takes, we'll find her." He turned to Celeste. "We'll be back as soon as possible."

The men drove the curricle to Fourth Avenue. Jonas parked as close as he dared to the library, noting Luke's carriage near the entrance and a landau across the street.

"Since I've not met Fordham or Miss Pringle," Jonas said, "I'll go inside to see what's going on. You pretend to inspect the wheel."

Noah's anxiety sharpened his senses, much the way it did before battle. His muscles tensed, ready for action, as he focused on the building. Minutes later, Luke sauntered outside. He glanced both ways and headed toward the curricle. He kept his back to the library entrance as he joined Noah in his examination of the wheel.

"He'll be coming out momentarily. I overheard him tell Miss Pringle he'd be away for a few days. We ought to—"

"Shh." Noah hissed and dropped to his haunches. "Someone's coming out."

Their suspect carried a large basket in one hand and some books in the other. He placed the items inside the landau and climbed onto the driver's seat.

Jonas and Caroline exited the building as Fordham drove off. Luke and Noah hopped into the curricle and followed Fordham at a discreet distance while Jonas turned the carriage and fell in behind them. Traffic was light, which helped them keep their quarry in sight.

Noah held his breath as they drew near Market Street, praying Fordham wasn't headed for the depot. When the way cleared, Fordham turned right, and Noah released a prayer of thanks. But this direction led to the ferry.

He and Luke exchanged a look of dread. If Fordham crossed the river, it would be more difficult to follow him. They might lose him entirely. Noah could lose their only link to Rose.

～

*R*ose's hopes of a quick rescue dimmed with every degree of the sinking sun. The servant boy either hadn't comprehended her message or didn't want to offer help. It could be hours before anyone realized she was in trouble, and how would they know where to search for her?

A crisp knock sounded on the room door.

Pierce donned his hat and jacket. He threw her a satisfied smirk. "By the way, your shoes and cloak are under the bed. But you won't be needing them for a while, I expect. Vernon plans to keep you busy here. Best get used to this room."

She faked indifference. "Vernon may get a few surprises. I don't give in easily."

Pierce yanked open the door, and Rose stood, stiff with apprehension.

The same serving boy entered carrying a large basket.

Vernon followed and blocked the way. His gaze wandered around the room.

The boy threw Rose an apologetic look as he set down the basket and picked up the tray of empty dishes, then hurried to the door. He caught the coin Vernon flipped his way before the door shut behind him.

Rose let her gaze slide to the floor as the men carried on a low-voiced conversation. Pierce grumbled something about being late, and Vernon answered gruffly.

Pierce jerked open the door and stalked out, leaving it swinging on silent hinges.

Vernon took quick steps to shut it and secure the lock. With precise movements, he removed his bowler and overcoat and hung them on the pegs near the door.

Turning toward Rose, he smoothed his hands down his embroidered vest.

She raised her head in defiance. She may not look the part—disheveled as she was—but she would behave like the lady she'd always been.

Frowning, he took two steps in her direction. "I apologize for the rough treatment Pierce inflicted on you, my dear. He does tend to overdo at times, but you'll recover soon enough."

He gestured toward the basket on the table. "Have you eaten? It's too bad I couldn't be here sooner, but I had important business to attend." He held out a chair and gestured her to sit.

Rose stiffened. "I've eaten."

"Then sit and watch while I eat. I confess I'm famished." Though the words held no threat in themselves, his tone brooked no refusal.

She managed to evade his touch as she obeyed. Perhaps she could grab some cutlery and force him to let her go.

∾

*N*oah and Luke sat beneath an old oak tree across the road from the inn. Noah counted three carriages in the yard besides Fordham's landau. A coach for hire passed them and rumbled to the front door. The inn was busy and seemed respectable, although not the best he'd seen. It was off the main road but seemed to maintain a steady business. Jonas and Caroline waited farther down the road in case a second line of defense was needed.

Following Fordham had proved surprisingly easy. He clearly had no fear of being watched. He didn't even glance around when he left his vehicle and entered the inn.

As Luke and Noah argued over who should go into the inn and make inquiries, Luke spotted a soldier exiting the building. "Look there. Is that Pierce?"

They waited for him to step into better light for positive identification.

"He's waiting for the hostler to bring his ride, I expect." Noah started to leave the curricle. "We can jump him. You go right and I'll go left."

Luke gripped his arm. "Hold up. We need to draw him away from the stables. I wonder if he likes to smoke?" He patted his pocket with the cigar he'd pilfered from Jonas's supply. "I'll get Jonas to play the part while you circle around."

Noah jumped to the ground and made his way around the coach being unloaded, keeping his head down and his shoulders hunched over. He paused when Jonas called out to Pierce about a light and the offer of a cigar.

Pierce stepped closer to inspect the stranger. When Jonas extended the bait, Luke and Noah sprang the trap. A clout on the head elicited a soft grunt, and the three dragged him to the carriage where Caroline waited.

Noah's plucky aunt pointed a revolver in Pierce's face.

"Where's Rose? We know you brought her here. What's the room number?"

The man smirked. "C'mon, lady. You won't shoot me, and I know this guy—" he jerked his head toward Noah—"ain't got it in 'im."

Caroline cocked the firearm. "Noah might not, but I sure do. You want to lose a leg over this?" She aimed the gun at his knee, and Pierce went white.

"No number. End of the second floor on the left. But you—"

Luke plowed his fist into the man's mouth, effectively stopping his words.

Noah regarded his cousin in some surprise. "Feel better?"

"Much."

Luke and Noah tied up their captive while Jonas took the pistol from Caroline. The three of them lifted Pierce into the carriage amidst a string of protests and threats.

"Oh, would somebody shut him up?" Caroline dug into her reticule and produced a lacy piece of cloth. "I don't mind sitting with him while you men go get Rose, but I won't listen to his foul language."

After the men gagged Pierce, they moved to the inn, Luke and Jonas covering the back while Noah went inside. He wandered into the busy taproom first, stashed his cap in his back pocket, and glanced around as if searching for someone. He didn't want to draw anyone's attention, at least not yet.

As he neared the stairs, the harried manager stepped in his path. "Do you need a room, sir?" His glance carried disdain for Noah's worn jacket then jerked up at the sight of his uniform trousers.

Noah raised his eyebrows to emulate his commanding officer's patronizing expression. Sometimes a display of arrogance accomplished more than words. "I do not. I'm meeting my associate in his room."

The man bowed and moved away. Noah continued to the

271

steps and up to the second floor, where he paused outside the door to listen and weigh his options for gaining entrance.

"Psst. Mister."

Noah whirled around to find a serving boy hovering a few feet away.

"Are you here to help the lady in there?" He lifted a bony finger toward the door at Noah's back.

"She's in there? Did she ask for help?"

The boy shook his head. "Only gave me a look, but I knowed she was in trouble when he brought her in. She was out like my granny gets after taking her medicine. Let me do the secret knock for you."

Noah figured it was as good as anything he'd come up with. He pointed the boy forward. The youngster rapped on the door and scampered off like a frightened bird, disappearing in the stairwell.

Commotion on the other side of the door sounded like a chair toppling over and dishes crashing. A man's roar of pain followed. Noah slammed his shoulder into the door and plowed straight into a startled man opening the door with bloody hands. Continuing his momentum, Noah straddled the man and slammed his fist into his jaw.

The act didn't satisfy, as his victim already lay in a faint. He raised his eyes to find Rose, frozen in stunned tableau, staring at him. She held a broken bottle, evidence of its last use dripping on the floor.

❧

*R*ose stared at the jagged glass, streaked with blood where she'd slashed it across Vernon's hands when he reached for her. Stunned that her ploy for escape had worked, she couldn't figure out how her attacker had landed on the floor.

"Rose, are you all right?"

Noah? How was he here?

He snatched a discarded napkin from the table and positioned it between Vernon's bleeding palms. Then, he bound the man's hands with a length of leather.

When did Noah arrive? Vernon lay motionless. Had she killed him? But then why would Noah tie him up?

Noah stood and moved to her side. "Are you hurt?" Gently, he urged the broken bottle out of her hands and laid it on the table. He gripped her shoulders and pulled her into his arms.

Noah was here.

He was here, and she was safe.

She burst into ragged sobs.

"Shh. You're all right. It's over."

She peered over Noah's shoulder as Luke spoke from the doorway, his pistol at the ready. "It's over?" He glanced around the room. "Well, shucks, Noah. You take all the fun out of playing a Pinkerton man. I wanted to get a hit on this character as well."

Luke prodded Vernon's inert form and holstered his weapon. "Let me get Jonas up here to help with this blackguard. I'll be right back."

Rose shuddered. "He isn't dead, is he?"

"No," Noah said. "I hit him pretty hard when he opened the door. Then for added measure, I planted a facer to keep him down until Luke could get here."

Noah pushed her tumbled hair aside, reminding Rose of her disheveled state. She glanced at the blood spatters on her bodice and shivered.

"Where's your cloak? And your shoes? We need to be ready to leave as soon as Luke and Jonas return."

"Under...under the bed, Pierce said. I haven't had a...a chance to look."

Noah righted the chair she'd knocked over when she

grabbed the whiskey bottle and urged her to sit. After she was settled, he peered under the bed and grabbed her things. He shook out her cloak and set it over her shoulders. "Here, I'll help with your shoes."

Rose braced herself against the table and lifted one foot.

Noah pushed on the first scuffed boot, then reached for the other. "Very serviceable," he said. His comment had probably been aimed to soothe her, but she could only nod.

Holding the second shoe, he paused and looked into her eyes. "Well, Cinderella, if this shoe fits, we must hurry to the carriage before it reverts to a pumpkin."

Rose found an answering smile, weak and wobbly though it felt. "I believe you've muddled your story line, sir, but I am quite willing to leave this place post haste."

He slipped the boot on her foot and tugged her to stand beside him. "Then let's find that carriage and deliver you to the palace."

Luke guffawed from the doorway. "Whether you mean my home or the refugee house, I doubt either can be classified as a palace, Prince Griffin, but it will suffice for the time."

Jonas entered behind Luke. "Glad to see you're unharmed, Miss Carrigan." He squatted beside Vernon. "Luke, grab that side, and let's haul this fellow down to the constable."

Luke took up a position on Vernon's other side but gestured for Noah and Rose to go ahead. She clung to Noah as he led her from the room.

He pulled her close and spoke into her ear. "The question is whether you'll settle for an Army Major in place of a prince."

She took a moment to formulate her response. "I would much prefer this Army Major to any prince."

Assuming she ever felt normal again.

CHAPTER 33

*N*oah found himself tossing about ways to broach the topic of his relationship with Rose.

After long hours spent explaining the circumstances of Friday—to the deputy who met them at the inn, to the Union officers connected to Pierce, to the residents at the refugee house—he could claim to have lost his voice, at least until he could sleep for a few hours. He'd delivered Rose into the arms of her sister and friends as soon as she'd given her statement to the authorities. He left strict orders for her to spend the next day resting.

"I'll come again on Sunday to see how you're faring." Noah hoped she understood more than his words, but he didn't press her. She'd seemed ready to collapse, and the day's events had sapped his energy as well.

That was Friday. Today was Sunday, and he allowed his hopes to rise for a better outing. With Pierce and Fordham taken care of, perhaps now they could make plans for the future.

He wanted to visit the home place soon, before he was forced to return to duty, and he wanted Rose with him. He'd ask Celeste to join them for the sake of propriety.

In less than two weeks, his family would commemorate the day of thanksgiving set aside by President Lincoln. He expected it to be a great celebration, with Eliza and Ben arriving with his parents' first grandchild. Introducing Rose as his future wife would add to their delight.

Noah waited for a farmer's wagon to pass before he crossed Broadway to the refuge house. As he reached the gate, the front door opened, and several women emerged. He could now name everyone without hesitation, but his gaze centered on Rose. Before he could utter a greeting, John Mark and Wade Spencer claimed his attention, clamoring for an account of Friday's harrowing expedition.

"Boys." Olivia called them back. "Not now. We should focus on giving thanks and lifting our praise to God. Time enough for tales of rescue and adventure when we return from church."

Everyone seemed determined to protect Rose from any outsiders, including Noah. The women clustered around her like a clutch of broody hens, leaving him to fall in line with the men and boys at the rear of the procession. The closest he could get during church was the bench behind her, where he bunched in with the other males.

Finally, he managed to slip next to her as they left the church. He raised his voice so everyone could hear and made his announcement. "I've been instructed to take Miss Rose to my cousin's house so Cook and Gertie and Victoria can see for themselves she is safe and well. Would anyone else care to join us?" He felt obliged to offer but fervently hoped nobody would accept the invitation.

Various excuses accompanied inquisitive glances until he finally settled Rose's hand on his sleeve and started off. They covered the first block in silence. When Rose still didn't speak,

Noah began to worry. Perhaps her recent experience had affected her health more than she'd let on.

"You are well, are you not? Recovered from the madness of the other day?"

"Yes, thank you."

The terse stiffness of her answer, though, told Noah she wasn't pleased about something. He cast about for the reason and came up with nothing. Braving the waters, he touched her hand and stopped walking.

"What's wrong? Do you not wish to go to Luke's house? If that's the case, I'll return you at once."

"No, it's..." She removed her hand from his arm. Looking skyward, as if in prayer, she drew in a ragged breath. "What you did back there, taking charge without asking me if I cared to go. Why do you men do that?"

Noah flinched and searched for an answer. "I don't know. I guess we're just used to taking the lead." He resisted the impulse to reach for her again. "Perhaps I've been in command too long. I issue orders without considering how they're perceived because it's what my men expect. I guess I need to accustom myself to being around women again. Please accept my apologies."

Rose directed her gaze across the street with the delicate shrug he'd come to recognize. "I apologize as well." A sheepish smile and sparkling eyes reassured him. "Perhaps I read too many of those suffragists' pamphlets at the library."

"Or perhaps you still haven't recovered from the events of the other day. I'd hoped we could have some time to ourselves. To talk."

A blush stained her cheeks. "We may not be able to talk at Luke's house either." She placed her hand on his sleeve again.

"At least there won't be as many people there to interrupt, and I don't think they'll hover over you like the others."

He urged her forward with a gentle nudge. "Aunt Caroline

has gone back to Frankfort with Jonas and the girls, so it's only Luke and Victoria with Cook and Gertie."

"I know. Olivia said she and her family plan to go over next week for a special meal. It seems she and Jonas are making progress toward mending things between them."

Noah hoped Rose wouldn't take offense at the suggestion he was going to make, but he dared not wait for another opportunity.

"That gives them even more reason to celebrate Thanksgiving. I'm hoping to go home myself for a few days. I'd like you to go with me. You and Celeste or whoever else you'd want to go along."

She paused to look at him fully. "Your home is close by then? I know Indiana is just across the river. Quite a few refugees from Georgia went over when it got too crowded here." Rose nibbled her bottom lip, her brow furrowed. "Janie Wilson mentioned she might go too if things don't improve here. She's afraid the children might get sick again this winter. Plus, it would be closer to Pete at the prison in Ohio."

"Perhaps we could scout the situation there for Mrs. Wilson. Maybe Ben and Eliza could help her find a position and place to live. My folks live in the country, not far into Indiana, but Ben's practice is in New Albany, and he knows most of the people."

"He's a doctor then?"

Noah chuckled and shook his head. "No, he faints at the sight of blood. Ben's a lawyer. Here we are." He gestured her inside the gate ahead of him and lifted the door knocker.

The door swung open to a frowning Gertie. "So, you do know how to knock and enter a house like a gentleman." She gave him a fierce scowl then turned to Rose. "And how are you doing, dear girl? We was so worried for you." The housekeeper murmured more words of comfort as she ushered Rose into the foyer past a grinning Luke.

Noah's cousin grabbed him by the arm and pulled him into

the house. "Come on in, Noah. She'll forgive you for barging in the other day, maybe in a year or two."

~

ose soon heard all about Noah's unmannerly entrance on Friday. Now that the Richardson clan had gone, the servants joined the family and guests in the small dining area. Gertie expressed her dismay at finding Noah in the hallway, calling for Luke, on that fateful day. "Then without so much as a howdy-do, he hauls off and punches Mr. Lucas in the jaw."

Lucas played his part, moving his jaw side to side and touching the uneven circle of dark blue. "It still smarts too."

Unperturbed, Noah stabbed a piece of potato with his fork. "For the record, I apologized and offered to let Luke hit me back."

Rose glanced from one man to the other. "But I don't understand why you'd hit Lucas."

Luke waved away the breadbasket Cook held out to him. "He had to vent some of the anger he'd built up on the way from the library. In his faulty reasoning, he thought I might've hooked up again with Pierce to settle earlier quarrels."

Rose remembered the tales Pierce had spewed about Noah. Should she ask about them? Perhaps later when they were alone.

Victoria, who'd followed the adult conversation with surprising interest, spoke up. "Who is Pierce, Papa?"

"Someone Cousin Noah and I used to play with when we were children. But he turned out to be someone we didn't like."

Confusion mingled with her alarm. "And he lives in our town? But I thought he was a soldier."

Noah hurried to assure her. "He was, Poppet, but the Army found out about the bad things he did and sent him away. Rest easy. You don't have to worry about him coming around anymore." His gaze slid to Rose to underscore his words.

She no longer fretted over what Pierce might do, but he'd stirred up a hornet's nest of worry about her relationship with Noah. Plus, she had her own secrets to share. Her fairytale dreams threatened to crumble into ashes like the mill that brought them together. As much as she dreaded the coming discussion, it had to happen.

In an obvious attempt to steer the conversation in another direction, Lucas asked Noah about news from the front and orders for his division.

"It'll take some time to get the Seventh refitted, and most of the men will get furlough over the next few weeks. I plan to take some time myself and head home. I'm hoping Rose and her sister will accompany me."

"I don't know whether Celeste will be able to leave," Rose said. "Though Mrs. Coker's regular cook is back in the kitchen, both women still rely heavily on my sister. Perhaps something can be worked out. Luke, do you plan to join your folks in Frankfort?"

Luke shifted in his seat, sneaking a peek at his daughter. "I believe we'll stay here and enjoy the quiet." When Victoria groaned, he added, "I was thinking of inviting Miss Emily and her family for Thanksgiving, though, so Victoria will have some company. Will that be too much trouble for you, Busy Bee?"

Cook swatted him playfully as she loaded dishes on a tray. "Now you know I'm happiest when I'm making a meal, and it's easier to cook for a dozen than for two or three. You just let me know how many to prepare for."

"I'm sure Emily and Ada will be glad to help with the preparations, Cook," Rose said. "We've all learned to pitch in wherever we can. Sarah Grace will be thrilled to see Victoria again." She turned to Lucas. "Do you still plan for Emily and me to continue coming here, now you're in town and your mother has left?"

Luke ran a hand through his hair. "Hmm. I could do most of my work from the store here. I wonder… Do you think Victoria is ready to attend a regular school?"

"I'm not qualified to say, but you could ask Miss Dodd at the school to test her."

All eyes turned to Victoria, who clutched her hands together in a gesture of prayer. "Oh, yes, please! I could be at school and not bother you and Cook and Gertie while you're working."

"All right," Lucas said. He pulled at his daughter's braid. "I'll go to the school tomorrow and ask. But remember, we must abide by the teacher's decision. You may have to wait until next year."

As the group moved toward the parlor, Luke pulled Rose aside. "You're free to go with Noah either way. I believe Emily would be willing to help if we need her."

Noah flashed a wide grin at Rose, sure of getting his wish, but Lucas provided her a choice. "However, you're welcome to stay and join us for Thanksgiving dinner if you decide you'd rather not go with my dear cousin."

"You know I could give you a matching bruise on the other side of your jaw," Noah said. "Don't make it so easy for her to refuse my offer."

Lucas fingered his jaw and winced. "You do pack some power there. But I think you owe me already. Maybe I should spend a few hours telling Rose about our younger, wilder days."

"You mean *your* wilder days." Noah poked Luke's chest. "I was the one who had to rescue you and Pierce, not always with the best results."

Rose drew a breath for courage and dared to interrupt their teasing. "Actually, Pierce told me some things on Friday while he was waiting for Vernon at the inn."

Both men looked at her warily. "What things?"

Rose made sure Victoria was occupied in the corner with her dolls and no longer listening to their conversation. "Something about leaving him in jail for a prank y'all pulled." She swallowed. "And Noah fathering a child with his sister Alice."

She tensed as both faces darkened in anger. Luke clenched his fists while Noah's jaw jutted to contain the words he likely wanted to release. "You remember," Noah said, "I told you early on that Pierce twists the truth to fit his warped view of things."

"Then there is some truth to what he said?"

Noah dipped his chin in acknowledgment. "Half-truths. He told you only enough to cast doubt on Luke and me. I'll try to explain, though I'd rather not expose you to such ugliness in the world."

"I think I can handle the story, Major. I've come across my share of ugliness in my life."

Noah's face was grim, but he offered his hand. "Come walk with me."

CHAPTER 34

*M*oah struggled to keep his anger at bay as he led Rose outside then paced away from her. Pierce still worked his evil, even from afar, sowing seeds of doubt. He returned to the bench where Rose sat. She held herself erect, braced for the worst, it seemed. Perhaps she dreaded to hear this story as much as he despised having to say it.

"Pierce's sister was, or is, a couple of years older than Pierce and Luke and me. She's right pretty but a little slow in her thinking. Some say she had an accident as a child that made her that way. Everyone who grew up near us knew how she was and accepted it. When new folks came in, though, they treated her differently. Either they made fun of her or took advantage of her."

Noah sat and took her hand in his. "One fellow played up to her with sweet words and promised to marry her. Alice was probably eighteen and had no experience with men. She fell for him and did whatever he wanted. After"—Noah wasn't about to spell it out—"he bragged about it to the fellers when Pierce wasn't around. By the time it was evident she carried a child, the rogue had left town, but not before spreading lies that both

Luke and me had...had opportunity to put Alice in such a predicament."

"Pierce believed those lies," she said.

Noah nodded. "Yeah, but instead of challenging us like a man, he came up with a scheme designed to get Luke and me into a heap of trouble with the law. Unfortunately for him, it backfired, and he ended up spending time in jail."

"He fell into his own trap, like it says in Psalms." Rose shook her head. "As much as I want to hate him for all he did, I find I feel sorry for him. He's truly a sad, mixed-up soul."

"I think that experience is the reason Aunt Caroline decided to move away, to get Luke away from Pierce's influence. Luke didn't want to move. He blamed me at the time, and we had a big row over it. Pierce tried to say we were fighting over his sister, but nobody believed that. Her father tried to blame one of us, too, trying to pawn her off on a family with more resources than he had. I think he ended up sending Alice to her aunt in Missouri."

Noah lifted Rose's chin with one finger. "Have I said enough to exonerate Luke and me? You're free to ask anyone in my family to assure you of the truth, if you're willing to make the visit next week."

"Your word is good enough for me. I well understand how misunderstandings can undermine someone's reputation."

She looked away and twisted her fingers. "One reason I've been quarrelsome today—and hesitant to accept your invitation —is that I have something to tell you about my past. You may want to sever our relationship when you hear it, and if that's the case, then I'll accept your choice."

He laid his hand across hers and squeezed gently. "Rose, I don't think you could tell me anything that would make me feel differently about you. I've seen you at your worst, and I hope you never have to witness any worse from me than what you saw on Friday."

She shook her head and tugged until he released her hand. "Friday's events are what made me realize I had to tell you. You see, it wasn't the first time a man held me somewhere against my will. Like Alice, the shame of it... It's the reason my family moved away from Tennessee."

~

*T*he familiar flush of shame washed over Rose as she began to recite those events. "Where I grew up, the boys tended to shun me because they thought I was snobbish. The truth is, I loved reading and learning about new things, and I wanted to share what I learned with others. Sometimes, I guess I tried a little too hard to instruct the people around me.

"Anyway, the summer before I turned eighteen, a new man came to work at the bank in town. He was nice looking and had good manners. Everyone liked him. Some of the church women played matchmaker, pairing him off with me. Strangely enough, it worked. Lawrence seemed smitten, and I felt gratified to have someone court me at last."

She glanced away from the tender compassion in his eyes.

"I guess it didn't turn out well?"

Rose gave a harsh laugh. "You could say that." She pinched her lips and blinked away the threatening tears. She stared at the house, seeing instead pictures from the past. She had to get through this tale.

"We were going on a picnic with some other young people but got separated from the group. I thought we were lost, but Lawrence knew exactly where he was and what he'd planned. We stopped to let the horse drink at a creek, and he announced the rear wagon wheel was cracked and too dangerous to drive. He assured me someone would come hunting for us shortly, and it was useless to start walking since we were lost. It started to rain, so we took cover in an old line-shack."

She wrapped her arms around her middle. "Evidently, he'd planned ahead. Everything was in place. He slipped something in my drink. I remember sitting in the chair, then waking up on the cot. Lawrence was gone, and it was dark. Fear kept me from leaving. When the search party found me, they assumed the worst because they knew we'd been together."

Noah muttered something murderous under his breath, but she pressed onward.

"The next day we found he'd left town. I was left to bear the shame of having trusted the bounder. The church leaders encouraged my father to move away. I think they discerned the truth, but it was easier on everyone for us to relocate."

Noah moved behind her and wrapped her in a loose embrace. "I believe there's a special punishment reserved for men who use women in such a despicable way. But why would he go to such lengths to compromise you? Had you embarrassed him somehow?"

"He was out for revenge." One tear slid down her face as she confessed the rest of the story. "He had the gall to leave me a note so I'd know. Lawrence was the older brother of a child who died while we lived in Ohio. We didn't recognize him because he lived with grandparents who put him through university. Turns out Lawrence was actually Lance, as we'd known him in Ohio."

Noah lifted a handkerchief to catch the tears she couldn't blink away. He pressed the cloth into her hands, and she dabbed her face and swiped her nose before continuing.

"Lawrence went to Maryville to get revenge against my family, me in particular. You see, his little brother slipped away while I was watching several children at our house. Mother was seriously ill, and I'd sent Celeste to find Da and the doctor. I couldn't leave the other small children unattended to search for one missing boy."

"The child was injured or lost?"

She nodded. "Kicked by a cow in the pasture. His mama nearly went mad with grief when he died. I guess that's what drove Lawrence. He'd hated me for years and figured the best revenge would be to ruin my life like I'd ruined his mother's life."

Noah gathered Rose in his arms, allowing her to weep until her knees threatened to give way. He sat on the bench, taking her with him, whispering comfort and pressing kisses to her temple. "While it angers me that he mistreated you so, I am greatly relieved you didn't have to marry the cad."

"Looking back, I don't think I would have, despite the repercussions. My father would have supported my decision."

She raised her hand to touch Noah's face. "That's why I find it hard to trust men. It's why I kept finding fault with you while we were in Georgia, pushing you away even when you were kind. I hated the idea of coming north, imagining all the men here were like Lawrence. When you said we'd be riding in closed in rail cars, it brought back visions of the tiny line shack where Lawrence took me."

Noah tipped his head. "The day you nearly fainted in Roswell, you envisioned a repetition of those events?"

"Yes. I panicked at the thought of being in a dark, closed place like a rail car."

They ceased talking for a few minutes, merely absorbing each other's presence. Rose's thoughts retraced her journey to Louisville. "When I received your first letter, I imagined you wrote only to accuse me of something, especially considering the way we'd parted in Marietta."

"Oh, my sweet Rose. I'm sorry. I had to review my thinking over those weeks. Issues I'd always considered black and white didn't seem so distinct. I wrestled with them, trying to fit everything into neat boxes, but I've found you can't always do so."

She fingered the top button of his jacket and traced the thread along the side. "One day you'll have to tell me about those times and how the women you met changed your thinking."

Noah lifted her chin to look him in the eye. "Do I detect a note of jealousy? Nothing to warrant it, I promise. But you still haven't said whether you'll come with me to Indiana."

She threw him a teasing smile. "Maybe. We'll see what Celeste thinks."

~

*A*fter a leisurely visit at Luke's, they went to Mrs. Coker's house to present the idea to Celeste.

"Mrs. Coker has retired for the night, but I'll ask her after breakfast tomorrow." She tossed Rose a teasing grin. "Although she really doesn't need me, and I'm afraid if I leave for a while, she'll discover the truth of it." She removed a dead leaf from the flowers in a vase on the side table. "But what if I don't go and the two of you decide to marry while you're there with his family? I would miss the wedding, and you wouldn't come back here, and I might never see you again or even know how to find you."

Rose laughed and swatted Celeste's arm. "You're jumping much too far ahead, Sugar. He hasn't asked me to marry him, only to meet his family."

She caught Noah looking their way from the room across the hallway. Rose lifted her shoulders in a helpless gesture. Herbert had invited Noah to view the late Mr. Coker's collection of pipes and firearms. Somehow the older man knew the women needed some time to themselves.

Celeste noticed the exchange with Noah. "Oh, he will ask you, and soon if I don't mistake it. Meeting the family is the proper first step. Once they approve his choice, which they are certain to do, it's only a matter of finding some privacy so he can propose officially."

Celeste blinked a few times but smiled. "So, I guess I'd better go with you, as your only family. I want to be sure they know what a jewel they'll be getting."

"Oh, Celeste." Rose squeezed her sister's hands. "How I've missed having you to talk with every night. I know it's best for you to stay here and not have to walk from the refugee house every day, but it's the longest we've been apart."

"Well, you'd best get used to it. Once you marry, we could be miles apart."

"I guess we always knew that might happen one day. We must contrive some way to get together from time to time, no matter where the future finds us. And at least we'll have a few days on our way to Indiana."

Noah stepped behind Rose. "I hope you've agreed to come with us, Celeste?"

She heaved a dramatic sigh. "I suppose I must. I can't have my sister going off with you alone. Besides, unless you're a decent campfire cook, Major, the two of you will be forced to eat hardtack on the road."

"I'm not that bad at cooking," Rose protested.

But Noah only laughed.

"There are places to get a meal along the way, and a few inns to keep us from traveling in the dark," he said. "I won't expect either of you to provide anything but your fine company."

"That's good to know," Rose said.

"It's getting late," Noah said. "I should take Rose back to the house. Before we leave town, I'll check to see if we might be needed to testify against Pierce and Fordham. It may take a couple of days to put everything in order, but we should be able to leave before the end of the week. Will that give you ladies time to prepare?"

Celeste motioned toward the kitchen. "I'll probably cook up everything I can find, some of it to take with us. Beyond that, I don't have much to do."

Rose frowned. "I want to be sure Millie and Baby Amy will be all right. I know Lydia and Dorcas take good care of them, but they don't have many resources."

"I can ask Luke to check on everyone while we're away," Noah said. "We'll be sure they know how to contact him if they need anything."

Celeste added her assurances. "I'll give them Mrs. Coker's address too. At least they won't have to worry about Pierce being there to bother anyone."

"All right then." Noah turned to Rose. "Let's be on our way so this good woman can start cooking everything in sight."

Herbert met them in the hall with a lantern. "Darkness is descending quickly, and it looks like we're in for some rain. I will light your way to the carriage, Major, if you don't mind."

"Not at all. I appreciate your consideration. When Luke offered the use of it, I didn't expect to need the lamps."

"One can never be too careful these days, with all the new people coming in and not finding sufficient work or supplies."

The men kept Rose between them as they rounded the corner to the mews in the twilight. The circle of light from Herbert's lantern caught movement near the stable door. Rose couldn't prevent her gasp of surprise to see three figures moving toward them.

~

*N*oah's right hand moved toward his weapon while he stepped in front of Rose to shield her from the men coming their way.

"Who's there?" Herbert called, raising the lamp higher.

"Herbert?" The voice sounded strained.

The center figure leaned heavily on the companion on his right. The visitors had a better view of Herbert and Noah, thanks to the proximity of the lantern.

Herbert responded. "Lieutenant Hart?"

Another voice called out to them, "Noah?"

"Yes," the first voice returned.

The stable boy called from the wounded man's other side. "It be Mr. Gideon, I mean Lieutenant Hart, and he be mighty ill."

Both groups moved closer, and Noah found his friend's face. "Cooper?"

"Major," the boy said to Noah, "your carriage is set to go, but de Lieutenant and Captain need my help. I can bring it 'round in a minute."

Cooper peered at Noah and echoed, "Major? Does he mean you?"

Herbert pushed the lantern toward the boy. "Here, Tom, you show the Major and Miss Rose to the carriage, and I'll help with the Lieutenant."

Cooper pressed on. "And Miss Carrigan is with you?"

Noah ignored Cooper's questions. He wanted to know how this lieutenant garnered the attention of Mrs. Coker's household. He pulled Rose to his side. "Lieutenant Hart, did you say?"

"Gideon Hart"—the man tried to stand taller—"of the Union Fifth Corps. I took ill on my way home from Virginia. I'm—"

"I found him passed out near the depot," Cooper said, "roused him enough to get directions to this place. He said he lives here."

CHAPTER 35

"*H*e's fortunate to have made it home," Rose whispered to Celeste as they eased the door shut. Though Celeste had prepared the broths and clean linens to care for Lieutenant Hart, Herbert hadn't allowed the women to enter the sick room until today.

"Yes, and to have someone as dedicated as Herbert to care for him night and day. I just hope Herbert doesn't take sick from it and delay our trip to Indiana."

Rose followed Celeste to the kitchen, where they deposited the dirty dishes and used linen in their designated areas. "You know we may have an addition on that journey. Besides Phoebe. Captain Bradley's home is in the same area."

"I heard him discussing it with Major Griffin yesterday when they checked on our patient." Celeste touched Rose's arm. "Does he, Captain Bradley I mean, seem...I don't know... somehow different from when we met him in Georgia?"

Rose bit her lower lip. The man did seem more serious, almost melancholy. "I suppose he is different. This war is changing us all, some for the better, and some otherwise. When it's over, I'm afraid the recovery is going to take a long time. Not many people have the perspective you and I do, having lived in both the North and the South, and reared by parents who loved people no matter who they were."

"I know. We are blessed, yes, blessed indeed."

Rose joined her on the last three words, one of their father's favorite sayings. The familiar chant provoked them to giggles as they linked arms and trooped to the parlor. They joined Mrs. Coker, who waited to welcome Lydia, Millie, and Baby Amy to the house for the winter.

When the elderly lady learned the refugee house still had no heat, she insisted in her crotchety way that Celeste prepare the unused nursery rooms for them. After several days, the suite had been declared acceptable.

Lieutenant Hart's dramatic entrance on Sunday forced them to postpone the moving day until his condition improved. This morning the doctor had assured Mrs. Coker that the lieutenant's condition was much better and presented no danger to the rest of the household.

When the little family's wagon stopped out front, Rose and Celeste rushed to fetch parcels while Noah stowed Celeste's carpetbag in the vehicle. Celeste and Rose led Lydia to the nursery. "You can use this armoire and that chest of drawers for your clothing. Mr. will show you where to find clean linens. Did you say Dorcas plans to come over and help some?"

"Yes," Lydia said. "She said she'd rather stay in town while Phoebe goes with y'all. I told her we'd be fine, but I suspect she doesn't want to miss her time with the baby. Heaven sure smiled on us when Dorcas came our way."

"That's the truth," Rose said. They retraced their steps to the parlor and exchanged amused glances when they found Mrs. Coker cuddling the baby in her arms while Millie watched. Little Amy cooed, and Mrs. Coker's face radiated contentment.

The other four women chattered happily, forgetting to keep their voices down in deference to the man recovering down the hall. Lieutenant Hart reminded them of his presence in dramatic fashion when he tottered into the parlor dressed in a robe that dragged the floor on one side and rode above his ankle on the other.

His face contorted in a scowl, and his voice blasted with surprising strength. "What in he...heaven's name is going on here?"

The lieutenant's color faded like a blanched beet as he looked around the room, settling last on Mrs. Coker with the baby in her arms. "Oh. Beg pardon, Grandmother. I didn't know you had company."

He clutched the doorframe to steady himself, executed an about-face, and shuffled down the hall. Celeste glared after him, but Rose covered her mouth to keep from laughing aloud.

Noah returned from settling the horses to find them all sniggering. He sat beside Rose on the settee. "Did I do something stupid to set you all to laughing?"

That set Rose off again, but she soothed his concern with a comforting touch. "No, not you. I fear you'll have to wait until I've recovered before I can explain."

Celeste pressed her lips together and rose with regal grace. "Lydia, could you assist me with the tea tray? I dare not interrupt Hattie's laundry duty or wake Herbert from his nap. The poor man has run himself ragged, trying to take care of everything."

For the next hour, they enjoyed a leisurely visit and discussed the upcoming trip to Indiana, which would get underway early on the morrow. Lydia and Millie learned about

Mrs. Coker's routine activities, Hattie's housecleaning schedule, and Herbert's vegetable garden.

Lydia expressed her gratitude again to Mrs. Coker. "You mustn't refrain from asking me or Millie to do any chores. We're both capable and, besides my days at the bakery, have nothing to occupy our time except caring for Amy."

Mrs. Coker waved away her concerns. "We'll figure it all out as we go along. I will caution you not to answer the door, however. Leave that to Herbert and ask him for anything you find you need. As for that grandson of mine, we'll soon put him in his place as well."

Rose could scarce believe this was same woman who had been frightened of her and Celeste when they'd first applied for a position in her house. Celeste's skills and gentle nature had secured Mrs. Coker's good opinion, and now Baby Amy had softened her heart.

Noah put aside his teacup and stood. "If everything is settled then, I'll convey Rose and Celeste back to the refuge house. We leave early in the morning."

"When do you expect to return to Louisville?" Millie asked.

"Around the first of December." Noah assisted Rose with her cloak as Celeste went to fetch hers. "My furlough is good for a month, but the weather can change suddenly at this time of year, and we don't want to get stranded somewhere on the way back."

Mrs. Coker pointed a bony finger in his direction. "Good thinking, young man. You take good care of our girls here."

"That I will, ma'am. You may be assured of it."

Rose and Celeste made their round of hugs and goodbyes to a chorus of prayers for a safe journey. Another state to discover, Rose thought, and one that nearly completed the circle back to their Ohio roots.

~

HARRISON COUNTY, INDIANA
SATURDAY, NOVEMBER 19, 1864

*N*oah watched the familiar countryside open in a wide vista of dormant fields. He rode Hercules while Cooper guided the carriage along the winding drive that would circle back to the house.

Home at last.

Traveling with women made for a long journey. He and Cooper could've made the trip in half the time, had they traveled alone. Not that the women had complained or caused trouble. They'd been agreeable to all suggestions and covered their fear at the ferry crossing like brave soldiers.

Only they weren't soldiers. The stops to answer nature's call came more frequently and took longer to answer. Meals taken along the road required a spread quilt and a rest for proper digestion. Landscape had to be admired or lamented, at length.

The delays grated on Noah's nerves. He considered the journey a mission to be accomplished, a necessary trial to be endured to obtain a goal. He'd chafed at each hour lost until yesterday when his frustration erupted.

After her initial amazement and blurring of those blue eyes, Rose had squared her shoulders and marched to the carriage, which he'd purchased so she could ride in comfort. While he and Cooper traded off driving and riding their mounts—in the cold and a few bouts of rain, no less.

She led her wide-eyed quiet companions to the vehicle, mounted the steps without assistance, and settled herself inside. Celeste and Phoebe followed. Cooper turned his back, but not before Noah caught the grin his friend tried to hide while he lashed Chief to the rear and made his way to the box. Noah stared after them until Cooper clicked to the horses and the wheels crunched over the scattered leaves in their path.

Several hours later, having swung the pendulum from self-assured justification to a mental thrashing, Noah recalled a summer day when he'd surrendered his theories on promoting justice. God's way was love, not force and anger. *Guess I have to keep learning that.*

He jumped down as they pulled up at the inn and strode to the carriage, opened the door, and stuck his head inside before they could alight.

"I must apologize to all of you for losing my temper earlier. I have no excuse beyond being eager to reach our destination. Please forgive me."

He moved aside and offered his hand to the nearest woman. Celeste stepped out. "Nicely done, Major. We are likewise sorry to have tried your patience."

Phoebe came next, wearing an amused smile. "You're a rare one, all right. I never knew my Pa to apologize to nobody."

He waited for Rose to slide toward the door, but she held back. He poked his head inside. "Rose? Are you all right?" In the dim light he found her, her hands over her face and shoulders shaking. Alarmed, he climbed in beside her and pulled her into his arms.

"Ah, Rose, honey, I'm sorry. I'm a brute to yell at you the way I did. Please forgive me."

When she lifted her face, he was stunned to silence. Tears flowed across her cheeks, but laughter floated through the air as she held him away. "Oh, Noah, I'm sorry I frightened you just now. Forgiveness granted and requested on my part as well."

"But why are you laughing?" He worried she might have dissolved into hysterics.

She calmed herself enough to answer. "I was thinking about this summer when we first met. Every time I saw you, we argued about something. Then we picked right up again when you arrived in Louisville. Only in our letters did we manage not to argue."

Lowering her eyes, she cast herself as the one to blame. "The

Book of Proverbs is full of warnings about living with a woman who rants and nags. Perhaps we should limit our relationship to letters?" She looked at him again with assumed innocence.

Recognizing the teasing ploy, he pretended to consider before he answered. "Where would be the fun in that?" He seized the opportunity to lean in for a kiss, but a knock against the doorframe interrupted.

Cooper cleared his throat in warning. "If you two are through making up now, the rest of us would like to get a meal."

~

*H*er stomach roiled as Rose watched the sprawling house come into view. Though it was more splendid than any place she'd ever lived, the extensive property itself didn't cause her anxiety. It was the people inside. What would Noah's family think of her? Though born above the Mason-Dixon line, she'd lived in the South long enough to consider herself a Southerner. Political association aside, she'd seen people's reactions to her accent in Louisville, and that city was protected from the conflict. On their journey, Noah had described the Confederate attack on Corydon and Mauckport, towns in the same county as his home, in July of 1863.

The story had brought surprising insight from Phoebe. "You mean to say the Rebels came here and burned down the buildings in July last year, then the Yankees went to Roswell and burned the mills in July of this year? It almost sounds like they was getting back at the South for what happened here, though I know Roswell wasn't the only place to get such treatment."

"I doubt if the reasoning was so clearly defined," Noah said, "but such things do happen in war."

Phoebe's eyes pooled with tears. "But if we keep up a tit-for-tat, back and forth fighting, we'll never see the end of this war."

No one could offer comfort as she wandered away from their resting place to mourn the loss of her world.

Now, a shout alerted Rose that someone at the house had spotted them. The front door opened, and two children spilled onto the wide porch. A side door revealed two women, their loose hair dancing in the breeze. The barn door was pushed wide, and an older man limped outside with a younger one following. Six pairs of eyes fastened on the carriage, and the boys on the porch shouted Noah's name. Waving wildly, they all converged on the new arrivals.

Noah and Cooper received hugs from the females, pounds on their backs from the men, and some teasing comments from all. The young man and boys guided Hercules and Chief to the barn.

Inside the carriage, Celeste and Phoebe tied on their bonnets. "Here, Rose." Celeste picked up the discarded bonnet and slipped it over Rose's hair. "Don't worry. You'll be fine."

Phoebe motioned to the coach door. "You should get out first, Miss Rose. You're the one he wants them to meet."

"No, let me go last. Please." Rose struggled to quiet her fluttering heart. Her fingers trembled over the ribbons of her bonnet.

The door swung wide, and someone let down the steps. Phoebe stepped out, then Celeste. Rose could hear Noah introducing them as she struggled to calm herself.

Celeste made her curtsey and moved aside. "And this is Miss Carrigan's sister, Rose."

She didn't release his hand.

"Rose, Celeste, Phoebe, please meet my family. That's Pop and Mary, my sister Katie, and Andrew is the baby. Jesse and Zachary are putting up the horses."

Polite greetings overrode their curiosity, though the youngsters couldn't contain their giggles.

Mary firmly took charge. "Let's all get out of the cold and go inside the house. I'm sure we'll have plenty of time to hear all the stories everyone has to tell. Cooper, you'll rest a bit before you head over the hill, won't you?"

The travelers followed her and Katie to the house while Noah's father circled back to help in the barn, promising a quick return.

Noah's step-mother patted the arm of her youngest. "Andrew, run tell Wilma to make up the yellow room," Mary said, "then you and Zach can join us for afternoon tea and a visit with your loquacious brother."

Rose regarded Noah with raised eyebrows. "Loquacious?" she whispered.

Noah rolled his eyes. "Mary's way of chastising me for not letting her know we were coming."

Rose stopped and stared at him in horror. "You didn't tell her? We've been two and a half days on the road, and you didn't warn her?"

"No letter would have arrived before we did. Hush, now." He gently gripped her upper arm and urged her forward. "All is well."

⌖

*N*oah tamped down his impatience as he waited for Rose in the yard. Lifting his eyes heavenward, he prayed for guidance and hoped he wasn't rushing things. With the weather turning colder, their excursion would be short. He thrust his hand into his trouser pocket to verify the circle of gold hadn't mysteriously disappeared.

At the squeak of a door, he spun around. Adorned with a refurbished bonnet, Rose wore a heavier cloak than the one she'd brought on their journey. She kept her eyes on her feet as she descended from the porch. New shoes, possibly on the large side. Noah crossed to assist with those careful steps. Leave it to Mary, he thought, to take care of whatever someone needed.

Once on level ground, Rose grinned. "The shoes will fit much better when Celeste finishes the stockings she's knitting, but she wouldn't let me wait for them. We settled for stuffing the toes with fabric clippings."

"I'm glad to see you found better gloves also. I'm an idiot not to have noticed your need sooner."

Rose waved away his apology. "How could you know? The weather in Louisville is much milder." She glanced around as he led her beyond the barn. "Where are we going?"

"Just over that ridge. You can't tell it from here, but this land is higher than much of the county. When we pass the barrens area, there's a small copse I thought you'd like to see. We work hard to keep the wildfires from coming that far."

They trudged in silence until they reached the place he'd scouted earlier. Rose spotted the line of white aspens across the meadow, interspersed with occasional evergreens, and cried in delight. "Oh, they are so lovely. I often imagine trees are lifting their arms to heaven in praise."

Noah slipped his arms around her and gazed over her shoulder. "And it doesn't matter whether they have green leaves or golden, or no leaves at all, their beauty remains."

She sighed with contentment. "Maybe that's what David had in mind in Psalm 121. He lifted his eyes to the hills because they directed him to the Lord, the Maker of heaven and earth. All creation reminds us our help comes from Him."

Remembering the last few months, Noah agreed. Several times his life had been spared— from serious injury on the railroad, from drowning while crossing flooded rivers, from getting skewered during Minty's daring saber attack. Prayers had covered him, and gratitude swelled. To be able to see his family again, to be in this place with those he loved, that was a blessing.

They stood there for several minutes, still enough to see a deer poke his head through the thicket and gaze back at them. When the animal flounced away, Rose chuckled. "I think he must be telling us to move along."

"And so we will. In a moment." Noah turned her to face him. "I've something to ask you first. I hope it doesn't come as a surprise, for I don't want to upset this day or this visit." Cupping her face in his hands, he swallowed the lump of emotion. "I love you, Rose Carrigan, and I need your special element of beauty in my life. Will you marry me while we're here with my family? I realize it's selfish of me when there's a war still going on. I don't know what the outcome will be, what we may face in the future, but for the rest of my life I want you beside me."

He stumbled to a halt and forced a half-smile. "Are you going to say anything, or do I have to find a way to convince you?"

Her lips trembled and her eyes sparkled. "I was going to say yes, but you kept going on. I think you should convince me." *The minx.*

"Oh. Well, I… Yes ma'am." He pulled her into his embrace and warmed her lips with his own. A few minutes later, he remembered the ring. Lifting his head, he tucked her close to his side and fumbled in his pocket.

"This was my mother's, handed down from her mother."

The ring slid on easily. Rose admired the tiny pink gem that resembled a rosebud. "Oh, it's lovely."

He tipped her chin with his finger. "Let me be sure I understand. You are saying yes, and we can hold the wedding while we're here?"

"Yes. And yes, we can be married here. Celeste predicted it would happen, and I can't disappoint her, can I?"

"Heaven forbid. I know a few others who'd be disappointed as well, including me."

Laughing at the woebegone face he made, Rose took pity. "I love you, Noah. God sent you to provide an ark of safety for some poor Southerners, and you stole my heart in the process. I've longed for a place to put down roots, to call 'home' and never have to leave. Now I know home isn't a matter of geography. It's a condition of the heart. Even if we move from place to place, my home is with you."

Noah kept his answering kiss short, which she responded to with a fervor that had his heart racing. Even still, he didn't miss the way she shivered in his arms. "We'd better get back to the house before you freeze. I'll leave it to you and the other ladies to decide on the details, but you should consider this. I've plenty of room in my bed, while you are forced to share with Celeste and Phoebe. I think sooner would be better than later, don't you?"

Laughing at his reasoning, Rose gave him a playful swat. "Oh, you Yankees are in a hurry about everything. I think we'll have to do some negotiating over coffee."

They'd barely made it inside the house before the others descended on them, eager to confirm their suspicions and predictions. Rose displayed the ring to the excited delight of every female.

James pounded Noah on the back with his congratulations, then dragged him toward the door. "Now you've accomplished your main goal, let's see if we can find that big buck over toward Bradley's land. Eliza and Ben will be here in a day or two, and we'll need all the meat we can scare up for this crowd."

"See if you can find a couple of those, James," Mary called. "We'll be celebrating more than the official day of Thanksgiving. What blessings. Eliza's new baby and a wedding to plan. Girls, we'd better start making a list of everything we'll need."

∼

EBENEZER CHURCH, HARRISON COUNTY, INDIANA
WEDNESDAY, NOVEMBER 23, 1864

"*T*his is like a fairy tale," Phoebe whispered as the carriage pulled up to the church in a flurry of snow. She stared in awe out the window then pulled back as the coach door opened and the stairs were let down.

After her companions left the carriage, Rose stepped out and lifted her skirts above the speckled ground, feeling much like the transformed heroine in a cherished children's story. Hurrying into the warmth of the church, she laughed as snowflakes christened her face and hands.

Greenery and ribbons decorated the front rows. A blue carpet ran the length of the aisle, darkened in spots from damp boots. Cooper Bradley's family sat on one side while Noah's family occupied the other. A few more folks had braved the blustery weather and clustered close to the pot-belly stove at the front.

Mary adjusted Rose's skirt and the yard of lace serving as a veil, then she slipped up the outside aisle to join her family.

The kind pastor Rose had met on Sunday faced them in front of his pulpit. He beckoned to the organist, who set hands and feet into motion. The huffing notes of a hymn finally found their pitch, rising in the pipes to fill the small building like a prayer.

Celeste moved down the center aisle and stood opposite Cooper, who was next to Noah. Rose placed her trembling fingers on Mr. Griffin's sleeve and stepped forward.

Noah's eyes traced her every step.

When they reached Noah at the altar, and the minister began the ceremony. It was simple and short, full of scriptures on love and commitment.

When the pastor gave Noah permission to kiss his bride,

Noah lifted her lacy veil and leaned in. "I never dreamed when I left home to fight, I'd find the woman of my dreams."

"You stormed my town and captured my heart."

Family and friends surrounded them, a blend of North and South, both sides conquered by love.

Did you enjoy this book? We hope so!
Would you take a quick minute to leave a review where you purchased the book?
It doesn't have to be long. Just a sentence or two telling what you liked about the story!

Receive a FREE ebook and get updates when new Wild Heart books release: https://wildheartbooks.org/newsletter

Don't miss the next book in the Rescued Hearts of the Civil War Series!

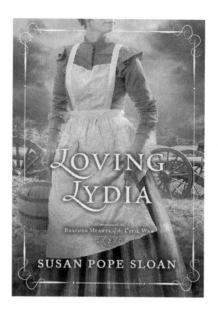

Loving Lydia
By Susan Pope Sloan

FRIDAY AFTERNOON, JULY 8, 1864
NEW MANCHESTER, GEORGIA

Hundreds of Union soldiers camped outside the village, their mere presence enough to set the locals on edge. The anxiety increased when small groups of them ventured into the outlying homes to seize food or whatever appealed to them.

Fear pushed Lydia Gibson to the hilltop, where she could see the farm below. Rumors at the mill had whirred as noisily as the wooden shuttles clacking back and forth in the weaving room. Stories were spreading of Union soldiers preying on helpless women.

I should've stayed home with Millie instead of going to work this morning. Their lack of funds had seemed the more immediate need. Lydia's job was their only source of income, and she needed to keep it, but not at the cost of Millie's safety. With all the family members she'd lost over the years, Lydia couldn't face losing another.

Although the mill was running again, it hobbled along like an injured bird after the soldiers had paid their visit last Saturday. Overgrown boys bent on devilment, they'd scattered cloth and thread across the floor, then ripped the belts from the machines to halt production. Shock had paralyzed the workers until the intruders left.

The enemy had arrived in their little corner of Georgia.

After hearing the reports, she'd pleaded illness and left her station early. Lydia skirted the white oak on the downward side.

She caught sight of two soldiers loitering near her front door and quickly ducked back behind the tree.

Her *open* front door. Each man held a burlap sack. She'd heard enough rumors to know those sacks would collect any property that took their fancy. Those scavengers were no better than the vultures that circled dying critters, waiting to pick them clean.

Before she could think what to do, one man yelled toward the house. "C'mon, Harris, we don't have time to dally with the girls."

A third soldier staggered out the door, holding a kerchief to his bloody nose, a limp sack dangling from the other hand.

Behind the tree, Lydia gasped, but the sound went unheeded as the soldiers snorted with laughter.

"Serves you right, Private. You'll learn your looks don't sway 'em all."

The younger man muttered an indistinct reply as the three tramped down the road.

Lydia released the breath she'd been holding, waiting until

they disappeared from sight before she left the shadows that shielded her.

Running on shaky legs, she rushed up the steps and halted at the entrance. "Millie? Millie, are you unharmed?"

Her blond stepdaughter ran to her, weeping. "Oh, Lydia, that awful soldier. Did you see him? Am I in trouble for hitting him? What will they do to me?"

"I don't expect you're in trouble." She stroked the girl's hair that rippled to her waist.

Millie pulled back from Lydia's shoulder. "Are you sure? Did you talk to him?"

"They were leaving when I arrived. I saw his bloody nose and figured you'd given him what for."

Millie nodded, her face flushing. "I hit him when he tried to grab me. He said..." She sniffled.

"Never mind that now. His friends laughed at him and said he got what he deserved. So I don't think you're in trouble. He's probably too embarrassed to tell anyone a girl hit him, especially one he was trying to sweeten up."

Millie scoffed. "Don't know why he'd even try, since my condition is obvious now. I can't get into any of my dresses but this one. Guess we'll have to let out the seams in the others." She patted her thickening waist.

Lydia wanted to wallop the man who'd weaseled his way into Millie's bed. It seemed life was as hard for a pretty girl as for a plain one. One had to ward off the men while the other could barely get them to notice her. Millie's bright hair and perfect complexion drew all eyes her way. Lydia often felt like a little brown wren next to the brilliant bluebird that was Millie, especially since she'd blossomed in the last couple of years.

Millie swiped her tears with her hands. "Why are you home early? Machines break down again?"

Lydia shrugged. "I wanted to be sure you were all right.

Motherly worries, I guess. Now go wash your face, and let's see what we can find for supper."

Millie padded into the kitchen, absently placing a hand at her lower back. She must be six months along now. Was she spreading in the rear? Didn't that mean a girl? *Oh, dear God, what are we going to do with a baby?*

Pain pierced her heart. She'd felt it over the years as women all around her were bearing children while she was not. Her desire for children was a large part of the reason she'd said yes to Cal. She wanted babies, and Cal already had Millie—eight at the time they married. But year after year had passed with no babies of her own to rock.

Then the war came. Cal enlisted right away, sure that he and his cronies could knock the Yanks to kingdom come. She'd wondered if his real reason was to get away. Away from the mill, away from the responsibility of a family, away from her and her "constant carping," as he'd often complained. He'd gotten away all right, right into the fire of enemy cannons.

Putting aside her sense of failure, she replaced it with the heady anticipation of a baby in her life. A grandchild, though she was only twenty-eight herself. It would be much like having her own. That sweet baby smell, cuddles and kisses, and watching him or her grow.

But reality always elbowed its way back in. Dear Lord, how were they going to manage? Especially now. The mill barely limped along, the army camped at their doorstep. What was to become of them?

"God, if You're there, we could sure use some help here."

Leave.

The voice rang so real, Lydia whirled around to find its source. All she saw was worn furniture, the door firmly shutting out even a slight breeze.

Was she losing her mind?

Perhaps.

Shaking it off, Lydia started for the kitchen again.

Pack and leave.

She froze in the middle of the small room. Could it be? Did God answer so swiftly someone who rarely searched for Him? She certainly counted herself a believer, but life had been so hard, she struggled just to keep herself going.

Now jolted into action, she found Millie at the sink, washing a couple of scrawny potatoes. A pot of water bubbled around three duck eggs.

"While I'm at work tomorrow, I want you to gather up our things and get ready to leave. We won't wait around here for the fighting to find us."

Millie dropped a potato and gaped. "But where will we go?"

"Dunno for sure. I think I have a distant cousin down near Columbus, where there's another mill. I'll see if I can find a name in Granny's Bible." She had brothers in Alabama, too, but she didn't want to be a burden. She'd have to think on which way to go. Farther south seemed the best direction, since all the fighting came from the north.

"But what about...what if someone comes looking for us? How will they know where to find us?"

Lydia pondered the question. She hadn't thought that far ahead. "I'll write to Pastor Bagley once we get settled, let him know where we are. I have a strong feeling we need to leave, not just sit around and wait for something to happen."

Later, she lay in bed and mulled over the day's events. Seeing the soldiers at her door had brought home the insecurity of their present situation. The Voice had only amplified it. Her faith had grown dusty with disuse over the years, but she had no doubt about Whose voice it had been.

Why would God speak to her? Her, Lydia Ruth McNeil Gibson. Oh, she attended church on Sunday and took part in each service. The music spoke to her weary soul, and she often gleaned a nugget of hope from Reverend Bagley's sermon. Even in that atmosphere, though, the cares of life seemed to press in, especially over the last few months.

Guilt weighed down her spirit. Despite repenting over and over, she figured forgiveness was out of reach. Her husband was likely lying in a common grave on the battlefield, a casualty of war. The official report was "missing" since the battle at Chickamauga, but if Cal had survived, surely he would've contacted her somehow while he was so close to home.

Her fault because she had pushed him to go.

~

Saturday morning, July 9, 1864
Georgia-South Carolina border

Wakened from a restless slumber by violent vibrations and thundering hooves, Seth Morgan reached for his weapon. How had he not heard the call to battle? Could he be dreaming?

No weapon met his hand, only the rough wood of a wagon bed. He pushed aside the hat covering his eyes. Memories marched in swift succession before halting at the present. He'd stashed his Confederate-issued bayonet under the wagon seat at the request of his female companions.

Looking about, he breathed deeply until his heartbeat slowed and took in his surroundings. The noise and shaking emanated from the wagon rumbling across a rickety bridge. Water sparkled below, shimmering under a hazy sky. Though the sun still climbed in the east, it poured merciless heat on the people in the wagon.

"We's come to the Georgia line, folks. Y'all might get a bite to eat at the farmhouse over yonder." The driver pulled his tired nag to a halt and pointed toward a structure south of their position. "I reckon y'all might find another wagon willing to take you on a ways."

Seth grabbed his knapsack and jumped over the side of the buckboard. Robby joined him, and both turned to offer their assistance to the three women. The men retrieved their weapons, and Seth waved his hand toward the driver.

"Much obliged for the ride, Moses. Maybe the private and I will catch you on our way back."

"I'll be here, Sergeant Morgan, if the good Lawd wills and the crick don't rise." He turned forward. "Walk on, Daffodil." The mule leaned into the traces and made a circle to reverse directions. Moses sang in his rich baritone as the wagon lumbered over the bridge again. *"Swing low, sweet chariot, comin' for to carry me home."*

Seth smiled, remembering how Moses's song had hampered the women's chatter earlier. Their grumbling about the wagon's discomfort had grated on Seth's nerves, but his upbringing had kept his mouth shut. His ploy to feign sleep had turned into blessed slumber. Heaven knows he'd had little of it lately.

He also had little patience for whiners. Two of the women had raged from one subject to the next. They castigated the State of South Carolina for not continuing the railroad beyond Greenville, which caused them their need to seek another means of travel. They reprimanded Moses for going too slowly and then protested when a faster gait bounced them off their seats. The older one, Mrs. Hobbs, had tried to stem the tide of the youngers' chatter, but her efforts had failed.

He could've told them about what their menfolk endured to the north. On top of the battles they fought, the conditions in camp tried the heartiest of soldiers. Lack of proper meals, combined with disease and the loss of limbs, eroded everyone's morale. Some men never returned from furlough. Others straggled at the rear of their units, disregarding orders about not plundering the towns and homes in their path, which incited the wrath and suspicion of civilians. What had started as a crusade for states' rights had denigrated to a vicious fight for survival.

Walking along the dusty road, Seth and Robby flanked the women to provide protection, slowing their longer strides to match the arthritic gait of Mrs. Hobbs. Oddly enough, she was the most cheerful of the group.

"Mrs. Hobbs, won't you take my arm and let me help you?" Robby extended his elbow.

Seth hid his smile, knowing the younger man chafed at the pace she'd set. Robby had always run, trying to keep up with Zeke, his older brother.

"No, thank you, Private Roland. I imagine you're as fatigued as I am since you've been traveling longer. We'll be able to rest in a few minutes when we reach that farm."

"Well, as to that, ma'am, our first day from Richmond was on the train, so it wasn't so bad. We stayed on it until we reached Greenville, with stops here and there. If it wasn't for the war, I expect the railroad would stretch all the way to Atlanta by now."

Somehow Robby had captured her arm to lend her his strength. She smiled up at him and patted his hand. "Yes, the war has put a halt to a good many things, I suspect. I've seen quite a few changes in my lifetime, and no doubt you will too. Sometimes I think we need to consider whether all those changes are for the better." She directed her attention to their destination. "Someone's coming from the house to greet us."

Seth looked over her head to verify the news. Indeed, a tall woman in a shapeless dress stepped from the porch to the yard. Her greeting fell short of hospitable. She clutched the handle of a pitchfork, its prongs pointed heavenward. Her stance indicated her readiness to fight the devil himself if he showed up at her door.

Seth took a step forward, and she flipped the pitchfork toward him. Surprised, he lifted his hands and stepped back.

Mrs. Hobbs pushed past him. "Good day, missus. I'm Elmira

Hobbs, and these are my sisters, Daisy and Thelma. These here are Sergeant Morgan and Private Roland. They're on furlough from the army in Virginia. These gentlemen have graciously watched over us on our journey from Charlotte, and I can assure you they mean you no harm."

The tall woman's eyes darted from Seth to Robby and back, but she returned the tool to its original position. "I seen you get off the wagon at the bridge. The last soldiers who come that way took our food and tore up the house, looking for any valuables, so now I don't allow no weapons inside my house. If you're looking for a meal, I got stew and cornbread for two dollars apiece. I can put up the women in the house, but you men'll have to stay out here."

Mrs. Hobbs looked at Seth to speak for them.

"That's fine, missus," he said. "We'll be glad to pay you in advance. Is there a place where we can wash up?" He stepped sideways to lean his rifled bayonet against an overturned wheelbarrow and motioned Robby to do the same. Seth pulled several bills from his breast pocket, extending the peace offering to his reluctant hostess.

Setting aside the pitchfork, she gestured to the side of the house. "The well's around that way. I'll bring your food out soon's I serve up the plates."

"Much obliged, ma'am." Seth led the way to the well. They pulled up the bucket and made quick work of washing their faces and hands. By habit, Seth surveyed the land for any threat or indication of problems. The area around the house resembled a patchwork quilt, with blocks of grass sprouting in sections against the reddish dirt.

The call of a crow directed his gaze to the roof, where a couple of loose shingles curled in the heat. If he could persuade the woman of the house to trust him with a hammer and nails, he'd climb up there and fix the problem. Otherwise, she'd have trouble with a leaky roof whenever it stormed.

Like many of the places he'd seen in the last several months, an unnatural stillness brooded over it. No chickens pecked in the yard. No dogs served as sentries of protection. Only one gray cat prowled the area.

In too much of the South these days, the healthy, boisterous sounds of life had faded, succumbing to the silence of impending death.

ABOUT THE AUTHOR

Born into a family of storytellers, **Susan Pope Sloan** published her first articles in high school and continued writing sporadically for decades. Retirement provided the time to focus on writing and indulge her avid interest in history. Her Civil War series begins (and ultimately ends) in her home state of Georgia with references to lesser-known events of that period. She and husband Ricky live near Columbus where she participates in Word Weavers, ACFW, and Toastmasters.

AUTHOR'S NOTE

I owe a huge debt of thanks to Mary Deborah Petite for her excellent scholarly work in *The Women Will Howl* (McFarland & Company, Inc., Publishers, 2008). Her book was my primary source of information, especially for the timeline of events related to the workers' journey from North Georgia to Louisville, Kentucky.

Another frequently-used source was the online Map Tour of 7th Pennsylvania Cavalry During Sherman's Atlanta Campaign —May to September, 1864 (https://7thpennsylvaniacavalry. com/map-tour-of-7th-pennsylvania-cavalry-during-shermans-atlanta-campaign-may-to-september-1864). This site helped me to understand the movements of Gerrard's division so I could plot Captain Noah Griffin's activity. Likewise, the Civil War Index provided movement of the 17th Indiana and Griffin's friend, Lieutenant Cooper Bradley.

For information on Mary Gay, I used her own work, *Life in Dixie during the War 1861-1862-1863-1864-1865.* I found samples of letters from soldiers in *Red Clay to Richmond: Trail of the 35th Georgia Infantry Regiment, C.S.A.,* and information on in-state travel and other conditions in *The War-time Journal of a Georgia Girl, 1864-1865.*

For weather, the National Weather Service website is valuable, and always Wikipedia is an excellent place to begin research on people and places.

Here are a few more websites I used:

www.civilwar.com/history/weapons-44543/railroads-79476.htm

https://tribupedia.com/louisville-military-prison-tribute/

https://civilwarwiki.net/wiki/Union_Insignia_of_the_Civil_War

I tried to stay as true to the timeline as I could, but sources vary on what happened when. Also, I could only speculate on some particulars, such as how the women obtained water at the refugee house, how they prepared meals, how many stayed in one room, etc.

From all reports, few if any of the women from Roswell could read and write, so it was important to provide a main character who was well educated elsewhere and recently moved to the town. The workers in New Manchester had more opportunities for schooling.

I also want to express my appreciation for my fellow historical writers with Civil War-era novels: Jocelyn Green, Stephenia McGee, Sandra Merville Hart, Jack Cunningham, Ann Gabhart, and others for their excellent research and writing, which inspired me to pen this story after years of procrastination. And a huge "thank you" to my former co-worker, Jim Mitchell, who first told me about the Roswell women.

Of course, I'm deeply grateful for the encouragement of my family, friends, and my writing community—Word Weavers International, the ACFW critique loop, my Toastmasters clubs (who heard speeches about my writing for years), and Word Weavers Columbus.

Jehovah Rohi always provided what I needed from start to

finish, when I didn't have a clue what to do next. It was a divine appointment when my friend Terri Miller shared my FCWC contest- winning entry with Erin Taylor Young, who recommended I contact Misty Beller at Wild Heart Books. To God be the glory!

If you love historical romance, check out the other Wild Heart books!

Marisol ~ Spanish Rose by Elva Cobb Martin

Escaping to the New World is her only option...Rescuing her will wrap the chains of the Inquisition around his neck.

Marisol Valentin flees Spain after murdering the nobleman who molested her. She ends up for sale on the indentured servants' block at Charles Town harbor—dirty, angry, and with child. Her hopes are shattered, but she must find a refuge for herself and the child she carries. Can this new land offer her the grace, love, and security she craves? Or must she escape again to her only living relative in Cartagena?

Captain Ethan Becket, once a Charles Town minister, now sails the seas as a privateer, grieving his deceased wife. But when he takes captive a ship full of indentured servants, he's intrigued by the woman whose manners seem much more refined than the average Spanish serving girl. Perfect to become governess for his young son. But when he sets out on a quest to find his captured sister, said to be in Cartagena, little does he expect his new Spanish governess to stow away on his ship with her six-month-old son. Yet her offer of help to free his sister is too tempting to pass up. And her beauty, both inside and out, is too attractive for his heart to protect itself against—until he learns she is a wanted murderess.

As their paths intertwine on a journey filled with danger, intrigue, and romance, only love and the grace of God can overcome the past and ignite a new beginning for Marisol and Ethan.

～

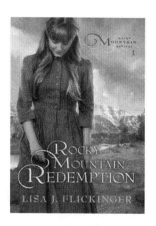

Rocky Mountain Redemption by Lisa J. Flickinger

A Rocky Mountain logging camp may be just the place to find herself.

To escape the devastation caused by the breaking of her wedding engagement, Isabelle Franklin joins her aunt in the Rocky Mountains to feed a camp of lumberjacks cutting on the slopes of Cougar Ridge. If only she could out run the lingering nightmares.

Charles Bailey, camp foreman and Stony Creek's itinerant pastor, develops a reputation to match his new nickname — Preach. However, an inner battle ensues when the details of his rough history threaten to overcome the beliefs of his young faith.

Amid the hazards of camp life, the unlikely friendship growing between the two surprises Isabelle. She's drawn to Preach's brute strength and gentle nature as he leads the ragtag crew toiling for Pollitt's Lumber. But when the ghosts from her past return to haunt her, the choices she will make change the course of her life forever—and that of the man she's come to love.

∾

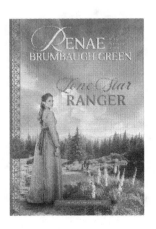

Lone Star Ranger by Renae Brumbaugh Green

Elizabeth Covington will get her man.

And she has just a week to prove her brother isn't the murderer Texas Ranger Rett Smith accuses him of being. She'll show the good-looking lawman he's wrong, even if it means setting out on a risky race across Texas to catch the real killer.

Rett doesn't want to convict an innocent man. But he can't let the Boston beauty sway his senses to set a guilty man free. When Elizabeth follows him on a dangerous trek, the Ranger vows to keep her safe. But who will protect him from the woman whose conviction and courage leave him doubting everything—even his heart?

Made in the USA
Columbia, SC
15 March 2025

55198665R00183